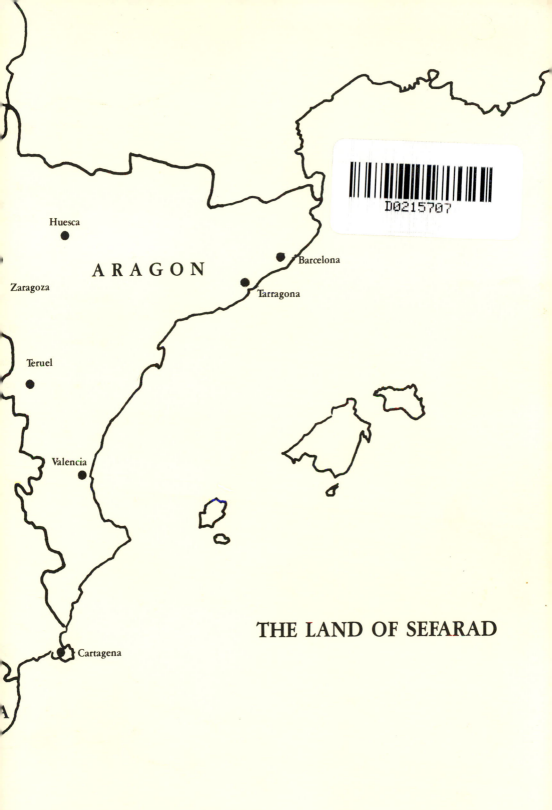

Huesca

ZARAGOZA

A R A G O N

Teruel

Valencia

Barcelona

Tarragona

Cartagena

THE LAND OF SEFARAD

THE ALHAMBRA DECREE

David Raphael

Carmi House Press

Carmi House Press
P.O. Box 4796
North Hollywood, California 91607

Library of Congress Catalog Card Number 88-71589

ISBN 0-9620772-0-8

To my wife
con todo mi cariño

TABLE OF CONTENTS

		Page Number
Part I:	The Land of *Sefarad*	1
Part II:	The Alhambra Decree	78
Part III:	Expulsion: 1492	232
Part IV:	Second Edict; Second Chance	326

PART I:
THE LAND OF *SEFARAD*

Chapter 1

Abraham Senior, Chief Judge of the Jewish communities of Spain, sat in the waiting room of the royal tent. Senior had been summoned to appear quickly before the King and Queen in Málaga because the city was about to surrender, and it was his business, Jewish business, to be in Málaga as soon as possible. Senior had received notice that several hundred Jews, most of them women, would need to be ransomed. Large sums of money would be required to ransom them, and he was to be directly involved in the negotiations. Senior had rescued Jewish slaves before. As the *juez mayor,* as the Chief Judge, he was being asked to do it again. He looked forward to the gratitude that the freed prisoners would show him — at the time of their release and forever thereafter. It was a joy to perform good deeds. It was a *mitzvah*. Yet he also knew the necessary ransom would be a burden to the Jewish communities of Spain.

As he sat there, his seventy-year old frame clothed in a mantle of silk, Senior thought not only about helping his captive brethren but also about his very fortunate past. Whatever the misery of his Jewish co-religionists, his lot had never been marked by hardship or misfortune. Always Senior had enjoyed prosperity and wealth. Indeed, he was exempt from many of the restrictions that applied to Jews everywhere in Spain. Senior, by special dispensation of the crown, was exempt from it all. Even though it was forbidden for Jews to wear any cloak of gold thread or silk or other rich trimmings, Senior and his family were permitted this luxury.

His retinue consisted of thirty mules, and always he was guarded while traveling from city to city. He rode as he walked: proudly, with a

1

royal bearing that had come from three decades of living close to Spanish royalty. Power he had always had to a relative degree, and he exercised it effectively and prudently as part of his vaulted position. But it was his wealth that was proverbial. Just how many millions of maravedis he had made in his activities as chief tax collector of the land was known to no one but himself and his wife Fortuna.They were both incredibly, astonishingly rich. Even the King and Queen had to borrow large sums of money from him. Ferdinand and Isabella themselves were indebted to Senior for several loans he had made to defray the vast military expenditures necessary in the war against the Moors.

But the indebtedness of the sovereigns ran deeper than that. On every major occasion that Senior met the King and Queen, the memory of that special debt came to mind, yet never found its way to speech. There was no need to remind the King and Queen of the historic circumstances that had produced an overlapping of their destinies. In appreciation of his many services, Isabella had granted Senior an annual lifetime annuity of 150,000 maravedis. But his reward was not to end there. From 1476 onwards, Don Abraham Senior was to be the supreme judge and the chief apportioner of taxes for the entire Jewish population of Castile.

In the capacity of supreme judge, Senior knew he was not a Hebrew scholar, much less a rabbi, a fact which at times disturbed him when he was asked to render a decision on community matters that required Talmudic learning. No one respected him as a man possessing any great knowledge, but they all stood in respectful awe of his power within the community and of his special relationship with the King and Queen. To maintain his position as *juez mayor,* as the supreme judge, he needed to consult learned rabbis on occasion. There were many of them in Castile: there was Rabbi Isaac Aboab of Guadalajara, the *Gaon* or 'genius' of Castile as he was called, whom everyone regarded as the greatest Talmudic scholar of the day. And then there was that newcomer from Portugal, Rabbi Don Isaac Abravanel, who was such a brilliant Biblical expositor that, within three or four years of his arrival, he had come to be regarded as the chief rabbi of Castile.

But the supreme Jewish judge of the kingdom of Castile was not expected to be a rabbi. His two immediate predecessors in that role — Shemaya Lubel and Jacob Ibn Núñez — had not been rabbis. They were expected to be tax supervisors, and good ones at that. And Senior was even better than they were; as the chief tax farmer of all Castile, he had introduced innovations in the techniques of harvesting the taxes due the crown. The increased revenues endeared him further with the sovereigns who were always in desperate need of funds. The tax farmers could not help but become enriched in the process. For every thousand maravedis collected, fifteen went to the local councils, fifteen for the tax farmer, and another fifteen for his assistants. Thus Senior had reaped millions of maravedis as a result. His lifetime annuity from Queen Isabella was an insignificant portion of his total income, but he accepted it as a token reminder of his privileged relationship with the sovereigns.

"Don Abraham, the King and Queen are ready to see you now", an attendant said softly. Senior, adjusting his gold necklace, left the antechamber and stepped into the luxurious main reception room.

"Welcome, Don Abraham, it is good to see you again", the King said as Senior bowed respectfully.

"Your Highness, it is my utmost pleasure when I am called to render service to my sovereign King and Queen. As always, I remain your faithful servant at your command."

The Queen now spoke:

"Don Abraham, health and grace unto you. We thank you for your prompt response to our letter requesting your immediate presence in the camp here at Málaga. The fortress is on the verge of surrender, and we understand that there are over four hundred Jews among the prisoners. You understand, of course, they are prisoners of war."

"Yes, of course," Senior answered cautiously, "and that a ransom will have to be paid for their release. I understand this perfectly well. However, I beg of the King and Queen that the ransom be one that our Jewish communities can bear. The Jews of your kingdom are already taxed beyond good measure, and the community will find it difficult to sustain an extra burden."

The King interrupted him,

"Don Abraham, the Jews of the kingdom, taxed though they may be, did not give of their blood as the Christian cavaliers have given. Fine young men, wonderful young men in the prime of their manhood, have given their lives to wrest this castle from the hands of the infidel Moor. We do not ask the Jews of our kingdom to do the same. We do not ask you to give your lives. We ask only for your support, for your maravedis, for your share of the war effort. The taking of Málaga cost us many lives and involved thousands of troops, troops that must be paid now if I am to keep their trust. That is why I must ask a ransom of thirty thousand Jaenese doblas for the release of the Jewish captives."

"Thirty thousand doblas. That is a very large sum, your Majesty.

Perhaps we can raise ten thousand. Do not forget that we are still recovering from the cost of the absorption of the many Jews that were forced to leave Andalusia at your command four years ago."

Ferdinand winced at the expulsion of the Jews from Andalusia that he had authorized, ostensibly to keep the Jews out of the war zone. Senior had countered with a reference to that unpleasant event in order to bolster his request for a lower ransom. The Queen joined the discussion.

"Very well, the ransom will be reduced because you are our trusted friend, Don Abraham. But we cannot accept any payment less than twenty thousand, or so we are informed by our treasurer."

"Then twenty thousand doblas it shall be, my Queen, if you so command. We do not now have a sum so large as this at our disposal, but we shall try to raise it to rescue our brethren. We will need at least six months time to do so, perhaps more. I hope you understand this."

"Your request for six months is granted", the Queen answered dryly. Senior nodded his head in ackowledgement of the agreement. Ferdinand took the initative once again:

"I wish to remind you, Don Abraham, that the royal treasury is practically empty. Do you realize that it costs us eight thousand maravedis just to equip a single cavalry officer with an armored steed, a metal breast plate, and a lance? Eight thousand maravedis for one man alone! The cost of outfitting our knights, the light mounted militia, the infantry footsoldiers — my God! It runs into the millions. We must find a way for increasing the tax revenues. I don't care how you do it, but you must get us more funds. Otherwise, we shall have to pawn the crown jewels and eat off earthenware."

Senior answered, "I understand your predicament, your Majesty, and I shall concentrate my efforts in getting additional funds for you. If I may, allow me to review the major sources of tax revenue for the crown."

"Proceed, Don Abraham", a subdued Ferdinand replied.

The chief tax collector proceeded to speak:

"It is obvious that the greatest revenue to the crown comes from the *alcalaba*, the tax on commercial transactions of all tangible and nontangible properties. It amounts to a tenth of each and every transaction. It has been brought to my attention by my assistant that there are many instances of fraud, especially in cases where the stated total is made deliberately low to avoid paying the *alcalaba*. Sometimes, the parties wish to hide the true terms from the royal officials. We need authorization from the crown to investigate these cases, and we also need an official statement that false declarations will be punished most severely."

"Consider it done", Ferdinand remarked.

"The people hate the tax, is that not true?", Isabella queried.

Senior answered, "All taxes are unpleasant, but the *alcalaba* is especially detested by the people. What is one to do? If the townspeople had their way, there would be no taxes, and then there would be no royal revenues, and then there most certainly would not be . . . ah . . .

". . . A King or a Queen", Isabella completed his sentence.

Senior half-nodded in agreement and continued:

"The transaction tax will last as long as there is a King and Queen in Spain. Now, there is also the matter of the extra ten million maravedis for the war effort that was voted four years ago at the General Assembly in Miranda de Ebro, which we have increased to twelve million maravedis this year. We are in the process of collecting it, despite continued opposition from many of the local delegates. Everyone accuses me of being harsh in collecting the money, of being arbitrary, and I have become a very unpopular individual, but I do what I am instructed to do. If you want more funds from this route, I will obtain them despite the attacks on my person and on my assistants. I would advise you, however, to wait one more year before substantially raising this war tax. In the interim, offer the cities judicial and legal reforms as you have done previously. This costs you nothing, but it will be valuable in obtaining their acquiescence to the next round of taxation."

Isabella concurred, "I believe that is what we have to do. Do you have any other ideas?"

Senior stroked his beard thoughtfully and asked, "What about the nobility?"

Ferdinand answered, "I do not have to inform you, Don Abraham, that the nobles do not pay taxes. I reward them with lands conquered from the Moors, and I confer upon them dignities and titles. In return, they provide me with loyalty and troops when I need them. No, Don Abraham, the nobles will not pay taxes. Nor, for that matter, does the Church . . . However, an idea has been proposed by which the Church could augment our revenues."

"How is that, your Majesty?"

"Well, Cardinal Mendoza has proposed that we re-petition the Pope for permission to levy a tax on the conscience of our subjects."

Isabella interjected, "I personally dislike this idea, I want you to know that, Don Abraham, but our hands are tied. We need the money desperately, and we must use every avenue possible."

Senior looked slightly confused, "This is a church matter and outside my sphere. Would you please explain to me what you mean by this?"

"What it means is this", Ferdinand elaborated, "If the Pope agrees to such a Papal Bull, then the faithful will be able to redeem their sins if they pay the crown a certain sum applicable towards the cause of this Holy War against the infidel. Thus, the believer will be able to lessen the punishment in Purgatory for himself and any other dead relatives he may have. Anyhow, what else is there to discuss?"

Senior replied thoughtfully, "There are the usual duties on imports, exports and circulating goods. There is little we can do to increase these and the same is true of revenues from the royal mines and salt pits. Perhaps we can raise the taxes for migrating sheep herds at mountain passes or raise the tolls at bridges and at seaports for incoming and out-going ships. I do not see a significant increase in revenues from these sources, and my personal recommendation is to leave them unchanged for the present. My advice to you is simply this: enforce the transaction tax. Raise the special levy taxes for the Granada war, but do so only after you have undertaken some legal reforms to pacify the townspeople. That is where you should concentrate your efforts."

"And obtain the Papal Bull for the Crusade", Ferdinand added, "Good advice, Don Abraham. Good solid advice. That is why we always listen to you. Do you agree, my Queen?"

"Yes, I do", replied Isabella. "Don Abraham, you know that we value your services highly . . . very highly."

Isabella never ceased to marvel at the mental sharpness of this old and trusted Jew who, at a crusty seventy years of age, was more useful to the crown than the colony of feeble-minded financial advisers who paraded ostentatiously in and out of her court. Senior was a genuine asset to the crown, he was a goldmine of information and advice, and he was worth every maravedi that he was receiving as chief tax farmer.

"Don Abraham, I realize that the demands of your present position are great, but we are in need of your skilled services once again. The Council of the Santa Hermandad, that is, the Holy Brotherhood, has been notified that it will be without the services of Pedro Gonzales de Madrid, who has been relieved of his position as treasurer. I would like you to consider accepting this vital position on the Council and to direct its taxation program in coordination with the chief royal auditor. What they need is guidance, direction, and most of all, financial expertise . . . expertise that only you can provide. Assessed payments have not been paid, and the Council is far behind on its collection of the required sum.

We must have someone on the Council who knows what we need and how to get it, someone we trust. You are that man, Don Abraham. At the behest of your Queen, I urge you to accept this position as Treasurer of the Holy Brotherhood."

Senior listened attentively to Isabella. It was not that he was unaware of the Brotherhood's weaknesses, or that he did not wish to help. It was just that a person could only do so much; to take on an additional task would be too much . . . far too much . . . especially for a man his age. Senior played with the idea of saying no to the Queen, of denying her request, of forcing her to search for someone else. He wanted to say no to her, just once.

"I will be honored to accept such a position, your Majesty, and to fulfill your royal command. However, in order to do so, I must insist on one condition."

"What is that?", asked Isabella, unaccustomed to her subjects imposing conditions, but, then again, Senior was no ordinary subject.

"I must insist that a significant portion of the chief tax farming duties be assumed by someone else, and I must be allowed to specify who that person will be. That is my condition, if you will, for taking on the position of Treasurer of the Holy Brotherhood."

There was silence in the air. Ferdinand and Isabella sat on their throne, grim and tight-lipped. Always the King and Queen went to great pains in their selection of key government posts, and Senior was robbing them of their choice of his replacement. An irked Isabella cast an angry glance at an equally sullen Ferdinand. This was not to their liking. It was not any mere violation of court protocol or even an improper request. It was a command, it was an ultimatum from Senior that they accept his choice, or the entire deal was off. Senior had outbargained them, had outmaneuvered the King and Queen into a position where they needed him more than he needed them. Isabella, the spite rising in her voice, asked sharply, "And who would that be?"

"My son-in-law, Rabbi Meir," Senior answered forthrightly, "He is obviously the best trained for this position. I have taught him all I know. He knows the tax trade thoroughly after years of working with me, and he knows it so well that I am ready this very moment to entrust him with all of the duties of chief tax farmer. That is how much I confide in him, and I ask of your Majesties to bring my son-in-law into your confidence. He is a loyal servant of the crown and is ready to do your will. Your Majesties, I beg of you, let him be your new chief tax farmer."

The silence and tension vanished. All was well again. Ferdinand relaxed back on his chair, and a soft smile found its way on Isabella's face. She was pleased with the choice.

"I believe that it is in our power to grant you such a request, Don Abraham," answered Isabella.

Ferdinand joined in, "Yes, Don Abraham, it is certainly a possibility, and we most likely will agree, but we must still give it further consideration. We have met your son-in-law, Rabbi . . . Me . . . uh . . . what is his name again?"

"Meir", Senior replied.

"Yes, Rabbi Meir", continued the King, "and he seemed to us to be a very intelligent and very capable individual. I trust your judgement in this regard is not affected by your relationship to Rabbi Me . . . Meir."

"It most assuredly is not. If at any time I find that my son-in-law is not performing adequately, I shall take charge of tax farming operations as before and remove him from office forthwith. However, I can guarantee you now, your Majesty, that this will not occur. I know what I am talking about."

"Very well", said the Queen, "I know and trust your choice in this matter is a good one, Don Abraham. Thus it is that we have trusted your judgment in other matters. Are there any specific problems of the Jewish community that you care to bring to our attention?"

Senior was aware that further concessions from the sovereigns would not be forthcoming, or at least not that day. It was enough that they had tentatively permitted his son-in-law, Rabbi Meir, to be the new chief tax farmer. There was no need to push whatever small advantage he had extracted from them in this regard. Meir would be delighted and so would his daughter Hanna. It was a position that would guarantee them an excellent livelihood, one that Senior wanted to keep within the family.

"Your Majesty is most gracious in wishing to hear about the problems that beset our community. However, I beg that you hear our requests on a day that does not have such pressing responsibilities as this one. If it pleases your Majesty, I request permission to begin forthwith making arrangements for our Jewish brethren who are to be ransomed. Money must be raised for their release, and then there are the problems of food, lodging, and transportation to other cities where they will be cared for and absorbed into the communities. Your Majesties, with your permission . . ."

"You are excused, Don Abraham. We shall meet with you before week's end to discuss these other matters", Isabella dismissed Senior.

"Good day, Don Abraham", Ferdinand offered.

"Good day, your Majesties", and with that Senior bowed once again respectfully and left the throne room. It was indeed a very good day, Senior thought to himself. He had satisfied the King and Queen, he had given them good advice and intelligent direction, and, most of all, he had satisfied himself.

As Don Abraham retired to his tent, he was briefed by one of his aides on the situation in Málaga. Senior was aware that he had arrived the day after the Moors of the city had surrendered; he was also aware that he had missed much of the excitement. It was perhaps just as well. He was tired from his journey, and he was not in the mood for the usual celebrations that followed each Christian victory. At seventy-plus years of age, he became easily fatigued. How much longer could he continue all these roles?

The irritating doubts circled in his mind endlessly, his tired muscles slowly lost their firmness, and he imagined he was losing control, losing his powers, sliding into oblivion, opening himself to the ebb and tide of a teetering limbo of consciousness that pulled him gently into the grasp of the night's sleep.

Senior woke up to the clanging of bells. The ringing in his ears grew, an unharmonious cacophony of thunderous vibrations that shook the Andalusian morning air. Unable to sleep further, he slipped into his clothes to witness whatever it was the untimely pealings were about.

The vanquished Moors were on display. The once proud Mohammedans walked slowly, their heads bowed in shame, the color gone from their faces as much from months of hunger as from the disgrace of defeat. Slowly, ever so slowly, they walked, thousands of them, of all ages, their headdresses flapping in the wind, parading themselves to the clanging din of church bells. One young Moor, able to speak the Castilian tongue, seeking to show some humor, shouted out, "You have no cows, but you have the mulebells?" A few laughed and passed on the joke, but it was not enough. The spiritless march of the beaten Moors continued as the Christian nobility, perched atop observation platforms, gazed triumphantly on this subdued herd of infidel foes.

Then with much fanfare and shouting and the raising of pennants in the air, the King and Queen emerged from the royal tent. A roar burst forth from the Christian camp as the Catholic sovereigns walked proudly, heads high with the elation of victory. Along with their daughter, the Infanta, the King and Queen found their way amidst the throng to the Granada gate of the city, where they received the six hundred emaciated Christian prisoners who had been held captive by the Moors.

As the prisoners emerged from the gate, some of them with crosses and royal pennants, they prostrated themselves on the ground and kissed the King and Queen's feet. They gave thanks to God, and broke into sobs of joy at their release. The King and Queen ordered their cavaliers to give the released prisoners food and drink, to remove their irons, to clothe them, and to give them enough money to return to their home.

El Zegri, the once fierce Moorish commander-at-arms of Gibralfaro castle, seeing that all was lost, submitted himself meekly to the Christian rulers. The irate King and Queen had El Zegri bound in chains and thrown into a dungeon to suffer what he had made the Christians endure.

After the ceremonies of surrender were completed, Senior went his own way to talk with the Jewish prisoners who had been separated from the Moorish captives and had been placed in a guarded area next to the city walls. He saw them from afar. There they stood — four hundred and fifty of his Jewish kinsmen, the young and the old, many of them swarthy, dressed in the Morisco fashion. The older men wore raggedy coiled turbans and dirty grey robes. The women had plaited headdresses and long flowing shabby garments. How different was their dress from that of his fellow Jews back in Segovia, Senior confided to himself, but they were Jews nonetheless, they were his brothers and his sisters, the carriers of the seed of Abraham.

A Morisco Jew, a gaunt, bearded man of fifty or so, spotted Senior, lifted the rope and broke away from the cordoned section; he raised his arms jubilantly, pointed toward Senior, and shouted for all to hear, *"Baruch Ha-Ba! Baruch Ha-Ba!* Blessed be he who comes in the name of the Lord!" The middle-aged Jew galloped down the hillside towards Senior, his legs churning up a white cloud of dust behind him, shouting his salutation again and again. He ran up to Senior, and falling on his knees, he kissed Senior's robe and the jeweled rings on the chief judge's hand. Senior lifted him up graciously and hugged him. *"Ahinu Atah"*, Senior said in his stuttering Hebrew, "You are our brother," as they continued to embrace. Tears came to the Morisco's eyes upon hearing these words; he cried with spasms of joyous happiness, upon knowing that his brethren had come to their rescue. *"Kulanu Ahim"*, the Morisco Jew answered him, "we are all brothers". Others now streamed down the hillside, despite the restraining efforts of the overwhelmed Christian guards, and joined the delirious jubilation down below. Senior was swamped by the ragged but grateful multitude that showered him with Hebrew blessings. Crying for help, arms raised to heaven, the crowd of people clung to Senior's garments. Teary-eyed young women thrust babies in his arms, others imparted an appreciative hug, turbaned old men lifted a cane into the air to get his attention and express their thanks — all of it became an intoxicating blur for Senior as he turned from one grateful co-religionist to another. He filled himself with their thanks and caringly assured them of their ultimate well-being. A group of men, both the young and the old, broke out into Hebrew song. It was a Psalm of Thanksgiving, of deliverance:

"Oh give thanks unto the Lord, for He is good,
"For His Mercy endures forever
So let the house of Aaron now say
For His mercy endures forever."

All the crowd in unison intoned the line, "For His mercy endures forever", adding special feeling to this often sung Hebrew psalm. It was into this overflowing wellspring of pulsating human emotion that Senior soaked himself and drank deeply of its waters, experiencing the transcendant feeling of being at one with his people, of capturing for himself at the moment that magical and mysterious linkage that connected all Jews, a sense of family that spanned the ages, of a kinship that defied boundaries and crossed castes and titles, of ties that broke all imposed barriers of society. Senior savored the warmth of the moment, prolonged it to a point of unreality, losing himself in the ecstatic interim, shedding the vanity of his vaulted position and his wealth, bathing himself in his own tears, forgetting who and whatever it was that he was, forgetting his heavy responsibilities and burdens, and became a child of Israel who was at peace with his people.

It was always in the darkness of the confessional that the Grand Inquisitor and the Queen would meet, she to disclose her failings, he to forgive them. Here, amidst the strangest of silences, they shared their darkest secret, allowing it to mature and gather strength in these secluded moments.

"Is it time yet?", the Grand Inquisitor asked.

In a hushed voice, the Queen replied, "No, it is not yet time. The King is not ready. There are still many of them in the court, and their influence on him is strong. His mind is on the war, but his heart is not yet set against them."

The deep-throated voice of the Grand Inquisitor reached out, "The time will come when it will be so. Soon the war against the Moslem infidel will be over, and then you must fulfill the promise that you made to our Lord."

The Queen answered, "I will fulfill my promise when the time has come. But I rule only over Castile, not over Aragon."

The voice of the Grand Inquisitor urged, "Work on the King. He can be made to see the need for such an action. Pray that he will see the light. Pray that he will join us."

The Queen paused, then continued, "I will pray, but you know that the King is not one to be influenced by prayer. He only understands gold and arms. This is the way to reach him."

"With gold?", the Inquisitor asked.

The Queen continued, "Yes, with gold, their gold . . . all the gold that they will leave behind. Just as you have been giving us money from the Converso estates. This is the way to reach the King."

The Inquisitor reflected, then added, "I shall work on a plan . . . a plan as you have described, a plan that will appeal to the King."

"Then do it, Grand Inquisitor, and the time will be soon upon us", the Queen said.

Chapter 2

Don Abraham Senior was returning exhausted. The three-week mule ride from Málaga to Segovia, across the harsh dry flatlands of Castile and then up the rockied pine-studded hills of the Sierra Guadarrama, had exacted a toll from his aging body. Each of his bones and muscles ached. He was getting too old for this sort of thing. There was no question in his mind about that. He would have to pass on the reins to his son-in-law.

From afar, the end of his trek came into sight. The narrow rocky road led to the massive Roman aqueduct, supported by 165 granite arches, that conveyed the city's water supply from the Río Frío. The aqueduct spanned the Plaza del Azoguejo, the principal entrance to the rest of the city. As Senior passed under its huge arches, a feeling of relief flowed through his body. He loved Segovia, and there was something special about his old mountain town, founded in ages past by the Celts, perched like a vast limestone sculpture on the heights of Castile. Here he had been born, and here it was that he wished to die. He would never leave Segovia, except when the dictates of duty forced him to do otherwise.

As the group proceeded down the narrow winding streets of Segovia, Senior experienced not merely relief at the journey's end, but a new-found strength. His bodyguards, atop Arabian steeds and with their lances poised for assault, came up alongside him as they rode into the city three across. From the plaza the group turned to the right as it entered the Calle Real, the principal thoroughfare. On both sides of the street were the white stone-walled tenements with their iron-gated win-

13

dows, their courtyards colorfully decorated with potted plants and flowers.

Senior recognized friends along the way who greeted him warmly. Curious lady onlookers on the uppermost tenements opened their windows to watch the distinguished retinue led by the famous Don Abraham Senior who was dressed immaculately in silken clothes and whose saddle and spurs were inlaid with glistening silver. It was an impressive sight.

The procession passed by the Casa de los Picos, its facade hewn with faceted stones. Proceeding along the Calle del Sol, they approached the *judería* or Jewish quarter with its four massive gates. The *judería* was located a few streets away from the massive Gothic Cathedral that loomed over it, their geography encompassing their relative positions, the church high on the hill, the *judería* and its synagogues in the spiraling vale below.

As the group approached the *judería*, more Jews came into view. Many were simple folk, artisans and the like, who made way for the chief judge of their community, greeting him with fearful respect.

While Senior was admitted to be the head of the Jewish communities in Spain, he did everything to do away with the outward signs of his Jewishness. Although the Laws of the Cortés of Madrigal required that every Jew wear a red circular patch on the right shoulder so as to make them identifiable among Christians, Senior and his family did not have to wear them because they had obtained an exemption from the King and Queen. Despite the prohibition on Jews wearing silk or fine scarlet cloth, Senior and his family were permitted to do so. Even though Jews were prohibited from living among Christians, Senior and his family were permitted to live outside the confines of the *judería*. Everything that demeaned and degraded the Jew, Senior found a way to get around. Some said that he was ashamed of being Jewish. Others said that he needed to be free of such degrading outward signs so as to be able to negotiate as a self-respecting subject of the crown. Whatever the reason, Senior was an enigma to his own people. His predecessors as supreme judge, such as Rabbi Bienveniste or Jacob Ibn Núñez, had been revered scholars who wore simple garments. Although they had been accorded this preeminent community position, they had not flaunted the power or the wealth that came with it. Don Abraham, however, was not one to cloak his might under a mantle of piety and meekness, and he made sure that the ceremonial honors and dignities due him were performed in accordance with custom.

Don Abraham was returning to Segovia with a feeling of personal accomplishment. He had gone on this mission to Málaga unsure of the outcome — unsure of the number of captives and unsure of the price to be paid. Yet despite some initial difficulties, all had gone well.

The four hundred and fifty freed Jews of Málaga had finally set sail on two galleys of the Castilian armada in order to be dispersed throughout the kingdom. As a preliminary payment on their ransom, the Christian rulers stripped the Jewish captives of all their valuables — jewels, silver trinkets, gold ducats — and all that was collected went into the Christian coffers. And yet it was far better than the treatment given the Moors. The eleven thousand captive Moors, stripped of their land, belongings, and valuables, were unable to secure payment of their ransom and were made slaves. They were sold like cattle in Sevilla and Jérez to the gloating of auctioneers and the bidding of feudal lords.

Senior thus felt that he had properly discharged his duties as chief Jewish judge and had spared his kinsmen the ignominy of such physical degradation. Indeed, he had even brought one notable Morisco Jewish family back to Segovia with him — the Alhadeff family, a family known for its erudition and piety. At the head of the family was the Hacham Isaac Alhadeff, and along with him was his lovely daughter, a dark-skinned beauty that his aides nicknamed "Morenica." In time, Senior mused, they would be an asset to the Segovian community.

Senior's group continued to progress down the alleyways until it arrived at the main entrance gate to the *judería*. Here there was heightened activity: homemakers bustled about, scarves on their heads, pails in hand from a recent trip to the river. Others carried food in cloth sacks over their shoulders. The pounding of hammers, accompanied by the blacksmiths' heat and smoke, carried a fearful din. Shoemakers displayed their samples of leather boots and sandals. The smell of the tanneries located further down in the Jewish district floated upwards to the entrance gate. Shopkeepers, silversmiths, bakers, kosher butchers, greengrocers — each and every little store had food or wares to sell, each and every proprietor added his voice to the dissonant street chorus in the *judería*. And now there was a muffled silence in the Jewish quarter as the mighty Don Abraham Senior made his entry. Merchants, artisans, customers, housewives taking care of Sabbath shopping needs, children wandering about — all stopped what they were doing to watch the procession led by Senior. The frenzy of business activity came to a standstill.

With Senior at its head, the group wound its way down the streets of the *judería* until it was but a turn away from his home. Senior's family was waiting for him outside his estate. Advance word of his party had been brought by a messenger, and all of them — his wife Fortuna, his son Solomon, and his daughter Hanna who was married to Rabbi Meir Melamed — all waited anxiously for the man who was the source of their pride, the man who had brought them fame and fortune.

Finally Don Abraham arrived. As he got off his mule, he was greeted with hugs and kisses from his relatives. Fortuna embraced her husband and then spirited him inside the house to avoid public display of affection. Don Abraham was accustomed to his wife's manner, to her insistence of social decorum, and he took it in stride. As they walked into the main living room, Fortuna led him past a servant who took his velvet coat and then past another who brought him a basin of water to freshen up. Then, Fortuna led him to the central huge patio where she made Don Abraham rest with his feet propped up on a large soft pillow. A servant came to take off his boots. Someone placed a bowl of fruit at his side and gave him crushed orange juice extract in a large wooden goblet to drink. All gathered about Don Abraham to hear his account of the latest battlefield reports, and Fortuna sat at his side to hear all the rumors and going-ons at court. Fortuna began the conversation, "Darling, it's so good to have you back after three months. Please, tell us about all that happened at Málaga. We will die from curiosity if you don't tell us what you did there".

Senior looked at his wife with a warm smile. Her sense of formality was matched only by her love of rumors and court scandal. Fortuna was seventy years old now, but she did not look it. She still looked and played the role of the refined aristocratic matron to perfection: her brown hair was parted in the middle and set with an intricately woven headpiece, the eyebrows arched high, the nose straight with narrow nostrils, the lips thin and tightly drawn, all within a waxen oval shaped face. And she was always dressed elegantly in the latest fashion.

Don Abraham put the goblet aside.

"Bring me a jar of wine," he said.

"What is it, Abraham?" Fortuna asked curiously.

Senior signaled for her to be silent. The servant arrived with the jar of wine and several glasses. Don Abraham took the jar himself, poured small portions in the glasses, and passed them out to all his family. He rose from the cushion, wine glass in hand.

"A toast," Don Abraham said.

"To your safe return, darling," Fortuna added.

"A toast . . .", Don Abraham continued holding them in deliberate suspense, "a toast to the new chief tax farmer of all Castile, Rabbi Meir Melamed."

Gasps of joy shook the air. Fortuna kissed her husband on the cheek and then sipped wine. Meir let out a yelp, drank his drink in one gulp, jumped into the air, and then came promptly over to hug Don Abraham in one long embrace. Then Meir kissed his wife who was crying with happiness; they hugged and rocked one another.

"This is wonderful, really wonderful," Meir said. Meir was turning fifty now, and this would be the climax in his career as a tax farmer. For years he hard worked long and hard alongside his father-in-law, and now he was finally reaping his just reward. The heavy jowls on his plump face took on a tinge of flushed red, his heavy-lidded eyes lit up with satisfaction. He was ecstatic. Nothing could have pleased him more.

Meir now led a new toast, "A toast to you, Don Abraham, for all the many wonderful things you have given us, for the wonderful wife you and Doña Fortuna have given me, and now for this wonderful position. What can I say? My life could be no happier than it has been as a result of my being a part of this great family. I thank you dearly, Don Abraham".

Then Meir and Don Abraham embraced one last time. It was only then that Don Abraham finally allowed himself to sit down on the cushion to tell of his deeds at Málaga. He related what he had heard of the battles between the Moors and the Jews, of how he had been appointed Treasurer of the Hermandad, of how their good friend Beatriz de la Bobadilla had nearly been killed by the Moro Santo, of how the King and Queen had dealt with his petitions on behalf of the Jewish communities. He spoke of these and other things well into the night, pausing every now and then to open up a saddlebag or two and disperse presents to the members of his household. For his wife, Fortuna, he pulled out a dazzling, gold-laced Morisco skirt made of purple velvet. His daughter was handed bagfuls of oriental spices — pepper, nutmegs, pimento, and cinnamon — obtained from an itinerant merchant in the Málaga camp. Solomon and Meir both got solid gold necklaces. The stories, the presents, the toasts, and the air of a joyful Sabbath eve continued well into the night.

The messenger told Rabbi Simon Maimi to expect a guest who was being sent by Don Abraham. As the Sabbath was nearly upon them, Rabbi Maimi was delighted to receive the guest because it would be a *mitzvah*, a good deed, to have honored guests at the Sabbath eve dinner table.

Rabbi Maimi was known for his hospitality, and whenever there was a new face in the synagogue, he would walk up to the newcomer in the midst of the religious service, and invite him and his family home for the Sabbath. He was fond of quoting the Pharisaic sage Shammai who used to say, "Say little and do much. And receive every man with a cheerful face." There was a saintly ebulliency about this bearded portly rabbi who loved people, who gave of himself to one and all. Rabbi Maimi's cheerfulness, good humor, and compassion endeared him to his congregants. Those who were sick looked forward to his visits, for it meant the telling of stories of the sages of old, and it meant pleasant words of encouragement and the communication of well-wishes from friends. Even for those who were not ill, just being around Rabbi Maimi made one feel better. He radiated goodness and cheerfulness, a loving kindness to all he came in touch with. He loved people, and people loved him. Had not the greatest of the Pharisaic sages, the Rabbi Hillel, said, "Be of the disciples of Aaron, one that loves peace, that loves mankind, and brings them close to Torah." So it was that Rabbi Maimi lived up to this measure.

As he looked out his window, Rabbi Maimi saw the train of plodding mules and horses emerging from the more affluent area of the *juderia*, where the physicians, courtiers, and the chief judge lived. The rabbi was content with his humble home in the poorer section of the quarter. It was all he and his wife needed. "Who is rich? He who is happy with his lot," he said to himself, quoting once again from the Talmudic tractate of Avot. His children, now grown up and married, were his treasure. And was not the wisdom of the Bible and the Talmud far more rewarding than worldly riches? Surely it was so. He stroked his white beard in expectation, scratched his balding head, clasped his hands nervously, wondering who it was that the mule train would bring him. His soft blue eyes studied the caravan as it passed into his part of the quarter.

He walked out into the street to receive his guests. All about him, people were popping their heads out of the windows of the overcrowded three-story stone tenements to see what was going on. Rabbi Maimi waited, a smile on his face, for his guests. He did not have to wait long.

"Blessed be those who have come in the name of the Lord," Rabbi

Maimi beamed, as he shook hands with the skinny turbaned Morisco Jew, then smiled at the young woman who had come with him. The Morisco Jew was emaciated and frail; he had sunken cheeks and hollow-looking eyes. His daughter was less undernourished, but even she had a thin, sickly look about her.

The Morisco Jew answered, "Peace be unto you, Rabbi. My name is Hacham Isaac Alhadeff, and this is my daughter. We are among the Jews of Málaga that were ransomed by Don Abraham Senior, God bless his soul, and we have no place to stay. Don Abraham told me you would be willing to share your household at least for the Sabbath until we can find a place for ourselves. You see, we have nothing . . ."

Rabbi Maimi cut off his apology, "My house is your house, and you are welcome to stay, not just for the Sabbath, but until you are ready to provide for yourselves. The community of Segovia will help you and your daughter as much as it can, I assure you of that."

"I know that we are a burden," Alhadeff said, "we will pay you back when we can."

"I will never allow you to do that. All Israel must be responsible for one another. Thus it is written. You should know that as a Hacham . . ."

Alhadeff remained silent, listening.

Rabbi Maimi continued, "Scholars are at a premium these days, and troubled days they are indeed for our communities in Spain. Is it not written that a person taken captive with his father and his teacher must first rescue himself, then his teacher, and then his father?"

"Yes . . . it is so written," answered Alhadeff.

Rabbi Maimi pushed his point further, "And is it not written in the Talmud that the ransoming of a scholar takes preference even to the King of Israel?"

"Yes, that is true," Alhadeff admitted, a look of surprise on his face.

Rabbi Maimi concluded, "Well, then, you are like a king in our home, nay, more than a king, and it is our honor and our privilege to welcome you. Please, Hacham, truly it is we who are blessed by your presence. Enter, please . . . my home is truly your home."

"You are most kind, Rabbi," said the Hacham, teary-eyed, with a glimmer of a smile on his cheeks. Accepting the offer, the Hacham and his daughter walked inside.

Rabbi Maimi then introduced his guests to his wife Sarah, who was in the kitchen busy preparing food for the Sabbath. Sarah was tall, reddish-haired and large-eyed, and she acknowledged the respectful bow of the Hacham with a bow of her own in return. She went up to the young girl and embraced her, saying, "Welcome to our house, daughter of Israel. If I may say so, you are very beautiful. With such beauty, you will have no trouble finding yourself a good Jewish boy to marry. How do they call you?"

"My name is Batya, but I like being called 'Morenica,' " she said.

"Then Morenica it shall be. It's a lovely name, don't you think so, Simon?", asked Ruth.

"Yes, yes, of course . . .," answered the rabbi politely.

"And how is it that you speak Castilian so well?", Sarah queried.

"I learned to speak it years ago," Morenica replied, "but I still do not speak it as well as I speak Arabic."

All faces turned towards the Hacham for an explanation.

"My daughter and I are natives of Málaga. When I was a young man, the Jewish community of Córdoba asked me to teach in their *yeshiva*, and I went there when Batya was but five years old. She grew up speaking Castilian until she was close to sixteen. My wife died, God bless her soul, and we were left alone in Córdoba, and we stayed there for several years despite the fact that all our relatives were back in Málaga. Ultimately, we were forced to leave because of an . . . an unpleasant incident."

"Unpleasant? It was terrible, father," said Morenica in a challenging tone.

Rabbi Maimi intervened, "Perhaps you should go to your room and wash up now and get ready for the Sabbath."

"What was it that made you leave, Hacham Alhadeff?", Sarah asked innocently.

The rabbi answered her, "Sarah, do not embarrass our guest. If he wanted you to know, he would have told you."

The Hacham explained, "As I have said, it was an unpleasant incident that made us leave. But because it is forbidden to speak of things that make one sad on the Sabbath, I shall tell my tale at some other time".

"I absolutely agree with this," said Rabbi Maimi, "let us all ready ourselves for the Sabbath. Let us banish unpleasant thoughts from our minds. Let us rejoice at your safe homecoming to Segovia, Hacham and Morenica Alhadeff, and let us be glad of heart today at the Sabbath table. Let us all have Sabbath peace."

"Amen," affirmed the Hacham, as did Sarah and Morenica. The Hacham and his daughter dutifully followed the rabbi as he led them to their room to wash and prepare themselves for the Sabbath.

While Morenica stayed at home with Sarah Maimi to help out with the cooking for the Sabbath, the Hacham and the rabbi walked slowly to the synagogue, talking and gesticulating as they went. The sinking sun in the east cast warm shafts of light along the corridors of the *judería*, giving the buildings a soft orangish hue, bouncing rays off the San Andrés Gate that led from the *judería* down to the River Clamores and making the quarter glow in the sunset.

The bustle of the day was gone. The gates of the *judería* were shut. Carts, horses, and other beasts of burden were absent from the streets in honor of the Sabbath, leaving all activity to the few pedestrians who strolled calmly and peacefully toward the synagogue. There Sabbath stillness soothed the soul and gave it rest. Here and there a father and his well-scrubbed children, all of them dressed in their very best clothes, walked hand in hand and sang Hebrew songs that the children had learned in school. The rabbi and his guest joined the casual promenade, much to the Hacham's delight.

In many homes, shutters were flung open showing lit Sabbath candles, burning brightly in silver candlesticks, their yellow flames adding to the aura of the eve. The last rays of the sun lingered on, only to be smothered by the softly falling curtain of darkness that became night.

The rabbi and the Hacham joined the congregation, a hundred strong, in the midst of evening prayers for *Mincha* and *Arvith*. The Hacham participated in the spirited chanting of the Psalms and in the prayers of welcome for the Sabbath. He felt all eyes were on him as he did so, everyone glancing a puzzled look at him from time to time, observing his odd Morisco dress and sizing him up at a distance. Children snickered in the aisles, pointing fingers at him and his turban, their hands covering their giggling mouths, adding to the Hacham's evident discomfort. When the service was finally over, amidst mutual exchanges of *"Shabbat Shalom!"* and "Sabbath peace!", the Hacham could not help feeling that he had undergone a communal inspection.

The Hacham was introduced to one person after another by Rabbi Maimi. Now his onlookers appeared to be as friendly as they had been curious, and the Hacham began to feel more at ease, and he, too, greeted them with the traditional *"Shabbat Shalom!"*

Finally the introductions were over, and the rabbi and the Hacham were able to walk home together under the canopy of the starry Castilian sky.

They knocked on the rabbi's door and kissed the mezuzah. The door opened and they were greeted by Sarah Maimi with a hearty *"Shabbat Shalom."* The rabbi kissed his wife, and Morenica kissed her father, and all exchanged well-wishes.

The table was set with a beautiful white linen cloth and glistening silverware. There were two loaves of freshly cooked *hallah*, the traditional Sabbath bread, covered by a red velvet cloth embroidered with gold Hebrew lettering. A gracefully shaped silver goblet filled to the brim with red wine was at the head of the table, together with the two Sabbath candles.

Everyone stood as Rabbi Maimi lifted the wine cup and intoned the *Kiddush*, the sanctification of the wine, and said, "Blessed Art Thou, O Lord Our God, Ruler of the Universe, who has created the fruit of the vine." He drank from the cup and he passed it around for the others to drink.

Then the group ritually washed their hands and proceeded to sit silently at the table. Rabbi Maimi held the two loaves, closed his eyes, and said "Blessed Art Thou, O Lord Our God, Ruler of the Universe, who bringest forth food from the earth." He then pulled off pieces of hallah bread, dipped them in a small heap of sprinkled salt, and passed them around the table for all to eat.

Sarah Maimi then brought servings of fish in lemon egg sauce. *"Pescado con huevo y limon,"* she informed her guests, "I hope you like it."

The Hacham sampled the dish and exclaimed "It's delicious, absolutely delicious. I've never eaten anything like it!" And he ate some more.

"Yes, I agree," said Morenica. "It's really very good. You must show me how to prepare this, Señora Maimi."

"It will be my pleasure," Sarah answered her.

The rabbi rounded out the compliments by saying. "After forty-two years of marriage to you, Sarah, I can honestly say that your meals keep getting better from year to year. I have only one misgiving about them."

Sarah braced herself for criticism, "And what is that, Simon?", emphasizing his name.

"I'm only sorry I didn't marry you sooner, so that I could enjoy even more of your good cooking." The rabbi laughed heartily, amused by his own joke.

Sarah laughed too and she gave her husband an extra helping of the fish. She returned to the kitchen and brought out more savory dishes — meat turnovers called pastelicos covered with sesame seeds, slices of roasted lamb cooked with garlic and onions, green beans, sliced cucumbers and peas.

"Ah, good, very good," the Hacham muttered as he gulped down huge helpings of the dishes, and drank generous portions of the wine.

"L'Hayim! To Life!", the rabbi would shout, as he filled his guest's wine cup every time that the Hacham emptied it.

"Eat! Eat! There's plenty more," said Sarah Maimi, urging her guests to indulge themselves. But the Hacham finally admitted he could not eat or drink anymore, and he sat back in his chair with a sated look. He was on the verge of dozing off when the rabbi suddenly beat the table rhythmically with his fist and began singing a rousing Hebrew Sabbath song. The Hacham shook off his weariness and joined in the rhythmic pounding on the table, the silverware and the plates nearly jumping off the table. The two women joined them in song, creating a merry atmosphere as they went from one song to another. After several songs Morenica asked, "How many Jews are there in Castile, Rabbi?"

The rabbi, still tapping out the beat of a song, thought about this for a moment and said, "My dear, there are probably about thirty thousand Jewish families in all of Castile, more or less."

"That many?", an incredulous Hacham remarked.

"Yes. But even though it sounds like a lot, we are no more than two or three percent of the total population of Castile. In Aragon, the Jewish population numbers about six thousand families, or so I have heard from Don Abraham."

Morenica probed further, "And what about the Jewish communities here in Castile — how are they structured, I mean, how do they govern themselves?"

The rabbi turned to the Hacham, "You have a very inquisitive daughter, Hacham. Very beautiful and very bright she is. It is good that she is curious about her new environment. Very good. I am sure she has this instinctive curiousity about the world from a man of learning such as yourself."

The Hacham nodded his head ambiguously, while Morenica lowered her large black eyes in embarrassment, her long black eyelashes blinking nervously.

"Now to answer your question, my dear. The Jews of Castile are governed by the *takkanot* of Valladolid that were drawn up in the year 1432 by Rabbi Abraham Bienveniste of sacred memory. These regulations, these *takkanot*, deal with various matters of community life: the provision for Hebrew instruction, the selection of judges, how to deal with slanderers, how to levy taxes, and also restrictions on extravagance in dress and entertainment."

The Hacham asked, "As a teacher, I am most interested in your school system. Could you elaborate further?"

The rabbi continued, "Of course. The funds for the school system come from indirect taxes on wine and cattle used by the community, along with other taxes from weddings and circumcisions and the like. Every community of fifteen families is obligated to hire a Hebrew teacher for their children. Communities of forty families or more must have a full-time teacher of Talmud and torah, a real scholar, who will head the school of learning, the *yeshiva*, and teach all who want to study Torah and Halachic Law. It is a very fine educational system, and it has produced some of the greatest scholars in the history of Israel. Our own *yeshiva* here in Segovia is one of the best in all of Spain, and perhaps we can find a place in the school for someone such as yourself, Hacham Alhadeff."

"You are most kind," said the Hacham, "Everyone knows that the Jews of Spain, especially those in Castile, exceed all other Jewish communities in their learning, lineage, and . . . wealth. Even the *yeshivot* of the Ashkenazim in France and Germany cannot begin to compare with the *yeshivot* here in Spain. I should know. I taught in the *yeshiva* of Córdoba.

The rabbi continued, "Yes, the Córdoba *yeshiva* has a very old, time honored tradition. It goes way back to the tenth century, when Abdul-rahman III reigned, at the peak of Moslem power in Spain under the Caliphate of Córdoba.

"It was Moses Ben Enoch who established the first *yeshiva*. He was a Babylonian rabbi by birth, and he and his family had set sail to seek their fortune in the new and rising Moslem Caliphate of the west. En route, he was taken captive and brought as a slave to Córdoba, where he was ransomed by the local Jewish community . . . as you have just been, Hacham Alhadeff."

"Shortly after he was freed, Rabbi Moses Ben Enoch was brought to the local school where a rabbi was expounding Talmud to his students. Hardly anyone paid any attention to the humble liberated slave who sat quietly in the corner listening to the exposition. At one point in the discussion, however, the local rabbi was baffled by a difficult Talmudic question that one of his students had raised. He did not know how even to begin to answer the problem.

"It was then that Rabbi Ben Enoch rose from his corner and quietly walked over to the local rabbi and whispered in his ears the solution to the Talmudic problem. The local rabbi was amazed at the ingenuity of the solution, and even more so by its source, and he asked the man who he was."

"I am Rabbi Moses Ben Enoch from Babylonia, and I was an instructor in the great Talmudic Academy of Sura."

"The local rabbi then said, 'Then, Rabbi, it is you who should be teaching this class and not I, for your learning in the Talmud and your wisdom far exceed mine.'

"So it was that Rabbi Moses Ben Enoch became the spiritual head of the *yeshiva* in Córdoba. The fame of his school spread far and wide, and students from all over Spain and North Africa came to study with this great man. His school was supported by local Jewish notables such as Hasdai Ibn Shiprut who was the chief adviser to Abdul-rahman III. It was then that Hebrew and Talmudic studies in Spain really began to develop.

"Perhaps, Hacham Alhadeff, you are the Rabbi Moses Ben Enoch of our generation. Perhaps it is you, a ransomed scholar, who shall kindle a rebirth of Jewish scholarship in Spain."

The Hacham shook his head knowingly, "You flatter me again, Rabbi, but, alas, I am not that man. I am a humble scholar with perhaps above average training, but I am no Rabbi Moses Ben Enoch. Although I wish I were, I must admit that I am not the man who will bring that Golden Age back."

Rabbi Maimi answered, "Nonetheless, I believe that you have something to contribute to our generation, to leave your mark on the pages of our history. We have fallen on difficult times lately, and when the Sabbath is over, I will discuss with you what some of our current community problems are and how you may be able to help us."

The Hacham inclined his head toward the rabbi, "Rabbi, this community rescued my daughter and myself from the curse of slavery and bondage, a fate worse than death itself. The least that we owe you are our lives. I will do my utmost to fulfill whatever the community requires of me and my daughter." Morenica silently nodded her agreement. Sarah Maimi put her hand gently on Morenica's, a look of sympathy on her face.

Rabbi Maimi looked pensive. Retreating in his own reverie of glories past, his eyes were glazed and unfocused. Then, returning from his moment of contemplation, he commented:

"It was a Golden Age as you say, Hacham Alhadeff. When I think of the many scholars and poets that came to be after Rabbi Moses Ben Enoch, it is truly amazing. Hebrew studies in Spain began to develop and flourish as they never had before. Yehuda Halevy, Maimonides, the Ibn Ezras, to name a few — who has not heard or been influenced by them? They were master thinkers, scholars who lived and breathed Torah, spiritual men who towered above their own and future generations, men able to inspire others through their writings and their own example. We are in desperate need of such leaders . . . leaders who are revered scholars, who occupy themselves day and night with study of Torah, who have their roots deep in our religious tradition."

"Are there any such leaders in Spain today?", the Hacham asked. The rabbi thought for a moment, "Yes, there are some, and you will meet them in due time. But their voices are muted by those who have power in the Jewish community and who wish to ingratiate themselves with the Christian authorities. It is these men, the men of wealth and position, who limit the activities and the statements of the pious for fear they will jeopardize the safety of the communities. Perhaps they mean well, but it does us no good. The sages of our generation, great as they may be, have mouths but are not allowed to speak. That is the tragedy of our generation, a generation that must suffer not only from Christian persecutors, but from our own Hebrew brothers."

The Hacham asked innocently, "Rabbi, if I may ask, who are these men in our midst who silence our sages?"

The rabbi cautiously replied, "I prefer not to name names. In any case, I have spoken too much tonight. Let us say the Blessing after Meals now, because tomorrow we must get up early for morning services. Besides, I see that you and your daughter are tired from the journey, and I think you should get some rest now."

And with that, the blessing after meals was recited, and everyone went to bed.

Rabbi Maimi and Hacham Alhadeff arrived early for Sabbath morning prayers. The Rabbi greeted everyone with a friendly smile and a handshake, introducing his exotic guest from the South to any who had not yet met him. At the very outset of the service, there had been barely a *minyan*, the quorum of ten men necessary for morning prayers, but people filtered in steadily throughout the service so that the synagogue was ultimately full to capacity. And as the liturgical service progressed, the intensity of the responsive chanting mounted, the worshippers fervently intoning in unison Psalms of the ancient Temple services, devotional hymns, and Biblical passages.

The chanting reminded the Hacham of the tunes he knew in Málaga; it brought back sweet memories of the humble synagogue there and of its golden-toned cantors. He felt much more at home now and he returned the stares of youthful onlookers with a wide smile of his own. Embarrassed, many who had lingered overly long in their curious gaze turned their heads away. The Hacham was beginning to like it here.

The Hacham looked about. The congregation sat on wooden benches; their heads were covered with traditional white prayer shawls fringed with blue. Most were praying diligently, but a few at the rear spoke in hushed tones. Off to the side was a partition separating the men from the women. This was done to avoid worldy distractions in the midst of an act of religious devotion. The Hacham looked around and tried to find Morenica; he finally saw her seated on the far side of the synagogue with the rabbi's wife. His daughter saw that he was looking at her, and she gave him an affectionate smile.

The pillars of the synagogue supported a vaulted ceiling, and the walls were painted white to brighten the interior. Sunlight entered through the interlaced woodwork of the arched windows. In the center of the synagogue was the *teva*, or podium, partially enclosed by a balustraded wooden barrier, from which the cantor led the ritual chanting. The cantor faced east, toward Jerusalem, facing the Ark and Torah scrolls on the opposite wall.

The synagogue was slowly filling up as people continued to arrive. Don Abraham Senior came in to the synagogue, put on his prayer shawl, and went down the aisle to take his reserved seat at the front of the synagogue, shaking hands with acquaintances and old friends along the way. His son-in-law, Meir, trailed behind him doing likewise. As they arrived at the area next to the Ark, Don Abraham continued on and walked up to where Rabbi Maimi was seated.

Rabbi Maimi, a warm smile on his face, rose respectfully seeing the Chief Judge approach him.

"*Shabbat Shalom*, Don Abraham, welcome back to Segovia. It is good to see you."

"It is good to see you again, Rabbi, and *Shabbat Shalom* to you too. I want to thank you for accepting Hacham Alhadeff for the Sabbath."

The rabbi answered, "It is our pleasure, Don Abraham. But please allow us to keep him for more than just the Sabbath. He is not a burden to us, and we as scholars have much to talk about. I assure you, it is our pleasure."

Senior stroked his beard, saying, "Ah, I am relieved to hear that. I was concerned that I might have unfairly imposed upon your hospitality."

Changing the subject, Rabbi Maimi asked, "How did things go in Málaga? Well, I hope."

"Very well," said Don Abraham. "Very well indeed. All of the Málaga Jews are free and they have been divided among our communities. The ransom price was twenty thousand Jaenese doblas."

"The rabbi was startled, "Twenty thousand! Vaya! That's a lot of money, Don Abraham."

"We had no choice," said Don Abraham, "we had to pay it."

The rabbi frowned, biting his lips, "Yes, we have no choice when it comes to liberating our brothers, however much it may cost us. But I do not need to remind you that our community is already saddled with so many taxes — the special war tax, the *alcalabas*, and now this. People cannot take much more. Before the war began, our annual community tax assessment was only eleven thousand maravedis, and this year it is unbelievable — it is over one hundred thousand maravedis! Don Abraham, I ask you, how much more is our community going to have to pay for this ransom?"

"Thirty thousand maravedis, more or less," said Senior matter-of-factly.

Rabbi Maimi sighed deeply. "Every year, the King and Queen find new ways to take away our hard-earned income. This is going to hurt, no question about that. People will complain. They will be angry — at you perhaps for negotiating such a deal, and God knows, maybe even at the Hacham and his lovely daughter for being such a burden to the community."

Don Abraham replied, "We must do our best to prevent ill feeling toward the Hacham. You understand that, of course."

"I shall do my best, Don Abraham. You can count on me."

"Good. By the way. I would appreciate if you would announce the good news."

"What good news?", asked the rabbi, unaware of any special tidings.

Don Abraham said pridefully, "That Rabbi Meir Melamed is to be the chief tax farmer for all Castile, and that I am going to be the new Treasurer of the Hermandad."

Rabbi Maimi's face beamed with joy. He grabbed Senior's hand and shook it enthusiastically, "*Mazal Tov*! That is wonderful! I'm so happy for you and Meir. The Senior family each year goes from one great honor to the other. We are all so very proud of you, Don Abraham, of your son-in-law, indeed of all your family. You bring us so much honor by your presence in this community."

"Thank you, Rabbi," said Senior, "Please inform the congregation that everyone is invited for a Kiddush wine and food reception at our home after services are over. And don't forget to bring along the Hacham."

The rabbi smiled at the Chief Judge, "I shall announce it during my talk. *Mazal Tov*, Don Abraham. This obviously calls for an *aliyah*, a going up to the Torah. We'll give you both a much deserved *aliyah*."

Satisfied with the offer, Don Abraham went back to his front row seat.

The service continued, the cantor intoning the passages in his distinctive chant, the members joining him in unison from time to time. A member of the congregation then proceeded to walk up to the podium to lead the bidding for the *mitzvot*, the ceremonial duties done in preparation for the recitation of the weekly Torah reading (the Parashah). Members would raise their hands to indicate their wish to bid, at times even stating explicitly the amount of the bid. And the member of the podium conducting the bidding, acknowledging the raised hands, would use a sing-song to announce the ongoing status of the bids:

Diez maravedis dan por hacer la peticha, diez maravedis dan
Veinte maravedis dan por hacer la peticha, veinte maravedis dan.

And so on it went. 'Hacer la peticha' was the ceremonial honor of opening the Ark, and of helping to take out the Torah scrolls within, 'meter los rimonim' related to the placement of the silver adornments and bells atop the torah scroll, 'hacer la hakamah' to the lifting of the Torah in full view of the congregation, 'hacer la gelilah' to the removal of the silver adornments and to the initial unraveling of the scroll, and 'meldar la haftarah' to the reading of the prophetic portion of the week.

Once the bidding for the *mitzvot* was finished, it led promptly to their actual ceremonial performance by the members who had purchased the special privileges. The Torah scrolls were taken out of the Ark, outfitted with silver adornments, and paraded to the central podium as the congregation lifted its voice in song. Upon being brought to the podium, the Torah scroll was divested of its bells and velvet mantle, and held up into the air for all to see.

In accordance with tradition, a Cohen and a Levy were the first to be called to the Torah. It was then that Don Abraham Senior, as the first of the Israelites, was called up to the Torah. The Chief Judge of the Jewish community was always accorded this honor if he wished, and the entire congregation rose respectfully as Senior, responding to his Hebrew name, rose from his bench and stepped toward the central podium. Don Abraham made the ritual blessing prior to the Torah reading, and the cantor, wishing to impress the Chief Judge, launched enthusiastically into the centuries-old mode of stylized chanting.

The Torah portion for this week was from the Book of Deuteronomy, and it was called "*Ve-Ethanen*", and the cantor chanted this discourse of Moses with an elegance of tone and with a voice so beautiful that it was a joy to listen to. When the reading was completed, Don Abraham made the required blessing and then was himself blessed by the cantor. Don Abraham donated several hundred maravedis to the general treasury of the congregation as an act of appreciation to God for his safe return to Segovia and for the successful completion of his rescue mission. The cantor spiritedly announced the donation within the formula of another stylized blessing, much to Don Abraham's satisfaction.

Then Rabbi Meir Melamed was called up to the Torah, and he, too, went through the age-old ritual of the *aliyah*, as the summons to participate in the reading of the Torah was called.

The fifth person to be called was the Hacham, but no one at the podium knew his Hebrew name. In addition to their regular name, Jews use their Hebrew name in the synagogue, a Hebrew name that is given to them when they enter the covenant of Abraham.

A youth rushed up to the Hacham, "Excuse me, sir, but we don't know how to call you."

"My Hebrew name is Yitzhak Ben Yosef."

The youth ran back up to the podium and whispered the information in the cantor's ear. Summoned by his Hebrew name, the Hacham responded to the cantorial call. It was an honor to be called up to the Torah. He was delighted. Yes, he was overjoyed. His face was radiant and his gait light and airy. It seemed to him that he was being transported like a leaf floating its way through the forest or like an angel on some spiraling skyward course to heaven. He wrapped himself tighter in the fold of his prayer shawl, basking in his own warmth, wishing as it were to circumscribe his inner glow and to prevent its dissipation.

"Blessed be the Lord, the Blessed One," shouted the Hacham as he stepped on the podium next to the cantor.

And the congregation replied, "Blessed be the Lord who is blessed for all eternity."

The Hacham then said, "Blessed art Thou, O Lord our God, ruler of the universe, who has chosen us from among all peoples and hast given us Thy Torah. Blessed art Thou, O Lord, who hast given us the Torah."

The cantor chanted the verses for the fifth *aliyah*. Following this, the Hacham, his voice choked and breaking at times with emotion, recited the final benediction, "Blessed art Thou, O Lord our God, ruler of the universe, who hast given us Thy Torah of truth, and planted among us life everlasting. Blessed art Thou, O Lord, giver of the Torah."

The Hacham returned to his bench, with the lingering feeling that it was all a dream, that Segovia was a mirage in the desert, that it would all fade away when his mind cleared. He still did not believe that all this was happening to him. He sat in his chair checking the reality of his senses. It was not a dream, he admitted, and yet it seemed so much like one. His daydream lasted through the rest of the Torah cantillation, through the reading of the prophetic portion, lingered on through some prayers until it was time for Rabbi Maimi to address the congregation.

Rabbi Maimi stood in the center of the synagogue, calmly looking at those gathered around him, waiting for silence. He tugged on his prayer shawl, and all was silent as he began his sermon.

"It is said in *Pirkei Avot*, the Ethics of the Fathers,
    'Look not at the pitcher but at that which is in it.'
That is, when one meets a person, one does not judge him by his outward appearance. One does not decide by his dress or by his outward looks what kind of a person he is. Rather, one must look inside the person to understand how his heart and his mind work. One must look into that person's very soul . . . I would like to tell you a story I once heard as a child from my grandfather of blessed memory.

"It was a story about Yehuda HaLevy, one of the great Sephardic sages and poets. This rabbi, Rabbi HaLevy, great as he was, had a problem: he had a daughter that he needed to marry. And his wife was worried, ay, so worried, that she was not going to find a husband for their daughter to wed. And she begged him to find a husband for their daughter, and she kept pestering him day after day, week after week, until the saintly rabbi did not know what to do. The rabbi looked through all of Toledo, contacting all the better families to find an appropriate match for his daughter, but was unable to do so. He wrote letters to Lucena and to Granada, but the heads of the Jewish schools there answered that they had no one who was learned to merit the hand of his daughter. Upon hearing this, his wife broke down and wailed and cried her heart out, and the poor rabbi was unable to console her any further. In a moment of frustration, not knowing what to do, Yehuda HaLevy swore that the next single, marriageable man to appear at the entrance to their home would marry their daughter, no matter who he was.

"It so happened that there was a knock on the door. His wife stopped crying, thinking of what the rabbi had just sworn to do. The rabbi went to the door and opened it. And there at the doorstep stood a poor Jew, dressed in filthy rags, his hair disheveled, his body thin and sickly looking. He was single and, therefore, marriageable. The rabbi's wife screamed hysterically when she saw this poor creature to whom their precious daughter had been promised, and she begged and pleaded with her husband to renounce the oath that he had made, but the rabbi refused. An oath was an oath, and it could not be undone.

"Rabbi HaLevy took in the young man and prepared him for the wedding. He gave him clothes to wear and food to drink and provided him with a dowry to get the young couple started in their new life together. Despite the protests of the rabbi's wife and the valley of tears that she shed, the wedding was to take place.

"The night before the wedding, Rabbi Yehuda HaLevy was at the synagogue working on a difficult acrostic poem, and he was unable to finish the last two lines of the composition owing to a problem with the rhyme. Exhausted by the effort, he fell asleep in the synagogue and did not come home for several hours.

"The rabbi's wife, a constant worrier, now worried why her husband did not come home as he usually did. Her new son-in-law was with her at the time, and they decided to go together to the synagogue to find out what had happened to the rabbi. When they arrived at the synagogue, they found the rabbi sleeping in his bed. On top of the desk, there was the poem that the rabbi had been working on, and the son-in-law picked up the piece of parchment to examine the poem. He immediately knew what the problem was. He picked up a pen and wrote in the last two lines of the poem — with perfect rhyme and meter, incorporating the last two letters of the acrostic.

"The rabbi awoke and thanked his wife and son-in-law for their thoughtfulness. Suddenly the rabbi looked at his desk, grabbed the poem off the desk, and shouted, 'My poem, it's finished! Someone finished my poem! Who did this?'

" 'I did,' answered the son-in-law.

" 'What? How can that be?,' the rabbi said, looking strangely at his son-in-law.

" 'You are not who you say you are. Only a master of Biblical verse and language could have written these lines. I insist you tell me the truth: Who are you?'

" 'I am Rabbi Abraham Ibn Ezra,' said the son-in-law, 'I had fallen upon bad times when I came unto your doorstep, and I was rescued from my misfortune by the oath you made to God Almighty.'

"And Rabbi HaLevy and his wife rejoiced knowing that their daughter was to be wed to such a great Hebrew scholar.

"So it was that Rabbi HaLevy's daughter was married to Rabbi Abraham Ibn Ezra, and they lived happily ever after. And so it is that this story illustrates what the Talmud says, and that is:

'Look not at the pitcher but at that which is in it.'

"We have in our synagogue today a new member of different appearance and dress, a new pitcher, if you will. He is Hacham Isaac Alhadeff, the former head of the Jewish community in Málaga. As you know, the community there was recently taken by the forces of the King and Queen. What happened to Rabbi Abraham Ibn Ezra in the story also befell the Hacham and his community: they fell on misfortune, and they were taken captive. Now he is a free man, and he is with us today as a free man because he has been ransomed by all of us — through our individual contributions, through the direct intervention of Don Abraham Senior, *juez mayor*, Supreme Judge of the *aljamas* of Spain, and most of all because it is the will of the Holy One, Blessed be He, that we perform this *mitzvah* in the name of heaven.

"Each and every community has agreed to accept the responsibility for the freed Jews of Málaga. We must do our share. It is not enough just to give money. We must accept fully the Hacham and his lovely daughter into our community. We must take them into our home and into our lives. They must become a part of us, and we must become a part of them.

"I have had an opportunity to examine this new pitcher from Málaga, and I have looked inside at that which is in it. And I liked what I found. I believe that you will too. Do not judge this man and his daughter by their outward appearance, but judge them by what you will find inside. Look not at the pitcher, my friends, but at that which is in it.'

"I would also like to take this opportunity to welcome back Don Abraham Senior from his successful rescue mission to Málaga. He has represented us well at the court of the King and Queen, he has rescued our Jewish brethren that were taken prisoner in Málaga, and now he has returned to us with new honors and titles. I will leave it to him to tell you today just what these honors are. All the congregation is invited to a party at the Senior home immediately after morning services. *Shabbat Shalom.*"

As Rabbi Maimi went back to his seat, the Hacham could not help but feel grateful for the rabbi's words of hospitality. He was touched. He would have to return the favor in some way. The Hacham was now convinced that his rescue had a spiritual purpose: that he had been chosen by the God of Israel to survive the famine in Málaga for some obscure reason, selected for some purpose relating to this Segovian Jewish community. What that reason was, what that higher purpose could be, was unclear to him at the present, but he felt that in due time it would become evident. The ways of the Holy One of Israel were unfathomable, and His mysteries were beyond comprehension, the Hacham said to himself, as he dazedly finished the morning prayers, his heady sense of unreality persisting.

Walking leisurely with Rabbi Maimi to the Senior home, the Hacham thanked the rabbi for his kind words. The cantor and others joined them as they walked down the cobbleways, talking animatedly about the war against the Moors, the situation of the Jews, and so forth.

The home of Don Abraham Senior was palatial. As the Hacham and other invited guests passed through the massive wrought iron doors, they entered a courtyard with neatly arranged benches and a cascading central fountain surrounded by potted plants and flowers. The mosaic path around the courtyard led into luxurious interior quarters, all painted a brilliant white. The guests were allowed entry only into the courtyard and two of the adjoining rooms.

After the *Kiddush*, the sanctification of the wine, there were toasts of homecoming and of well-wishes for Don Abraham. All congratulated the chief judge and his son-in-law on hearing of their new titles, and the wine cups were filled to the brim again for successive rounds of merry toasts and rousing salutations in their honor.

Then the food was brought out. There were heaps of cheese-filled pastry turnovers, squares of spinach and cheese souffles, pots filled with flan custard layered with honey, wound egg bread loaves, and various fruit jellies. Guests reached into bowls to pull out the '*huevos haminados*', the eggs cooked all night over the smouldering coals of a brazier until they were dark brown. On another table were apples, grapes, oranges, olives, quinces, figs, and other fruits. Some guests sat on benches, others hovered about the tables, and the rest stood talking on the paths.

Elegantly dressed, Fortuna Senior walked from one bench to another, greeting her guests and gossiping with them. Fortuna greeted Sarah Maimi and Morenica as they ate.

"*Shabbat Shalom*! How are you, Sarah? Ah, and who is this? Ah, I know . . . I know . . . the girl from Málaga . . . I hope you are enjoying yourself here, my dear," said Fortuna to Morenica, "I've heard so many good things about you and your father from my husband. He is delighted to have you here, and so am I, and so is the rest of the community. Welcome to Segovia."

Morenica put aside her food tray, rose from her bench in deference to her hostess, and bowed respectfully.

Morenica responded, "Señora, it is I who am grateful for the many good things that you and your husband have given us. Our thanks know no bounds, and our debt to you knows no end. Truly the delight is ours."

Fortuna nodded her head slightly in acknowledgement, and said, "Please, my dear, there is no need for such a testimony of your gratitude. Here, sit down on the bench, finish your meal, and enjoy the entertainment. Maybe later on today we'll have a chance to talk."

"Thank you, señora," said Morenica humbly, seating herself on the bench. Fortuna turned to Sarah, "Take good care of her, Ribisa Sarah. She's a real beauty. I'll speak to you later."

Sarah smiled softly as Fortuna walked to another bench, and welcomed another group of guests.

Rabbi Maimi came up behind his wife, placing his hand on her shoulder, "Ah, what a wonderful party this is. Good food, good wine, good company, what more can one ask for?"

"How about a good wife?", said Sarah jokingly, placing her hand on his, ". . . or is that too much to ask for? How are Don Abraham . . . and our new chief tax farmer, Rabbi Meir Melamed?"

The rabbi, squeezing her hand lovingly, answered, "Senior, as always — the eternal realist, never happy, never sad, never allowing the situation to get the better of him. Meir is just the opposite; this is his first taste of glory, and if the glory does not go to his head first, then all the wine that he is consuming will. He had better stop drinking to all those toasts in his honor, if he knows what is good for him."

Rabbi Maimi and his wife strolled back toward the courtyard. They came upon two elderly gentlemen absorbed in a chess match. They stopped a while to watch the game.

One onlooker asked the rabbi, "Rabbi, I was under the impression that Maimonides had forbidden the playing of chess?"

The rabbi smiled and stroked his beard, "No, my son, it is permitted provided that one does not play for money."

"I see," said the youth, his curiosity returning quickly to the game in progress.

The Sabbath party was slowly coming to an end. Guests began leaving; a few lingered in the courtyard singing the Spanish ballads called *romanzas*. Others sat enraptured around the Hacham, devouring his tales of faraway Málaga. The chess game came to an end, and the pair of elderly gentlemen departed, taking their avid youthful audience with them. The hosts, Don Abraham and Fortuna, bid everyone gracious farewells. Rabbi Maimi and his wife told the Seniors how wonderful the reception was and they extended their official congratulations once again to the Chief Judge and his son-in-law. At the last moment, the Hacham and Morenica joined the queue of departing guests, and they, too, thanked the Seniors for the reception.

It was a slow easy walk back to the rabbi's home. The rabbi, his wife, the Hacham, and his daughter — all took their time in the unhurried tranquil spirit of the Sabbath.

When they returned, all retired for a rest. By late afternoon, the rabbi and the Hacham walked to the synagogue for the closing Sabbath prayers. After prayers they returned home for *Havdalah*. Morenica lit the candle, and the rabbi held up a glass of wine for the closing benediction.

Pouring the remaining wine on the candle wick and extinguishing its flame, the rabbi kissed his wife and said, "*Buenas semanas*!"

"*Buenas semanas*! Good week!," said the Hacham as he kissed his daughter. The traditional greeting was exchanged, accompanied by handshakes, embraces and kisses. A new week had arrived.

Rabbi Maimi was very disturbed. Two weeks after Senior's return, he had been invited to the home of the Chief Judge to discuss the new taxes on Segovia's Jewish community. But the Rabbi's mind was not on money; he was worried about the Conversos. The Conversos, *that* was the problem — and that infernal Inquisition.

As he walked slowly toward Senior's home, logbook in hand, Rabbi Maimi thought about the Converso problem. It had all begun over a century ago, in 1391, when there were widespread massacres of Jews throughout Spain. Led by the Dominican priest Ferrante Martínez, the blood-thirsty mobs had destroyed many of the Jewish communities of Spain, slaughtering over one hundred thousand Jews. The surviving one hundred thousand Jews struggled to recover their prosperity, but it was difficult.

The Converso problem existed only because many Jews had chosen to convert to Christianity rather than be slain. Tens of thousands of Jews, perhaps as many as a hundred thousand, had preferrred conversion to death. But forced conversions were bound to be insincere. The new converts to Christianity, *Conversos* or New Christians as they were called, found ways of practicing their former religion secretly.

A new crypto-Judaism was developing throughout Spain. Moreover, the Conversos were often helped by their Jewish kinsmen: secretly, rabbis and other Jewish teachers encouraged the Conversos to maintain their identities as Jews.

The secret activities were not without great risk. As far as the Catholic church was concerned, once baptized, that individual was forever regarded as a Christian. And, although religious backsliding was heresy, Conversos continued to practice the faith of their fathers.

After nearly a century, the Christians became alarmed. On the advice of a Dominican monk, Ferdinand and Isabella were made aware of the great laxity of observance among the New Christians. So critical was the situation that the Holy Office of the Inquisition was established in 1481 to investigate and punish the heretics among the New Christians.

The Inquisition quickly began its deadly work in Sevilla: thousands of Conversos were imprisoned, tortured, and burned at the stake. The Jewish accomplices of the Conversos were also punished. The Inquisition ordered that on January 1, 1483, all Jews had to be expelled within a month's time from the bishoprics of Sevilla and Córdoba, that is, from all of Andalusia. The claim was that the Jews helped the Conversos be unfaithful to the Christian faith. The crown added that it would be to the benefit of the Jewish communities to relocate away from the battle zones, because the war with the Moors was about to begin again.

And now the Inquisition had extended its activities to Segovia. Entire Converso families accused of Judaizing activities had been thrown into the prisons of the Holy Office. And today, this Sunday, was the date set for Segovia's first *Auto-de-Fe*. The city's first group of convicted Judaizers were to be publicly burned at the stake. Fearing a Christian outbreak, Rabbi Maimi and Don Abraham Senior had ordered that the gates to the Jewish quarter be kept shut. Jews were forbidden to leave the quarter during the entire day of the mass execution.

As he walked down the cobblestone street, Rabbi Maimi heard the commotion outside the Jewish quarter. There were thousands of people; many were rural peasants who streamed in from the countryside to witness the spectacle. The whoops and the shouting choked the morning air as if some wild uncontrollable bedlam was ready to break loose.

Rabbi Maimi arrived at Don Abraham's home and was led into the Chief Judge's office.

"Good morning, Rabbi. Please take a seat."

But Rabbi Maimi seemed not to notice either Senior's entry or his greeting. He continued to look out the window in the general direction of the plaza where the *Auto-de-Fe* was taking place. All he saw in the distance was pain, the pain of his Jewish brothers and sisters. He could see the smoke rising from afar, indicating that the flesh of his brethren was being charred beyond recognition. He heard the intermittent roar of the crowd and its raucous cries of approval. There was a doleful faraway look in his eye, a grieving in his heart for his kinsmen who had been set aflame in the death pyre, a spiritless feeling that it had happened before and that it was happening again. As he looked out, he quoted a passage from Lamentations:

"For these things I weep
Mine eye swelleth with tears
Because He who comforts me . . . is far from me,
Even He that should refresh my soul,
My children are desolate,
Because the enemy hath prevailed.
Zion spreadeth forth her hands,
But there is none to comfort her."

"What are you mumbling about, Rabbi?," said Senior gruffly, as he kept on checking the logbooks without looking up. Senior flipped a page indifferently, uncaring whether he elicited an answer to his question.

Rabbi Maimi replied, "I was reciting a . . . a lamentation, a lamentation that it is my lot to have to see my people suffer so."

Senior laughed, "*Your* people? Ha! They are turncoats to our faith and, mind you, they are unfaithful Christians, too, traitors even to the cause they accepted."

Senior licked his index finger and flipped the page. He continued, "Let's see . . . four thousand maravedis to his credit . . . Good . . . yes. They left us once, and that was enough. There is no turning back. Now, let us get back to the tax matters of the *aljama*. If you consider . . ."

Rabbi Maimi slammed the logbook in Senior's startled face, "Forget your taxes . . . and listen to me, "Chief Justice" Senior. They *are* Jews just like me and you. They are Jews whether you like it or not. They are of the stock of Abraham, Isaac, and Jacob — and that makes them our brothers and sisters. They are our brethren, whose only misfortune was to have weak-hearted ancestors, who were forced to become something they could not be — forced to be Christians against their will, forced to abide by a decision not of their making."

Senior rose from his chair, and looked straight into the rabbi's accusing eyes. "Circumstances force us to abide by the law of the land. The law states that those individuals out there are Christians, not Jews — and if they engage in Jewish activities, they are to be punished as heretics.

"They disobeyed the law? That . . . out there . . . is their punishment. Understand? . . . Law and order, that's what Ferdinand and Isabella stand for . . . Law and order! . . . You can't run a country without it. And if you can't accommodate yourself to that fact, then be prepared to resign from your present duties as Chief Rabbi of Segovia."

The rabbi looked Senior in the eye, "I am resigned . . . resigned to the fact that you of all people, our Chief Jewish judge, are willing to put the concerns of the state over the sufferings of your people."

Senior replied, "I am a functionary of the State. I cannot run my business if people do not obey the law — whether they be the Jews of my community, those who think they are Jews, and those who never were."

"We must help them," said the rabbi.

"Let God help them," said Senior, "has He helped us?"

Rabbi Maimi could take no more. He spurted out his rage, "How dare you speak that way, *juez mayor*?"

Senior returned the rage. His voice broke as he jabbed a finger into the rabbi's chest, "I'm telling you, Rabbi Maimi, if you dare aid these Marranos in any way, I will cut off your salary and deprive you of all your social privileges. Endanger my position . . . and it'll be your neck on that stake."

Rabbi Maimi glared at Senior and Senior glared back at him. It was a standoff.

Rabbi Maimi stormed out of Senior's office and slammed the door loudly behind him.

When Rabbi Maimi returned home, he was surprised to find his wife, Hacham Alhadeff, and his daughter, Morenica, talking animatedly about the *Auto-de-Fe*. He did his best to mask his agitation after the meeting with Senior. But Sarah could tell he was upset.

"Is everything all right, Simon?," she asked.

"Why, you cannot expect me to be unaffected by the events of the day."

"Your meeting with Don Abraham . . . how did it go?"

"Fine, fine," he answered quickly.

Sarah kept quiet but sensed the meeting had not gone well.

Hacham Alhadeff, unaware of any problem, remarked,

"Rabbi, you and your wife, Sarah, have shown me many kindnesses. In return, I would like to tell you the story I could not tell on the Sabbath because it was not appropriate then. But today's events bring it back to mind. I would like your permission to tell it now."

"As you wish," said Rabbi Maimi, anxious for diversion. "I want you to understand that you are under no obligation to do so."

"Rabbi, it is a story that I must tell and that you must hear. Please sit down."

The rabbi sat down next to his wife.

The Hacham began his account thus, "I was a Hebrew teacher for the small Jewish community left in Córdoba after the great massacre of the previous century. They paid me a modest salary but it was, thank God, enough to support me and my daughter. One day, I was approached by Conversos to teach Hebrew to their children. I knew that this was very dangerous work, and I was unsure whether to take the position or not. But they pleaded with me to do so, and I finally accepted their offer. I did this work secretly for nearly two years.

"At night, I would sneak into the Converso neighborhood, and I would teach their children about Hebrew and about Jewish customs. It was very satisfying work. It was strange to meet young people who wanted so badly to be Jewish, but who were forced to pretend to be Christians.

"One day, I was teaching in the Converso quarter. I had four adolescent pupils with me who were studying the weekly Torah reading in a small room. It was dark, and the only light we had was what came through the cracks in the window. As we were studying, I heard chanting from afar. I went to the window to look out on the street below. It was a Catholic religious procession. There were altar boys who were waving incense containers, and at their head was a Dominican priest carrying an image of the crucified one. The priest's head was shaved on top but not at the sides, as is the custom of the Dominicans. Stragglers joined the procession as well. They were chanting a church hymn as they entered the Converso quarter.

"Many of the Conversos closed their doors. I saw shopkeepers grabbing their wares and running into their homes. I could see people running back and forth, trying to get out of the way. Those who could not run away stayed respectfully at the sides of the street to watch the procession go by. Everything would have been well, except that the procession suddenly stopped singing. Their silence as they went through the Converso quarter caught some of the residents by surprise.

"A Converso family was busy cleaning up its home and apparently they did not hear the procession coming. The father was fixing a wooden table with a hammer and was banging away. The mother was scrubbing the floor with her daughter. The mother wrung out the washcloth in a pail of dirty water and gave it to her daughter to throw away. As the procession was just turning the corner, the Converso girl threw the pail of dirty water on the street, that is, in front of the procession. The water splattered on some in the procession. The young girl, realizing that she had committed an error, quickly ran back into the house and closed the door behind her.

"A blacksmith shouted that the Converso girl had poured urine on the procession. Another crowd member shouted that the Jews had insulted their savior. Shouts of 'Kill the Jews! They've thrown urine on our savior' and 'Death to the Jews!' could be heard. The fury spread among the rabble. The screaming mob beat on the door of the Converso family, and tried to push it in.

"My four pupils begged me to let them see what was going on, but I kept them away from the window, thank God. I could see the look of horror on their faces. They were afraid they would be caught while studying Jewish customs. I told them not to leave the secret meeting room, or they would be in great danger. It was good they listened to me. We hid our Hebrew books in the wall in case we were discovered, and we prepared to escape if the situation demanded it.

"Anyhow, let me keep my story brief. The mob broke into the home of the Converso family. The father, hammer in hand, tried to fight back. He struck one assailant, then another, but they overpowered him, and he was thrown to the ground. His hammer was taken from him, and they used it to beat him brutally on the head until blood spurted from his nose and his mouth and his ears.

"Some of the mob attacked the mother, and she tried to fight them off with a broom and kitchen knife, but she was no match for them. She was beaten and killed, too.

"The little Converso girl, the one who had thrown the pail of water, ran out the back into an alleyway. The child jumped over a ledge, but she was spotted and the mob set out after her. Her pursuers also included several children. The young girl stumbled and slipped as she tried to get away, and her pursuers gained on her. She ran into a sidestreet only to find someone there ready to catch her. The man grabbed at her blouse and it tore in his grasp, and he was left holding a piece of cloth. The girl ran back a short distance in the opposite direction and then up a steep side street, only to find that it was a dead end. The child, realizing that no escape was possible, stood there petrified, and I saw her back up slowly as the angry mob slowly closed in upon her. They grabbed her and she screamed for mercy, but they began to beat her like savage animals. One man ripped off her clothes while others pinned down her arms and legs. A woman came up and ripped off tufts of her hair while she was still down. Then the men kicked her and spat in her face, and they kicked her in the stomach, and everywhere else they could think of until she was bleeding from head to toe. Although the child was unconscious, they did not stop: one man brought out a whip and they flayed her back until it flowed with blood. I could see the eyes of my students wince every time they heard one of the lashes strike her body. But she was still breathing. Finally, the blacksmith who started it all twisted her neck until he broke it, and then the poor thing stopped breathing, and she finally died. God bless her soul.

"But the rioters did not stop there. They set fire to the homes of the Conversos, and there was much looting and killing.

"Alonso De Aguilar, the commander of the fortress of Córdoba, came to the defense of the Conversos. The blacksmith hid in a church when he saw De Aguilar and his men coming, but De Aguilar tracked the blacksmith down and persuaded him to come out to talk. When the blacksmith came out of the church, De Aguilar threw a lance at him. It speared him in the chest and killed him. But that still did not stop the rioting.

"Peasants from the countryside came to help the blacksmith's men fight the Conversos, some of whom had armed themselves. It was in the midst of all this that . . . my students and I managed to escape. I found my daughter, Batya, who had returned home when she heard of the rioting. We quickly gathered our belongings and prepared to leave. When night was upon us, we left the city by going through the fields, far from the main road, until we were able to make our way safely back to Málaga. I have been in Málaga ever since. When Málaga fell to the Christians, I was afraid that they would kill us all as they had killed the Conversos in Córdoba.

"But God has been merciful to us; He has brought us to safety and shelter under the protective wings of Don Abraham Senior and of kind souls such as yourselves who offer us your food and your home with open hearts. I only hope that my daughter and I will prove worthy of your generosity, and that someday we will be able to return your great kindness."

There was complete silence when the Hacham finished.

It was Rabbi Maimi who finally broke the silence. "What you have told us, Hacham, is a real tragedy. Terrible, as your daughter put it. I am sure that all of us here have witnessed similar incidents."

"I am sorry that I ever asked to hear it," said Sarah Maimi.

"No, we must hear it," said the rabbi firmly, "we must not close our eyes and ears to the world about us. We must be forever on the alert against their evil designs against us . . ."

The Hacham interrupted him, "What for? There is nothing we can do to stop them."

The rabbi said, "On the contrary. We can do exactly what you did . . . we can teach Torah to those Conversos who want to learn it, we can bring them back to Judaism, we can undo through careful teaching all that the Christians have been trying to do to us through force."

"Yes, but it is not without risk," said the Hacham. "It is dangerous. They will kill you if they catch you. The Christians have no mercy when it comes to such things. You need to have someone who is brave, a committed Jew, preferably someone the authorities do not recognize, someone who is . . . a . . . a . . newcomer."

Suddenly the thrust of what he was saying struck the Hacham. "Someone like . . . me," the Hacham stuttered, suddenly realizing why he had been brought to Segovia.

Chapter 3

It was Sunday. Only a week had passed since Segovia's first *Auto-de-Fe*. It had kindled the religous zeal of monastics and laymen. Antonio De la Peña remembered the event as if it were yesterday, so intense had been its effect on his very being. He was a stodgy Dominican friar of no special distinction, whose life was guided by monastic vows of poverty and chastity. Dressed in his traditional garb of scapular, cowl, and white robe fastened by a leather belt at the waist, he felt that today after years of discipline of mind and body, he had finally summoned the inner strength to do what he had sworn — to begin his evangelical ministry. Today, Fray Antonio de la Peña knew his days of preparation were ended.

As he climbed up the rocky terrain of the Eresma Valley, his rosary swinging from his belt, De la Peña felt a new power surging through his body, expanding his chest, animating his stride, uplifting his being. Truly, he believed, it was his burning zeal to do Christ's will that had inflamed him so, his passion to set out his vocation as an apostle of the church.

As he looked back behind him, he saw the monastery of Santa Cruz la Real with its carved facade and small Gothic spires. It was there at Santa Cruz that his evangelical zeal had been nurtured; it was there that he had studied the sacred works of Scripture, of Augustine and of the Church Fathers, of Thomas Aquinas, and of other Biblical commentators. It was there that his decision had been made; and it was there, just today, that he had tried to awaken others to the heretical dangers in Segovia, of the dangers of the diabolical Jews, and he had bidden them to follow

44

him in his crusade for Christ. The monks would not listen, so he went to preach to the simple shepherds and farmers of the countryside. They, however, responded to his plea to join him in his march against the forces of unbelief.

De la Peña had seen the fire of Christ in the flames of the *Auto-de-Fe*, flames that had devoured the heretics and destroyed them utterly. He felt such a burning fire within himself: an uncontainable blaze of faith that was the source of his newfound power. And now the fire — the Dominican detestation of the heretics, the incinerating will to crush and consume the unbeliever — overtook him and propelled him towards his destiny. The Auto had shown him the way; its incandescence had illuminated the dark recesses of Judaic heresy in Segovia itself. But De la Peña knew that the fire did not stop with the Converso, the renegade Jew in Christian disguise. It could only stop when it had scorched and devoured the seedbed of the infestation, when it had come to the temple of the Jewish unbelievers and razed it to the ground. Only then could the flames abate from lack of tinder, only then could the fire extinguish itself out. He would only be content when the Jews, depraved and blinded as they were, would see the light of his fire, when they would come to Christ through him, through the benefit of his preaching. And if they rejected him, if they rejected Christ, the Jews would suffer that which they deserved: death by fire.

De la Peña was buoyed by the message he carried. He had become a fisher of men who could rouse the faithful to action. He felt their faith in him, faith in his proclaimed purpose, in his ability to do as he preached. As the group he led entered the city gates, they were joined by other peasants from the countryside, many of them simple folk who had returned to Segovia this Sunday in wishful expectation of a repeat performance of the previous week's Auto. Word quickly spread among the peasants of the Dominican friar from Santa Cruz monastery who was marching on the city's heretics. The people of the town, prompted by curiosity, came out on the street to observe the commotion. Others trailed behind the main group as it headed toward the central plaza, with De la Peña in his white robe leading the way. The word continued to spread until De la Peña's following arrived at the central plaza facing the Cathedral.

Domínguez, the Hermandad officer, watched the group with De la Peña without any reason for concern. It was not uncommon to see friars giving sermons on a Sunday in the city's principal plaza. It mattered little, he thought to himself. Dominicans did good work; they ran the

Inquisition, they supported him as head of the Hermandad. It was, he thought, an action obviously prompted by good Christian faith, just as the *Auto-de-Fe* last week had been. No harm would come of it, it would please the Sunday crowd, it would be for a good cause, he admitted to himself. So much for that. He returned to his duties and paid no further attention to the matter.

De la Peña arrived at the central plaza when people were streaming out of the cathedral after morning mass. He climbed atop the platform used for the Auto a week ago and looked about him. He flipped the cowl backwards over his nape and let it dangle, exposing the baldness of his head to the rays of the morning sun. Then in a sudden dramatic gesture, he raised his arms, lifted his head, and closed his eyes in meditation. He stood there saying and doing nothing — as people gathered about him, wondering who the strange and silent friar was. Then De la Peña lowered his arms and directed his attention to the two hundred persons or so gathered about him.

"My dear brothers and sisters, I stand upon a site where the stench of heresy lingers. I smell it here in the ashes of the Act of Faith that took place here last week, I smell it in the streets of Segovia as I walk by certain quarters, I smell it even now among those of you who have just come to mass. The smell is everywhere. Do you hear me . . . everywhere! It is, Christ's name be blessed, even in our monasteries where, even if one were to set fire to them, one would not be able to drive out all the wolves there who prey upon our holy faith. Of what do I speak, brothers and sisters? What is this foul odor that I speak of, this rottenness in our midst?

"It is the stink of the Jew. It is the Jew that I speak of. Yes, he and all those corrupted by him. His stink is all over us — we breathe the air he gives off; he gives off an odor that sticks to our clothes, an odor that sticks to our bodies and that penetrates to our souls. Our wise King and Queen saw the need to separate these creatures, to protect good honest Christians from their corrupting presence; they saw the need to identify Jews by having them wear badges on their shoulders, so that we could see them at a distance and have nothing to do with them. But what has happened? These wolves have disguised themselves as Christians and have penetrated into our midst. They act and sound like Christians; they pray, they kneel, they confess like we do, they even partake of the Holy Eucharist, desecrating it week after week. They are everywhere — in the Church, in the universities, even in the court of the Catholic sovereigns. Everywhere you look, you will find them and you will smell them —

these swine, these Marranos, these filthy pigs. But fear not, we will find them, and we will smell them out, and we will burn them alive as we did a week ago. That is why we should thank our King and Queen for establishing the Holy Office of the Inquisition. Through the Inquisition, we can rid ourselves of the Marranos in our midst, we can blot out the stench of heresy from our land. Through the Inquisition, we can become a Christian nation pure of soul as we once were.

"But the Inquisition, great as it is, is not enough. Its powers are limited. It can find and punish these false Christians, these Marranos, but it cannot touch the root of the problem. It cannot touch the cursed Jews. Yet we know, you know, I know that the Jews are the core of the problem, that they are the ones who are the first and the last causes of all that is rotten in Spain today. They poison the Conversos with their heresy and with their depraved Judaic rites; they teach the Law to all who listen to their lies and deceits, and they defy the orders from our kings to refrain from such forbidden activities. Yet they continue. They refuse to stop, as if our ordinances and our warnings mean nothing to them. They laugh at us, they mock us, they look down upon us — because these Jews know that the Inquisition cannot touch them, because they know, yes, they know that all unconverted Jews are outside the jurisdiction of the office. They are a subtle people, these Jews. They think they are clever, that their usurers can rob us and that we will not miss the loss, that they can corrupt us and that we will not be offended, that they can transgress the law and that they can escape punishment. But it shall not be so today. No, my Spanish brothers and sisters, it shall not be so today, because today the Jews will pay dearly for their sins — against us, against Spain, and against our Lord Jesus Christ!"

The crowd roared its approval upon hearing these impassioned words. Applause shook the cool plaza air. De la Peña was gratified by the response. Emboldened by their enthusiastic support, he preached on.

"Yes, my Spanish brothers and sisters, the Jews must pay not only for their sins against us, but for their sin against our Lord Christ. It is their sin for eternity, it is the greatest sin of all time — the mortal sin of the Jews against our Lord when he appeared unto them in Jerusalem, when he came as a gentle lamb into that vicious den of wolves. And the Jews, animals that they are, rejected his teachings.

"They made our Lord stand trial, they mocked him and jeered at him, and spat at him and humiliated him till tears came to our Lord's face for the way they made his body suffer. Our Lord Jesus Christ was scourged and tortured by the Romans, but what pained him most was the rejection of his own people, the Jews, a people corrupted and perverse and unable to see truth when it presented itself in the body of Christ himself. On the day Christ was crucified, he cried with pain, he cried from the thorns that tore into his flesh, he cried from the nails driven through his hands, he cried from the weight of the cross, he cried from the spear that was thrust into his chest, and most of all, he cried from the betrayal and rejection of his own people. Yes, he cried because of what the Jews did to him."

The crowd was silent. A few were sobbing from De la Peña's words; others wiped their tears away. De la Peña knew that the crowd was on the verge of catching his fire. There was no stopping him now.

"And the Jews who mocked Christ said, *'His blood be upon us and upon our children'.* It was Christ's blood that the Jews shed nearly one thousand five hundred years ago, and it is Christ's blood that they shed today. *'His blood be upon us and upon our children'!* Yes, that is what the Jews said then and that is what they do today: they spill the body and blood of our Lord Jesus in vain every Sunday when they come to communion in the disguise of Christians.

"We know this from many confessions that the Inquisition has obtained from Conversos. They pretend to drink of Christ's blood at communion, and then they spit it out when they go back to their homes, rinsing out their mouths instead. Others eat of Christ's body, the sacred host that we know as the Holy Eucharist, and they keep the host in their mouths till they return to their pews at church, and then, when no one is watching, they spit it out between the pages of their missal so that they do not have to swallow it. *'His blood be upon us and upon our children!'*" Have you not heard enough? Is there no end to their diabolical desecrations?

"No, there will never be an end! Scripture tells us what the Jew is. It reveals his identity once and for all. In the Gospel of St. John, chapter eight, Quote:

'The devil is your father, and you prefer to do what your father the devil wants.'

And in the Book of Revelations, it is said not once but twice that their synagogue is the *'synagogue of Satan'.* The Jews are the sons of the devil, and they do the devil's bidding. The Jews are the enemies of Christ on this earth, and they will do all in their power to destroy the Catholic Church that Christ has built. Just as Jesus Christ came to redeem the world, Satan seeks to destroy the world through his agents, the Jews.

Just as Christ struggled with Satan, so we Christians must struggle with Jews who serve Satan. We must fight the Christian battle for truth and salvation, we must fight for Christ, we must fight the Jews and all other infidels who oppose us. It is a war to the finish, for Satan will not stop until all mankind is under his rule. Who will rule over us — will it be Christ or will it be Satan? If you are for Christ, if you are against Satan, then you are against the Jew — against the Jew who as scripture says, is 'an enemy of the human race', the Jew who is the devil incarnated, the Jew who seeks to exterminate us all.

Over there, my friends, in the Jewish quarter is the synagogue of Satan, over there in the *judería* you will find the enemies of Christ, over there you shall find all that is rotten in Spain today. I go there now to fight Christ's battle, to open the eyes of the Jews to the truth of the holy Gospel. And if they refuse to receive Christ today as they have refused in the past, then Christ's blood will be avenged! Join me, Christian brothers and sisters! Heed the call to battle in Christ's name! Let the Jews hear the sacred words of the Gospel, and if they will not have any of it, then by God, we will not have any of them in Christian Segovia by nightfall!

"On to the Jewish quarter! On to the *judería*!"

A roar exploded in the plaza. Once again it was the fire of De la Peña that prompted the crowd's outcry; it was the fire that swept into their souls and aroused them to vengeance against the Jews.

De la Peña stepped down from the podium to the tumultous din of the crowd's approval reverberating in his ears. The priest pulled out a wooden crucifix and raised it high for all to see as he led the way to the Jewish quarter. It was Christ leading the way, not he. He was but the Lord's obedient servant, a humble Dominican gatherer of men, who came to stir the believers to action.

The mob poured down the city streets. Most of them were simple folks, shepherds, farm hands, minor artisans, muledrivers. They were the simple people, *el pueblo menudo*, of simple faith and simple needs. They only asked from life the most elemental necessities. Their faith was pure and their devotion to the Church was total. And what was expected of them was that they not only love Christ, but that they hate the Jew. Sermon after sermon told them the Jew was Satan incarnate — half man, half devil, with horns on his head and a tail from behind. It was the Jew who robbed the Christian with his underhanded business dealings. It was on account of the tax-collecting Jews that many Christians were supposedly kept poor and forced to till the land with hard manual labor, whereas the Jews found plush managerial positions by which they could exploit the hard-working poor. This was what the simple ignorant folk believed about the Jew, and it was because of this that they came to detest Jews, one and all.

As the crowd marched on the Jewish quarter, an Hermandad sentry ran to the local station and, between gasps, related to Domínguez what was taking place. Domínguez jumped from his chair and rushed outside the building. He had barely gone twenty paces when he saw the surging mob in the adjacent alleyway. He estimated there were two hundred people or so, and that it would be difficult to control them. He could summon his dozen Hermandad officers to try to stop their advance, but what if the mob went wild and turned against his handful of men? His men would not be able to withstand the onslaught of such a crazed multitude. Then again, what would the local Inquisition have to say about his intervention in such an instance. Would they cut off his funds? Would he be the local hero who had set fire to Jews one week ago at the *Auto-de-Fé*, only to become their protector the following week? And what about that decrepit Jew Senior, the Hermandad treasurer — would he report his failure to intervene to the King and Queen, and would they strip Domínguez of his position? Moments passed as Domínguez tried to decide what to do. It did not take long, because he knew that he was a compromised man. He made the sign of the cross, spun on his heels, and returned quietly to his office. There was nothing he could do.

The mob reached the gates of the Jewish quarter. The two guards at the gate were overwhelmed and the doors were forced open. They poured into the *judería*, with De la Peña leading the way, his crucifix raised even high. Onwards they went — past the closed bakeries and butcher shops, past a series of plain brick homes, as they made their way to the principal synagogue of Segovia. Upon hearing the distant trampling, fearful Jews slammed their doors and shut the windows everywhere. The mob pressed on, meeting with silence rather than resistance. Indeed, it was the strange silence of the main street of the *judería* that surprised those who penetrated into the inner sanctum of the Jewish quarter. There was an eeriness about this silence, a feeling that this was a diabolical trap. De la Peña walked on because he knew the reason for the stillness of the quarter, even though his followers did not.

De la Peña knew it was *Rosh Hashanah*, the day of the Jewish New Year. Morning services had begun a short while ago, and the cantor's melodious voice had provided a moving rendition of the opening prayers to the attuned ears of a capacity audience. However, his cascading cantorial trills soon found themselves competing with an ill-defined focus of dull sounds from afar. The noise outside troubled Don Abraham Senior and his son-in-law, Rabbi Melamed; Hacham Alhadeff tried to dismiss the distraction and concentrate his energies on repentance on this holy day. All in attendance heard it coming — Morenica, the rabbi's wife, everyone heard it.

The dissonant clamor continued, a thunder that reverberated endlessly and increasingly in one's ears. The cantor's voice, ordinarily sonorous and full-throated, seemed muted by the approaching discord. Prodded by the rabbi, the cantor continued on half-heartedly, his voice dimming in intensity as the thunderousness grew by the moment. Whatever it was, it was getting closer. The congregants, their faces taut with fear, were numbed by the persisting rumble that was coming their way. The cantor stopped his singing. The approaching noise became louder, and suddenly a horrendous blood-curdling noise shook the windows and the synagogue. It was upon them.

Pandemonium broke loose as De la Peña and his supporters burst through the synagogue doors. A few of the congregants tried to stop the advance, but they were pushed aside. Some women tried to escape through a side door, but they were caught and thrown to the ground. Most of the congregants, sensing the futility of struggle and the impossibility of escape, wrapped themselves tightly within their shawls shivering with fear. Many thought it was the beginning of the end, and they started intoning prayers — prayers of forgiveness, supplications for redemption and divine intervention — in anticipation of a terminal bloodbath.

Rabbi Maimi was outraged and demanded an explanation of the intruders.

"How dare you enter our synagogue on such a holy day?," he shouted, "Get out of here, all of you!"

A fist slammed into the rabbi's face, throwing him to the floor. Two other congregants rushed to his side to help him, but he was able to signal to them that he was, despite his dizziness, still able to function.

Don Abraham Senior was furious. As one accustomed to dealing with manifestations of power, Senior knew that he would have to speak firmly with the person responsible for the disturbance. He approached one of the intruders.

"Who is in charge here? Who is responsible for this?," Senior asked him.

The ruffian sneered at him and answered him, "Shut your mouth, Jew."

Senior, his face flushed with embarrassment from being insulted in front of his co-religionists, persisted. "I demand to speak to the person responsible for this. I am Don Abraham . . ." Before Senior could finish his sentence, the ruffian shoved Senior on the chest, and sent Don Abraham reeling and tottering backwards into the outstretched arms of his son-in-law. Senior looked at this rowdy ill-bred fellow with disdain, but felt he could do little against such lawless hooligans. Where was that Hermandad yokel Domínguez when you needed him? By God, he would make Domínguez pay dearly for allowing such a thing to happen, and he would make sure that the ringleader of such an outrage was fittingly punished. No one could do this to Don Abraham Senior and get away with it. The King and Queen would see to that. By God, he would make them pay.

His son-in-law, Rabbi Meir Melamed, said, "Let me at him, Father. Let me at him." Senior looked at his well-meaning over-weight son-in-law and extricated himself from Meir's heavy torpid arms. Don Abraham frowned at Meir. The last thing he needed was a fat, slow-footed Meir getting himself hurt. Besides, Meir could not defend himself, much less anyone else. Senior stated it sharply, "Just stay where you are, Meir, and keep out of this."

Fray De La Peña walked around in the synagogue, crucifix in the air, his face beaming with victorious pride. "I am Fray De la Peña, and I have come to bring you eternal salvation through our Lord and redeemer Jesus Christ. I offer his salvation to you in the name of the Father, the Son, and the Holy Ghost."

Don Abraham cleared his throat. It was obvious that the priest was the instigator. Senior cautiously approached the priest and said:

"Pardon me, dear curate, may I as head of this community be allowed to say something?"

"You may," answered De la Peña suspiciously.

Senior collected himself. He phrased his words slowly and carefully.

"Pardon me, dear curate, for saying so, and please do not take offense at my words. However, it is my duty to inform you of a ruling, a ruling of our royal majesties Ferdinand and Isabella, that . . . ah . . . Christian demonstrations of this sort, however well-intentioned they may be, and however praiseworthy they may be insofar as your Christian beliefs are concerned, are . . . by special order of our royal majesties . . . ah . . . they are . . . forbidden in the Jewish quarter."

"Never!," De la Peña screamed into Senior's face. "The word of our Lord knows no boundaries, it knows no prohibitions, it knows no limits set by any man, be he commoner or king or queen. You shall hear the word of the Lord today. Most of all, it needs to be heard in this synagogue of Satan. Do you hear me, all of you here, do you hear me? You shall hear the word of the Lord on this New Year Day, for I have sworn that it will be so — that Christ will enter your hearts today, and he will do so if you will but let him. Begin this New Year with a Christian heart and a Christian soul. Break your pact with Satan. Let Christ come into your soul and let him cleanse you of your sins! Be redeemed in the blood of the lamb and live forever! Listen and be not afraid, for I bring unto you the truth to which you and your forefathers have been blinded for so long. Sit on your benches, and listen to the truth that is in Christ . . . now! Sit in your chairs!"

Senior, head bowed, obediently took his place on a prayer bench, as did his son-in-law. Rabbi Maimi picked himself off the floor and did the same. Others in the synagogue followed suit. Hacham Alhadeff shook his head in disbelief at what was occurring. Was it Córdoba all over again? Was it happening here too? Was Morenica all right? He spotted her beyond the partition, and knew that she was uninjured. That was all that mattered. He sat down to listen to the sermon. Like it or not, this was a distraction that he could not ignore except at his peril.

The mob closed off the lanes between the pews so that none of the Jews could leave. When the shuffling noises had subsided, De la Peña walked up to the podium and began his sermon.

"Children of Israel, I bring unto you the good news that you have been waiting for. The good news is that the Messiah has come in the person of Jesus Christ. He came as God incarnate, as the son of God in the flesh to redeem you from the original sin of Adam. Through Adam, sin entered the world, and through sin came death, and death spread throughout the whole human race because everyone has sinned. And only through Christ is it possible to be saved from death and live forever. It is Christ only who can save us from the sin from which we cannot redeem ourselves. It is the sin that tainted man and made him mortal and impure; it is the sin from which your souls can be cleansed if you will but accept Jesus today. Today, let your souls be pure. Today let your souls be clean. Today, on this first day of the Jewish New Year, accept Jesus in your hearts and be ye baptized. Let today be a new beginning for you, let today be a new life for you, a life everlasting, by accepting the salvation that comes through faith in our savior Jesus.

"The prophets foretold his coming and of how he would suffer at the hands of your ancestors. The prophet Daniel spoke of the 'Son of Man,' and Isaiah proclaimed the coming of God's Anointed and of the universal salvation that the Anointed One, the Messiah, would bring. And when our redeemer Jesus came to earth, he was born of the virgin Mary and made himself known to all mankind and to your ancestors. But despite the wonders and miracles that Jesus performed, you Jews did not believe your eyes, and you did not listen to him, but rather you persecuted him, and you killed him. Jesus died because of you and because of what your fathers did. Yet despite the severity of your error, despite your terrible crime of killing God's only begotten son, you and your fathers never repented of your sin nor were you willing to accept the truth of the Gospels as preached by his holy apostles. You persisted in your error, and you persisted in your sin. You are as guilty today by not accepting Jesus as your savior, as your ancestors were guilty of killing him. The sin is for you to bear, and you must decide today whether you will persist in your sin, or whether you will find eternal salvation through him. Today is the day of judgment. Today you must decide whether you will live through Jesus, or whether you will pay the wages of sin. Today you must leave the clutches of Satan and be reborn in Christ. Today . . . and not tomorrow.

"Redemption is possible, if you will but believe in our redeemer. He is the light, he is the way. Believe in him! He is the road to your salvation, and not through your abominable Law. Because, as Saint Paul has said, the Law does not save, it cannot bring you redemption. It makes you aware of sin, but cannot save you from it. You must leave the Law that does not save. You must leave the Talmud that cripples you and blinds you, as it blinded your forefathers, to the truth of our faith. Come and accept Jesus — be circumcised of the spirit, and not just of the flesh. Come and accept him. Jesus waits for you, he wants your redemption, he wants your salvation. Remove the yoke that is between your eyes, and behold the truth of the word made flesh. Break the shackles of the Law and come join us . . . now, this moment.

"Which of you shall be the first to have Jesus in your heart? Shall it be you . . . or you . . . or you? I wait for you. Jesus waits for you. He has waited too long, he wants you to join him. God has sent me here today to bring you his offering of life eternal. He has sent me here to let you know that He sacrificed his only begotten son that you might live . . . that you might live today and forevermore, so that you might live and not die. Come forward, be not afraid. We will protect you from those who try to prevent you from joining us. Come . . . Jesus is waiting. Come and be baptized."

No one moved. There was an utter silence in the synagogue, a total absence of even the faintest sound. There was not even the slightest trace of movement as people remained fixed in their seats, their faces indifferent to what had been said.

De la Peña fumed with anger. "Oh, ye sons of the devil, how long will you be stiff-necked and sinful? Has Satan so corrupted your souls that you cannot see the truth? If you choose Satan as your master, then sin is your due, and you are truly beyond redemption. By rejecting life eternal through Jesus, you have shown yourselves to be subjects of Satan . . . yes, in this your last chance to have Jesus, you have rejected him again. You have chosen death and not life. Verily, verily indeed, you have chosen."

Suddenly De la Peña stopped his preaching, and there was total silence again. He turned to face his followers now, his eyes burning like hot coals, his spirit aflame with vengeance against those who would not listen to him. It was all over as far as he was concerned. The Jews had missed their moment of truth. They had rejected the Lord, they had rejected his preaching . . . then, by God, let the Jews join the devil in hell where they belonged!

As De la Peña was about to pronounce his judgment, a furious onslaught began. The synagogue door burst open and armed cavaliers brandishing swords surged into the synagogue. The newcomers ripped into the ruffians, disabled one with a swipe of the blade, cut a gaping hole into one intruder's thigh, and held another at bay with the point of a sword. The uncouth mob was no match for the armed cavaliers, and their resistance dissolved immediately. The conflict was over almost as quickly as it began.

De la Peña watched the collapse of his support with dismay. He had failed his Lord as much as his supporters had failed De la Peña. He had failed to bring the Jews to Jesus Christ, and he had failed to bring them to justice. He had come ever so close to doing what he had set out to do. And now, he knew, Satan's henchmen had stopped him from accomplishing God's will.

Andrés de Cabrera, governor of the Alcazar castle, walked into the synagogue and assessed the situation. It was obvious he had come in time. On hearing of the disturbance in the plaza, he had quickly gathered a force of able men to quell the disturbance. As the local governor, Cabrera knew that such a disturbance would have to be stopped immediately before it became out of hand. Besides, it was important to make sure riots did not become directed at him personally. Cabrera himself was of Converso origin, and there had been a time in his life when the entire city had revolted against him. He signaled to his men to apprehend De la Peña. The disturbance was over.

De Cabrera went to where Senior was sitting. He had known the old Jew for a long time. He remembered years ago, when, Bishop Dávila had organized the revolt of the townspeople against him, and how the mob had stormed the courtyard of the Alcázar. Isabella had heard out the grievances of the mob against Cabrera, had found the charges to be groundless, and had reinstated Cabrera as governor of the Alcázar. In her investigation of Cabrera, Isabella had paid close attention to the testimony of Senior. It was Senior, along with others, who had evidently saved him.

It was also Senior who had persuaded Cabrera in 1474 that Henry IV was unfit to rule, and that he would be wise to turn over the city and the Alcázar fortress to the newly proclaimed sovereigns Ferdinand and Isabella. It had been sound advice in the end. He owed much to Senior as well as to the Queen. To the Queen, he owed his total allegiance. Because Jews were officially the property of the crown, any damage inflicted on the Jewish community was injury to the crown, and Cabrera, faithful servant that he was, intended that no such injury would ever come to pass. And, besides, his old friend Senior was in danger, and he was not about to let anything happen to him.

"Don Abraham, how are you, dear friend? Are you hurt?," Cabrera asked as he shook the hand of this long-time comrade.

"Don Andrés, praised be the Lord for sending you here," Senior said, his voice shaking with emotion as he embraced Cabrera. Tears of joy streamed down his face. "Praised be the Lord. Truly, you have saved us. I thought for sure that we were all going to die today."

Cabrera replied, loosening himself from Senior's embrace, "Did you think I would let such a thing happen? I can assure you that will not be the case, not today or any other day. The situation is now completely under control. We shall take this instigator and keep him in my custody until the matter can be brought before the King and Queen."

Senior said, "I tell you, I can hardly believe what happened. My God, he wanted to kill us all. I personally am going to file a formal protest against this lunatic and make sure that he is properly punished. God Almighty, I thought I was going to die, that it was all over for me."

Cabrera remarked, "It is almost like old times, is it not? Except that then, it was I whom the mob wanted to kill."

Senior looked up into Cabrera's eyes, understanding immediately what the governor was alluding to in his remark. He replied, "Yes, Don Andrés, it is almost like old times. Thank you, dear friend, for being just that . . . a dear and true friend. You are, as I am, one who is faithful to the laws of friendship. I owe my life to you today, as do all the members of this community. We will be always eternally grateful, Don Andrés."

"I am touched by your gratitude, Don Abraham, and I remain at your command should you ever need me," Cabrera said. "I will have part of my men stay behind to make sure that there are no further interruptions of your religious service. Please, continue with your service . . ."

"So we will," said Senior, "And we will think of you, and of your great deed, in our prayers."

Senior and Cabrera embraced each other one last time and bade each other farewell.

Held by two men, one on each side, De la Peña watched this display of noble friendship with disgust. Struggling to get free, De la Peña screamed loudly, "You traitorous *Converso* . . .Do you, too, make your peace with Satan? Do you, too, deny the word of God? Because what I say cannot be denied. It is the truth, the everlasting truth, the truth which cannot be refuted. It cannot be denied — not by you, Cabrera, not by you, Senior, not by anyone here. I dare you to answer me, Senior, if you can. But you cannot, because you know that what I say is true. Is that not so, Don Abraham Senior, chief judge of the Jews, supreme priest of the Pharisees? Is that not so? I dare you to answer me."

Cabrera was steaming and drew his sword, but Senior grabbed his arm and held him back. Don Abraham stood there nervously, holding on to Cabrera's arm. He sensed that all the eyes of the congregation were on him. Even Cabrera's eyes were on him. Senior was not a scholar nor trained as a rabbi, even though he was popularly thought to be a court rabbi. What was he to say? If he evaded the challenge, he knew he would lose face. Yet if he tried to engage this Dominican in a debate, he would lose even more.

"I will answer you," said a deep voice. But the voice was not Senior's. It was a voice from the back of the synagogue. People's heads turned in the direction of the voice, as did Senior's, wondering who it was that had responded to the challenge. There, in the darkness of the rear, stood a tall bearded figure, his prayer shawl covering his face and shoulders, his identity shrouded in a veil of mystery. The figure moved away from the shadowy rear and began to walk toward the front of the synagogue. From the way he walked, it was evident that this was no ordinary man. His body was straight as a lance, his demeanor was commanding — even overpowering. As he came out of the shadows, the figure pulled his prayer shawl down and let it rest on his shoulders. Now it was possible to see his face. There was a series of surprised gasps among those present who recognized the mystery man. It was evident that he had penetrating eyes, a straight handsome nose, and small lips that were buried in a flowing well-kept beard that reached to his chest. The mystery man continued walking, oblivious to the wave of whispers that he had generated, taking large, confident steps toward the podium. He walked by Cabrera and Senior and paid no attention to the astonished look on their faces. He walked by De la Peña and likewise paid him no heed.

The mystery man was none other than Don Isaac Abravanel, chief rabbi of Castile, whose presence in Segovia was as unexpected as it was welcome. Abravanel stood there, arms at his sides, gazing out calmly at the congregation, and began his response to De la Peña's challenge.

"In ancient times, the pagans worshipped many gods — gods of lightning, gods of rain, moon-gods, and sun-gods. There were gods of the Earth, and there were fertility goddesses to which people paid homage. Our blessed father, the first Jew, Abraham, was the first to see the folly of idols. Because of Father Abraham, Jews became unique among the peoples of the Near East in believing in a God that was invisible, of which no idols or images could be made.

"Jews believe that no human being should be worshipped as a god. No person — not Antiochus, not Caesar, not Jesus — not anyone should be worshipped as a god. God does not have human form. The God of Israel, the God of the universe, is beyond human form; He is beyond representation. There is no idol or picture or mental image that can capture the form or the essence of His being.

"It was into this strict anti-idolatrous environment that Jesus of Nazareth was born. As a Jew, Jesus believed that God was incapable of pictorial representation or bodily incarnation. And as a Jew, Jesus would have regarded as blasphemous the claim that a human being, including himself, could be worshipped as co-equal with God. Indeed, in the New Testament, Jesus himself admits, 'Why do you call me good? Only God is good,' indicating that Jesus did not consider himself divine.

"The Jews of Judea were familiar with the man-gods of other religions and nations. In Egypt, the Pharaoh was revered as a supernatural being, as the incarnate form of the god Osiris. Alexander the Great demanded and secured recognition of his divinity.

"In Roman imperial religion, the god Apollo was supposed to be god-the-father of his two begotten sons, Julius and Augustus Caesar, who, according to the Roman senate's decree, were to be worshipped as gods. Augustus was made into a god while he was still alive and, following his death, people were willing to testify that he ascended to heaven.

"It was in light of this historical pattern of the making of gods out of mortal men that Judaism viewed the attempt to make a god, or a son of god, out of Jesus. Because Judaism is opposed to the idea of worshipping humans, Jews regard Jesus as but another human who was mistakenly elevated to the status of divinity. Jesus was a human being — and nothing more.

"Many of the teachings of Jesus were unrealistic. He instructed his followers not to resist evil. In fact, he encouraged his followers to turn the other cheek whenever one was struck. To *not* fight against evil was and is contrary to Jewish teaching, and in this regard Jews regard Jesus as being wrong. On the contrary, Judaism has always regarded the battle against evil and injustice to be a Jewish ideal. Despite Jesus' teaching to turn the other cheek, Christians are among the most warlike of peoples; in generation after generation, they have slaughtered thousands in the name of Jesus, killing Jews and Christians alike. But even Jesus himself could not live up to his own teachings: he taught people to love their enemies, but Jesus could not bring himself to love the Pharisees, whom he criticized as 'hypocrites, serpents, and offspring of vipers.'

"Jesus claimed that the Kingdom of Heaven was immanent and that all that he prophesized would come to be before his generation passed away. He taught men to give away all their earthly possessions, for they were of no importance in the world to come. He taught people to forget about trying to change the social order, 'To give unto Caesar the things that are Caesar's.' 'This generation shall not pass away, till all be fulfilled', he said.

"But it did not come to be. The Kingdom of Heaven, that Jesus had predicted, never materialized. The generation of Jesus passed away and still the world was no different. The world was still full of war and poverty and disease. The coming and going of Jesus had made no difference. And yet his followers continued to wait; perhaps Jesus had meant it was the next generation, or the one after that. For centuries to come, the early Christians kept waiting and waiting, denying themselves the pleasures of life, denying themselves earthly possessions in preparation nalingr.

for the world that Jesus spoke of. But it never came. The Christians isolated themselves from society, living lives of hermits and ascetics, building monasteries where they could avoid contact with the real world about them. Ultimately, the Christians were forced to reinterpret the passages that related to the Kingdom Come that never came.

"This is why we feel that Jesus was mistaken with his other-worldly preoccupation and with his doomsday preaching of repentance. He should have been more concerned with the social and political problems of his day.

"As to Jesus being the Messiah, it must be understood that the Jewish conception of the Messiah matured during Roman rule in Judea. The Messiah was never supposed to be a supernatural figure. "Messiah" comes from the Hebrew word *Mashiah*, which means "anointed." The prophet Samuel was the "anointed one" of Israel, and so was King David. They were all men, yet they were all "anointed," all *Mashiah*, in the name of God. The Jewish Messiah was supposed to be a man anointed by God who would fulfill certain ideas. The Messiah would be descended from King David, he would overthrow the hated Roman rule, he would gather in the dispersed Jews from all over the world, and he would usher in a new Messianic era following the Day of Judgment.

"Jews did not accept Jesus because he did not satisfy the Messianic criteria. Jesus made no attempt to overthrow the evil Roman government; indeed, he preached submission to Roman rule. He did not gather in the Jewish exiles, nor as the prophet says, did he 'rule from sea to sea, and from the river unto the ends of the earth'. In fact, Jesus did not rule over anyone. During his lifetime he was persecuted by his enemies and was in constant hiding from them. In the end, he fell into their hands and was not even able to rescue himself. How could such a person be expected to help the people of Israel from their plight? Both during his lifetime and after his death, Jesus had absolutely no dominion over anyone. Therefore, because he did not gather the dispersed ones of Israel, because he did not usher in a new Messianic era for the world as was expected, because he ruled over none of the peoples of the earth, as far as Jews are concerned, this was sufficient evidence that Jesus was not the Messiah.

"As to the genealogies in the New Testament stating that Jesus was descended from King David, the accounts are conflicting. One author traces it through Joseph, and another traces it through Mary. If Joseph is claimed to be the father of Jesus, then a Christian may claim that Jesus is perhaps the Messiah; however, at the same time, he cannot claim that Jesus is the son of God. On the other hand, if the Holy Ghost rather than Joseph is presumed to be the father of Jesus, then a Christian may claim that Jesus is the son of God, but since the Davidic seed of Joseph is not involved, the claim may not be made that he is the Messiah. Therefore, Jesus cannot inherit through Joseph because the Christians say Joseph was not his father. If Mary is claimed to be descended from King David, this is of no avail either because Jesus cannot inherit the Kingdom according to the laws of the Torah, for it is written that daughters and their seed do not inherit whenever there is a male descendant and, in the generation of Jesus, there were many such male descendants. Therefore, Jesus cannot inherit through his mother.

"Most of the early followers of Jesus were Jewish. They viewed him as their Messiah, as the man who was to usher in the New Kingdom. They did not view him as divine, however, because as Jews, this belief would have been regarded as blasphemous. The Jewish followers of Jesus would have remained an insignificant sect had it not been for the appearance of Paul, a man who never even met Jesus.

"It was Paul who changed the nature of the Christian movement. After having undergone a mystical conversion, Paul was moved to devise a scheme of redemption involving the death of Jesus that had little to do with the historical Jesus. Indeed, Paul seemed to act as if he knew more about Jesus than Jesus did about himself. Whereas Jesus had said, 'Go not unto the Gentiles, but unto the lost sheep of the House of Israel', Paul decided to do precisely the opposite and started preaching unto the Gentiles. Whereas Jesus never mentioned anything about Original Sin, Paul asserted that Jesus' death was meant to be a sacrificial atonement for the Original Sin of Adam which had led to the condemnation supposedly of all men. Whereas Jesus had said that he had not come to change one iota or tittle from the Law, Paul contradicted him and said that the Laws of Moses did not save and should be abandoned, and that the dietary rituals and the covenant of Abraham should be abolished.

"The effects of Paul's preaching was to permit the entry of large numbers of non-Jews into the early Christian movement. The ranks of the Christian movement swelled with these pagan converts who brought with them their pagan ideas, until the movement was entirely in their hands.

"When Paul preached to the pagans about Jesus being the son of God, the pagan converts took him at his word and saw Jesus as born of a virgin as were the pagan gods. Since the pagan gods looked like men and women, so under the influence of the pagan converts, the Christian god took the form and appearance of a man in Jesus.

"The concept of dying and resurrected gods was very well known to the pagans who made up the bulk of the Christian converts. For example, the cult of the lord god Adonis was popular and involved the mock burial and the resurrection of Adonis.

"In another cult, the cult of Dionysus, the believers ate a sacramental meal where they ate the flesh and drank of the blood of the dying god who later enjoyed resurrection.

"In Egypt, Osiris died and was resurrected, assuring his believers that all would be saved who had made the magical declarations of faith in Osiris. So too, in Asia Minor, the death and resurrection of Hercules was celebrated annually.

"To compete with the pagan cults, Christianity became like them. It, too, developed sacramental rites for initiates to attain salvation and immortality. As the followers of Dionysus had a special communion meal involving bread and wine, so, too, the Christians through the bread and wine of communion partook symbolically of the body and blood of their lord Jesus. Just as faith in Osiris and the secrets of Dionysus guaranteed one immortality and salvation, so too faith in Jesus was made to be the criterion for securing the afterlife. Just as Hercules, Dionysus, and Osiris had died and been resurrected, so too Jesus was said to have died and been resurrected.

It took three centuries for the damage to be done. It took only this long for the God of the universe — invisible, and beyond representation — to be reduced promptly in Christian hands to the status of a god that differed little in form from the gods of the pagans. Whereas the Jews had worshipped one God alone, the Christians claimed that there were three parts to theirs — a father, a son, and a holy ghost. Whereas in Jewish Jerusalem, it had been prohibited for any statue of any man or deity to defile the sacred city, it was commonplace in Rome and in Spain and elsewhere in the Empire to find statues and icons portraying Jesus, Mary, the apostles, and other saints.

It is easy for us as Jews to see the mistake that Christianity has made: they have fashioned themselves a god in the image of man, a god in the image of the Jew known as Jesus. This is the fundamental error of Christianity, and yet incredibly it is the foundation of their religion. We know that their claim is utterly false, yet they proclaim it to be ultimate truth. They have taken our Holy Scriptures, taken passages out of context, and invented forced interpretations to make the prophetic portions fit events. They pretend to be the New Israel, they who have done everything possible to subvert all that is sacred in Judaism.

"Yet for all their pronouncements, the Christians fear us and what we have to say. That is the reason why, when Christianity became the official religion of the Roman Empire in the year 315, it was made a crime punishable by death for anyone to convert to Judaism. That is why in every Christian country, regulations are passed restricting the rights and privileges of Jews. That is why we Jews are restricted in the occupations we can practice, that is why we are forced to wear different clothing from the Christians, that is why we are herded in separate quarters. That is why they persecute us, and that is why they will do everything in their power to silence and destroy us.

"Today we are gathered here on this first day of the Jewish Year to prepare ourselves spiritually to seek atonement for our sins. Judaism has always held that a man should be held accountable for his own sins. The belief that someone should suffer to atone for the sins of another is totally foreign to Jewish thinking. For this reason, the death of Jesus to atone for the sins of mankind makes no sense to the Jew.

"We Jews have never had any belief in the idea of Original Sin. After the Garden of Eden account in the Book of Genesis, there was no further mention of Original Sin in the Bible or in the Talmud, which gives one a clear idea of its utter unimportance. No sacrifices were ever made in the ancient Temple to atone for a so-called Original Sin. And because Jews have never believed in any kind of inheritable blemish on their souls that required someone to save them, there is no need for a savior.

"Furthermore, in Judaism, true forgiveness for one's sins is obtained without an intermediary. Through sincere repentance, anyone can obtain forgiveness from the Holy One, blessed be He. *Teshuva*, the returning to God and to His commandments, the returning to a state of holiness and repentance, is possible even to the worst of sinners.

"Now it is time for us to answer to God Almighty on this *Rosh Hashanah* day. Let us now purify ourselves from sin. For those sins we have committed against each other, let us ask forgiveness from those we have injured. For those sins we have committed against God and His Holy Torah, let us ask for His divine forgiveness. It is said in the Psalms, 'God is near unto all who call upon Him, who call upon Him in truth.' Let us do so today, let us achieve the redemption from sin as individuals, as the people of Israel, that we may deserve in this generation the speedy coming of the Messiah."

"Amen," the congregation intoned loudly in unison. Abravanel turned toward the Ark, covered his head as before with his prayer shawl, opened his prayer book, and bowed respectfully in prayer. No sooner had he done so than the cantor, his composure and full-throatedness regained, began to sing again at the point where the religious service had been previously interrupted. The congregation, charged with newfound energy, joined the cantor in his animated singing. Every verse became charged with an excitement and a meaning that the Hebrew words had never experienced before, every inflection became imbued with a new tingle of exaltation, every rhyme became a matchless poetic thrill of beauty. The feeling was wonderful.

Hacham Alhadeff, his face aglow, his eyes glistening, felt the warm shivers go up and down his body. Rabbi Maimi, overcome with excitement, went up to Abravanel and embraced him. Don Abraham Senior and Rabbi Melamed also climbed on the podium, shook Don Isaac Abravanel's hand, and hugged him dearly like a long-lost relative. Many came up to Abravanel to express their gratitude for preserving the honor of Israel. Truly, Don Isaac Abravanel had lived up to his reputation. Although a newcomer to Spain, Abravanel had established himself as the prime spokesman of Spanish Jewry. As his family claimed descent from King David, Abravanel came to be regarded as the latest Lion of Judah who carried on the tradition of the noblest family line in the House of Israel. All in attendance agreed that here was a Jew, a rabbi, a leader, the likes of whom they had never seen before.

Don Isaac Abravanel was born into one of the great Sephardic families of the Iberian peninsula — the Abravanel family, a family that for generations had served as financial counselors and political advisers to kings and nobles in the royal courts of Castile and Portugal. It was a family that had produced prominent Jewish leaders and patrons of Jewish learning.

Each of his ancestors for at least five successive generations had been individuals of exceptional ability; and the consciousness of being an Abravanel, of being of the royal House of David, of being destined for greatness, had been inculcated in young Isaac from a very early age. Great deeds were expected from him, and he spent his youth preparing himself for a lifetime of service of the highest order. His father, Don Judah, had been the financier to Prince Fernando, son of the Portuguese King João I. His grandfather, Don Samuel Abravanel, a patron of scholars, had served as financial adviser to the kings of Castile. His great-grandfather, Don Judah, had been the treasurer of Fernando IV in Seville. And then his great-great-grandfather, Joseph

Abravanel, a learned Jewish sage, had attained distinction in the court of the Castilian King Alfonso X. Such was the pedigree of Don Isaac Abravanel when he was born in Lisbon in the Year 1437.

He was schooled in the Hebrew scriptures, in the Bible and in the Talmud by Rabbi Yosef ben Abraham Hayyun. He studied the Jewish philosophical writings of Maimonides, Albo, Crescas, and others. His initial love of philosophy, its rational axiomatic approach, deductive logic and syllogistic argument, was intense; and his pursuit of truth led him to explore the writings of non-Jewish philosophers such as Aristotle and Averroes.

But his love of philosophy did not blind him to its limitations for the philosophers offered no satisfying solutions to the questions of fundamental importance that had aroused the curiosity of the young Isaac. Abravanel then mastered Latin, the language of medieval scholastic discourse. He poured over the Latin classics — Tacitus, Cicero, Suetonius, Marcus Aurelius, the poet Virgil, and the Spanish-born Seneca. He read the Latin Vulgate and delved into the writings of St. Augustine, Aquinas, Jerome, Origen, Ambrose, and of the modern-day monastic scholars. His intrinsic curiosity took him far astray into diverse fields such as medicine, law, and mathematics. Although Abravanel had exposed himself to the alleged knowledge and wisdom of the western world, he had found it lacking. He had studied the sacred writings of Christendom and found them unconvincing. And now it was time to return to his own tradition, to be a proud part of it and to enrich it with the knowledge that he had amassed. While still a youth, Abravanel composed his first religious work, *Crown of the Elders*, in which he expounded his views on divine providence and prophecy. Soon thereafter, he was providing elegant lectures in the Lisbon synagogue on the Book of Deuteronomy, much to the pleasure of his proud parents. It was his dream one day of writing a learned commentary on the prophets of Israel, the prophets who had articulated the perfect truths of love, justice, and mercy.

But the far-flung business undertakings of the family began to make inroads into his time. His father Don Judah was ailing, and young Isaac, groomed to follow his father, stepped in to fill the void. While still in his twenties, he married Esther Benaroya, daughter of a Portuguese grandee family, who in a matter of a few years bore him three healthy sons — Judah, Joseph, and Samuel.

Called to ransom 250 North African Jews who were captured and enslaved as a result of the Portuguese conquest of Arcila in 1471,

Abravanel labored feverishly for their rescue. He went everywhere, caring for the captives, negotiating with their taskmasters, and raising funds from the Jewries of Portugal and Italy to liberate them. Abravanel and his Lisbon committee raised the ransom of ten thousand doubloons to free their people from bondage and brought them to Portugal.

By 1475 Abravanel held an advisory position in the court of King Alfonso V. The King, a broad-minded patron of scholars who relished the company of learned individuals, had a special liking for the erudite Jew whose humanistic spirit was, in certain ways, so much like his own. When Don Judah Abravanel died, Isaac succeeded his father in the role of treasurer to the crown and came to be the highest placed and most respected royal councillor in the land. Privy to the King's confidences, entrusted with guiding the monarch on matters financial and otherwise, Abravanel had truly soared to the heights of courtly success.

His rapid rise in court was due in part to his involvement with the Braganza family. The Braganzas were, without question, the richest nobles in the land, and their holdings exceeded well over a third of all Portugal. Abravanel had been in their employ as a financial adviser for several years, and he had become the beneficiary of their generosity and gratitude for his services. As a result, Abravanel became an immensely wealthy man. He lent over a million reals to the crown to help cover the expenses of the debilitating war against Castile, a war Abravanel had advised against.

But when Alfonso V died in 1481 from the plague, things took a turn for the worse. The new regent of Portugal, João II, was of a different breed; the new King disapproved of the nobles' power and wealth, and particularly the all-powerful Braganza family against whom João had a longstanding personal desire for vengeance. Modeling his policies on those of Castile and other European countries, João II embarked upon a ruthless course of centralization. To gain the favor of the townspeople, he began enforcing the anti-Jewish regulations. He commanded all the magistrates of the cities to swear their exclusive loyalty to him as king, much to the discomfiture of the nobles. Although Abravanel continued for some time as royal advisor, he knew his position as a close con-fidante of the Braganzas would compromise his standing with the King.

The Duke of Braganza and the Count of Faro secretly planned an insurrection of the nobles against the King. João was informed of the planned rebellion, and he countered with an immediate purge of the nobles beginning, of course, with the Braganzas. The Duke of Braganza was arrested on his arrival at the royal castle of Evora. The following day other conspirators were summoned likewise to the Evora castle to appear before the king. Thus it was that, the day after the Duke's arrest, Abravanel set off for Evora to comply with the royal summons. En route to Evora, he spent the night in Arreyolos, a township under the Duke's control. There the villagers told Abravanel what had happened the preceding day, and a messenger informed him that he, too, was suspect. Abravanel protested, but it was doubtful that the King would believe he was innocent in light of Don Isaac's long and close ties to the Braganzas. Urged to flee the country, he made immediate preparations to do so. Don Isaac dispatched a close friend to inform his family of his decision to flee, what plans he had to rescue them, and what measurues should be taken to salvage the family fortune. On May 31, 1483, barely two days after the Duke had been arrested, he left Portugal and crossed over to Castile.

Abravanel settled temporarily in the town of Segura de la Ordén, in the region of Badajoz, close to the Portuguese border. He maintained an active correspondence with his friends and family and addressed a series of letters to the King, insisting on his innocence. He expressed resentment against the false charges against him and pleaded with the King to deal with him justly by pronouncing him innocent of treason. The pleas, the supplications, the entreaties were not without effect. In due time, João II, unable to secure convincing testimony of subversion on Abravanel's part, relented and allowed Abravanel's wife and three sons to join him in Castile.

Abravanel attributed his downfall to a misguided sense of service. Instead of serving the King of the Universe, the Lord God of Israel, he had wasted years of his life in the service of an ungrateful earthly king. Instead of committing himself to a lifetime of study and to the unselfish pursuit of Torah for its own sake, he had allowed himself to be distracted by the opulence of court and his material success, by the titles and riches that he knew were evanescent. He resolved to use his solitude as an opportunity to make amends for his sinful oversights. It would be the first step in the fulfillment of his dream of a new commentary on the prophets, the first step on the road of his self-directed spiritual salvation. The prophet Micah had said it simply, "He has shown thee, O Man, what is good, and what the Lord requireth of thee, but to do justly and to love mercy, and to walk humbly with thy God."

He needed to learn humility. His downfall was a blessing in disguise, an opportunity to forever set his lifetime priorities straight.

Abravanel used his stay in Segura to work on a commentary on the minor prophets, interweaving scholarly insights with interpretive comments that drew on his experiences of political intrigues at court. Within six months, he had written the full commentaries on Joshua, Judges, and Samuel, and part of Kings. Only after half a year was Abravanel ready to resume his career of public service. He had learned his lesson. He vowed that he would stay close to a *yeshiva*, a rabbinical center of Jewish learning, so he could continue his writing and maintain contact with people of piety. This would keep his spirit from being corrupted by wealth and power. He would never make the same mistake again.

An opportunity arose in 1484 to meet with the Spanish sovereigns, Ferdinand and Isabella. The sovereigns had heard of the financial skills of Don Isaac and of the circumstances under which he had been forced to flee. During their meeting, the sovereigns wasted no time in recruiting the former treasurer of Portugal, and they appointed Abravanel to work alongside Don Abraham Senior as a tax farmer. Together, Senior and Abravanel were assigned the task of raising large funds to conduct the costly military campaign against the Moors, a war already in its third year. Year in and year out, Ferdinand and Isabella were forced to call on the combined financial genius of Don Isaac and Don Abraham to raise new funds to continue the war effort.

By 1485, Abravanel had come to the attention of Cardinal Mendoza, the "third King of Spain," and Don Isaac assented to take charge of the cardinal's tax-farming activities in Alcalá de Henares, Guadalajara, and other nearby localities. The Portuguese refugee succeeded in raising millions of maravedis for the Cardinal, who belonged to the powerful Castilian family of Mendoza. Abravanel's star was on the rise again. But the lesson he learned from his stay in Segura stayed with him. Whatever wealth he might gain, he would disperse generously to those in need. Whatever power he had, he would use to help his Jewish brethren. All that he would do, as courtier, as religious thinker, as a leader of his people, he did in the name of the Holy One of Israel, Blessed be He.

Abravanel settled initially in Alcalá de Henares to be at the center of his tax-farming district. But there was also another reason — Alcalá was but a short distance away from Guadalajara, where Rabbi Isaac Aboab, the *Gaon* of Castile, had established a renowned Talmudic academy. Abravanel developed close ties with Rabbi Aboab and with the students of this academy, and he sought every opportunity to spend time there to study, to learn, to teach, to pray, to be in the company of pious Jews who shared his commitment to Judaic scholarship. It was in Guadalajara that he found the spiritual counterbalance to his secular activities as a tax-farmer, and he resolved to move there as soon as his duties permitted.

It was with Senior that Abravanel sensed a special kinship because of their mutual interests in the royal court and the Jewish community. Senior had recommended Abravanel to the King and Queen to assist him in tax-farming. But Senior's plans for the former head of Portuguese Jewry went beyond tax-farming; Senior planned to introduce Abravanel to the people, the problems, and the structure of Jewish communal life throughout Spain. Everywhere he went, Don Isaac made a strong impression on all who heard him speak. His brilliantly crafted sermons, ripe with learned wisdom and delivered with a marvelous inspiring style, packed the synagogues to the rafters in Tudela, provoked rousing cheers of approbation in Zaragoza, stirred people to tears in Valencia. Everywhere he went, people flocked to hear him. They were touched by Abravanel's encouraging words, by his sense of mission for the welfare of his people. Most of all, they were touched by his vision of the historic destiny of the people of Israel.

Abravanel gave generously of himself during this tour, inspiring his tormented kinsmen with an optimism that bordered on millenial expectations. Yet words, Abravanel knew, words of hope and encouragement, however well said, were not enough. His words would have to be matched by deeds that would put a stop to the anti-Jewish ordinances and demonstrations. This was what he and Senior were working for.

First they would have to advance money to the crown to meet the war debts. Senior and Abravanel loaned millions of interest-free maravedis to the King and Queen, hoping thereby to obtain royal favor and appreciation. The grants in aid were not without effect, and, as a token of their gratitude, the sovereigns gave Don Abraham and Don Isaac freedom to formulate and execute royal financial policies. But this was not enough for Senior and Abravanel; they wanted to extend their influence beyond their financial responsibilities. It was their goal to influence the Catholic sovereigns to annul much of the harsh anti-Jewish legislation urged by representatives of the Inquisition at court, and to foster a more enlightened and tolerant royal attitude toward their harassed constituency.

And now, after the outbreak in Segovia, Abravanel heeded the call to duty. Senior had requested of Abravanel that he make a formal protest at the itinerant royal court now in Baza. Senior himself had dispatched a sharply worded complaint concerning De la Peña to the chancillery at Valladolid and had rebuked the Hermandad head, Domínguez, for failing to take adequate measures to protect the local Jewish community from harm. But if such an outbreak could happen in Segovia, where the Chief Judge Senior resided, it could happen anywhere. It was urgent that the King and Queen be informed immediately of what had taken place in Segovia. It was imperative that the instigator be severely punished, and that the crown be persuaded to issue a warning prohibiting demonstrations against its Jewish subjects in Segovia and elsewhere.

In earlier days, Senior would have gone himself and personally taken care of such a matter. Now, Senior was exhausted from his recent trip to Málaga, so he asked Abravanel to go in his place.

The royal court was now at Baza where the King and Queen were laying siege to the Moorish fortress. Abravanel entered the royal tent at Baza. As he entered it, Abravanel immediately noticed the Grand Inquisitor, Tomás de Torquemada, standing off to one side and staring at him with menacing brown eyes. As in the past, Abravanel and Torquemada exchanged hostile cold glances. Time and again the two had met on such royal terrain, pitting their strengths against one another, probing for signs of weakness in their antagonist's defense, hoping to dismantle all that the other wished to achieve.

Abravanel knew that Torquemada was the architect of the anti-Jewish and anti-Converso policies of the crown. It was Torquemada, the former prior of the Dominican monastery of Santa Cruz in Segovia, who as Grand Inquisitor supervised the Inquisition and presided over its Supreme Council. It was Torquemada who sought to blot out heresy in the land by conducting a campaign of terror, torture, and executions against all who stood in his path. It was Torquemada who had ruined the lives of countless people throughout Spain, and who had ruined small and large towns alike through the widespread confiscations and persecution of the Holy Office. It was Torquemada who had advised the King and Queen to expel the Jews from Andalusia. It was Torquemada who was the Queen's confessor and filled her ears with reports of the iniquities of her Jewish subjects. Thus, it came as no surprise to Don Isaac Abravanel that De la Peña, too, was from the very same Santa Cruz monastery in Segovia.

Yet the fate of these two individuals, in this world, was ironic. Abravanel, a child of wealth, helped the poor and persecuted Jews, while Torquemada, the other-worldly priest, erected the worldly means for the extermination of Christian unbelievers. Abravanel, once fallen from courtly greatness, sought redemption in selfless devotion to his people; Torquemada, trusting to heaven, found need to surround himself with 70 archers and soldiers to protect him. Abravanel, the conosseieur of aristocratic refinements, uplifted himself with the vestments of the spirit. Torquemada, the avowed man of religion, became a torturer of human flesh.

And it was the flesh of Don Isaac Abravanel that Torquemada wanted most to flay. He had gotten a disturbing report from the Segovian Inquisitor Lucero concerning De la Peña's activities; admittedly, the report was garnered from local hearsay and rumor. But what was disturbing was not that a priest from his own monastery acted irresponsibly. This was at most deserving of a friendly admonition to the priest. No, that was not it. Rather, it was the response to De la Peña's sermon that troubled him. Based on Lucero's account, a rabbi named Isaac reportedly made such sacrilegious remarks that, had the rabbi been less important, he would have been arrested and interrogated for blasphemy. Torquemada had no doubts about the truth of the report and of the involvement of Abravanel, yet he knew he needed substantial evidence against Don Isaac to justify his arrest. He knew that he would have to bide his time until Abravanel made another false move. Torquemada swore to himself that one day he would remove all unbelief from Spain. More, he would bring the arrogant Jew Abravanel to his knees and to accept Jesus Christ in his heart.

Abravanel's attention focused now on the King and Queen as he approached the throne.

"The court announces Don Isaac Abravanel," proclaimed a voice. Don Isaac placed himself squarely in front of the King and Queen. He doffed his hat, bowed respectfully, and looked up to his sovereigns. As soon as the Queen nodded, Abravanel began his address:

"Your most royal highness, on behalf of the Jewish communities of the kingdom, I bring you wishes of health and property. All Spain speaks of your glorious victory over the Moors at Málaga."

Ferdinand, clearing his throat, remarked, "And what success we enjoyed was in no small measure due to your assistance, Don Isaac."

A gratifying look flashed across Abravanel's face at hearing this statement of royal appreciation. It was obvious he was getting off to a good start in this presentation.

"Your Majesty, to have served in such a noble cause is its own reward. Your good favor is the most excellent compensation one could possibly ask for."

A short distance away, the Grand Inquisitor listened carefully to what was being said. A Franciscan priest came up to his side and whispered a question, "I hear this Jew Abravanel loaned the King 1,500,000 maravedis for the campaign. Is it true?"

Torquemada nodded and bit his lip.

"What do you know about him?," queried the friar further.

"He is the real leader of the Jews," said Torquemada matter-of-factly, his gaze still directed toward the throne, paying lttle attention to the Franciscan.

"But what about the Chief Judge, Abraham Senior?", the friar asked again.

"Senior means nothing," Torquemada said softly and without emotion, "He is a senile pompous old goat. Senior may have more power at court, but Abravanel is the one the Jews respect and look up to."

"Oh, I see," said the friar, withdrawing quietly from the Grand Inquisitor's presence.

"Is there some favor, Don Isaac, you wish to ask of us?"

Abravanel answered, "Yes, your Majesty. If I may be so bold to ask on behalf of your loyal Jewish subjects, our requests that Jewish quarters not be the site of Christian religious demonstrations have gone unheeded. In a recent outbreak in Segovia, there was a near riot as the result of the preaching of a Dominican priest called Antonio De la Peña. His sermons encouraged the local townspeople to do violence to the members of the Jewish community, and even Don Abraham Senior was nearly injured."

The Queen interrupted, "We heard about this scandalous incident, and it upset us. Don Abraham Senior filed a formal protest with the chancellery at Valladolid, and a copy of his petition has been forwarded to us. Please be assured, Don Isaac, and you may assure our good friend Don Abraham Senior as well, that the Dominican priest will be duly punished for causing this disturbance. We have issued an order that the priest, Fray Antonio de la Peña, be brought personally before us for chastisement. Furthermore, this priest has been ordered not to preach to anyone whatsoever, nor is anyone to be permitted to listen to his sermons. It is our intention now, as it has been in the past, to protect the Jewish subjects of the crown from physical harm. We will not permit any more acts of provocation, for it not only causes great confusion and harm, but it is also a great disservice to our Lord."

Abravanel listened to the Queen's words; he felt relieved that measures were being taken to keep De la Peña under control. He wanted further assurances, however.

"Your Majesty, such words are the words of justice; they are the words of law and order for which you have become highly esteemed throughout the land. Am I to understand, then, that no further religious demonstrations will be allowed in the Jewish quarters, either by Fray De la Peña or anyone else?"

This was a much more searching question, and Abravanel wanted a general affirmation of community protection from the Queen. Isabella furrowed her brow, reflected upon the question, but hesitated before replying. Abravanel waited for an answer.

Torquemada suddenly stepped out of the crowd.

"If I may be allowed, your Majesty, to answer this question."

Isabella, catching a deep breath, looked relieved. "Ah, Grand Inquisitor . . . please proceed."

Torquemada advanced to the throne. He tugged once again at the rope around his waist, holding firmly on to the crucifix at his side. He looked at Abravanel, thinly disguising his dislike of the man, and said:

"Perhaps I should remind Don Isaac Abravanel that the Jewish quarters — the inhabitants and the domains therein — are all properties of the crown. A Christian crown, I should add. This is a Christian country, with a Christian King and a Christian Queen, and all of us as Christians are engaged in a holy crusade against the infidel, to spread the dominion of the word of Christ. And wherever the King and Queen have dominion, the word of Christ will be heard there. And Jewish quarters, being as they are under royal control, are no exception. The Gospel of our Lord will be heard there and, indeed, must be heard there. Therefore, in response to your question, Fray de la Peña will, of course, be kept out of the *juderías*; however, this does not mean that the Evangel will no longer be heard in the Jewish quarters of Spain. It will be heard time and again throughout Spain, but only under circumstances where there is no threat of physical injury to the Jews of the community."

"Until, I presume, all the Jews of Spain are converted to Christianity?," Abravanel asked.

"Don Isaac, I am dismayed by your question. Surely you are aware *that* is our professed intention," said Torquemada forcefully.

Isabella was satisfied with the Inquisitor's clarification of state policy. Ferdinand, uneasy about the direction of the exchange, cleared his throat again, and finally asked, "Hrumph . . . well . . . is there anything else, Don Isaac?"

Don Isaac Abravanel stood silently in place, acutely aware that any move he made would elicit a countermove by Torquemada. He looked in the King's eyes and sensed Ferdinand's desire to change the topic. Isabella, judging by her pleased look, was eager to let Torquemada continue to represent her position on matters affecting the Jewish community.

Abravanel allowed himself to continue, "Yes, there is another matter. I have been approached by the Jewish family members of a certain Abrahan Harache, of the village of Aguilar, concerning the family estate and certain family members. All of their property, it seems, has been confiscated by the Inquisition. Also, two young sons of the family have been taken for questioning by Inquisition authorities, and nothing further has been heard about them. It is my understanding that the Inquisition has no jurisdiction over the Jews of the kingdom. If such is the case, why has this taken place, and what has become of the two boys?"

Isabella, intruding upon the exchange, said curtly, "We do not interfere with the workings of the Holy Office of the Inquisition, Don Isaac. This is an improper request."

Torquemada glared at Abravanel and replied in a biting tone, "I am familiar with the case you mention. The Jew you call Abrahan Harache uttered blasphemies and other ugly words against our glorious Virgin Mary, and an authorization has been issued for his arrest and to bring him to trial for his abominable crime. In the interim, all his belongings — his home, his land, and other possessions — have been sequestered. As to the two sons of this sinful blasphemer, it is apparent that they, too, have engaged in unpardonable utterances against our glorious Virgin Mary. Such impudence will not go unpunished. No blasphemer, Jew or Christian, is outside the jurisdiction of the Holy Office of the Inquisition, and that even includes you, Don Isaac Abravanel."

Abravanel smarted from the flung implication. It would be unwise to continue with this damaging exchange much longer. Torquemada had placed him on the defensive, and the sooner he got off this subject, the better it would be. Nonetheless, he still wanted one more bit of information.

"But are they alive?," Abravanel asked once again.

"It is their sinful soul with which we are concerned, not the fate of their bodies," said Torquemada.

Abravanel, unable to contain his frustration, was insistent. "Answer my question, Grand Inquisitor," he demanded.

"No Inquisitor of the Catholic faith need answer to arrogance such as yours, Don Isaac Abravanel," Torquemada retorted.

Abravanel countered, "Perhaps because the utterance of the truth is too much for them to bear."

Torquemada fumed upon hearing such a remark. His face turned red with rage, his nostrils flared with indignation, as an overpowering impulse to wreak vengeance on Abravanel overtook him.

Ferdinand quickly stood up and shouted, "Silence! Enough squabbling! Don Isaac, you will watch your tongue in the presence of the Grand Inquisitor. Inquisitor, you, too, must learn to watch what you say. The audience is over."

Everyone stood as the King and Queen left the room. Torquemada looked disdainfully at Abravanel, but the Jew ignored him. Leaving the courtroom, the Grand Inquisitor vowed death and destruction to the unbelievers. He stormed down the side, snorting and grimacing as he went, pounding one fist into the palm of the other hand, kicking at the dirt floor, furious for allowing the foul-mouthed Jew to speak to him that way. He was the Grand Inquisitor of Castile and Leon, and no one could speak to him this way.

A hand reached out and firmly grabbed Torquemada's arm. Torquemada was startled momentarily. Quickly he recovered his composure. It was the Queen. As she stood hiding in a darkened corridor, she exhibited a peculiar cunning look on her face, as if she were ready to play a clever trick on one of her friends. Torquemada wondered what the Queen was doing there, hiding in a corner with that silly grin on her face. The childish look surprised Torquemada, and he disapproved of it because it was so unbecoming of her royal highness. He would have to bring this to her attention during the next confession.

"Fray Tomás, I have something to tell you," the Queen said coyly.

"Your Highness, I am at your command," answered Torquemada seriously.

In a slow deliberate voice, the Queen revealed the strategem behind the look on her face.

"*Now* is the time," she said, opening wide to reveal the white of her eyes.

Torquemada understood the statement perfectly. He had waited so long for these words, and now, when least expected, the words had been said.

"It is time," the Grand Inquisitor said, his face flushed with understanding.

"It is time," echoed the Queen, "You must see the King at once."

"Very well, your Majesty," Torquemada said, "I will do so immediately . . ."

The Queen took her hand from Torquemada's arm. The Inquisitor was now free to leave her presence. He bowed respectfully and said in parting, "It is time to do God's will."

Isabella nodded her head in agreement.

The King was indignant.

Ferdinand screamed, "What do you mean by that, Grand Inquisitor, trying to make a mockery of the royal court?"

"My humblest and most sincere apologies, your Majesty," said Torquemada, his head bowed in humility.

Ferdinand pointed a finger at Torquemada, "Damn your apologies. You respect the dignity and the manners of the court. Is that clear?"

Torquemada stayed bowed in respect of the request, and continued, "Yes, your Majesty. I remain your faithful servant . . . Your Majesty, I have entered your chamber with the best intent, even though I have withheld my thoughts on this matter until the incident today."

"What in damnation are you talking about?," asked Ferdinand.

"Your Majesty realizes that I have been entrusted with the responsibility for eliminating heresy from the land. It is the opinion of the Supreme Council of the Inquisition that the task is impossible so long as Jews are present in the kingdom. The Jews secretly teach the New Christians to observe the ancient Jewish practices, and they circumcise the children of the Conversos. Thus, the New Christians persist in the error of their ways. It is the opinion of the Holy Office that you consider expelling the Jews from all of Spain just as you drove them out of Andalusia five years ago.

Ferdinand shook his head at this absurd proposition.

"Have you gone mad? The Jews are a valuable people. Abravanel put up much of the money for the campaign against the Moors, as did Abraham Senior who is our chief tax collector. And you want me to expel them? . . . Ha! Others, as you well know, are physicians, men of commerce and wealth. It would have disastrous results for the kingdom."

"Ah, but their wealth would not go with them," said Torquemada.

"Wha . . . what do you mean?," asked Ferdinand, a puzzled expression on his face.

Torquemada replied, "To impoverish Spain would be to weaken the cause of Christendom. Of course, their valuables — their gold, their silver, and other properties — would stay behind."

"But they would smuggle it out," said Ferdinand.

"A small amount," answered the Inquisitor, "There would be inspectors and guards at every port and every road."

Ferdinand was beginning to show interest. He placed his hand on his chin, reflected for a moment, and stared frankly at the Inquisitor to make sure there was no misunderstanding. Ferdinand looked him straight in the eye and said, "And, of course, the Crown would be entitled to its share of the confiscated property, eh?"

Torquemada understood the intent of the question, and answered, "To all of it, your Majesty. My interest is only our holy Christian faith. I leave the worldly matters to you."

"An interesting proposition, Grand Inquisitor," said Ferdinand good-naturedly.

"Thank you, your Majesty," said Torquemada.

The King turned his back on Torquemada. Looking out through the window, hands behind his back, Ferdinand wondered about the armaments outside, the multitude of soldiers, the array of colored tents that filled the landscape as far as the eye could see. He wondered how much the entire enterprise was costing him. In a thoughtful tone, he remarked, "You realize, of course, that the Crown is in great debt as a result of the war."

Torquemada said, "So I have heard."

Ferdinand paused again before continuing. He stood silently at the window. Then, as if interrupting his reverie, he said softly, "The loans have to be repaid somehow . . . and funds will be hard to come by when the war is over . . . Let me think about this matter further."

Ferdinand, his anger gone, turned to face Torquemada.

Torquemada excused himself, "Of course, your Majesty. May I bid you good day?"

Ferdinand answered him, "Why, yes . . . good day."

Torquemada left the room, leaving the King alone. Ferdinand returned to the window and gazed outside again, thinking about the ramifications of the Inquisitor's proposition. It was a solution to the disturbing financial problems besetting the crown, and it could all be done in the name of religion. That was the beauty of the proposition.

He would think about it. Perhaps there would be a time when he would do as Fray Tomás suggested.

PART II:
THE ALHAMBRA DECREE

Chapter 4

January 2, 1492

It was a day like no other. It was a day all Christian Spain had envisioned as the day of its national purification, the day when the last taint of infidel control over their Spanish soil would be eradicated. Nearly 800 years ago, in the year 711, the Moors had crossed the Straits of Gibraltar and planted the Islamic crescent throughout the Iberian peninsula. Year by year, the movement to reconquer the peninsula grew and animated one Christian combatant after another with the spirit of the holy crusade against the Moorish infidel. Christian kings succeeded in forcing the Saracen menace southwards, depriving the Moors of their hegemony and shrinking the extent of their borders. By the year 1212, all that the Mohammedans had left was the small kingdom of Granada. Since the Moors no longer posed a significant threat, the Christian crusade was forgotten. But the Moorish attack on Zahara a decade or so earlier reawakened aspirations in Ferdinand and Isabella to complete the task that previous generations had left undone, namely, the Christian reconquest of the Kingdom of Granada. One after another, the Moorish cities — Zahara, Loja, Málaga, Moclín, and others — fell to the Christians. And today, after a bloody eight month siege, the last Moorish city of Granada was about to fall.

The cream of the Moorish warriors were gathered in Granada for the final confrontation. In skirmish after skirmish, the Moorish defenders fought courageously, their scimitars slashing through the air, their turbans flying in the wind alongside the pennants of the noblest Moorish families of Al-Andalus. But, outmanned and undernourished, the proud Moors could not long continue.

No one realized the hopelessness of the Moorish situation better than Boabdil, the Moorish King of Granada. Often called *El Rey Chico*, "The Little King" because of his small stature, he was propelled by the knowledge of the misery and humiliation that awaited his inevitable surrender to Ferdinand.

It was a lost cause, despite the remonstrances of Moorish zealots who wanted to fight to the last. Even his mother Zoraya wanted him to continue fighting. But the prospect of sure defeat, and a critical food shortage in the city, caused Boabdil to surrender the city of Granada to Ferdinand and Isabella.

Boabdil signed the treaty of surrender in the last few days of December, 1491, agreeing to turn over all Moorish fortifications and the Alhambra castle. As a pledge of his capitulation, Boabdil also gave his son along with 400 other Moors of noble Moorish blood to be held hostages of the Christian crown until the city itself was turned over. Despite his written surrender, there were thousands of Moors in Granada who, at the urging of a few instigators, were still fighting.

In a subsequent letter to Ferdinand, Boabdil disassociated himself from the persisting local agitation. He further urged Ferdinand and Isabella to move the Christian army in as quickly as possible to claim the city to prevent the disturbance from getting out of hand. The King and the Queen, on receipt of Boabdil's letter, readied their forces to take the Alhambra on the second day of January, 1492. This was the day of celebration of the Three Magi, the day when three Oriental Kings had brought gifts to the newborn babe Jesus, the day when the Catholic kings in like manner would offer the conquered city of Granada as a personal gift to their Lord.

The day had come. Isabella awoke, invigorated by the excitement of the day. Her face, her hands tingled with joy, and taking deep breaths of the crisp, cold Andalusian air, she shuddered with delight. It was the day of militant Christianity triumphant, the day dreamed of by all Spanish Christians. For eight centuries, it had been the illusory substance of dreams, a happenstance in the distant future, an expressed wish that time itself would hopefully bring. And now the surreal matter of her daydreams had found form on this waking day, transmutating itself as it were into the substance of the new Spanish reality. The phantasm of yesteryear, of even yesterday, was no more. Spain was one, Spain was whole again, today and forevermore.

Her intoxicating euphoria was shared by her chamber servants. Amidst an animated babble of voices, Isabella found herself being dressed in a purple silken raiment that covered her from head to toe in a nun-like vestment. Atop her head, she wore a smooth-topped wide-brimmed hat, likewise made of silk, that was tied underneath her chin. Satisfied with the simplicity of her dress, she stepped out of the royal tent.

It was cold outside. The snow-capped mountain peaks of the Sierra Nevada abutted against the blue Andalusian sky, its white crests shimmering in the early morning sun's rays. It seemed to Isabella that nowhere else in the world did the sun shine today as brightly as on the face of Spain, and nowhere in Spain did it shine brighter than on Granada, now the citadel of the new illumination, the fortress that had succumbed to the brighter light of Christianity. The sun's rays gave her cheeks a rosy glow. She put her hat back on, slipped on her leather hand gloves, and walked towards her readied chestnut-colored horse. An aide helped Isabella mount.

Ferdinand was already waiting for her. Sitting proudly astride his own chestnut horse, the King sat erect of bearing, his jeweled golden crown perched atop his wavy hair, a purple mantle draped over his shoulders. He, too, was happy. Ferdinand watched Isabella's stately approach with satisfaction. This day to be theirs was fulfillment as King and Queen, the day all Spain would remember as the greatest achievement of their reign. Together, for ten years, they had battled the infidels. Together, they would enter the walls of the fabled Alhambra castle and reap the fruits of their greatest victory.

Cheers of jubilation echoed as the King and Queen rode majestically through the camp. The Christian cavaliers were glistening and radiant in their embroidered cloaks and lavish plumery. Some were holding lances, some were in armor. The foot soldiers carried crossbows, primitive muskets, bows and arrows. Even the lombard cannons were polished. Everyone, everything was ready for this glorious day of celebration. It was a day of fiesta.

Trumpets sounded a fanfare. Drums rolled. The banners of the various military orders unfurled and caught the wind. The royal army rumbled forward, led by the forces of the Count of Tendilla and the Duke of Escalona. Tens of thousands rode behind the King and the Queen, and alongside the rulers rode Prince John, the Infanta Juana and her sons, the Master of the Order of Santiago, the Marquis of Cádiz, Cardinal Mendoza, as well as other counts, knights, prelates, and bishops.

When the army came within half a league of the city, it stopped at the bank of the Río Genil. As they waited, a band of Moors on horseback was seen to exit from the Alhambra gates. The Moors galloped their way down the winding road and onto the broad plain where the Christian troops were gathered. A silence prevailed as Boabdil and his men steadily approached the royal army.

Ferdinand and Isabella at the head of their troops waited to receive the Moorish King. When the Moors came within fifty yards of the Catholic Kings, Boabdil continued on alone, a small bearded figure atop of a huge black stallion.

Boabdil rode deliberately toward the King, with downcast eyes and cheeks flushed with shame. The Moorish King was surrendering his honor as much as his kingdom.

"Your Majesty, I humble myself in your presence. Allow me to show proper respect on my knees."

Boabdil tried to dismount and to kneel, but Ferdinand reached out his hand to stop him, and said, "There is no need, Boabdil. We know that you will be our loyal servant. The Queen and I accept your surrender."

Boabdil then tried to grab and kiss the King's hand, but Ferdinand withdrew it out of reach. Nonetheless, Boabdil grabbed the King's arm and kissed it instead. Having done so, the King of the Moors handed the keys of the city to Ferdinand.

"Take it, your Majesty, the keys of the city, for I and those who are in the city of Granada are yours."

The King acknowledged the admission of surrender. He took the keys and gave them to the Queen, and the Queen gave them to the Prince, and the Prince passed them on to the Duke of Escalona and the Count of Tendilla who, in turn, were to lead the first contingent of forces into the Alhambra and to take possession of it. The contingent, three-thousand strong, set forth.

A teary-eyed Boabdil was reunited with his son amidst embraces and kisses. He held his son to his chest, clutching him tightly. They separated, the son and the father, sobbing for the fate that had befallen them. Boabdil returned to his horse, as did his son. The Moorish royal family was now together again — Boabdil, his defiant mother Zoraya, and the male royal heir. They were detained from making their departure until the advance forces had penetrated and secured the Alhambra.

The Alhambra palace, the "Red Fortress" as it was called in Arabic, stood majestically on the steep hill overlooking the intervening vega. Its massive stone towers and walls formed a forbidding oriental outline in the distance, soft reds of stone abutting criss-crossing greens of foliage.

Everyone waited. It seemed as if they waited for an eternity. The King and Queen sat expectantly on their horses, their eyes transfixed on the distant castle. The entire army stood poised, noblemen and footsoldiers alike, as all waited for the signal that the Alhambra was theirs. And then it came.

From atop the highest tower of the Alhambra fortress, the Christian cross was raised. This was followed by the banner of Santiago, St. James, the patron saint of Spain. Upon seeing the risen cross in the distance, the King and Queen dismounted and got on their knees. This was their Holy Cross, the standard of Jesus Christ that they had carried with them throughout the campaign. It was only fitting that they give thanks to their Lord. A chorus of Archbishops and priests broke piously into the *"Te Deum Laudamus"*, a hymn of thanksgiving. The hymn was followed by benedictions and chants that created the aura of a ritual mass.

Then the pennant of the royal army bearing the insignia of King Ferdinand was raised into the air. The troops broke into loud cheers. Hats were thrown into the air. Fellow cavaliers hugged each other, their faces beaming with exultation. In this spirit the King and Queen acknowledged the felicitations of the grandees of Spain. The rulers were overjoyed, and they thanked each one of the grandees for their contribution to making such a glorious day possible.

"Castile! Castile!", shouted the troops. "Castile for our invincible King Ferdinand and Queen Isabella!" "Ferdinand and Isabella!"

Boabdil and his retinue left at this mortifying movement. The Moors left quietly, defeated and subdued. Boabdil, the king without a kingdom, rode to a hilltop where he could take a last view of the city he had once ruled. He was flanked on one side by his mother, on the other by his son, the heir-to-be, the heir to never be. The Moorish ruler sighed deeply one last time, the heaviness on his chest more than each breath could seemingly bear. His face in agony, with tears flowing from his eyes, Boabdil turned to his sullen dark-eyed mother Zoraya and asked:

"Oh mother, could greater misfortune happen to a man than to lose the jewel of the Alhambra?"

Zoraya answered him, "It is well you should weep as a woman for what you were not able to defend as a man. Come, let us go."

Zoraya looked at Boabdil with disdain, kicked her horse angrily, and left Boabdil to his weeping. Boabdil sighed one last time, he wiped the tears from his eyes, and he rode after his mother.

The trumpets blared once again. Drums rolled, and the pennants and lances were thrust once again into the air. The army of King and Queen, knights and foot soldiers came to life again. It was a stately, dignified advance, a parade of resplendent dress and polished armament, paced by the stirring hymns of the churchmen. Row by row, regiment after regiment, the foot soldiers marched with precision to the cadence of the drums.

The knights on horseback marched through the arched Alhambra entrance gate, the trouncing patter of hoof and boot landing sharply on cobblestone. Cheers were heard from bystanders at the gate, welcoming the victors. Amidst this sonorous ambience, a new swell of cheering and shouting was heard as King Ferdinand and Queen Isabella made their triumphant entry into the Alhambra. Ferdinand was riding magnificently on his chestnut horse, the crown on his head, a smile on his face, a joy in his heart. Isabella rode with equal sense of elation, her countenance radiant and happy, with tears welling in her eyes. The Catholic sovereigns nodded benevolently, acknowledging the accolades. They rode into the Alhambra, conscious of the historic moment. Eight hundred years Christians had waited for this day; eight hundred years were erased by the planting of the cross on the Alhambra. The festivity continued throughout the day.

Ferdinand and Isabella dismounted and got on their knees, as did the nobles who were with them. At this moment the rulers gave thanks to their Lord for having brought the war to a successful conclusion. They gave thanks that the victory was granted to them as King and Queen to subdue the Moorish kingdom of Granada for the greater glory of the Holy Catholic Faith. Then the King and Queen arose to take full possession of the kingdom of Granada. The noblemen of Spain, the powerful grandees, one by one came up to the King and Queen and kissed their hands as the new rulers of Granada. The Count of Tendilla was appointed as governor of the Alhambra in their name and was instructed to protect the castle with his men.

The remaining Moors then formally turned over the castle to the King. But the Alhambra was more than a fortress, more than an amalgam of jutting parapets and heavy walls. It was a structural masterpiece, a marvel of Islamic art. The Alhambra was the pride of the Moors, the subject of their romantic legends and the architectural evidence of their greatness. The jewel of the Alhambra, the matchless "red castle" the Arabs called *al Qal'ah al Hamra*, was theirs no more. It had a new ruler.

The victory party walked through the majestic chambers of the palace. Some gasped in amazement, others walked in awed silence. Huge arches, intricately decorated with abstract arabesque script and floral motifs, opened to ornate chambers. The weave of flowing script, interlaced in a complex, repetitive pattern, extended from archway to adjoining wall to chamber room. The ceilings in some of the rooms were honeycombed cupola-shaped domes, their recessed cells illuminated by shafts of light filtered through the lace of arched windows. The geometric decorative pattern, devoid of images and representations in accordance with Koranic dictate, showed a variegated ornamental form.

Graceful columns supported smaller interior arches that encircled the courtyards. Pools of sparkling blue water were fed by gushing central fountains, their jets of water splashing in tiered ponds, creating a cascade of interconnected pools. The surrounding foliage bathed in the soothing murmur of perpetually tumbling water. Shaded walkways, hedges of myrtle, orange groves, woods of elms, and fragrant flower gardens added to the fairy-like aura of the castle.

On and on it went, fabulous patios leading to luxurious salons, all inlaid with azulejo tile and the ever-present graceful cufic script, the mosaic floors carpeted with oriental rugs. The new King and Queen of Granada walked into the Court of the Lions, its central fountain bordered by a dozen lions carved out of marble, with an arcade of more than a hundred marble columns enclosing elegantly roofed footpaths and adjoining living quarters.

It was far more than Ferdinand and Isabella had expected. The Alhambra was an artistic wonder, a trophy of war beyond compare.

No church in all of Spain could compare with it. Yet art was not everything. Such beauty could not save, it could merely comfort. And the Moorish Arabs, torn by dissension for centuries, had finally succumbed, their talents for art undermined by their propensity for political disunity. In the end, they had fallen, victims to forces of their own creation.

The King and Queen walked down one of the paths and entered one of the outlying towers. Even there the arabesque inlays covered the interior walls. That the embellishment extended even to the insignificant structure added to the monarch's sense of amazement.

Isabella remarked, "Truly mine eyes have never seen a thing so wondrous as this . . . It is as beautiful as I have been led to believe."

Ferdinand joined in, "Yes, indeed it is. Something worth fighting for."

Isabella said, "Now I understand why the Moors fought so fiercely for this last of their treasures."

Ferdinand approached an arched window, took in a deep breath of cold air, and scanned the countryside. In the gorge below, he could discern his troops at rest and, further on, the broad expanse of the once fertile vega of Granada, now scorched beyond recognition. As far as he could see, from vega to mountain crest and beyond, from the Andalusian coast to the snow of the Pyrenees, over every Castilian and Aragonese town and its inhabitants, he reigned as King.

"Yes, this magnificent palace is ours now," Ferdinand affirmed. "It and all the rest of Spain belong to us . . . and to us alone."

Isabella nodded her head in agreement.

"So it is on this glorious day . . . and forever more."

Ferdinand thought out loud, "For more than a decade, we have dreamed of this glorious day. We led our army in the valiant struggle, never once questioning our resolve. Now, after much blood, we have finally emerged victorious. The dream of eight centuries has come true. The struggle is no more. The rapture of the moment will slowly fade; yet I am proud, I am content with our achievement. Isabella, today is more than a day of joy. Today we have achieved greatness together. Today, my Queen, we have become immortal in the chronicles of history."

"Yes, we did it together, Ferdinand, you and I," Isabella said smilingly. Ferdinand took Isabella's hand and held it in his.

"There is still one more dream I have, my King, and I wish with all my heart and soul that you would make it your dream too."

"And what is that?", Ferdinand asked curiously.

"To make Spain one, to make Spain Christian, to rid it of Mosaic infidelity . . .," Isabella said.

Ferdinand interrupted her, letting go of her hand. "To rid it of Jews, is that not what you mean? That is not your dream, Isabella. It is Torquemada's dream. He is the one who has put this idea in your head."

Isabella was insistent, "It is my dream now. And I intend to use all of the powers at my command to make it come true. The campaign for our Lord cannot end here at the Alhambra today. It must continue until Spain is rid of all unbelievers."

Ferdinand gazed into Isabella's determined eyes. He had seen that rock-hard look before.

"If that is what you wish," Ferdinand said, "On such a day as this, when God has seen fit to reward us so, who am I that I should not consider such a proposition."

"Think of it well, Ferdinand," replied Isabella, "It is my wish. In the meantime, let us enjoy the festivities of the day."

Chapter 5

Hacham Alhadeff waited breathlessly. So did his son-in-law Aaron, a poor schoolteacher like himself, as did the others who crowded in the humble stone tenement. They winced with every scream Morenica made from the adjoining room, their anxious eyes and ears turned towards the door from which the cries came. The screams became more intense and more frequent, piercing the drone-like hum of women's voices that came from beyond the wooden partition. The Hacham paced back and forth nervously, fidgeted with his fingers, and looked for a prayerbook to occupy his mind. It was no use; he could not read. He would stare blankly at a Psalm, only to look again in the direction of Morenica's cries. Somehow, he felt guilty that such agony, however much it might be ordained by Scripture, was not his burden to bear. It pained him to hear Morenica cry this way, but at least it pained for a purpose.

The shrieks stopped, and the erratic soft sobbing of his daughter persisted instead. The Hacham looked at his son-in-law, their eyebrows raised in anxious expectation, their eyes darting nervously about. What was it to be?

The proud midwife stepped out. "It is a boy!"

It is a boy! The Hacham clapped his hands loudly, let out a whoop of delight, and jumped into the air. He grabbed his frail son-in-law and hugged him tightly, kissing him on the cheek. Acknowledging the good wishes of those about him, he went from one person to another, shaking hands and receiving congratulations. He was jubilant. He grabbed the wine bottle and poured drinks for his guests. He let out another whoop.

"*L'Hayim*! To Life!," the Hacham toasted, raising his goblet.

"May the boy grow up with Torah and good deeds! *Mazal Tov*!"

"*Siempre en alegrías*!," joined in another. "May we always meet on such happy occasions!"

The wine spread warmth to everyone present, flushing out their spirits from restraint. The Hacham's cheeks, rosy from the wine, were two reddish mounds connected by a fixed crescent of a smile. His excited brown eyes gazed at one well-wisher after another with a look of distant contentment.

The years in Segovia had been good to the Hacham. His once emaciated body looked much improved from the four years he had spent in this Old Castilian city. He had grown in body and soul. While his robust face had become indeed the antithesis of his earlier emaciated self, the well-being he felt today was a well-being of the soul, nurtured to health by scholars and pious friends through the medicaments of human tenderness and solicitude. He had become a part of their lives, as much as they had become a part of his — friends with whom to share one's sorrows, friends with whom to heighten one's joys. And on the birth of his grandson, the Hacham was whole again, as he reveled in the companionship of cherished friends, happy to be alive and healthy, happy to be a grandfather.

At his side was his son-in-law of two years, Aaron Benoliel, a scrawny, long-nosed, withdrawn scholar, who loved his daughter and provided her with the basic amenities his scholar's income permitted. He had allowed the newlyweds to move in with him, and their combined incomes provided a table of plenty for the Sabbath.

The mid-wife reentered the room and announced firmly, "You may come in now, señores, two at a time."

The Hacham and his son-in-law were the first to enter. Although the room was now strangely silent, the broad, smiling faces of the two women guarding the doorway reassured them. The yellow hue of candlelight filled the room. The flames cast an endless dance of flickering forms on the white stone walls and on the proud faces of the Hacham and his son-in-law as they entered the bedroom.

Morenica, sitting upright in bed, was radiant in her motherhood. Her black shining hair was still wet from the sweaty strain of her labor, her olive-complexioned skin still showing beads of perspiration. Her delicate face was flushed with contentment, most evident in her brown eyes, glowing and serene. Cradling her baby snugly in her arm, she leaned back on the pillows exhausted from the agony of the delivery. Giving the child a gentle hug, she turned its face toward the timid, hovering father.

Aaron kissed Morenica on the forehead, then crouched next to her to see the baby better. Aaron looked in amazement at the child, then back at Morenica with a loving smile, then back at the child again. Morenica said, "Is he not the most beautiful child you have ever seen?"

"Oh, absolutely . . . Absolutely! I just cannot believe it. Our child, Morenica, yours and mine. It is incredible . . . simply and utterly incredible! I thought this day would never come, my dearest."

"I wish that you could feel, Aaron, the sweetness of feeling that I am feeling now, the knowledge that this child came from within me, that it grew inside my womb, that it is part of me and part of you, my beloved, something that is a product of our love, and yet something that now has become the object of our love . . . our child, Aaron, yours and mine."

"Our child . . . beautiful, is he not?"

"Of course he is. He has your nose, big and straight, like the cedars of Lebanon."

"Ahh," said Aaron, checking his nose for comparison, "Why, so he does. A sapling like the old cedar tree himself. And what color eyes does he have?"

"Dark brown, like mine."

"With my nose and your eyes, he will be a handsome child beyond compare . . . the nose of Castile, the exotic eyes of the Moor, by the stars of heaven, what better combination can there be, my love?"

"None, my darling."

The slender-faced Aaron patted the infant gently on the head, stroking its thin tuft of hair with excessive caution, rolling his hand under its chin, letting his finger trace out the child's eyebrows, feeling the nose he had given to his first-born son. There was a magic tingle in his fingers when he touched the fragile flesh. The infant burst into a loud wail, and Aaron withdrew his probing hand, content to observe the noisy phenomenon at a safer distance.

The Hacham came up to the other side of the bed, kissed his daughter, and took the sobbing child out of her arms.

"There, there, come to Grandfather . . . now, now," the Hacham said tenderly, a proud look on his face, as he rocked the child gently in his arms, whispering soft nothings to its face, pressing it caressingly to his chest, then lifting it slowly to his bearded face for closer study. After some more rhythmic rocking and grandfatherly cooing, the child was lulled back into sleep, to the amazement of all.

"Aha! You see? He needs his Grandfather."

Morenica said, "There was never any question that he would take a liking to you, Father. After all, we are naming him after you."

The Hacham smiled. He looked back at his grandchild, trying to picture himself in its rounded face.

"So, little Isaac, little Iziko, you are going to grow up and be a Hacham like your Grandpa, eh? You going to grow up and study Torah and perform good deeds and be a master of the Talmud? You say yes? Ahh . . . and are you going to listen to your mama and your papa, and to your Grandpa too? You say yes? Ahh . . . then you going to be a big big scholar in Israel, oh little one, a big big scholar, a *tzadik*, then you be no longer little Iziko, but big Iziko, and we all will be very very proud of you."

"Amen," said Aaron, nodding his head.

"All right, Iziko, now you go back to your mama, and you be a good boy, eh, until Grandpa sees you again."

The Hacham kissed the child and gingerly returned it to its mother. Sighing, he mused, "Would that your dear departed mother could see you now, Morenica. She would have been very happy for you, my daughter, and she would have been delighted to see her own first grandchild. She would have been very proud of you, Batya, as . . . as I am today."

The Hacham put his finger to his eyes to keep back his tears. Morenica took his hand and pressed it, saying nothing, yet expressing in her grasp an understanding of his feelings. The handclasp between father and daughter, the mother's embrace of her child showed the connecting ties of one generation to another — from Isaac to Batya to little Isaac, the cycle of life whirling on, the life-blood of one generation flowing into the next.

Only Sephardim named their grandchildren after grandparents who were alive. The Ashkenazim of Central and Eastern Europe did not do so because they were afraid it would shorten the life of the grandparent. The Hacham was proud his grandchild would carry his name, and he hoped that whatever merits, whatever *zacuyot*, accrued to his name in his lifetime, would be passed to his grandchild. This Iziko was verily "the flesh of his flesh, the bone of his bones," an extension of his physical and moral self, a scion of the dispersed greater family of Israel. Eight days hence, the child would be circumcised to become a member of the covenant of Abraham. Then the familial line of transmission would be intact, from Father Abraham to the present day, the dictates of the holy covenant maintained, the physical manifestation of one's Jewishness cut permanently into one's very tissue. The night before the *Brit Milah*, the circumcision ceremony, members of the community would gather in the Hacham's home to sing hymns like the ballad, *"Cuando el Rey Nimrod"*, which told the story of the ancestral birth of Father Abraham. And thinking of the festive ceremony to come, of the ballads he would then sing, of the foods he would eat and the wine that he would savor, a Hebrew phrase kept recurring in his mind as he looked down on little Iziko. It was the traditional blessing that would be chanted at the circumcision ceremony as the infant would be stately led to its Hebraic rite of passage:

"Blessed be he who comes in the name of the Lord!"

*   *   *   *   *

Don Abraham Senior was troubled. Whenever one community problem was solved, another arose in its place. Not only did his constituents argue and bicker continually, but they no longer respected his authority. People were listening less to what he had to say; others openly flouted his decisions as supreme court justice and paid him no heed. In an earlier day, the word of the *juez mayor* had been law, his opinion had been beyond question. The erosion of community confidence did not result from his legal decisions, but rather from his inability to prevent the economic devastation inflicted upon the Jewish communities largely through new legislation passed by Ferdinand and Isabella.

People no longer saw him as their protector. Despite his efforts to prevent the legislation, Senior was roundly criticized for his failures. People said he was too old and infirm for his duties; such responsibilities should have been delegated to a younger, more persuasive, and, therefore, more effective person. Everyone agreed that an 80 year-old man had no business directing the affairs of all Spanish Jewry. A committee of concerned laymen and rabbis, Rabbi Maimi included, approached him discreetly and raised the matter of his voluntary retirement from public office. It was suggested that Senior quietly step down from office and allow someone new to take his place.

Senior was furious at such a proposition. "I will have you know, distinguished rabbis and señores, that my appointment as *juez mayor* of all the Jewish *aljamas* of Spain comes from none other than our sovereign majesties Ferdinand and Isabella. They it is who have placed me in a position to serve them, and this I have done as their faithful servant for the last fifteen years. I have never once failed them, nor have I neglected to represent the welfare of the Jews at the royal court. I bitterly resent the implication of this committee that I am not capable of properly discharging my duties as Chief Judge. Ailing though my body may be, my mind is alert and my voice is strong. Yes, I am aged in years, but rich in knowledge of the ways of the royal court. I know it better than each of you, or anyone else for that matter. How dare you insinuate otherwise! Do you know the mind and the heart of the King and Queen as I do? Do you know their dislikes, their tastes, their private thoughts? Can you influence them as I have?

"None of you know them and, therefore, you are unqualified to sit as judges of the supreme judge. Shall the tail wag the dog? Shall a delegation of the flock guide its shepherd? Ha! You are greater fools than I thought you were. I tell each and every one of you that, as long as my heart beats, and my mind is clear, and provided I continue to enjoy the good graces of our majesties, I will persevere, nay, I will prosper in my position of Chief Judge to my last breath! . . . I will never relinquish this position, do you hear me? . . . Never! Now, all of you foggy-brained dolts, leave me immediately. I cannot stand the sight of you. Out of my house!"

Thus Don Abraham Senior disposed of the committee. Yet the committee had delivered a telling message to Senior; there was a disturbing element of truth in their suggestion that he was too old.

He sensed his end as a courtier was near, and the only qualified successor was Don Isaac Abravanel. Don Abraham wished his son-in-law, Rabbi Meir Melamed, were capable of succeeding him, but Rabbi Meir, gifted as he was in finance, was not a *leader*. It was apparent to Senior that the sceptre of judicial supremacy, which he had wielded for more than fifteen years as the arbiter of the Jewish communities of Spain, would soon pass to the eminently deserving Don Isaac Abravanel.

Senior did not doubt his capabilities at court. He had worked hard to overturn the ordinances that kept Jews in a degrading position. He had bargained, cajoled, and pleaded with his King and Queen, argued with them as friends, appealed to their sense of justice, exercised every stratagem of flattery — all to no avail. Ferdinand and Isabella were willing to exempt Senior as an individual from the law, but it remained in effect for the Jews as a people.

Senior had secured privileges for himself and his family which had placed them well beyond the realm of anti-Jewish ordinances dealing with dress and deportment. He had sought and accepted such privileges with the hopeful expectation that other Jews — wealthy merchants, physicians, traders, and others of note — would likewise acquire such a status. In the long run, Don Abraham hoped that the day would come when all Spanish Jews would be freed from the restrictions. Unfortunately, Senior remained the single exception. To others it appeared that he had obtained his personal freedom at the expense of the community's well-being. This feeling was particularly rife among the artisans of the community, subject to malicious legislation that made it nearly impossible to eke out a livelihood. They it was who saw Don Abraham's subtle intrigue as an effort to better himself and his family, without the slightest attempt to alleviate the miserable conditions suffered by other Jews. All that Senior had done in the past for the community was forgotten. The community began to question his ability, his age, indeed, his concern for community problems.

It pained Don Abraham that people thought of him like this. While he had been solicitous of Senior family interest, and his family did indeed come first in his life, that was only natural. Never in his career as Chief Judge, however, had he betrayed the Jews of Spain. Always, he had promoted its best interests, regarding its prosperity and as being coincident nearly with his own. Always, he had been the faithful servant of the community, ready to do its aggregate will, provided it did not conflict with his own sense of duty to family. He had proved himself before and, even now in his old age, he would prove himself again to one and all. He would quell the suspicions, dispel the resentments, and once again earn the people's respect and admiration. They did not understand the difficulties he was encountering; they did not know the Queen. Senior resolved to do something so spectacular that it would allay all doubts and force others to acknowledge his unequaled skill. This masterful deed would forever inscribe his name with shining glory in the annals of the Jewish people. This was what he would do as a fitting and final monument to himself.

The problem was Senior did not exactly know what it was he would do. He studied the official court pronouncements of the past few years, hoping they would contain the clue he needed. Perhaps an imaginative interpretation of some existing law might provide a masterful way out of the quandary, if only he could discern the right legal approach. Somehow, the solution lay in the documents of the royal archives of Valladolid. Copies of court pronouncements were kept on file in the Valladolid chancellery, and Don Abraham requested permission to review all available documents pertaining to the Jews of the kingdom.

Senior sat alone in the reading room of the chancellery, studying the learned tomes and manuscripts. The lonely seated figure of the *juez mayor* seemed curiously at odds with his customary role. Far from the pomp and the glitter of court, he was left quietly to himself, a supreme judge left to dwell on matters of jurisprudence.

Don Abraham took the parchment documents from a stack and unraveled them, one by one. He took down brief notes as he went, quickly summarizing the essence and effect of each pronouncement, questioning its legality, comparing it with precedent, challenging the spirit and the letter of the rulings.

There were hundreds of such documents, and Don Abraham decided to restrict himself to the court decisions of the last four years. A new ordinance or restriction had more chance of being reconsidered than an older one already entrenched by years of practice. He picked up the first document and read it. It dealt with his own community of Segovia.

Within the city of Segovia, the King and Queen had ruled that no fish could be bought by Jews on Friday or fishdays, but that they could buy live meats during restricted hours on that day.

Don Abraham asked himself: Is it worth fighting to overturn this law, and is it achievable? The answer was "no" on both counts. The Christian merchants of Segovia were doing their utmost to shut the Jews up in their restricted quarter, and out of their local economy. The resistance was too great, and the King and Queen's acquiescence to their demands was an indication of the power of local financial forces. He would not waste his time on this. On to the next document:

"From Don Ferdinand and Doña Isabel, to the magistrate of the city of Soria or to your councilman in the same office, health and grace unto you. We have been informed by certain residents of that city that the Jews who live in that city, contrary to the tenor and form of the law made by us in the Cortés de Toledo, have gone to live and reside outside of the Jewish quarter that borders on the Church of St. Gil; they have back-to-back houses with windows facing the said church, so it is not possible to celebrate the divine cult without their seeing it, by manner of which God our Lord is much disserved. And they have beseeched us and requested our favor with regard to a remedy of justice which we should provide as our mercy sees fit, and we have taken it to ourselves for good.

"Therefore, we now hereby order you that you look into the aforesaid matter, and if it is stated before, you shall execute justice as befits you, according to the tenor and form of the said Law of Toledo. And you shall not do the contrary of what is ordered.

"Given in the city of Jaén in the year 1489. Diego decanus Plazentinus, Iohanes doctor, etc. . . ."

Senior said softly. Laws of the Cortés of Toledo. Old laws. Fixed laws. A Jew has to live in the *judería*. Unable to change that. On to the next document.

"Don Ferdinand and Doña Isabel, to our chief justice and to the councilmen of our House and Court and Chancellery; and to the councilmen, judges, and justices of the city of Vitoria and to all the magistrates and judges of all other cities and villages and habitations of our kingdoms and domains, those which are and those which are yet to be, to each one of you and to whomsoever of you this letter is shown or its translation thereof as signed by a public scribe, health and grace unto you. Know ye that the *aljama* of the Jews of the said city of Vitoria has informed us through its petition that was presented to the Council, stating that they have been and are maltreated by the inhabitants and residents of Vitoria, who pelt them with stones and break their skulls whenever they walk the streets, this being unjust and uncalled for, and who call them many disgraceful and dishonorable things without any cause whatsoever, and furthermore, they go at night to the Jewish quarter after the Jews are walled up in their houses and they break their windows with stones. And the worst yet has occurred in that, when the Jews were in the synagogue praying, the Christians entered suddenly where the Jewish women were located, spitting upon them and hitting them with their fists and kicking them in such a manner that such Jews and Jewesses did not dare stay in the Jewish quarter in not having any security of protection. In all this, they state that they have received much harm and affront, as a result of which they supplicate us and plead for mercy through our provision of a remedy of justice, sending unto them our letter of security and aid in the form prescribed by law, for such has not been done to date, as our mercy would see fit. And we have taken their request for good.

"For the present we take and receive all the Jews and Jewesses of the said *aljama* of the said city of Vitoria and their belongings under our security and aid and royal protection, and we prohibit all the inhabitants and residents of the said city of Vitoria, as in other parts, that they not dare to do, nor cause to be done, the aforesaid things; nor that they injure, kill, wound, take, nor restrain the affected persons and their belongings; nor cause, nor order to be caused neither harm nor hurt nor offences whatsoever as much in their persons as in their belongings which, being contrary to reason and law, ought not to be done. . .

"Given in the very noble city of Burgos on the thirtieth of July in the year 1488 of our Lord Jesus Christ. The constable Don Pedro Fernández de Velasco, et cetera. . ."

A sign of the times, Don Abraham Senior said quietly to himself. He had seen similar petitions for royal protection from other small communities, such as those of Orense and Valmaseda and Trujillo. And although royal protection had always been granted, it had not stopped anti-Jewish sentiment from growing throughout Spain. In the small villages, in the countryside, even in the larger cities such as Segovia, feelings against the Jew festered, ever on the verge of violent outbreaks. Here, too, these dark irrational forces were beyond Senior's control, indeed, almost beyond regulation by the King and Queen. A sign of the times, indeed, Senior admitted, but not something he could influence and, therefore, not what he was looking for.

Don Abraham quickly went through several additional documents, scanning the stylized judicial openings and closings, in order to get the documents' legal essence. He scratched his head, wondering if he would ever find what he was looking for.

One document dealt with the complaint of Jews concerning the royal letter which prohibited them from remaining more than three days in the city of Cuenca. The complaint was under investigation.

A similar document dealt with a recent ordinance prohibiting Jews from being found or staying overnight in the Basque city of Bilbao upon penalty of a thousand maravedis fine. The reason given for the ruling was that no living quarters were available for Jews in the city. The ordinance was overruled by the royal court.

Still another was an official letter to the magistrate of the city of Trujillo ordering him to investigate the recently passed ordinance prohibiting Jews from going out in the streets of Trujillo after dark. The penalty was two hundred maravedis and the loss of one's clothing.

Another court document, addressed to the magistrate of Plascencia, ruled that Jews were prohibited from residency outside the Jewish quarter, as the laws of the Cortés of Toledo demanded, and ordered that appropriate measures be taken against those Jews who left the confines of the *judería* and resided side by side with Christians, much to the disservice of the Christian God.

On and on it went, in one document after another, the peasantry clamoring for the destruction of the walled up Jews, the merchants and town councilmen passing ordinances to prevent the participation of the Jews in the local economy and, finally, the King and Queen revoking some of the ordinances but allowing others to remain in force, depending on the city and parties involved.

There was the case, for example, of the Jews of Medina del Campo, where the famed annual fair was held. The fair was a major event for traders and merchants from all parts of Europe. At first, the King and Queen had forbidden the Jews from having any stores or booths outside of the Jewish quarter. Then the sovereigns had reversed themselves, permitting such stores and booths outside of the *judería*, provided that the Jews did not live in them. Finally, the original decision to disallow such stores and booths was upheld, because, it was argued, some Jews had gone out of the Jewish quarter to live among the Christians, and this, of course, was in no way to be tolerated. A minor concession of sorts was made in that Jews could set up small tents in the central plaza by day to display and sell their merchandise; but by nightfall, the tents had to come down and the Jews had to return to the *judería*. Jews could live in the *judería*, and nowhere else. That was the law.

And yet, Don Abraham mused, it had not always been so. Before Ferdinand and Isabella had caused the old Laws of the Cortés of Toledo to be observed and enforced, many a Jew had lived side by side with their Christian neighbors, some of them becoming good friends. So it had been in Aragon where he had grown up; so it had been in Castile up until twelve years ago. Things had changed . . . and obviously for the worse.

And if Jews did not have problems enough from without, they created their own from within, as in the case of the feud that had broken out in the city of Trujillo . . . all because of a ladder! Don Abraham remembered that one.

Senior had been called by the local magistrate to arbitrate the dispute. Apparently, a new ladder had been constructed inside the synagogue of the city of Trujillo so that the Torah could be carried up and down the ladder in accordance with the Sabbath service. Certain members of the community protested because they preferred to use the old ladder, as was the custom. So intense had been the confrontation over this issue that members started engaging in rock fights and sword duels. Don Abraham Senior adjudicated the affair, resolving it on behalf of the plaintiff. Senior ruled that the new ladder could not be used for the raising up and lowering of the Torah; only the old ladder, as was the custom, could be used. He further declared that anyone who violated the ruling would be subject to a fine of six thousand maravedis. But his ruling was soon ignored, much to Senior's dismay. The proponents of the new ladder neither respected his opinion nor were they willing to comply with it. In fact they threatened to excommunicate anyone who abided by Don Abraham's ruling, and they made everyone use the new ladder for carrying the Torah scroll.

For the decision of the Chief Judge to be ignored was unheard of. Senior was outraged. Never in his life had he experienced such open disrespect. He would teach these quarrelsome natives of Trujillo a thing or two - especially that the *juez mayor*, even at eighty years of age, was not a person to contend with. The six thousand maravedi fine per person was exacted, and a new fifteen thousand maravedi fine for each violator was announced. On hearing that the recalcitrant Jews were still unwilling to comply, Senior swiftly enforced his larger fine with the full force of the law enforced by the local Hermandad. That broke the resistance.

So much for the document on that forgettable affair, Senior muttered, an affair which had, to his great embarassment, come to the ears of the King and Queen. It had been shameful.

Senior plodded on through the massive stack of documents through the afternoon. He did not find what he wanted. It was exhausting work. His body tired so easily nowadays, and he felt he would have to stop soon. He would examine a few more documents and then call it a day, before his mind too began to feel the effect of undue strain.

At the bottom of the stack of documents, he came across the royal command that ordered the trial of the Niño de La Guardia to be transferred from Segovia to Ávila. He was instrumental in getting the trial transferred, and he took satisfaction in that achievement. Nonetheless, the cause of the trial sent shivers of fear down his spine. This was no trivial dispute about a ladder, this was no petty confrontation over whether Jews could buy fish at the market or about some other minor community trifle. The La Guardia affair was terrifying because it could lead to the destruction of the Jewish communities of Spain.

"Niño! Niño! Niño de La Guardia!"

That was what the angry Christian mobs were shouting when they tried to attack the Jews in their walled-off quarter. It was the centuries-old blood libel, and Don Abraham realized immediately that the Grand Inquisitor Torquemada was behind it all. According to the Inquisition, an innocent four-year old child from La Guardia had been murdered by conspiring Jews and Conversos. The child's still throbbing heart had been allegedly ripped out by the blood-sucking Jews for their demoniacal ritual purposes. Outbursts of Christian rage and violence of unprecedented intensity resulted. "Niño!", they cried out. "Avenge the Niño!"

It was one thing for Senior to know that Torquemada had master-minded the monstrous fabrication. It was quite another to thwart the malicious intentions of such a powerful cleric who had the full backing of the crown. How could he possibly hope to prevail against him?

Senior was at a loss about what to do. In a moment of exasperation, he pushed the documents roughly aside. That was enough for today, he concluded, and enough of that infernal Niño de La Guardia.

*   *   *   *   *

The Grand Inquisitor had reason to be content. His plan to rid Spain of Jews was entering its final phase. The details of the plan had been proposed to Ferdinand, and he had finally agreed to it provided certain conditions were met.

The conditions Ferdinand imposed were directed at safeguarding the assets of the crown, both property and other valuables. The King was insistent that all confiscations be done under proper legal guise ("What did he pay all those jurists for, anyway?") and that it all be done in the name of the Christian religion ("What . . . and be accused of robbing my own subjects? No, my dear Inquisitor, if *you* want the Jews out, *you* must rob them for me in *your* name"). The final condition Ferdinand imposed was that some of the Jewish tax-farmers must stay behind to prevent collapse of the crown's revenue collection system. That meant that either Senior, Abravanel, or Melamed would stay behind to run the system, or else the deal was off. Without the tax-farmers the crown would be ruined. So would the economies of Castile and Aragon. Ferdinand had no desire to be a rich king one year, and a beggar the next. "If no Jewish tax-farmers stay behind, not one Jew will leave Spain . . . accept it or leave it," Ferdinand told Torquemada.

Torquemada accepted it all. And having agreed to abide by those conditions, the Inquisitor and his *Suprema* promptly drafted a provisional edict of expulsion that incorporated all that had been agreed upon. It was simple: the plan was to wall the Jews off, strip them of their resources, and then to cast them out of Spain.

Another aspect of Torquemada's master plan was to incite hatred against the Jews.

There was much work to be done. Fortunately, there was no lack of friars to go about the countryside and stir up the rural folk against the Jews. What Torquemada wanted, however, was a priest willing to go beyond the law, someone who detested Jews so much that nothing — not the law, not fear of others, not even his own conscience — would stop the man from pursuing his single-minded obsession. The Grand Inquisitor wanted someone with hate and revenge in his heart; and he found such a priest in the person of Fray Antonio De la Peña.

Ever since his humilitating rebuke by Ferdinand and Isabella, Fray De la Peña had been quietly retired in the Santa Cruz monastery in Segovia. He was rarely seen in public and was never allowed to address his former congregants. Returning to a life of study and contemplation, De la Peña reflected often upon his ill fortune in having his evangelical career terminated almost as soon as it had begun. His mood, which was never good, was now gloomy and withdrawn. His conversation, always sparing, now became curt and bitter. Wherever he walked, the aura of disgrace followed him, a dark hovering cloud that clung to his being. Shame . . . disgrace . . . failure . . . the words circled in his brain endlessly, a whirring medley of reproach, a hurt and slur upon his name. He kept to himself, with his cowl pulled well over his head. He prayed fervently, hoping to forget himself and his distressing thoughts in prayer. But it was to no avail. The sense that he was a broken, beaten man, beaten by Jews no less, sent him into a tailspin of depression.

He prayed fervently for his redemption, and one spring day in 1490 when De la Peña was sweeping the floor of his cubicle, his prayers were answered. The Grand Inquisitor Tomás de Torquemada appeared at the door of his cell. Holding two books, the steely-eyed Inquisitor looked into the startled eyes of De la Peña.

Putting the broom aside and wiping his dusty hands on his cassock, the monk walked up to Torquemada, kneeled, and kissed his hand. "Your Holiness . . .", said De la Peña, who prostrated himself before the Inquisitor. Terrible thoughts flashed through his mind: "More punishment to follow . . . more disgrace. Is it the end? What will become of me? Am I through as a Dominican?"

Torquemada placed his hand on De la Peña's shoulder. "Stand up, Fray De la Peña, for you have been unduly punished for seeking to perform God's will in Satan's court. I bring unto you today, if not the immediate relief of your agony, then the means whereby you can recover your honor and clear your good name. The devil Jews have brought you low through their wicked influence on the King and Queen. However much you have been punished, and it is great indeed, it is but a trifle of what will soon befall those who have caused your dishonor. Do not ask me to divulge how this will come to pass, for it is not in my authority to do so, but trust my words. Trust everything that I say and do exactly as I instruct you — and not only will you be reinstated to all dispensations that have been taken away from you, but you will avenge yourself a thousand-fold upon the devil's henchmen."

De la Peña rose slowly, his face suffused with gratitude. "Your Holiness, I am yours to obey. Do what you will with me. My disgrace can be no greater, and my spirit no more cast down. All that I am to suffer, I would bear willingly if only I could avenge myself upon those accursed Jews, the enemies of Christ. Give me the chance to prove that I am worthy of your trust, and I will prove to you a most obedient and unquestioning servant, ready to do your command."

"You will have the chance that you seek . . . to prove yourself worthy, Fray De la Peña. It is not my trust alone that you will bear, but the trust of this Spanish nation whose Christian religion we friars have vowed ourselves to safeguard, whatever the cost and, if need be, by whatever the means. We could perform no greater disservice to our homeland than to fail to take the most extreme measures in dealing with these Jewish infidels. No good comes without pain; no purification of the soul comes without mortification of the flesh. What self-flagellation is to the friar, the Inquisition is to all Spain. It pains, it hurts, but it purifies. Join me in my sacred task, brother, for there is much godly work to be done against the infidels. You have felt the power that these Jews are able to wield. You have seen how they manipulated the Queen against yourself.

"But now a plan, a secret plan, has been devised to unleash the greatest power in all of Spain, a power greater than all the Jews and their tax collectors, a power greater than King Ferdinand and Queen Isabella themselves. What is this awesome power of which I speak? You know it well. Indeed, you were on the verge of tapping the source yourself until you were stopped. Yes, Fray De la Peña, the ultimate source of our power is the pure Christian faith of our people. It is the force that will stop the Jew. As we met Moorish might with Christian military might, we will likewise do battle with the diabolical Jew in his very element. And what is the Jew's element but his resort to fiendish lies. Lies and more lies! Lies against our savior, lies by Conversos that they are believing Christians, lies against all that we hold dear.

"We must be ready to fight the lie with a lie, to fight it with a lie so terrifying that it will crush the Jew and all of his machinations, a lie so unbelievable that only those of unquestioning faith would believe it. To unleash the greatest power in all of Spain . . . that is my goal. For that, I need someone willing to transform the unbelievable lie into a believable reality. I ask you, Fray De la Peña, are you that man? Are you willing to do battle thus against the enemies of Christ?"

De la Peña spoke. "Your Holiness, allow me to say but this to you: speak and I will listen. Command and I will obey. Confide in me and your secret will never pass my lips. Give the charge of this holy task to me, and I will prove that no greater executor of your slightest wish could be found in a person other than myself. I will speak the lie, commit the deed, as you desire, if only you will release me from the sentence of my forced confinement."

The Grand Inquisitor was pleased. "It will be done, Fray De la Peña. As of today, you are under my protective custody. You will be accountable to me alone. From now on, you will work with two other Dominicans from this monastery in conjunction with the Holy Office, and you will do as I tell you. Have faith, my Dominican colleague. Your days of shame are ended."

The Dominican friar knelt once again, kissed Torquemada's hands gratefully, and did exactly as he was told.

Fray De la Peña was assigned to Inquisition headquarters in Segovia. He was to serve as the special assistant to the Inquisitor of Segovia, Fray Domingo Lucero, also trained at the monastery of Santa Cruz. The two knew each other quite well from their years together in the monastery.

It was a welcome relief for De la Peña. Instead of a dark cell, he had a sparkling white-walled spacious office. The room was sparsely furnished: a wooden desk and table, a few writing implements, a crucifix on the wall, his spartan bed off in the corner. But it was all he needed to accomplish his task.

De la Peña's first assignment was to forge letters. These fabricated documents, ostensibly written by escaped Jews in distant lands to their brethren in Spain, were to be intercepted by Inquisitional authorities. Their sordid contents would be revealed and then widely publicized to further inflame popular feeling against the Jews. De la Peña wrote furiously, composing one vitrolic letter after another. One of the letters which bore the signature of a Jew in Constantinople and was addressed to a Jew in Toledo, encouraged Jews to become Christians in the following manner:

"Because the King of Spain has confiscated your property and belongings, you should make your children merchants, so they may rob all that which belongs to Christians. Since you say that they take away your lives, make your sons into apothecaries and physicians to take the lives of Christians. Since they destroy your synagogues, make your sons into priests so they may destroy the Christian churches."

Copies of such allegedly intercepted letters were distributed by the Holy Office to priests throughout the country. Circulars with quotes from the letter were nailed on the posting boards of public meeting places. The popular outrage provoked by the letters and circulars was enormous. Everywhere — in the marketplace, in the taverns, in the fields — the seditious and evil intentions of the Jews were on people's minds and on their lips. They stopped going to Converso physicians, fearing for their lives. Jewish and Converso businesses suffered, and many simply closed. And behind it all, behind the flurry of virulent letters was Antonio De la Peña, author anonymous, priest become provocateur become propagandist.

Chapter 6

Don Isaac Abravanel was in a hurry. The flat Castilian terrain facilitated his haste. The broad landscape was dotted with low-lying brush, clusters of sunflowers, and an occasional poplar tree. In the coolness of a bright spring day, Don Isaac rode his mule along the road flanking the banks of the Río Henares, heading towards the town of Guadalajara, his new home. 'Guadalajara' came from the Arabic *Wad-el-Hajarah*, meaning 'river of stones'. Such a name was perhaps a reflection of its stony riverbed, others attributing the name disdainfully to its propensity for shrinkage during times of drought. Yet for Don Isaac, this little river had become a familiar companion, providing him with relief from the dusty path, reminding him of his own need to maintain touch with the poor and humble.

Many a time it had been when, upon returning home with his aides on a hot summer day, he had dismounted from his mule, taken off his leather boots, and waded in the cool blue water of the Río Henares, its gentle currents nibbling at his feet, its foamy jets of water splattering onto his thighs. Scooping up the water with cupped hands, he would splash it on his face, only to see it end as shimmering ribbons and shiny beads of water on his handsome well-trimmed beard. Having allowed himself this small measure of frolic, Don Isaac would retreat to the shade of a poplar grove, sit against a tree, and rest his head on its trunk. Then he would take out his canteen, drink its minty beverage, and eat the cucumbers and dates and other dainties that his wife had packed for him. Ordinarily, he would have eaten sliced portions of bread as well, but Passover was a day away, and he had taken every precaution to rid

104

his bags of the slightest speck of leavened bread. Once he was rested, it was Don Isaac Abravanel's custom to take out a prayer book, recite a few Psalms, and read some selections from a Talmudic tractate. Most of all, he loved to take out his Hebrew Bible and dwell on the writings of the prophets of Israel. He was still writing a commentary on the prophets, but he was too busy to get very far with it. Yet moments of pure pleasure such as these helped him to harness the reflections that he would ultimately write down. The soft fluff of clouds overhead, the feel of a cool glistening grass carpet underneath him, the gentle breeze whistling through the tree tops — all contributed to his sense of inner serenity. At times, his mind would wander vacantly. In the free flow of ideas and images, the 'river of stones' became a symbol of the fluctuating fortunes of the people of Israel — a river which, in time of affliction, hardened itself to stone to weather the hard times. Verily, Israel could be likened to Guadalajara, to a 'river of stones'. Who was he, Don Isaac mused, but a mere pebble caught in the midstream of Spanish Jewish history, unable to alter its course, unable to perceive the end of its serpentine journey. Who was he but a pebble, an oversized pebble perhaps, but a pebble nonetheless, whose cavortings and perpetual tumblings would, in the course of time, grind him down layer by layer into a few minuscule grains of dust. Who was he but a pebble to the Rock of Israel, the Holy One, blessed be He, who was the Creator of the universe, the source of all knowledge, who had set all life, all pebbles, adrift into the unfathomable swirl of existence. Abravanel answered himself with a quote from *Avot*: "It is not up to you to complete the task, yet you are not free to desist from it." The pebble had work to do. He arose from his reverie and continued on his way.

As soon as Don Isaac Abravanel arrived in Guadalajara, he proceeded directly to the Palace of the Mendozas to report on the tax collection activities of the day. Along the way, he took note of the activity on the narrow cobblestone streets. There were mule-drawn carts carrying grain and vegetable crops. Sheepherders gathered at the central market hoping to exchange their wool for foodstuffs. Hawkers selling sundry wares — pottery, sheets of cloth, swords, leather vests — could be heard in the distance, offering unheard of bargains. Men gathered in taverns, drinking their frothy beverages while standing. Scarved women with colorful laced blouses walked in pairs, jabbering continuously as they went. From all the goings-on, it could have been any small town or village in Spain. And yet it was the provincial home of the Mendoza family, the most powerful house of grandees in all Spain.

The Mendoza Palace towered above every other building in town, except for the Cathedral. The palace's facade was studded with project- ing bosses and an ornately carved shield held by satyrs. Within the pala- tial structure, balustraded columns surrounded an inner patio teeming with fountains and multi-colored flowers. Oriental rugs with stellate and criss-crossing design patterns covered the interior marble floors, and decorative tapestries lined the walls. Ivory and jade artifacts from the Indies, furniture with Moorish style insets, alabaster vases, gilded frames of individual portraits — all contributed to the aura of opulence within. The possessor of this wealth was Don Iñigo López de Mendoza, the Marquis of Santillana, the second Duke of the *Infantado* in whose employ Abravanel had served for nearly two years as the chief accountant.

Iñigo López de Mendoza, the Duke of the *Infantado*, had vast feudal holdings, at one count exacting tribute from ninety thousand vassals dispersed over eight hundred localities. Having heard from his relative, Cardinal Mendoza, how successful Don Isaac had been in farming the taxes in the bishoprics of Siguenza and Guadalajara, he had recruited Abravanel into his service. The war against the Moors had drained the Duke of the *Infantado* of money and men, and the Duke needed to find someone who was able to replenish the Mendoza coffers one way or another.

Abravanel waited for Don Iñigo in the luxurious anteroom. It was just a short wait before the Duke entered. Don Iñigo wore a striped red- and-white cloak with silvery tabards. His cropped black hair hung loosely over his bony face. He showed little sign of emotion, always addressing others with great reserve and meticulous attention to propriety.

"Good day, Don Isaac, how fares my chief accountant this week in securing the tribute of my vassals?"

"It has gone well, Don Iñigo. I am happy to report that people are paying their fees, perhaps because many expect the fees to be substan- tially less next year. By this I mean that, with the war against the Moors now finished, there are those who feel that taxes in the duchy should be reduced accordingly. This is a reasonable expectation. Some, I dare say, have insisted that such a reduction in their dues be effected as of this moment, and they have refused to pay their levied assessment."

"Who, for example?"

"Rodrigo de Marchena, the olive grower . . ."

"A stubborn old goat. Does this every year. But he will pay the full amount. You shall see to that, Don Isaac."

"Yes, sir. There were a few other holdouts, but I managed to secure written promissory notes from them without an undue amount of trouble. All in all, the collection process went smoothly."

"And the total collected, Don Isaac?"

"Three hundred and forty-six thousand maravedis, Don Iñigo, which I shall proceed to register immediately in your vault. Another thirty-four thousand maravedis are still outstanding as collectibles in the form of the promissory notes which I mentioned. . .all payable within a month's time.

"Very well done, Don Isaac. Your financial skills never cease to amaze me. May I have the honor of your company at a dinner I am giving this Saturday in honor of the Count of Cuellar?"

"Thank you, Don Iñigo, you are most gracious to extend such a kind invitation to a humble servant of yours such as myself. However, I must excuse myself — not from want of desire or interest on our part, but rather owing to religious obligations which we, as observant Jews, must fulfill. Tomorrow eve the festival of Passover, the *fiesta de pan cenceño*, the feast of unleavened bread begins. And my wife and I and all my family will be preoccupied with its observance for the next eight days."

"Yes, I have heard quite a bit about this ritual meal that you Jews eat during Passover."

Abravanel was attentive to the ambiguous nuance of Don Iñigo's statement. Rumors about how Jews allegedly drank Christian blood during the ritual service had become widespread in the wake of the Niño de La Guardia trial. Abravanel wondered what the Duke meant.

"You are most welcome to join us for the ritual Passover meal, Don Iñigo. We would be greatly honored to have you as our guest."

"The climate is not right, Don Isaac. In earlier days, thirty, maybe forty years ago, I could have done so with impunity. But the Cardinal is related to me, and the Holy Office has its agents everywhere. The religious climate has changed in Spain . . . for the worse, even though I regard myself to be a religious man. No, the climate is definitely not right. But I thank you for the invitation, Don Isaac."

"And I thank you most kindly for yours, Don Iñigo."

"One last question, Don Isaac, before you leave . . ."

The Duke of the *Infantado*, his brow furrowed, looked concerned. "If the climate should get worse, Don Isaac, I want you to know that you and your family can count on protection from our House of Mendoza."

"That is most generous of you, Don Iñigo. But if I may say so, I fail to understand the sense of alarm that provoked such a statement."

"There are intimations of . . ." the Duke paused again.

"Of what, Don Iñigo?"

"Of . . . of . . . trouble ahead."

"Trouble? What trouble?"

The Duke shook his head. "I cannot tell you. I have been sworn to secrecy."

"But if the fate of my people is in danger, if the lives of thousands of innocent people may be at stake, can you not give me a hint of the nature of the danger you are alluding to?"

"I have sworn by my honor that I would not tell. Already, I have said more than I should have. Do not press me for details, Don Isaac Abravanel. Forgive me, but I can tell you nothing more, so help me God."

"Very well, Don Iñigo. I must respect your vow. But, you have not asked me your question."

"Question?", the Duke repeated, "Ah, yes, the question. Do not be offended, but is there anything I may offer you, any monetary inducement or grant of land or whatever else you may wish, that would make you consider becoming a Christian?"

"Never, never will I become a Christian. Whatever inducements or trouble lies ahead, I will remain a Jew to my dying breath."

"I suspected as much, Don Isaac. Forgive me for believing that a man of your character could be swayed from your faith. Believe me when I say that I respect your religious devotion. Nonetheless, come what may, my offer of protection still stands."

"I accept your apology and I do not misunderstand your gracious offer. Let us hope that we never have to witness a time when it is necessary. For the meantime, let us remain friends, Don Iñigo, as we have always been."

"Yes, friends, Don Isaac, that we shall always be."

They shook hands firmly and bid each other farewell.

Don Isaac Abravanel was disturbed when he left the Mendoza palace. Trouble, the Duke had said, but he refused to elaborate on its nature. Trouble — what kind of trouble? Assuredly, it would take the form of some new measure against the Jews of Spain. A new prohibition, perhaps, limiting the livelihood of Jews in the *juderías*? Trouble yes, but hardly something that would provoke the Duke of the *Infantado* into such a disclosure.

Or would the trouble come in the form of riots, organized riots, against the Jewish quarters — pillage and destruction, the slaughter of innocents, the vicious rabble gone wild at the urging of religious fanatics like De la Peña. But what of Ferdinand and Isabella's guarantee of physical protection? Surely the King and Queen would intervene to stop any such bloodshed . . .

A religious disputation perhaps, such as the ones of Tortosa and Barcelona in centuries past, where Jew was pitted against Christian in theological debate? But for Abravanel, that was not trouble. It was a welcome ideological challenge. . .

Abravanel thought on. A new incident such as that which had involved the Niño de La Guardia? More charges of host desecration and ritual murder? That would be trouble indeed . . . if that were to be the case.

Passover, that was it, Abravanel concluded. As Passover approached, so did Holy Week. That meant Easter and Holy Friday and the traditional Christian commemoration of the trial and the crucifixion of Jesus . . . and the Jews, the unforgiven Christ-killers, would be vilified once again in sermons throughout the land as to their historical complicity in the horrendous deed. Surely that was the nature of the ill-defined trouble. Surely it was this that had prompted Don Iñigo López de Mendoza to warn Don Isaac of forthcoming adversity. It was a warning which Don Isaac took to heart and he made a note to himself to send messages to as many Jewish communities as possible to inform them of potential outbreaks of violence during the time of Holy Week.

As Don Isaac Abravanel entered the *judería* of Guadalajara, its poorly fortified walls and gates sufficient to separate but not to protect the Jews in the town, he wondered what the effects of the trouble, if any, would be in this defenseless locality. He had come to love this small town, the inner warmth of its Jewish quarter, its lively people filtering their way through its narrow crowded streets, and he wished no harm to come to it. He had made friends here, dear friends, from all walks of life, who reciprocated with hospitality what he had shown them in consideration. Those in the Jewish quarter were, for the most part, simple artisans — weavers, shoemakers, tailors, and the like. Don Isaac had opened his home to them, as they had graciously done for him, bringing them closer to one another in a binding friendship borne of their mutual love of Torah and one another. The spiritual leader of Spanish Jewry wanted to root himself in this simple ocmmunity, to exhibit once and for all in his lifetime the proper balance of *Torah u-Malachah*, of study and work, of the fine meshing of his spiritual endeavors and community commitments with that of his worldly occupations. This balance, he felt, he had finally achieved in the rustic environs of this Castilian town.

The *judería* of Guadalajara had a longstanding reputation of being a center of Jewish mysticism, of Kabbalistic learning, dating back to the thirteenth century. The town also had the first Hebrew printing press in all of Spain, which published several compies of Kimhi's commentaries on the prophets and the *Tur Even Ha-Ezer* of Rabbi Jacob Ben-Asher. It boasted four synagogues and well over a hundred families, and it seemed to be on the edge of a veritable renaissance.

Don Isaac Abravanel could ask for little more. He needed the tranquil surrounding to continue his commentaries and, in a larger and more important sense, the Jewish community surely needed to recuperate from its wounds. Rest, and not trouble, was what they all needed.

His wife, Esther, petite and blue-eyed, with a soft white bun, was waiting at the entrance to his house. She saw Don Isaac from some distance away as he rode slowly up the winding street on his mule, waving salutations to one person after another. Arms crossed, she smiled as she saw him do so. It was her husband's way to reach out to one and all, never failing to give of himself in a friendly personal way. She saw herself as a partner in his life venture — sharing his dreams, partaking of his accomplishments but, most of all, creating a Jewish home that would fulfill his intimate domestic needs, providing him with the calm that every scholar requires, bearing and rearing his children in the ways of the Torah. Their three children were now adults. Their son, Judah, was physician to the Queen, and Judah and his family were expected to arrive soon to join them for Passover. The other two sons would also be making the journey to Guadalajara this year to be with their mother and father. She was elated at this. So was Isaac. They were both very proud of their children who, like their father, had demonstrated qualities of leadership in both the religious and secular spheres. She had wanted the family to be together this year for Passover — her three sons and, of course, Judah's first-born son, their precious grandchild, Isaac. She looked forward to the holiday. She waved to Don Isaac, and he waved back as he approached her.

"Welcome, beloved, we have all been waiting for you," said Esther.

"Ah, Esterica, if you only knew how much I missed you on that dusty road to Siguenza."

Esther Abravanel smiled. They kissed each other on the cheek.

"How did it go with the tax farming this week?"

"It went very well. Don Iñigo was most pleased. Tell me, is Judah here yet?"

"No, we expect him sometime tonight."

"Ah, good . . . very good. I have many things I want to discuss with that physician-philosopher son of mine. He has a mind of his own and, as you well know, he has this infatuation with love itself. Love, love, love . . . that is all he ever talks about. A love of love . . . and he loves to talk about it . . . I hope he changes the subject this Passover."

Don Isaac laughed light-heartedly at his own suggestion.

"Well, Isaac, you must admit to an occasional excess of your own. Besides, I must admit that there can be no finer emotion worthy of philosophical study than love . . . in all of its forms and gradations. Judah has a brilliant mind, and he has chosen a subject worthy of his intelligence. I, for one, find what he is doing to be of the greatest interest."

"Forgive me, dearest, for injecting levity where none was truly intended. I merely wished that Judah would show more balance in his philosophical investigations. That is all. My apologies .. *my love*."

Esther smiled again. "Ah, that is better. Besides, I can assure you that the conversation this Passover will not be exclusively about love."

"And how can you assure me of that?"

"We have a guest in the house who also is only interested in one subject . . . and who loves to talk about it . . . and it is *not* about love."

"Who might that be?", asked Abravanel.

Esther pointed her head. "Why don't you go into the living room and find out for yourself?"

Abravanel walked into the central patio area and searched for his mystery guest. Don Isaac spotted him and recognized him immediately. The guest was a nervous excitable sort, a short bearded figure who paced about the courtyard. His black cloak was wrinkled and unkempt. His head bobbed with each step that he took. Round and round he went, his being immersed totally in thought, his thick eyebrows drawn tightly into a menacing brow. He prowled on, his undulating frame weaving to and fro in the air like an upside-down pendulum, oblivious to all about him. Don Isaac watched this circular peregrination with mild amusement, and called out to his old friend.

"Zacuto! You Salamantine star-gazer, wake up!"

"Abravanel! You . . . you displaced Lisbonese alien . . . Aha! Thought you'd never see me again, eh?"

The two embraced each other heartily.

"What brings you here, Professor Zacuto?"

"Well, certainly not your invitation, Don Isaac. I had to invite myself to your Passover Seder, if you want to know the truth."

Don Isaac Abravanel laughed, asking, "Do people of your sort require an invitation?"

"Only by those who would deny me one. To those who would not deny me, I do not ask."

Don Isaac nodded his head in understanding. "I am then so fortunate as to be considered in the latter category."

"Yes, that you are."

"And I should, I presume, count my lucky stars."

"Nay, it is I, the astronomer, some would say astrologer, who should count them for you . . . and I shall formulate the constellation of your astral destiny in two words . . . *Mazal Tov*! Good luck."

"Why, thank you, Professor Zacuto. May it be from your lips to God's ears. What else do the stars say?"

"This is a year of destiny, a year of awesome deeds and unheard of accomplishments.Yet more than the deeds, it is a year of evil as well . . . on a scale never before seen. It is a year like no other . . . like nothing we have ever seen before in our lifetimes."

Abravanel asked, "Aha! And for the people of Israel? What do the stars hold for us?"

Zacuto paused for a moment, cleared his throat, and sighed deeply. "Trouble."

"Trouble?", Abravanel said apprehensively. "What kind of trouble?"

Don Isaac had the peculiar feeling of a strange cyclical disquiet. He had heard all this before, had he not?

"The constellations do not indicate the specific details of events to come, but merely provide a hazy foreshadowing of the future. Anyhow, I do not wish to distress you with omens that I only half-believe myself. Astrology is not a science, Don Isaac. I indulge myself in it only because my patron, the bishop of Salamanca, is forever hounding me for favorable signs of the times. I see, by the worried expression on your face, that I have indulged myself too far. And that, far from bringing good cheer to a friend, I have brought gloom into your heart with my baseless premonitions."

Zacuto shook his head guiltily. Don Isaac put his arm on Zacuto's shoulder to put his scholarly friend at ease.

"I, however, have reason to believe that there may be more truth in your presentiments than you are perhaps aware."

"But your *Mazal*, Don Isaac, your fortune . . . it is a good one by comparison. You will be spared the worst of the calamities. But please, Don Isaac, enough of this astrological nonsense. Otherwise, we will start believing it ourselves. Let me tell you instead of something that has brought great joy and pride into my heart. Have you heard of my new discovery?"

"No, tell me of it," said Abravanel, appreciating the change in subject.

"My new astrolabe! It is the finest, the most precise instrument of its kind. Before, it was impossible to navigate the sea without a large margin of error. But now, my astrolabe, together with the Alfonsine tables that I have drawn up, allow navigators to determine latitude without any need to know the meridian of the instrument."

"It sounds very important," Abravanel remarked. "Congratulations, Professor."

"Thank you. That is why I have become the new head of the astronomy department at the University of Salamanca. This instrument has changed my life . . . and it will utterly transform the navigation of the seas! Bartholomew Dias used it on his expedition four years ago round the southern tip of Africa. Every Spanish and Portuguese sailor who is of any worth uses *my* nautical tables and uses *my* astrolabe. I have even prepared a new treatise on solar and lunar eclipses that is also coming to the attention of all mariners."

"Speaking of mariners, have you heard of a certain mariner by the name of Christopher Columbus?"

"I most certainly have. I was on the Talavera commission that evaluated his proposal . . . the man wants to reach the Indies by traveling west. A wild-eyed idea, but one worth testing, or at least that was my feeling at the time."

"Then why did the commission reject his proposal?"

"Why, the decision was not all up to me. It was composed mainly of ecclesiastics, as you well know. Talavera, once the Queen's confessor, was the head of the commission, and Diego de Deza, an Inquisitor no less, was part of it too. These are men whose decisions are influenced by dogma, not facts. You know well the theologians and their fixed way of thinking.

"This Columbus, brash and arrogant as he is, had to come down to their level and use the same types of argument, quoting one Biblical verse after another, with references to Ezekiel, and to the many 'isles in the sea', and so forth and so on. But it was to no avail, and perhaps for good reason. There were no funds available at the time; the war against the Moors had drained the royal coffers dry. And then, I must confess, I made a formal presentation to the commission that dealt the mortal blow to his proposal."

"But, Zacuto, how can that be? You have just told me that you were in favor of Columbus' proposal."

"I was, and I was not. I was *for* the proposal because it was an exploratory expedition, a thrust into the darkness that lies to the west. It might lead to the discovery of new islands, like the Azores, discovered forty years ago by the sailors of Prince Henry the Navigator. But, alas, that was not what this Columbus was proposing. He was claiming that he could reach Japan, the island of Cypango, and estimated that it was a mere distance of one thousand leagues to the west. The proofs that he presented to support such a claim were weak and drawn from Aristotle and Marinus of Tyre and the Moslem geographer Alfragan. The proofs did not convince me, and I proceeded to submit computed astronomical evidence to the contrary to this commission. As much as I wanted the expedition to be approved for royal sponsorship, for exploration's sake if for no other, I could not sacrifice my scholarly integrity by pretending to take Columbus' claim seriously."

Don Isaac noted, "You appear to have some reservations about your opinion, Professor, or so it seems to me."

Zacuto shrugged his shoulders. "Bah! What is done is done. My presentation was correct yet it led, my intuition tells me, to the wrong decision. Perhaps I did my scholarly duty too well."

"But why so downhearted, Professor? Surely you must know that this past January Columbus finally secured the financing for his expedition."

"Yes, that I do. From what I understand, the Queen acted on the recommendation of the Talavera commission, and told this Columbus that the answer was definitely no. Yet a certain Luis de Santangel, the Converso keeper of Ferdinand's private purse, intervened and offered to raise the money for the expedition from private sources."

"I am one of them," added Abravanel. "I have invested well over ten thousand maravedis in the expedition."

Zacuto jumped out of his chair. "What? You . . .?"

"Yes, Professor Zacuto. You see, I let my intuition get the better of me."

Zacuto slapped his thigh and laughed uproariously. But then, as if catching himself, Zacuto slapped his forehead sharply in astonishment.

"Ay, no, oh my! . . . Don Isaac, what have you done to me?," said

Zacuto in a mock wail, walking nervously to and fro again, his hands fidgeting with his beard. "By the stars above, I swear that this expedition has your blessing. Ay, no, oh my! . . . I know now what will happen: Columbus will discover the route to the Indies by traveling west, and we of the Talavera commission will be made to appear as utterly brainless fools. Ay, no, oh my! The expedition has your blessing, the blessing of the chief rabbi. Oh, woe to my reputation! Had I known you were involved, Isaac, I would never have gone against your forecast of good fortune. Oh, woe is me!"

Don Isaac Abravanel looked on, a curious grin on his face, wondering whether to take Zacuto seriously or not. "Surely you attach undue importance to my financial participation in such an enterprise," he remarked. "Besides, does this Columbus not use the astrolabe that you invented?"

"Why, yes, he does indeed. Columbus, I know, uses my Alfonsine nautical tables as well. Why . . . ahh . . . that means if he finds a western route to the Indies, it will be said that my astrolabe made it possible."

Abravanel interjected, "Your fame, and that of your astrolabe, will spread far and wide. It will be said that previous mariners failed to find such a route because they did not use your instrument."

Zacuto slapped his hands, his cheerful spirit returning.

"Fame! Not the fame of a lifetime, but fame for all generations to come. Fame beyond belief!" Zacuto, an ebullient look on his face, relaxed back into his chair. "What need have I to worry? If Columbus does not reach the Indies, I and the commission will be vindicated, and my reputation will be untarnished. And if he should find a way, then I will become even more famous because he used my astrolabe. Either way, my reputation, my good name, will be the better, and not the worse, for it."

"There, you see? You have every reason to be content. 'Better a good name than fine gold', the Psalmist says. Is that not so, Professor Zacuto?"

"Better than all the gold in the world, Don Isaac, . . . better than all the gold in the world."

Zacuto sighed deeply and finally allowed himself to relax in the chair, his face aglow with contentment.

Abravanel smiled and stroked his beard understandingly. It would be a beautiful Passover this year, he said to himself, with a fascinating guest such as Abraham Zacuto at the Seder table. It could not fail to be otherwise. It would be a beautiful Passover, indeed, this year in

Guadalajara, as it had been in other years, a festival of freedom, a festival to be savored and made meaningful, one that would be forever memorable.

Chapter 7

The King and Queen had summoned Senior and Abravanel to present themselves immediately at the Alhambra palace. Hardly two days of the Passover holiday had been celebrated when royal couriers came to their doorsteps ordering them to appear at once in Granada. And Don Abraham and Don Isaac, leaving family and friends behind in the midst of the Passover observance, undertook the difficult journey to Granada to comply with their sovereigns' command. Both of them wondered what was the cause for so much urgency.

As they paused to rest during the journey, Abravanel queried Senior, "Tell me, Don Abraham, I have heard the strangest things about King Ferdinand's origins. Am I to believe the popular stories about him?"

Senior chuckled knowingly. "I dare say there is more truth in them than you can probably imagine."

Abravanel looked puzzled.

The Chief Judge took a sip of wine from a gourd and wet his lips.

"So you want to hear the story of Palomba and her son, eh? Very well, I will tell you. It happened a few generations ago as I understand it, but I will tell you the story as I heard it when I grew up in the Jewish quarter.

"There once was a very beautiful Jewish girl named Palomba, which means 'dove' in Spanish, and she lived in the village of Llerena. In fact, she was the most beautiful of all the Jewish girls in the *judería*. She was happily married, she had slaves and maids, and she loved to wear gold-lined dresses. One day, she went to visit her ailing mother in a nearby town. As she did so, she caught the attention of the Admiral of Castile, who was second in command only to the King of Aragon. The Admiral was a warrior type of ruler, and he was accustomed to having his way. He first inquired who the young beauty was and then arranged for agents to secretly abduct the young Jewess during her visit and to bring her to him. The Admiral then forcibly seduced Palomba, and after having satisfied himself, he set her free to return to her husband.

"Palomba returned home and told her husband all that had happened. When her husband heard what she had to say, he separated himself from her and refused to have any further relations with her. Palomba became pregnant with child and then bore a son. Palomba weaned the child and brought him up. The child was extraordinarily handsome and she loved him dearly. There was one problem, however."

"What is that?", asked Abravanel curiously.

Senior continued. "The problem was that the Admiral had no children of his own. But the Admiral had heard from his aides that Palomba's child, who was then about six years old, was a handsome lad to behold, and that he had radiant features worthy of the Admiral and of his station.

"The Admiral commanded his aides to go to Palomba's house and to take the child away from her. Although Palomba was able to hide the child successfully for a few days, ultimately the Admiral's aides took her son away and brought the child to the Admiral. Poor Palomba! Twice she had been robbed, once of her honor and later of her only child.

"The Admiral proceeded to treat the child as his very own son, which indeed he was. Thus the child became the proper heir because the Admiral had no other children. The child grew up in the King's palace, and he was educated in the arts and letters of the court. And the Admiral bequeathed to the youth all of his wealth, his cities, and his title, and everything else that belonged to him. Thus, when the Admiral died, the youth took over his position and acquired his title, and so he became the new Admiral of Castile.

"The new Admiral, son of the Jewess Palomba, eventually had four daughters whom he wedded to various kings and dignitaries. The first one he married to an aristocrat from Portugal, and two others he married off in Spain according to his wishes. One of the daughters, however, did not find a suitable husband and she remained at home with her father.

"In those days, the King of Aragon, John II, was a widower, and had a son named Carlos. Upon hearing that John II had been widowed, the Admiral of Castile sent his remaining daughter, Juana Enríquez, to the King with an eye to marry. Juana Enríquez found favor in the eyes of the

King, and he took her for a wife, and she bore him a son whom they called Ferdinand."

"Aha! Now I see," exclaimed Abravanel. "Most interesting."

Senior smiled. "There is more. Allow me to continue. Ferdinand's mother, Juana, was a very ruthless woman. During the last part of her pregnancy, she made a special journey to assure that Ferdinand would be born on Aragonese soil. From the day that Ferdinand was born, it is said that she hated the King's other son, Carlos, Prince of Viana, who was heir to the throne. It is reported that she plotted to have Carlos killed so that her son Ferdinand would inherit the throne. It so happened that Carlos became ill and the Queen ordered the attending physician to poison her stepson. As the young Carlos drank the herbal potion that the physician had prepared, he screamed, 'Death in the pot! There is death in the pot!' And Carlos died shortly thereafter.

"With Carlos now out of the way, the Queen knew that her son Ferdinand would one day reign as king. Because Ferdinand was now the heir apparent, it was only fitting that his supporters start looking for his queen. I was one of those supporters."

Abravanel interjected, "You were then a courtier in the Aragonese court."

Senior replied, "That is so. Ferdinand was only about seventeen years of age. And I must admit that his principal interests at the time seemed to lie in horsemanship, weapons, and women. Hmmm, actually, Ferdinand's interests have not changed at all since that time. Anyhow, where was I? Ah, yes, I remember now. A few of us in the court came to Ferdinand one summer day in 1469, and we proposed a secret plan to win the hand of Isabella, sister of Henry IV, Princess of Asturias, and possible heir to the throne of Castile. Much to our pleasure, the plan caught the fancy of young Ferdinand. I had already made contacts in Castile with certain nobles who likewise saw the political value of such a marriage. You must be aware, of course, that there were many suitors for Isabella's hand. Castile was a rich and powerful country, and Aragon by comparison was poor and had little to offer. We had to work secretly if we were to be successful in this enterprise, because there were many opposed to such a union.

"I set up a secret network of Jewish messengers. Official emissaries of the Aragonese court would have been detained at the border with Castile. But who would suspect lowly Jews of carrying such potent political correspondence? Through my messengers, we hand delivered a painting of our Prince Ferdinand to young Isabella. She loved the way he looked and she wanted very much to meet him. So we worked out a plan for a secret meeting between the two. By we, I mean Don Pedro de Acuna, the Count of Buendia, and Don Fadrique Enríquez, Ferdinand's grandfather."

Abravanel was surprised. "You mean that you knew Ferdinand's grandfather, Palomba's son?"

Senior smiled again. "Certainly, I did. He was a very shrewd old man, very tough, very wily. We all knew about him and his family. In fact, everyone in the Jewish community knew about Ferdinand's partial Jewish extraction. We even had a nickname for Ferdinand. We called him Palombino, because of his descent from his great-grandmother Palomba. As you can imagine, he was very well liked by all the Jews of Aragon. As far as I was concerned, I was advancing not only my personal interests, but also the interests of the Jews of the kingdom."

"The secret meeting was to take place in Valladolid. It was raining very hard that night. We were all supposed to meet in the *judería* of Valladolid at the home of a certain Rabbi Jacob Altaras. We had instructed Ferdinand to disguise himself as a muleteer and to pretend along the way to be the servant of the courtiers who were to accompany him. At the home of Rabbi Jacob, Ferdinand exchanged his shabby clothes for royal attire. All of us left the *judería* and walked to the house of a prominent and loyal Valladolid family. We were met there by Don Alfonso Carrillo, the proud archbishop of Toledo, who formally introduced the prince and the princess to one another. As you well know, history was made on that day, and I was part of it. The initial encounter between Ferdinand and Isabella lasted no more than two hours, but that dark and soggy night in Valladolid was a night of destiny for me. That night, we courtiers knew all that we needed to know: Ferdinand and Isabella were to be wed. By the morning, all of Valladolid knew. Within a week's end, all of Spain knew of the upcoming nuptials."

"And our people, how did they respond?," asked Abravanel.

"They went wild. In the Jewish community of Valladolid and in many others as well, people were deliriously happy. 'Palombino is going to rule over us!', they all shouted. 'Viva Palombino!' 'Palombino is going to rule over us! Our brother of Jewish blood, the flesh of our flesh, will rule!' You should have seen the celebration that we had in the *judería* of Valladolid. What a fiesta that was! Ay, what a fiesta! For two full days, people celebrated. It is a full twenty-three years since that day, and yet I remember it as if it were only yesterday. That night, Don Isaac, was the glory of my career as a courtier.

"Ferdinand and Isabella were indebted to me, and they have repaid me a thousand times over. I was made Supreme Judge of the Jews. Because of that night, I became the wealthiest of men by being appointed chief tax collector of the crown. One night, Don Isaac, was all it took to change my life forever."

When they finally arrived in Granada, there was no time to admire the Alhambra palace. Senior and Abravanel were hurriedly directed to the throne room where the King, the Queen, and several other court dignitaries were waiting for them. From the look on the faces of the rulers, it was obvious to Don Isaac that there was trouble ahead, perhaps the 'trouble' that Don Iñigo had cryptically alluded to.

Senior and Abravanel bowed respectfully on entering, but their presence was not acknowledged in accordance with court protocol. Instead, the Queen stared icily, and the King scowled. Don Abraham was disturbed by the breach of court etiquette, but even more by the coolness of his reception. Abravanel sensed that something was afoot, but said nothing, preferring to wait for the King and Queen to open the conversation.

Ferdinand spoke first. "Be seated, señores. I have been waiting for you."

Senior, continuing to stand up, asked, "A most unexpected visit on our part to the court, your Majesty. Is something the matter?"

Ferdinand said without emotion, "We have some bad tidings for you, Don Abraham and Don Isaac."

A distressed Senior asked, "Bad tidings, your Majesty?"

Abravanel spoke up. "Your displeasure, your Majesty, is a call for action. Tell us of it and we shall do our utmost to change it."

Ferdinand explained: "Both of you . . . have been loyal subjects of the crown, always ready to place your resources at our disposal. Without the two of you, the war against the Moors would have been harder to win. And the Queen and I are prepared to reward you most handsomely."

Abravanel remarked, "Your Majesty, no recompense is necessary, I assure you. Thanks to your bountiful kindness, my family has never been lacking."

"I feel likewise equally grateful," Senior added. "But what is this talk of . . . of bad tidings?"

Ferdinand took a deep breath. "I shall speak straight to the point. The Queen and I, in conjunction with the Holy Office of the Inquisition, and after much consultation with many of the ministers of state, have decided to expel all Jews from the kingdom."

Both Senior and Abravanel were speechless. Abravanel closed his eyes, his mind not yet prepared to accept the new reality, the new 'trouble', that was about to be inflicted on his people. He felt the torrential force of the decision and understood the human toll that such a calamity would exact. He perceived the pivotal role that he must play in making sure it never came to pass, and resolved to resist it to the utmost.

An outraged Senior was the first to respond. Don Abraham indignantly demanded an explanation, "Expel us, your Majesty? I . . . I do not understand this at all . . . Why?"

It was Isabella who answered, "Because Jews have been involved in incident after incident of flagrant Judaizing activity among the New Christians, and discourage them from being loyal to the Christian faith. Just this week, we caught a band of New Christians observing the Passover. This must stop, and it will stop by virtue of this decree."

Abravanel entreated, "But surely they must be only a handful . . . it cannot be sufficient reason for blaming the entire Jewish community."

A figure suddenly appeared from behind a curtain and shouted, "Your Majesty!" It was Torquemada, the Grand Inquisitor, who was now the center of attention as he walked toward the sovereigns. He talked forcefully as he approached the throne, "Do not be deceived, your Majesty. As long as practicing Jews are around, the New Christians will persist in the error of their old Jewish ways — clinging to the rituals of their fathers, tens of thousands of them all over the country, corrupted by these Jews who make them blind to the truth of our faith."

Isabella, responding to the Inquisitor's admonition, seemed to explain, "It is a matter of faith . . . of purity of faith . . . It was such purity that allowed us to be victorious over the Moors. And just as God has given us the faith and the strength to crush the Moslem infidel from without, so we must find the faith and the strength to eliminate the disease of unbelief from within. All Jews must convert or leave Spain. There is no other way."

Abravanel pleaded, "Your Majesties . . . I cannot believe what my ears have heard. Would that I could not hear and the words never spoken! Your Majesties, I am shocked that you, our protectors, would consider such a program . . .

"Why will you do this to us? Why do you order us, your loyal Jewish subjects, to leave our homeland — to be uprooted and cast forth as a driven leaf? Have we not supported you in your darkest hour when your campaign against the Moors was at its lowest ebb, indeed, when you stood in the shadow of defeat? Did we not stand by you and pray for you?

"Have mercy on us — the *great* majority of us Jews — blameless men, women, and children — who have done you no harm, who have sought only your good, who have been your faithful servants time and again."

"Have mercy on us, your Majesties. Have mercy for my people Israel . . . have mercy for your loyal subjects who love you so."

The King's face showed traces of anguish at Abravanel's plea. The Queen listened without emotion, neither approving or disapproving, although seemingly willing to listen further.

It was Torquemada who spoke out. The Grand Inquisitor grabbed the crucifix on his chest and pointed to it, "As you showed *him* mercy when he presented himself to you, thus we shall show you mercy."

Ferdinand waved the Inquisitor off. "Enough, Grand Inquisitor."

Senior made his appeal. "Your Majesties, we beg of you to reconsider your decision. I beseech you to consider the practical losses to the crown — in commerce . . . in the sciences, medicine, mapmaking."

Ferdinand replied calmly, "We have considered the losses, and we will take measures to reduce any massive outflow of wealth. Quite frankly, Don Abraham, Jews will not be allowed to take out any gold or silver with them."

Senior shook his head, the color of blood rushing to his face. "So that is it! No gold or silver, eh? Is this your gratitude for all that the Jews of this kingdom have done for you?"

Isabella interjected reassuringly, "But, Don Abraham, you and Don Isaac are to be exempted because of past services you have rendered. This is the recompense the King was referring to . . . each of you will be allowed to take a thousand gold ducats if you decide to leave. If you convert, however, nothing will be taken away from you."

Senior was further incensed. "Convert? Convert . . . or be allowed a small amount of gold and silver? My Queen, what kind of talk is this?"

Abravanel, looking at Ferdinand, remarked, "If money is the problem, the Jewish community would be willing to pay the crown a most generous sum to . . . uh . . . help pay off its obligations."

Senior caught the gist of Abravanel's offer. Directing his words likewise toward the King, he added, "Yes, yes, of course. If I may, your Majesty, be allowed to discuss this matter privately with Don Isaac."

Ferdinand, to the astonishment of the Queen and the Grand Inquisitor, answered, "Please do, Don Abraham."

Isabella and Torquemada looked at each other, extremely upset by this unexpected behavior on the part of the King. It had been agreed that the decision to expel the Jews was final, that it would not be reconsidered. Now Ferdinand, contrary to their shared understanding, was undermining their unity. Ferdinand, ignoring their stares, awaited the response of the two Jewish leaders.

Gesturing animatedly, speaking in whispered tones, Senior and Abravanel consulted over the amount they should offer the crown. Community resources were estimated; imagined levies on the larger *juderías* were stretched to the limit; and both agreed to liquidate most of their assets. There was to be no holding back. Nothing less than a massive sum of money was required, without equivocation, if the decree were to be averted. The two ended their discussion, and Don Isaac turned around to face the King.

Abravanel declared, "Your Majesties, on behalf of the Jewish communities that we represent, we are prepared to raise for the crown a sum of 300,000 ducats . . . in return for the annulment of any and all plans of expulsion."

Ferdinand was staggered by the amount. It was a huge sum. Nonetheless, he said cagely, "Is that your maximum offer?"

"It is open to negotiation, your Majesty," Senior noted. "But it is a realistic sum. Your Majesty, for God's sake and the sake of your country, we beg of you to allow us to stay."

Torquemada, breathing heavily, spite rising in his voice, said, "Your Majesty, if I may . . ."

Ferdinand sharply cut him off again. "No, Grand Inquisitor, you may not."

Torquemada was taken aback by the affront. Like a wounded animal, he looked for support from the Queen, whose sense of surprise was equally great, but the support was not forthcoming. Ferdinand, who ordinarily did the Queen's bidding in matters of church and state, was in command today. The wresting of control from Isabella in such a critical issue, in the very presence of the Grand Inquisitor was as much an affront to Isabella as it was to Torquemada, and it was an indication to Don Isaac that there was less than full royal agreement on the need for this edict. If it was the King's desire to have greater say on this and other matters, it was to Don Isaac's benefit to strengthen the King's hand.

The Queen looked at the King with profound disapproval, but remained silent, deferring the expression of her anger at Ferdinand's heavy-handedness.

Abravanel, sensing the unstated difference of opinion, argued impressionably upon the King. He continued on, "Your Majesty, in the name of Heaven, I urge you to accept this sum as a gift of love and affection from the Jews of the kingdom. Do not betray them . . . do not betray their trust in you as their ruler and as their protector. Be the good and wise king that we believe you to be."

Ferdinand said, "Well . . . perhaps we will think further on this."

Isabella, incensed, burst out of her silence, "I thought this matter was already decided, Don Fernando." Her words were tinged with bitterness.

Torquemada quickly followed suit, saying, "You gave me your word, your Majesty."

Ferdinand looked at the two, discerning the displeasure that he had provoked and stated, "I, as King, must give this matter further thought."

Torquemada seethed with indignation at this latest slight. In a violent fit of temper, he pulled the crucifix off his chest, and thrust it angrily into the air. Holding the cross over his head, he walked up to the King and roared, "Judas Iscariot betrayed our Lord for thirty pieces of silver. And now you sell him again for your ducats and your doblas. Take him . . ."

Torquemada furiously threw the crucifix on the floor in front of the King, and shouted,

". . . And sell him to the Jews!"

Torquemada stormed out of the reception hall, slamming the door behind him.

There was a strange, uneasy silence. The two Jewish courtiers, unsure how to proceed, looked for a sign from Ferdinand allowing them to continue with their case. The King looked instead at Isabella, who stared at him with evident disapproval; he then looked at the courtiers whose desperate hopes he had encouraged by offering them the prospect of negotiations. Caught up in his quandary, the King replied, "We must think on this matter further. Court is adjourned."

When they returned to their rooms in the Alhambra, Senior and Abravanel were greatly vexed by the proposed edict to expel the Jews. A confused jumble of feelings, ranging from disbelief to anger to wounded pride, assailed them. Don Abraham Senior's sense of agony was the greater, because the expulsion was proposed by life-long friends, a King and Queen whose marital union he had once facilitated. It was inconceivable to him that the sovereigns would actually execute the cruel plan. Surely it was a ploy and nothing more.

Senior slammed his fist on the desk. "It is a bluff, I tell you . . . The

King . . . the Queen . . . even that bastard Torquemada . . . they are bluffing . . . they have got to be."

Senior slammed his fist on the table again. "First, they threaten to expel us . . . and then we believe their story, gullible fools that we are . . . and we offer to pay them . . . Ha! *Pay them* handsomely to allow us to stay . . . what a brilliant tactic. What will they not do to squeeze . . . and squeeze . . . and squeeze every last maravedi out of their Jewish subjects, eh?"

Abravanel expressed his disagreement. "Senior, do not be a fool . . . this is not time for wishful fantasy. The King and Queen . . . certainly the Queen . . . did you see the look on her face? I am of the opinion that they mean what they say. They want us out. They want to expel us — I sense it . . . I feel it in my body and soul."

Senior laughed. "Body and soul, the man says! Ha! . . . Body and soul! He feels! He senses! Let me tell you something . . . what do you know about them, eh? I tell you that they need me . . . and they need you. They cannot collect any taxes without us. Give them the 300,000 ducats that they probably want . . . and the threat is gone. Like that! Overnight!"

Abravanel scratched his beard, "If that is so, why did they not accept the offer?"

With a wink of an eye, Senior answered, "Well, Isaac, why else? . . . They want more money."

Abravanel took a deep breath and shook his head. "I am not going to continue this absurd line of reasoning any further. Money is not all that matters here, Don Abraham. Surely you understand that. Isabella said it plainly and simply, 'It is a matter of faith'. Do you understand: *a matter of faith*! I have no doubt in my mind that the Grand Inquisitor is somehow behind all this . . . after all, did not the King give him his word? My God, the King gave him his word that he would expel us! No, my dear *juez mayor*, if you want to ignore this threat and pretend it is merely a game to get more ducats from us Jews, I can not join you in your blindness . . . I am going to speak to the Marquis of Cádiz and to the Duke of Medina-Celi about this."

Senior said, "And you think *they* can influence the King?"

Abravanel walked up slowly to Senior and placed his arm on the Chief Judge's shoulder. "Senior, I want you to understand one thing: we are in great danger. *Great* danger. There is still hope that this threat will not come to pass. We need help from powerful people in the court."

Don Abraham walked away from the hand on his shoulder. Hands behind his back, a pained look on his aged face, Senior walked out on the balcony that overlooked the garden below. In shadowed silence, he stood there pensively, trying to fathom the turn of events, attempting to come to terms with the new reality he was still inclined to deny.

"What can I say to you, Isaac? That I do not see the immediate threat, that I cannot bring myself to admit the possibility of catastrophe? Of course, I can. But, I must confess, I do find it difficult to think of the consequences, as much for the Jews of the kingdom as for myself. Look at my position. Here I am, Chief Judge of the court, the richest Jew in the land . . . admittedly by virtue of being chief tax farmer, and suddenly . . . suddenly all my wealth, all my power and influence, all that I have fought and worked for — for myself and for my family . . . absolutely everything that I have worked for is as if I had worked for nothing at all."

"We will both be ruined, Senior. I have been ruined before in Portugal, and I have come back . . . Believe me, it is not the end."

Senior closed his eyes, held them shut for a prolonged moment, and opened them again. "It would be for me. I am eighty years old . . . I cannot start all over . . . very well, we will do as you say. I will take it upon myself to meet with the Duke of Medina-Celi, and it will be your responsibility to contact the Marquis of Cádiz. These two noblemen have always been our friends, and they have the ear of the King and Queen. It will be to our benefit to have them plead our case. There are others, too, who may be willing to help. Beatrice de Bobadilla in my hometown of Segovia, she is a childhood friend of the Queen, and she is married to a Converso. She will help us."

"And in Guadalajara, the Duke of the *Infantado* may be willing to put in a good word for us," added Abravanel.

"Maybe, maybe not. Do not forget that he is related to the Cardinal of Spain. The Cardinal undoubtedly knows what is happening, and Don Iñigo may be compromised for this reason. I suggest you not involve him in this matter."

"As you say, Don Abraham. In the meantime, we have work to do. *Esperanza*, my friend . . . Hope . . . it is all we have."

Isabella was infuriated with Ferdinand's flagrant violation of their stance vis-a-vis the Jews. It was one thing to disagree privately on matters of principle; it was quite another to display that disagreement in court and to bring ridicule upon themselves. The Queen resolved to

impress on her husband the importance of adherence to this wise principle of conduct. She wanted to make it clear to her husband that she
would not tolerate any dereliction with regard to the expulsion of the
Jews. At stake was the crucial objective of the complete Christianization
of Spain, an objective which clearly could not be effected without the
expulsion. Also of concern to her was that Ferdinand's opposition on
this matter suggested she was not exclusive ruler of the territories of
Castile and Leon. If need be, she would enforce the agreement that they
had long ago concluded.

At the time of their nuptials, Ferdinand and Isabella had signed a
marriage contract limiting their respective domains of sovereignty.
Ferdinand, the princely suitor from the impoverished and weaker kingdom of Aragon, had secured the heart of his Castilian bride-to-be, but
little more. As a result of the wedding negotiations, Ferdinand was to
retain his rights as heir to the throne of Aragon. However, he was to be
nothing more than a nominal King in Castile, bereft of any real power;
he would have no right to make appointments to state offices where the
finances of the Castilian crown were involved, nor for that matter to
offices in the church. He could effect no law, command no army,
proclaim no edict in Castile without the prior approval of the Queen. To
certify the agreement, Castilian coins were minted with the head of
Isabella higher than that of Ferdinand's. For an ambitious manly prince
like Ferdinand, such a shackling agreement could not go unchallenged.

Perhaps it was because of these imposed handicaps that Ferdinand
engaged in several illicit amorous escapades with ladies of the court. He
sired several illegitimate children, much to the distress of Isabella whose
courtly reputation for chastity was proverbial. Whether it be from fault
of moral character alone, or whether it be from the inhibiting legal
provocations, Ferdinand had proved repeatedly his infidelity to
Isabella, at first on matters of the flesh and now, it so appeared to her, on
a serious matter of the spirit. She could excuse lustful indiscretions, as
men were wont to be men. But Isabella could not condone Ferdinand's
non-compliance on the expulsion; in part because it violated her
Christian pledge to rid Spain of the national Mosaic infidelity, but
also because she religiously viewed it as her husband's ultimate act
of infidelity.

Later, at dinner Isabella asked Ferdinand, "Why do you oppose
me on a matter that is so dear to my heart? Why now, after you gave
me your word in January of this year, after you promised the Grand
Inquisitor . . ."

"Leave the Grand Inquisitor out of this," Ferdinand said. "Promises to Fray Tomás mean nothing to me."

"Very well, then, my lord, then let it be so . . . just between you and me, as it should be," Isabella stated.

"No, it is not so, my Queen . . . and it is not as it should be. It is merely the way it is, at least here in Castile, and that way is your way, my Queen, whatever your will may be. Concerning this matter of the expulsion of the Jews, which you say is so dear to your heart, the decision will be mine. I care little for the religious glories that you pursue. I care little for religious titles, such as the 'most Catholic' sovereigns that the Pope gave us, however sweet they may sound in your ears, especially if they do not enlarge our nearly empty treasuries. What is necessary, my Queen, is to increase the wealth of our kingdoms. If I reconsider my decision to expel the Jews from all the territories under our rule, it is only because I am concerned about our material interest. My concern is also that what may be best for Castile may not be appropriate for Aragon. Your reasons for wanting to expel the Jews are not the same as mine. Quite frankly, I have come to question yours, Isabella. Over the years, I have given in time and again to your religious fanaticism: I have allowed the restrictions to be applied against the Jews in Aragon as much as in Castile. I have allowed the Inquisition to operate in Aragon with its *Autos-de-Fe*, despite the many protests that I have received from sincere Christians regarding the many injustices of the Holy Office. Yet, I permitted this because I knew that it brought in large sums of money from confiscated Marrano estates. It suited our interests perfectly. And now you ask me to expel the Jews. You ask me because you obviously cannot do this alone. Because if Castile expels its Jews when Aragon does not, all the Jews of your kingdom will simply go into mine. So in order for the expulsion to work, we must both be in accord. Well, I must tell you, I am not in accord. Perhaps we have gone too far. Perhaps it will cost us too much in the end. The Jews are a steady, exploitable source of income; they are utterly defenseless, and, they are always ready to do our bidding to assure themselves of our royal protection. I say: take their money, take all the gold that they can raise, and let them stay. They will be eternally grateful, these Jews, and they will pay dearly in the years to come."

Isabella listened to Ferdinand's explanation, her eyes alive with fire. "Ferdinand, I cannot believe that they have made you into what you appear to be."

"Oh, what am I now?," said Ferdinand . . ."and who is it, pray tell, that has made me this time?"

"You know," said Isabella.

"No, I do not know," Ferdinand said innocently.

Isabella colored with anger. "By God, that does it. Yes, you want to hear it . . . Well, I will tell you to your face . . . you are a puppet, you hear . . . a puppet of the Jews!"

Ferdinand scoffed. "Oh, don't make me laugh. Me, a puppet of the Jews? Surely you mean a puppet of the Queen."

Isabella frowned, "You have always been their puppet. You know why . . ."

Ferdinand responded cooly. "No, I do not know why. Tell me."

"*Because* . . .," Isabella said, the anger restrained in her voice.

"Because what?," asked Ferdinand, irritated.

Isabella exploded, "*Because you are part Jew yourself!*"

Ferdinand rose angrily from his chair, and said threateningly, "Don't you *ever* say that again."

Isabella raised her voice in response to the threat, "Admit it . . . everyone knows it. Your great grandmother was Palomba, the Jewess, who was seduced by the Admiral of Castile."

Ferdinand's face became contorted with rage, "I said, shut your mouth."

Isabella kept on shouting, "Palombino the people called you. Palombino, the great grandson of the Jewess Palomba, will rule over us . . ."

Ferdinand furiously answered her. "Isabella, I am warning you for the last time."

Isabella said mockingly, "Well, is it not true? The people know it. Everyone in court knows it. Even I know it . . . and I know that Abraham Senior set up our marriage . . . well, didn't he? He did it because he knew you had Jewish blood in you — and that as King you would never hurt the Jews. What do you say to that, Palombino? Isn't that the real reason you don't want to expel the Jews?"

Ferdinand, grabbing a glass goblet from the table, raised it into the air as if to throw it. "You pompous Castilian bag of hot air, I am going to empty you of all your phony pretenses. I have had enough of this."

Ferdinand threw the glass at Isabella but missed. The goblet smashed against the back wall.

Isabella grabbed a wooden chair and placed it between Ferdinand and herself. "Don't touch me, you Aragonese primitive!"

Ferdinand took off his shoe and threw it at her. The shoe glanced harmlessly off Isabella's shoulder.

Isabella mocked him savagely, "Ha! Palombino . . . Palombino."

Ferdinand took off his other shoe and advanced toward Isabella. He did not want to miss this time. As the King came closer, Isabella dropped the chair and ran for the door. Ferdinand ran after her and threw the shoe with full force. Isabella shut the door the instant before the shoe crashed against it. The King picked the shoe off the floor, opened the door again, and threw it at her again. Blind with rage, he shouted after her, "Take that, you . . . you Castilian windbag!"

Ferdinand slammed the door shut again. He propped his back against the door and sighed heavily. It was too much for him. The Queen had beaten him at his own game. He sighed heavily a second time and picking up Isabella's chair, he flung it at the wall. Next he pushed the kitchen table over, sending the silverware, plates, and glasses crashing onto the floor. Then he staggered to a nearby mirror, his legs wobbly and weak. He studied his features carefully, felt the profile of his nose, and outlined the bones of his face. He saw himself, Palombino, in the mirror, and he could not escape the truth of his own image. Using the handle of his sword, he smashed the mirror to fragments. Unable to handle the pain of this self-admission, he leaned on the broken mirror, moaning and whining, burying his head in his arms, and knowing that in order to avoid more pain he would have no choice but to do as Isabella willed.

Within a matter of days, the Alhambra palace was alive with rumors of the threatened expulsion of the Jews and everyone was aware of the fierce struggle between the Jewish courtiers and Torquemada. It was reported that the Grand Inquisitor had won the initial confrontation, much to the consternation of the Jewish representatives who thought that the sovereigns could be readily bought for the right amount of gold. The Jewish courtiers, Senior and Abravanel, altering their tactics, had enlisted the services of various noblemen to persuade the King and Queen to rescind the edict. Whether the courtiers would succeed in staying the decree, or whether they would suffer its consequences if they failed to do so, was the topic on everyone's lips.

The first to respond was the Marquis of Cádiz. Upon the taking of Granada, the famed warrior had retired to his Marquisate, its boundaries now substantially enlarged by royal grants of territory conquered from the Moors. The Marquis had always been outspoken in matters that violated his sense of justice. In the year 1480, when eight thousand

Conversos had fled to the territory under his rule to escape from the newly formed Inquisition, he protected them. Only after religious threats of excommunication had he surrendered the refugees to the Holy Office. Many of the Conversos were burned at the stake in the *Autos-de-Fé* that followed in Sevilla. The fate of those Conversos, many of whom the Marquis had come to know personally during their brief stay of refuge on his estate, weighed heavily on the conscience of this Andalusian grandee. Forced to consign defenseless people to the flames, the Marquis became a vehement opponent of the Holy Office and its ruthless methods.

Befriending Jews and Conversos alike, he developed strong ties with those of Hebrew descent, among them Don Isaac Abravanel, making it clear to them that he was a friend who could be called upon in time of need. Thus when Abravanel appeared one evening at his estate, entreating him to intercede on behalf of the Jews of the kingdom, the Marquis unhesitatingly offered to speak with the King and Queen in the hope of changing the rulers' minds. It was the least he could do, for his old friend Don Isaac, but especially to assuage his feelings of guilt. It was something he had to do, for the Jews' sake as much as for his own.

Upon his arrival in Granada, the Marquis found the King practicing with a crossbow in the archery range. With the King were several cavaliers who were engaging in mock combat with their swords. A few ladies and other onlookers were casually observing the activities. Ferdinand, raising his crossbow to his shoulder, took aim, fired, and watched enthusiastically as the speeding arrow struck a distant dummy with a turban-shaped Moorish helmet on top. The King gloated, "By San Fernando — I've done it again. Ha!" The onlookers applauded politely at this feat.

A page walked up to the King. "Excuse me, your Majesty, the Marquis of Cádiz is here and would like to speak with you."

"Aha, the Marquis of Cádiz, my good friend . . . of course, I shall speak with him."

The Marquis of Cádiz, bowing respectfully as he approached, "Your Majesty, I bid you good day."

"And a good day it is, Marquis. Welcome, welcome . . . How long has it been since that glorious day when we entered the Alhambra palace, eh? It has been months . . . and yet it seems like years."

The Marquis smiled and nodded his head in agreement. "Truly the sweetest day of my life, your Majesty."

Ferdinand put the crossbow down. "And there will never be another like it. For ages to come, the children of Spain will tell the story of the conquest of Granada, and of the part played by tthe greatest warrior and cavalier of his day, the Marquis of Cádiz."

The King continued. "You made it possible . . . you and your men. But tell me, what brings you here for a private audience?"

Ferdinand picked up the crossbow again and reset it with another arrow. Observing this, the Marquis said, "Your Majesty, forgive me for being so bold to ask . . ."

Ferdinand dispensed with formalities. "Come now, out with it We are friends . . . we have been friends for years, Marquis. What is it? Boredom because there are no castles to take? Or is it because there are too many vassals to feed?" Not waiting for an answer, Ferdinand took aim with the weapon, looking down its shaft in the direction of the dummy.

The Marquis spoke, "Your Majesty, I shall speak directly. Is it true that you intend to expel the Jews?"

Ferdinand, still aiming the crossbow, tensed. "Why . . . uh . . . yes, the matter is under consideration." Ferdinand fired the crossbow, the arrow swiftly speeding through the air, but striking wide of its mark. He put the crossbow down again.

"Damnation," the King muttered. He began to walk away from the archery range. Walking beside Ferdinand, the Marquis spoke freely. "Your Majesty, I have fought the Moors and I never questioned the need to fight them. I will fight against the enemies of Spain whenever and wherever you so command.

"But the Jews? The Jews? They are harmless. They are *not* our enemies. They are Spaniards like we are . . . Spaniards who have roots in our land for centuries . . . good citizens who contribute to our country each in their own way." The Marquis paused for a moment.

"Go on," said the King. "I am listening."

The Marquis continued. "I tell you as a friend . . . it is a mistake to expel them. A great mistake. If there are Jews who persist in helping out the New Christians, then find them and punish them. But do not let *all* the Jews suffer.

"This Converso problem, who created it? We, the Christians, created it. We let the religious fanatics in our midst run wild one hundred years ago, killing thousands of Jews, and forcing tens of thousands of them to become Christian against their will. Why should these Conversos believe as we do, when our own Catholic priests either murdered their ancestors or dragged their forefathers to the baptismal fountain? My King, I know it is your wish to make this a more Catholic Spain. And, my King, it is my duty to obey your dictates as a loyal subject of the crown. Yet my conscience, as a Christian if not perhaps as a subject, impels me to express that which sorrows my heart, even if it kindles your anger against me. I want only what is best for my motherland, your Majesty, and only what is best for you and the Queen. Yet my disservice would be far the greater for failure to report my misgivings to you, even if it would spare me your anger, than it would be for me to present myself and my case, as I am so doing now, with regard to the error that, I feel, your Majesties are about to commit.

"My dear King, it is a truism of wisdom that things done to excess are never good. Just as the Converso problem arose from an outbreak of Christian fanaticism, so, too, the problem cannot be solved by the very means that created it. More fanaticism, more religious zeal, cannot undo the damage that such zeal has already inflicted. As I have spoken to you on previous occasions, these fanatics, operating under the protection of the Inquisiton, see no violation of Christian principle when unfortunate Converso backsliders are tortured into a state of fear and dread, or when they are burned at the stake. These fanatics, my King, are gaining strength day by day. Given enough time, they will be the undoing of all that is good and true in Spain, and the time has surely come for you to stop them.

"I will repeat myself, your Majesty. The problem is not with the Jews; they are *not* the enemy. The enemy is within us; the problem is the Holy Office, which is out of control. It is this institution that is teaching us to be unfaithful to the highest principles of Christianity. If we shall listen to the fanatics, we will become like them — zealots breathing the fires of hate and intolerance.

"Do not expel the Jews, my King. Be strong. Do not give in to these fanatics. I tell you, the expulsion of the Jews is a needless act of fanaticism, and nothing more."

Ferdinand continued walking, finding it hard to believe that these words were coming from the Marquis. How could he tell the principled Marquis that his sole interest in this was financial? How could he tell him that Isabella was the mainspring of this religious zeal, that it was she whose Catholic ardor waxed so intensely? Indeed, what would Isabella herself say to the Marquis when she would hear him speak this way? Plucking a leaf from a nearby hedge, Ferdinand put the thought of this forthcoming confrontation out of his mind, content to let the Queen tell it to him straight.

Yet he had to tell the Marquis something. To say that the Jews helped the Conversos and therefore merited expulsion, as the Inquisition maintained, would only confirm the Marquis' argument that the tribunal was indeed responsible. Actually, the King valued the Inquisition greatly. It had enriched his royal coffers and it could be used to keep dissidents in check, ambitious noblemen as well as religious heretics. It would be wiser to sidestep criticism of this institution, which he had helped to found, as long as it remained useful to him. Rather he would tell the Marquis that the source of the hatred against the Jews originated elsewhere.

Ferdinand spoke simply, "But the common people . . . they do not want the Jews."

The Marquis answered him. "The common people will believe whatever you want them to believe. As long as those Dominican priests run about the countryside preaching hatred of the Jew and distrust of the New Christians, of course they will hate the Jews. How can you expect them to think otherwise? I tell you once again, my King . . . stop these fanatics and their rabble-rousing, and you will stop the hatred."

Ferdinand replied, "And you think that I can do this? Change their beliefs? Keep those extremist priests in line?"

The Marquis said frankly, "You are the King, aren't you?"

Ferdinand, seemingly stung by the remark, frowned upon hearing this. He was the King, and yet, in a certain sense, he knew he was not.

The Marquis continued, "Your Majesty, you are the only one who can stand up to them. Even we nobles are not safe. Everyone lives in fear and dread of the Inquisition."

"It is not as easy as you think," replied Ferdinand. "Answer me this. Do you really think the Jews are so valuable that their expulsion would be to our detriment?"

"Absolutely," said the Marquis. "I would not be here if I thought otherwise."

The King now questioned the grandee, "Did someone send you here to speak with me? Abravanel? Senior perhaps?"

There was no response from the Marquis.

Ferdinand, judging what the answer was from the silence, remarked, "I trust then that you do speak for yourself. Very hard words, Marquis, all that you have said. Very hard words."

"I felt it was my duty, your Majesty, to let you know what my feelings on the subject were before it was too late."

"Ay, Marquis, I am afraid that it may already be too late . . . fate has a way of tying one's hands, even the hands of a King."

The Marquis did not agree. "It is never too late if you will it so."

"I do not rule alone," said Ferdinand. "No, by no means do I rule alone."

The goings on at the Alhambra continued. First it was the Marquis of Cádiz, then the Duke of Medina-Celi, each willing to plead the case of the Jews and their permanent retention within the kingdom. Other notables also came to their support. Even Beatrice de Bobadilla, the childhood friend of the Queen, was recruited, coming all the way from Segovia to Granada to make her point. This was taken as a measure of the intense pressure being exerted on the sovereigns by Senior and Abravanel.

Yet no one knew whether the rulers had been swayed from their original course. From day to day, it so seemed, the fate of the Jews hung in the balance, a few good words from one nobleman tipping the scales slightly in their favor, making the ominous spectre of expulsion slightly less probable. Then, on another day, the scale would turn the other way, as Torquemada rallied his supporters into making presentations to the rulers of the widespread Mosaic depravity; the Grand Inquisitor would remind them of the Niño de La Guardia atrocity, of the Jewish practice of usury, indeed of their utter non-integrability into the body of the Christian nation.

Spokesmen for the mercantile class were called into action by Torquemada, and they expressed their opposition to the participation of Jews in the business and commercial affairs of Castile. It was one more reason to get rid of the Jews.

Every day that passed without a royal pronouncement seemed a partial victory to Don Isaac and Don Abraham, an indication perhaps that their collaborative effort was having its desired effect, that perhaps all was not lost. After two more meetings, Ferdinand and Isabella refused Senior and Abravanel the privilege of a repeat audience, although the sovereigns permitted invited noblemen to speak on the Jews' behalf. When such grandees would emerge from their private meeting with the rulers, the Jewish courtiers would ask them if the King and Queen were receptive to their suggestions, whether there seemed to be any prospect of a reversal of their stated intention. From all accounts, the rulers had listened politely but had promised nothing.

Each extension of time seemed to the courtiers, as to a captive prisoner awaiting the verdict, as much a reprieve as a penalty, the defendants at times preferring to enjoy the bliss of ephemeral ignorance than to risk the knowledge of a potentially unhappy sentence. As testimonies and counter-testimonies were submitted to the judges, as friends were summoned and accusations rebutted, as every known device and strategem was employed to ward off the catastrophe, Senior and Abravanel each found ways to make the waiting more bearable.

Don Isaac Abravanel found comfort in prayer. Each morning as he awoke to the break of dawn, Abravanel would begin his prayers, refracting the golden brilliance of morn into the receptacle of his soul. Putting on his phylacteries, winding its strap around his forearm and its square box on his forehead, binding thus symbolically body and mind, he was ready, his total self was ready, in thought as in deed, to engage in the worship of the Holy One, Blessed be He. Covering himself with a large prayer shawl, Don Isaac would walk out in the balcony, feeling invigorated by the cool crisp air of the Sierra and its splendorous landscape. Opening his soul for guidance, seeking an answer from on high to his labyrinthine quandary below, the Chief Rabbi directed his prayers heavenward, yearning for the answer that was not yet his, endowing his entreaties with all the fervor at his command, pleading earnestly for the speedy salvation of his people. "May it be Thy will, O Lord our God and God of our Fathers, to save us today and every day from the brazen and the impudent, from evildoers and from evil impulses, from malicious friends and neighbors, from plague, from vileness of eye and tongue, from the painful decree and those who decree it, whether he be a son of the covenant, or not one of the covenant." These words, recited daily by Don Isaac as part of the opening prayer of *Shaharit*, gathered increasing relevance in light of the portents of the present. Abravanel prayed alone, a lonely shrouded figure in an isolated balcony, a solitary voice in the wilderness of Al-Andalus, a supplicating voice that unaided tried to accomplish for his people what they could not do for themselves. He prayed profoundly, losing himself in a trance of piety, hoping that his humbly offered prayers would be sufficient to save the day.

Don Abraham Senior did not believe in reverential retreats, viewing them as withdrawals from reality. Pushing his infirm body to its physical limits, the aged Jewish statesman roamed the hallways of the Alhambra, cornering one court official after another, urging them to speak favorably to the King and Queen concerning the Jews of the kingdom. If there was any hesitation, Senior discreetly slipped into the man's hand a

small bagful of ducats to help persuade the official. Yet for all his out-
lays of time and money, Don Abraham had not achieved his goal. Were
he to accomplish this, it would be a stunning and brilliant finish to
his role as a courtier. What he had not found in the legal archives of
Valladolid, he had found now in the corridors of this Moorish palace —
an opportunity beyond compare, an opportunity to stave off the
greatest threat ever hurled at Spanish Jewry, an opportunity to attain
historical greatness. It would be a feat that would bespeak the greatness
of his own personage. Only he, and no other, could hope to do so, if but
the rulers would grant him an audience.

It was in the midst of a rainstorm that Senior finally obtained his
audience. The waters had been tumbling from the skies, drenching the
palace complex with one torrential sheet after another, causing its many
fountains and pools to overflow. The brightness of day had given way to
a continuous damp, dark pelting, adding to Don Abraham's growing
sense of melancholy. Weary of waiting, plunged into despondency and
now into a wet darkness, the Supreme Judge had summoned all his
energies for one last assault: he *demanded* an audience with the King.
And when the courier returned to tell Don Abraham that the King had
agreed to his request, Senior knew that he had his opportunity.

Abraham Senior sat on a wooden bench in the corner of a large
poorly lit hall. A few candles burned, casting flickering shadows on the
wall. The loose window panes rattled from the incessant downpour.
Occasional bolts of lightning illumined the night sky beyond and
flashed into the hallway within, only to be promptly followed by the
associated claps of thunder. Senior sat alone — pensive, haggard-
looking, despondent. He looked sadly out into the bleakness of space,
glassy-eyed, his face worn heavy with his fourscore years of age. Ready
to face the present, he allowed himself to relish in his accomplishments,
savoring their sweet memory.

In his mind's eye, he remembered that wet dark night in Valladolid
when he had helped to arrange a secret rendezvous between Prince
Ferdinand with Princess Isabella. He remembered it all, even the pounding rain on that day, and the role that Jews and Conversos had played in
helping Ferdinand to win the hand of the Princess. He remembered how
a near penniless Ferdinand was forced to borrow twenty thousand
sueldos from the Converso Jaime Ram to pay for the expenses of the
royal entourage to Valladolid. He remembered how, on many occasions,
Don Isaac Abravanel and he had rescued the King and Queen from

financial ruin, granted them one interest-free loan after another, reorganized their tax structure, and supervised provision of supplies to the troops engaged in the Moorish campaign. He remembered how, at the outset of the war against the Moors, the rulers had forced all Jews out of Andalusia "for their own protection." Well, the war was over, and Jews were still not allowed to return to the south. Had the sovereigns lied to him? Had it all been one deliberate massive deception and he the unwitting fool? He had been lied to, yet for what reason?

If the expulsion of the Jews had taken place prior to the completion of the war, many Jews would have fled to the Moorish kingdom of Granada, strengthening the hand of the Islamic infidel. As a temporary measure, it was necessary for the rulers to transplant the Jews to an area far away from the war zone, not for their own protection as was claimed, but to make more difficult their defection to the Moorish enemy. Don Abraham Senior came to this conclusion after much thought. The expulsion of the Jews had been planned long ago. And he, trusted friend and aide of the sovereigns, had been made an unknowing accomplice in this devious scheme. That would no longer be possible. Mustering all the powers at his command, he swore to disrupt the royal plan, piece by piece, argument by argument, making sure it never came to fruition. Now, in this moment of opportunity, he would collect, he would demand payment of the personal debt due him by Ferdinand and Isabella. He would demand that they call off the expulsion.

In and out of the darkness, a figure loomed in the shadows, his footsteps smothered by the din of the downpour. He stood there silently for a while, watching. Suddenly, out of the blackness, Ferdinand's voice boomed out, "You asked to see me privately, Don Abraham, on a day such as this . . . Why?"

Senior, awakened from his reverie, looked up at the King. He got up from his chair, searching for the right words. "Oh, your Majesty, forgive me for disturbing you . . . but I must be allowed to speak to you this once."

"About what?," Ferdinand asked curtly.

Senior spoke firmly. "I wish to speak to you about that which troubles my heart in the hope that it will soften yours. I ask you to hear me out, to listen to the things I have to say."

"No!," said Ferdinand bluntly.

Senior persisted, "Your Majesty, I am your faithful servant. You know what I have done for you . . . all the many services through the years . . . from the very beginning."

Ferdinand replied, "Do not remind me of them. Your friends have reminded me enough."

Senior would not let go. "But, your Majesty . . ."

Ferdinand raised his voice. "You are too late, Don Abraham. Do not speak to me anymore about this . . . this matter is *closed*!"

The King turned his back on Senior and walked away. He strode the length of the hallway and disappeared again in the surrounding darkness.

Senior sat back on the bench — a beaten man, his body limp and drained. His one chance for glory was gone as quickly as it had come. It was all over. He was finished, the Jews were finished, finished with Spain as Spain was with them.

Isabella was immensely gratified that her husband had finally come around to her point of view. Perhaps he did so to disprove rumors of his partial Jewish origin. Perhaps it was because the Jews had not offered him enough gold to satisfy Ferdinand's greed. After all, the estimated value of the property of the Jews of the kingdom was close to 30,000,000 ducats. And the courtiers had offered him only a mere one percent of that. Whatever the reason was, Isabella did not press her husband for an explanation. She was content to have gained her way in the end.

It was at this time while she was basking in this serenity, confident of the rightness of her decision, that she was visited by her onetime confessor, Hernando de Talavera, now the Archbishop of Granada. The saintly priest was supervising a missionary campaign to convert the defeated Moors. He had long advocated that Church-sponsored conversion efforts be of a peaceful nature, and that force never be employed. Talavera had long questioned the methods of the Inquisition, and had strongly opposed its establishment in Castile. His protests, along with those of others within the clergy, represented a minority that could not withstand the well-organized campaign of Fray Tomás de Torquemada and his Dominican followers. Even now, Talavera struggled to protect the Moorish converts in his custody by declaring them exempt from Inquisitional investigation for a forty-year period.

Talavera showed the same qualities of love and simple piety that had once attracted Isabella so closely to him. He loved her dearly, despite her close attachment to Torquemada who had supplanted him as the Queen's confessor and had led this trusting creature of God astray. It was out of his love for her and for Spain that Archbishop Talavera saw the need to speak with his Queen.

"My dear Isabel, long has it been since I once spoke to you concerning your pursuit of virtue and abstention from vice. I remember warning you of unbecoming frivolities such as dancing at *fiestas*. As a Queen, you have come to shine above all others. And as a woman of Christian faith, there is not praise enough for your attempts to curb the moral laxities of the court. You have cultivated the qualities of chastity and purity both within yourself and within others. You have raised the banner of the Christian faith above the Alhambra castle to the greater glory of our Lord and all Christendom. And you have authorized me further to spread the word of the Evangel to the Moors of this kingdom of Granada, to bring them to the bosom of our Christian faith. Yet, my dear Isabel, as the Archbishop of this diocese, as your former confessor and as one who has known the innermost secrets of your heart and who loves you, I come here today to warn you that you are about to commit a mortal sin."

Isabella was taken aback. "Archbishop, how will I trespass? Teach me as you once did that I may serve my Church and my God. Tell me, Father, tell me what is this sin of which you speak?"

The Archbishop, putting his hand on her shoulder, said gently, "My daughter, the sin you are about to commit is the expulsion of the Jews."

"Oh, Father, how can it be so?," a fretful Isabella declared. "Fray Tomás tells me that what I am about to do is an act of great Christian faith. He tells me to combat the Mosaic heretics by all means possible. Indeed, I have sworn by our Lord that when the time came, I would drive all Jewish infidels out of the kingdom. If thus I have been made to swear, if I faithfully keep the word that I made to Fray Tomás in the name of our Lord, how can this be a sin?"

The Archbishop smiled in understanding at Isabella's plight. "My daughter Isabel, there are many ways to please the Lord. Some use the methods of fire, as does the Holy Office of the Inquisition. Others such as myself use the gentler waters of baptism, supported by the teaching of the Evangel. But, my dear Queen, the transgression I am referring to is not one of water or fire. It is not one of simple method. Rather the transgression lies in the human consequences of the action that you are taking. Remember, Isabella, you are not dealing with a single individual. You are dealing with an entire people. Yes, these Jews are unbelievers, but they are children of God nonetheless. And they are no ordinary people. They are of the stock of the patriarchs Abraham, Isaac, and Jacob of which our Lord was a part. If you maltreat this people, however great their blindness may be in not accepting our faith, if you cause them to suffer hardship, indeed, if so much as one Jew suffers or dies as a result of this expulsion, you must answer for this to God. Any harm that comes to these Jews, Isabella, if it occurs at all, will be by your hand, and by your hand alone. This is the sin which you may commit if you keep your vow to Fray Tomás de Torquemada."

"And if no Jew comes to harm?," asked Isabella anxiously. "If no Jew is hurt or killed as a result of the exile, what then?"

Archbishop Talavera answered, "Then, my Queen, you will have committed a great service for Spain. All generations will hold you forever grateful for your cleansing this Christian country of its unbelievers."

"Oh, Archbishop, verily you have brought confusion into my heart."

"And a good heart it is, my Queen. Yet my conscience bade me come here when I saw how you were risking your soul, yes, carelessly risking your soul in a deed that, it seemed to me, sinned greatly against heaven. Far be it from me to deprive you of an awareness of the danger to your Christian soul, my most Catholic Queen. And now, when I perceive that you had no idea of your spiritual peril, I am relieved that I came to warn you in time. Now I have discharged my duty to you, to my conscience, and to God Almighty."

"Archbishop Talavera, then you would have me undo my vow to the Grand Inquisitor?"

"That, my dear Isabel, is between you and Fray Tomás and God Himself. You, as regent, must decide what you will do. You alone will bear the burden of responsibility for what you do to any child of God who suffers through your acts. Isabel, I bid you good day. May Christ be in your heart and may peace reign in your soul."

Isabella kissed the priest's ring, and the Archbishop kissed her affectionately on the cheek like a daughter. The Archbishop walked out slowly, leaving Isabella to meditate his words. Taking his counsel to heart, Isabella for the first time began to question the advisability of the expulsion. Neither the practical appeals of the noblemen, nor the friendly advice of Beatrice de Bobadilla had shaken her as had the fearful prospect of losing her own soul. Unable to resolve the dilemma, she retreated to her chamber, her being frantic and agitated, as she struggled to come to terms with this unforeseen problem.

She searched nervously through the books in her devotional library, looking for the answer that would set everything straight again. She flipped the pages of a missal, scanned the lines of the *Imitation of Christ*, pushed aside an anthology of homilies, but did not find what she was looking for. It was all no use — not this set of books, nor any other. The answer was one that only she could provide. The answer, somewhere, somehow, was buried deep within herself, and she had now to search into her subconscious, to unearth the answer as to what it was she must do.

She went into the chapel to seek an answer and was joined in prayer by her handmaidens who knelt beside her in silent devotion. Underneath the statue of a crucified Jesus above the altar, the muted whisper of their gathered prayer was heard. After reciting a few opening prayers, Isabella tried to go beyond mere recitation. Isabella reached back to the time when she was a young girl with many questions and few answers. Yet somehow, in that faraway time, the answer had been planted. Somehow, the answer was given to her then and was made to grow with her as she matured in years. She needed to recall that moment of implantation. And she did.

It was when she was twelve years of age. The moment was not much unlike the present — the altar richly decorated, the lingering odor of incense in the air, she herself kneeling as now, with Torquemada at her side. Through the mist of her recollection, she felt his imposing presence on the other side of the semi-transparent cloth that covered the aperture in the wooden confessory. Humbly, Isabella began, "Forgive me, Father, for I have sinned. My last act of contrition was three weeks ago . . ."

Isabella then confessed to her venial sins, grateful her penance was only three Hail Marys. Isabella crossed herself and began to get up.

"Isabella?," Torquemada said.

"Yes, Father," answered Isabella attentively, returning to her knees.

The priest paused and said, "One day you will be Queen of Castile."

"Oh, Father, you forget Juana, my niece."

Torquemada repeated himself, "I say to you you will be Queen. And you will lead Castile in battle against the Moors."

"Father, truly I do not understand you."

Torquemada phrased his words carefully. "You are but a child now, and yet you are no ordinary child. You are a princess, and I say to you you will become Queen."

Bringing his head closer to the Princess, Torquemada said, "Isabella, listen carefully to what I have to tell you."

"Yes, Father," she answered respectfully.

Torquemada's tone suddenly became darker, "If Heaven wills that you be Queen of Castile, yours will be the task to uphold and defend our Catholic faith against unbelievers. I ask you now to swear before our Lord Jesus Christ that if God grants you the grace to be Queen, you will expel all the infidels — the Moors and the Jews — from the kingdom."

Isabella obeyed. "Yes, Father, I swear it. I swear that if I am ever Queen, I will fight against the Moors and expel the Jews."

The words reverberated in Isabella's ears, "I swear it . . . I shall expel the Moors and the Jews . . . I swear it . . . I shall expel the Jews . . . I shall expel them."

Those echoes from afar surfaced in her memory as she knelt now in her private altar, eyes closed, conscious of what she had sworn to do. She made the sign of the cross and arose slowly. She had her answer. "There is nothing more to consider. It is done. It is finished."

"Yes, your Highness," answered one of the handmaidens dutifully.

Isabella got up from the pew and walked away. She needed to see Torquemada immediately, and she summoned the Inquisitor to the chapel.

The words of the Archbishop were still fresh in her mind, yet she knew that fate had already committed her to a course of action that forced her to reject his words of caution. Too much of her being had been committed to the expulsion enterprise, and it was too late for her to change, too late to alter a resolve that had stayed with her for years. This doubt of hers was not enough to stop her from her deed. Yes, she would bring suffering to a great many people, but it was right for her, for Spain, and for God.

And as the Grand Inquisitor arrived to receive her confession, Isabella wondered whether she should confess to the deed or to her doubt. All she could confess with absolute honesty, she uttered in her opening sentence, "Forgive me, Father, for I have sinned . . ."

Chapter 8

Abravanel and Senior found little reason to hope. The King's refusal to hear out Don Abraham on that dark soggy night meant that the two monarchs had now reached a mutual accord to expel the Jews from the kingdom. Senior's many friends confirmed this because both the King and Queen would no longer listen to their entreaties. It was only a matter of time, a few days at the most, before a pronouncement would be forthcoming.

Sensing that the situation was worsening, Don Isaac and Don Abraham began to discuss alternative plans of action. If the expulsion were to take place, and there was every indication that it would soon occur, it was imperative that messengers be sent to the emissaries of various lands to see which lands were willing to accept Jews and on what conditions. Then they could discuss the number of vessels required to transport the exiles who wished to depart by sea. For those exiles who sought to leave on foot to neighboring countries such as, say, Provence and Portugal, routes with aid stations along the way would have to be set up. And then, of course, there would be a need to purchase two-wheeled carts by the thousands to transport the exiles' belongings. Both Abravanel and Senior had experience in such matters as supervisors of supply transport for the warring Christian armies. They now had cause to put their experience to good use. Now, as before, they used their individual contacts to make the necessary preliminary preparations. That they forced themselves to think about such matters, both large and small, matters that as of one month ago would have bordered on the unthinkable, was an indication of the seriousness with which they perceived their imminent peril. The time of disaster was closing in, and there was nothing they could do to stop it.

It was in the midst of this crisis that Don Isaac's wife, Esther, came to visit him in Granada. He was delighted to see her. They embraced and kissed each other as if they were young lovers long separated from one another. In this moment of tenderness, Don Isaac felt their love for one another was the most precious of his possessions. Whatever Spain would take from him — wealth, property, or books — this was something that could not be taken away. Their love could withstand anything.

"My dear Esther, my heart could know no greater joy than to see your lovely face again. How good it is to see you again, *querida*."

"Oh, Isaac, forgive me, I wish not to interfere with your responsibilities at court, but I missed you. I missed you terribly. When you left us suddenly at Passover even with our sons in the house, it was not the same. Your astronomer friend, Abraham Zacuto, began to tell me about all the bad omens that he had seen in this year's forecast of the stars. What awful nonsense he said, but it frightened me nonetheless. And then, when you were summoned by the King and Queen, I thought of what had happened to you and the Braganzas in Portugal and of how you had narrowly missed coming to harm. The thought that it might happen here, too, left me sleepless for nights. Zacuto's warnings, the courier's disturbing message, brought dread into my heart.

"And when our sons all left, I knew that I had no choice but to be at your side. With my two assistants, I have come here to Granada to be next to the man I love."

Abravanel spoke tenderly. "My dear Esther, as it was God's will to send me forth on a Passover mission on behalf of our people, so it has been God's will to send you here to me. As birds have wings, so, too, angels know the mysteries of flight. Let me kiss you, my dove, my angel with wings from heaven." They kissed each other once again.

Don Isaac and his wife walked through the city together. Descending through the Gate of Justice, and then down through a trail lined by elms and myrtles, they came upon the stone houses of Granada. Through the narrow streets, the handsome Moors walked to and fro, creating a hectic bustle of activity. Artisans — weavers, shoemakers, potterers, and the like — displayed their wares outside their shops. Fruits, pastries, and sundry meat dishes were on sale. Colorful carpets hung from overhanging posts. Trinkets of all kinds were sold by loud barefoot children at each street corner. The plaintive wail of the *muezzin*, and the exotic sound of the Moorish oboe added to the chorus of street noise.

Merchants from the aristocratic families of Al Andalus rode through the streets on Arabian steeds. Christian cavaliers could also be seen going from one shop to another, buying trinkets and carpets and other wares to take back home. The Christian presence was much resented by the local Moors, and many rebellious incidents had taken place. To avoid trouble, Don Isaac took along a native guide as their interpreter. It was at times like these that Don Isaac wished that he knew Arabic. It troubled him that he, an admirer of Arab philosophy, a student of the great Averroes, would be regarded by the local populace as a detested outsider, as an affiliate of the barbaric Christian conqueror. There was no time to explain that he was not one of them, that he was an outsider even to the Christian outsiders themselves. What little time he did have, he spent with his wife in enjoying the many sights of the city.

Before nightfall they returned to the palace to celebrate the coming of the Sabbath. Upon their arrival, a royal summons was delivered to Don Isaac Abravanel to appear the following day at noon in the Hall of the Ambassadors. He put the summons away. He wanted to enjoy the Sabbath without interference from the affairs of the world. He wanted to enjoy the day of rest, to sing the songs of Sabbath peace with his loving wife, but he had a premonition that this joy would be shortlived.

The Hall of the Ambassadors was full. Aristocratic courtiers, scribes, priests, and armed guards walked about. Others were seated on benches admiring the intricately carved walls and the vaulted ceiling of this palatial chamber. Light streamed in through the upper layer of windows illuminating the throne area. On the back wall, above the two centrally placed chairs, were the outstretched flags of Castile and Aragon. It was unclear to those in attendance what was the purpose of this assembly. It was clear, however, that something important was about to happen.

After reciting morning prayers, Don Isaac Abravanel walked toward the Hall with Esther. When Isaac had told her the previous day of the possible expulsion order, she expressed disbelief, then anger, and now was resigned to it. She knew only too well when her husband was disturbed, and she wished that she could find the words to lessen his apprehension.

"Oh, Isaac, I see the worry in your eyes. It pains me to see you this way. Have faith, darling, have faith . . . perhaps our greatest fears will not come to be."

Abravanel replied, "In faith I am not lacking, beloved. It is the faith of others that I have come to distrust. Wait for me here . . . I shall not be long."

Esther squeezed her husband's hand tenderly, "Isaac, be careful."

Don Isaac smiled lovingly and walked away. As her husband entered the Hall of the Ambassadors, Esther walked to the adjacent court.

When Abravanel entered the Hall, he went over to Don Abraham Senior.

"Good day, Don Abraham," said Abravanel. So worried was Senior, that he did not even reply.

A court crier came to the center of the throne area and addressed the crowd, "Order in the Court! Their Majesties Ferdinand and Isabella, by the grace of God, King and Queen of Castile and Aragon."

Everyone rose as the sovereigns made their entrance. Wearing embroidered cloaks and jeweled gold crowns, Ferdinand and Isabella walked to their thrones and seated themselves. Tomás de Torquemada, the Grand Inquisitor, stood next to Isabella.

The crier announced, "Everyone, please be seated." Everyone sat down. The crier continued, "The crown calls forward Don Abraham Senior and Don Isaac Abravanel."

"This is it, Isaac," whispered Senior. "Oh my God, this is it."

Abravanel and Senior rose from their bench and walked toward the throne area. Senior bowed and said respectfully, "At your service, your Majesties." Abravanel also bowed.

Ferdinand spoke. "The Queen and I have reached a decision, Don Abraham Senior and Don Isaac Abravanel. Let the edict be read."

A reader with a scroll stepped forward, stood directly in front of the two Jewish courtiers, and proceeded to read.

"Don Ferdinand and Doña Isabella, by the grace of God, King and Queen of Castile, Leon, Aragon, and other dominions of the crown — to the prince Don Juan, to dukes, marquees, counts, the Holy Orders, priors, knight commanders, lords of the castles, cavaliers, and to all the people of the towns and places and cities of our territories, and to all the Jews, men and women of whatever age, and to anyone else this letter may concern — health and grace unto you.

"You well know that in our dominions, there are certain bad Christians that judaized and committed apostasy against our Holy Catholic faith, much of it the cause of communication between Jews and Christians. Therefore, in the year 1480, we ordered that the Jews be separated from the cities and towns of our domains and that they be given separate quarters, hoping that by such separation the situation would be remedied. And we ordered that an Inquisition be established in such domains; and in the twelve years that it has functioned, the Inquisition has found many guilty persons. Furthermore, we are informed by the Inquisitors and others that the great harm done to the Christians persists, and it continues because of the conversation and communication that they have with Jews, such Jews trying by whatever manner to subvert our holy Catholic faith and trying to draw faithful Christians away from their beliefs.

"These Jews instruct these Christians in the ceremonies and observances of their Law, circumcising their children, and giving them books with which to pray, and declaring unto them the days of fasting, and meeting with them to teach them the histories of their Law, notifying them when to expect Passover and how to observe it, giving them the unleavened bread and ceremonially prepared meats, and instructing them in the things from which they should abstain, both with regard to food items and other things requiring observance of their Law of Moses, making them to understand that there is no other law or truth besides it. All of which then is clear that, on the basis of confessions from such Jews as well as those perverted by them, that it has resulted in great damage and detriment to our holy Catholic faith.

"And because we knew that the true remedy of such damages and difficulties lay in the severing of all communication between the said Jews with the Christians and in sending them forth from all our reigns, we sought to content ourselves with ordering the said Jews from all the cities and villages and places of Andalusia where it appeared that they had done major damage, believing that this would suffice so that those from other cities and villages and places in our reigns and holdings would cease to commit the aforesaid. And because we have been informed that neither this, nor the justices done for some of the said Jews found very culpable in the said crimes and transgressions against our holy Catholic faith, has been a complete remedy to obviate and to correct such opprobrium and offense to the Christian faith and religion; because every day it appears that the said Jews increase in continuing their evil and harmful purposes wherever they reside and converse; and because there is no place left whereby to more offend our holy faith, as much as those which God has protected to this day as in those already affected, it is left for this Holy Mother Church to mend and reduce the matter to its previous state inasmuch as, because of our frailty of humanity, it could occur that we could succumb to the diabolical temptation that continually wars against us so easily if its principal cause were not removed, which would be to expel the said Jews from the kingdom. Because whenever a grave and detestable crime is committed by some members of a given group, it is reasonable that the group be dissolved or annihilated, the minors for the majors being punished one for the other; and that those who pervert the good and honest living in the cities and villages and who by their contagion could harm the others, be expelled from amidst the people, still yet for other minor causes that would be of harm to the Republic, and all the more so for the major of these crimes, dangerous and contagious as it is.

"Therefore, with the counsel and advice of the eminent men and cavaliers of our reign, and of other persons of knowledge and conscience of our Supreme Council, after much deliberation, it is agreed and resolved that all Jews and Jewesses be ordered to leave our kingdoms, and that they never be allowed to return."

There was a great commotion in the chamber. "The Jews are going to be expelled!" The phrase was on everyone's lips, being repeated by one and all as if to assure themselves that they had indeed heard correctly. Against the backdrop of such whispered tumult, Don Abraham Senior and Don Issac Abravanel remained at attention, their bodies erect and unbudging, impervious it so seemed to the flood that rocked the room.

The tumult continued. "Order! Order in the Court!," shouted the crier.

Esther Abravanel, seated quietly on a bench outside the hall, heard the roar from within. She saw an excited cavalier emerge from the hall and start to speak to one of the guards. She overheard the conversation.

"Listen, Pedro," said the cavalier, "You will not believe what is going on inside."

The guard offhandedly asked, "Oh . . . what could that be?"

The cavalier said, "They are going to expel the Jews . . . every single last one of them."

"What! I do not believe you!"

The cavalier shot back. "You do not believe me, you son of a Moor? Step inside. They are reading the edict this very moment."

Esther walked up quickly behind the distracted guards and slipped into the rear of the Hall of the Ambassadors. She moved slowly down the side of a huge Moorish arch, her back to the wall, until she was safely out of their view. From her vantage point she could see what was happening. She could see her husband and Don Abraham standing in front of the King and Queen. It was happening after all, Esther thought to herself, and she whispered '*Shema Yisrael*' under her breath, as the reader continued to recite the edict.

"And we further order in this edict that all Jews and Jewesses of whatever age that reside in our domains and territories, that they leave with their sons and daughters, their servants and their relatives, large and small, of whatever age, by the end of July of this year, and that they dare not return to our lands, not so much as to take a step on them nor trespass upon them in any other manner whatsoever. Any Jew who does not comply with this edict and is to be found in our kingdoms and domains, or who returns to the kingdom in any manner, will incur punishment by death and confiscation of all their belongings.

"We further order that no person in our kingdom of whatever station or noble status dare to hide or keep or defend any Jew or Jewess, either publicly or secretly, from the end of July onwards, in their homes or elsewhere in our reign, upon punishment of loss of their belongings, vassals, fortresses, and hereditary privileges.

"And so that the said Jews may dispose of their household and belongings in the given time period, for the present we provide our assurance of royal protection and security so that, until the end of the month of July, they may sell and exchange their belongings and furniture and other items, and to dispose of them freely as they wish; and that during said time, no one is to do them harm or injury or injustice to their persons or to their goods, which is contrary to justice, and which shall incur the punishment that befalls those who violate our offer of royal security.

"Thus we grant permission to the said Jews and Jewesses to take out their goods and belongings out of our reigns, by either sea or by land, with the condition that they not take out either gold or silver or minted money or any other items prohibited by the laws of the kingdom.

"Therefore, we order all councilors, justices, magistrates, cavaliers, shield-bearers, officials, good men of the city of Burgos and of the other cities and villages of our reigns and dominions, and all of our vassals and subjects, that they observe and comply with this letter and all that is contained in it, and that they give all the help and favor that is necessary for its execution, subject to punishment by our sovereign grace and by confiscation of all their goods and offices for our royal statehouse.

"And so that this may come to the notice of all, and so that no one may pretend ignorance, we order that this edict be proclaimed in all the plazas and usual meeting places of any given city; and that in the major cities and villages of the diocese, that it be done by the town crier in the presence of a public scribe. And that neither one nor the other should do the contrary of what was desired, subject to punishment by our sovereign grace and by deprivation of their offices and by confiscation of their goods to whosoever does the contrary. And we further order that evidence be provided to the court, in the manner of signed testimony, regarding the manner in which this edict is being carried out.

"Given in this city of Granada on the thirty first day of March in the year of our Lord Jesus Christ — 1492.

"Signed, I, the King, I, the Queen, I, Juan de Coloma, Secretary of the King and Queen, which I have written by order of our Majesties."

The reader rolled up the scroll, bowed deferentially toward the throne, and stepped aside. There was complete silence in the courtroom. The two Jewish courtiers standing at attention were expressionless. The two pillars of Spanish Jewry, Senior and Abravanel, would not add to their nation's humiliation by debasing themselves at this time through a disgraceful exhibition of whining pleas for mercy. The time for such entreaties had long since past. And the two proud statesmen, mindful of the burden of responsibility that they bore, now had to deal with the disaster of the moment.

The Grand Inquisitor Torquemada stood next to the Queen with a look of triumphant satisfaction. The Queen seemed the human counterpart of the edict itself, harsh and unmerciful. Alongside the Queen sat Ferdinand, cool and indifferent. He calmly addressed the Jewish courtiers standing before him.

"Inasmuch as both of you are the heads of the Jewish community, I am sure that you wish to say something concerning this matter. One of you will be allowed to speak freely for the last time, without any restriction or limitation. It will be the only argument to be heard, and then the matter will be closed. Which of you wishes to do so?"

Senior turned towards Abravanel.

"Isaac, you speak. I have done what I could behind the scenes. There is nothing more that I can do. Now it is up to you, Isaac, to speak for all of us."

Before Abravanel had an opportunity to answer, Senior turned promptly towards the King and Queen, loudly proclaiming, "Your

Majesties, Don Isaac Abravanel will speak on behalf of all the Jewish communities of Spain." Without further ado, Senior removed himself from public view and sat quietly in a nearby chair.

All eyes were on Don Isaac Abravanel. The Jewish statesman turned to face his audience. His light brown eyes penetrated through his onlookers, his bearded visage was fierce and prophet-like.

Abravanel began to talk. "Your Majesties, Don Abraham Senior and I thank you for this opportunity to make one last statement on behalf of the Jewish communities that we represent. Counts, dukes, and marquees of the court, cavaliers and ladies . . . it is no great honor when a Jew is asked to plead for the safety of his people.

"But it is a greater disgrace when the King and Queen of Castile and Aragon, indeed of all Spain, have to seek their glory in the expulsion of a harmless people."

There was an angry shout. "Is there no end to these insults to our King and Queen. I say . . . Enough! Out with these damn Jews!"

Don Isaac Abravanel whirled about furiously to face the sovereigns. His eyes raged with a fiery incandescence. He advanced toward the King and Queen and gazed at them contemptuously.

Don Isaac sternly informed the rulers, "I will not tolerate any interruption. Do I or do I not have complete freedom to say what I please?"

Isabella answered him spitefully, "You may say what you please, Don Isaac, if you think it will make a difference."

Ferdinand said to Abravanel, "And you, Don Isaac Abravanel, finish what you have to say."

Don Isaac Abravanel felt new strength enter his body. A newfound power had overtaken him, investing him with the feeling of righteous invincibility. As a lion in the jungle, as an incontestable prophet in the wilderness, he felt more than a match for his opponents. Girding his loins, steeling his voice, he went forth with his slingshot of words to slay the Spanish Goliath.

Abravanel spoke. "I find it very difficult to understand how every Jewish man, woman, and child can be a threat to the Catholic faith. *Very, very* strong charges.

"*We* destroy *you*?

"It is indeed the very opposite. Did you not admit in this edict to having confined all Jews to restricted quarters and to having limited our legal and social privileges, not to mention forcing us to wear shameful badges? Did you not tax us oppressively? Did you not terrorize us day and night with your diabolical Inquisition? Let me make this matter perfectly clear to all present: I will not allow the voice of Israel to be stilled on this day.

"Hear, O heavens, and give ear, King and Queen of Spain, for I, Don Isaac Abravanel, speak unto you. I and my family are descended directly from King David. *True* royal blood, the blood of the Messiah, runs in my veins. It is my inheritance, and I proclaim it now in the name of the God of Israel.

"On behalf of my people, the people of Israel, the chosen of God, I declare them blameless and innocent of all crimes declared in this edict of abomination. The crime, the transgression, is for *you*, not us, to bear. The unrighteous decree you proclaim today will be your downfall. And this year, which you imagine to be the year of Spain's greatest glory, will become the year of Spain's greatest shame.

"As honor is the reward of individual virtue, so too the worldly renown of kings and queens is their proper due for noble deeds. So, too, when unseemly acts are committed by an individual, that person's reputation suffers. And when kings and queens commit shameful deeds, they do themselves great harm. As it is said, the greater the person who errs, the greater the error.

"Errors, if recognized early, can be corrected. The loosened brick that supports the structure can be reinserted into position. So, too, a mistaken edict if caught in time can be undone. But religious zeal has undermined reason, and misguided counsel has perverted sound judgment. The error of the edict will soon become irreversible as the very deed which it proclaims. Yes, my king and queen, hear me well: *error*, your error, profound and uncorrectable, the likes of which Spain has never seen before. You and you alone are responsible.

"As arms measure the might of a nation, so arts and letters measure its finer sensibilities. Yes, you have humbled the Moslem infidel with the force of your army, proving yourselves able in the art of war. But what of your inner state of mind? By what right do your Inquisitors go about the countryside burning books by the thousands in public bonfires? By what authority do churchmen now want to burn the immense Arabic library of this great Moorish palace and destroy its priceless manuscripts? By whose right? By whose authority? Why, it is by your authority, my king and queen.

"In your heart of hearts, you distrust the power of knowledge, and you respect only power. With us Jews it is different. We Jews cherish knowledge immensely. In our homes and in our prayerhouses, learning is a lifelong pursuit. Learning is our lifelong passion; it is at the core of our being; it is the reason, according to our sages, for which we were created. Our fierce love of learning could have counterbalanced your excessive love of might. We could have benefited from the protection offered by your royal arms, and you could have profited the more from our community's advancement and exchange of knowledge. I say to you we could have helped each other.

"As we are reminded of our own powerlessness, so your own nation will suffer from the forces of disequilibrium that you have set in motion. For centuries to come, your descendants will pay dearly for your mistake of the present. As it is might of arms you most admire, you shall verily become a nation of conquerors — lusting after gold and spoils, living by the sword and ruling with a fist of mail. Yet you shall become a nation of illiterates; your institutions of learning, fearing the heretical contamination of alien ideas from other lands and other peoples, will no longer be respected. In the course of time, the once great name of Spain will become a whispered byword among the nations: Spain, the poor ignorant has-been; Spain, the nation which showed so much promise and yet which accomplished so little.

"And then one day Spain will ask itself: what has become of us? Why are we a laughing-stock among the nations? And the Spaniards of that day will look into their past and ask themselves why this came to be. And those who are honest will point to this day and age as the time when their fall as a nation began. And the cause of their downfall will be shown to be none other than their revered Catholic sovereigns, Ferdinand and Isabella, conquerors of the Moors, expellers of the Jews, founders of the Inquisition, and destroyers of the inquiring Spanish mind.

"This edict is a testimony to Christian weakness. It shows that we Jews are capable of winning the centuries-old argument between the two faiths. It explains why there are 'false Christians,' that is, Christians whose faith has been shaken by the arguments advanced by the Jew who knows better.

"It explains why the Christian nation would be as injured as it claims to be. Desiring to silence Jewish opposition, the Christian majority has decided not to argue further, but rather to eliminate the source of dangerous counter argument. The opportunity to the Jews is not to be granted after today.

"This is the last opportunity on Spanish soil to state our case. In these last few moments of freedom granted to me by the King and Queen, I, as the last spokesman of Spanish Jewry, will dwell only on one point of theological dispute. I will leave you with a parting message, although you will like it not.

"The message is simple. The historic people of Israel, as it has traditionally constituted itself, is the final judge of Jesus and his claims to be the Messiah. As the Messiah was destined to save Israel, so it must be for Israel to decide when it has been saved. Our answer, the only answer that matters, is that Jesus was a false Messiah. As long as the people of Israel lives, as long as Jesus' own people continue to reject him, your religion can never be validated as true. You can convert all the peoples and savages of the world, but as long as you have not converted the Jew, you have proved nothing except that you can persuade the uninformed.

"We leave with this comforting knowledge. For although you have the power, we have the higher truth. Although you can dispose of our persons, you cannot dispose of our sacred souls and the historical truth to which only we bear witness.

"Listen, King and Queen of Spain, for on this day you have joined the list of evil-doers against the remnant of the House of Israel. If you seek to destroy us, your wishes will come to nought, for greater and more powerful rulers have tried to finish with us, and all have failed. Indeed, we shall prosper in other lands far from here. For wherever we go, the God of Israel is with us. And as for you, Don Ferdinand and Doña Isabella, God's hand will reach out and punish the arrogance in your heart.

"*Woe unto you*, authors of iniquity. For generations to come, it will be told and retold how unkind was your faith and how blind was your vision. But more than your acts of hatred and of fanaticism, the courage of the people of Israel will be remembered for standing up to the might of imperial Spain, clinging to the religious inheritance of our fathers, resisting your enticements and your untruths.

"Expel us, drive us from this land that we cherish no less than you do.

"But we shall remember you, King and Queen of Spain, as our Holy Books remember those who sought our harm. We Jews shall haunt your accomplishments on the pages of history . . . and the memories of our sufferings will inflict greater damage upon your name than anything you can ever hope to do to us.

"We shall remember you and your vile Edict of Expulsion *forever.*"

Don Isaac Abravanel turned and strode out of the hall. As he made his dramatic exit, the crowd made way for him. At the far end stood his wife Esther waiting for him, tears in her eyes, glowing with pride in her husband. Esther smiled, came up quickly to join him, and took him by the hand. They walked out man and wife, Jew and Jewess, unbeaten and unbowed. As they left, bedlam once again erupted in the hall. Goliath, if but for a moment, had fallen.

The decree was proclaimed throughout Spain. In every city and village, in every public square and meeting place, the Edict was read aloud to the local citizenry. The Edict sent each *judería* into a state of panic. Incredulous at first, the Jews then despaired.

In Segovia, as in other cities of the kingdom, the announcement of the Edict came near the end of Passover. Those who heard the Edict in the main plaza of Segovia ran through the *judería*, shouting out the frightful tidings at every door. Elderly women pulled the scarves off their heads and tore out their hair. Young and old alike buried their heads in their hands, unsure of what the future held for them and their families. In a sudden rush, the *judería's* huddled populace flooded the narrow cobblestone streets, a mass of screaming people, cursing the King and the Queen, hugging their children, embracing one another, asking God's help in this time of despair.

Rabbi Maimi, the chief rabbi of the city, was greatly troubled. The rabbi knew that he would have to act fast to prevent the hysterical crowd from getting out of control. Realizing what he had to do, he ran to get a Bible, and then stood on a platform.

"Señores and señoras, listen to me," the rabbi exclaimed. "Listen to me, listen to the words of the prophet Isaiah."

People pointed to the rabbi, and the din in the street subsided as Rabbi Maimi began to intone the prophetic passage: Isaiah 41:8-14:
"But thou, Israel, My Servant,
Jacob whom I have chosen,
The seed of Abraham My friend;
Thou whom I have taken hold of
    from the ends of the earth,
And called thee from the uttermost parts thereof,
And said unto thee: 'Thou art My servant,
I have chosen thee and not cast thee away;
Fear thou not, for I am with thee,
Be not dismayed, for I am thy God;
I strengthen thee, yea, I help thee,
Yea, I uphold thee with My victorious right hand.
Behold, all they that were incensed against thee

Shall be ashamed and confounded;
They that strove with thee
Shall be as nothing, and shall perish.
Thou shalt seek them, and shalt not find them,
Even them that contended with thee;
They that warred against thee
Shall be as nothing, and as a thing of nought.
For I the Lord thy God
Hold thy right hand,
Who say unto thee: 'Fear not, I help thee.'
Fear not, thou worm, Jacob,
And ye men of Israel,
I help thee, saith the Lord,
Thy Redeemer, the Holy One of Israel."

The rabbi looked up from the bible and addressed the attentive crowd.

"Señores and señoras, the Holy One of Israel, Blessed be He, is with us today. As He has promised, so He shall fulfill. The Holy Presence, the *Shehinah*, is ever ready to receive our supplications if we will bend our hearts toward Him in full repentance for our sins. If the God of Israel is to listen to our plea for help, we must first purify our souls. Only then can we ask the God of Israel to intervene on our behalf so that this evil decree may be averted.

"As the chief rabbi of Segovia, I hereby proclaim a fast day. I proclaim a day of prayer for every Jew of Bar Mitzvah age or older, both men and women alike, with the exception of pregnant women and the sick. Everyone is to join us now in the synagogue for the penitential prayers. Join us now, my brothers and sisters, that we may bring about our own redemption."

In response to the rabbi's words, people streamed into the synagogue until it was packed to capacity. Prayer books containing the order of service for a fast day were pulled out and distributed to those in attendance. The prayers began: "God, save us! Our King, answer us this day that we call upon Thee!" The elderly prostrated themselves on the ground, tearing their clothes, wearing sackcloth and covering themselves with earth from the fields. "Forgive us, our Father, because in our thoughtlessness we have sinned! Pardon us, O King, because great are our sins, O God, who art most forgiving and compassionate, the giver of all mercies." The community self-affliction continued throughout the day and night. Despite the structured order of the service, the agonizing cries of the congregants pierced the air; the torment of these individuals was too great to be contained in the fixed ritual of the fast day. On and on it went, prayers and pleas, cries and implorements, the recurring beseechment repeated again and again: "God, save us! Our King, answer us this day that we call upon Thee. Answer us, O Lord, answer us!," was the endless phrase on everyone's lips. It was recited with such fervor that it seemed an answer from on high must be forthcoming. "*Anenu*! Answer us, O King, in this day that we call upon Thee!"

Rabbi Maimi was swept up by the zeal of his congregants. Swaying his body from side to side, he seemed caught up in the gathering swoon. The entire synagogue shook from the rafters above to the floor under his feet. "God, save us! answer us, have mercy upon us, O King, spare us and save us for thou, O God, art a merciful and gracious King," pleaded the rabbi ardently, adding his voice to the thundering chorus about him. The window panes rattled from the intensity of the community cry. Their prayers now became as one, forged into a tool of supplication before the divine tribunal, shaking the very gates of heaven.

The children of the synagogue gathered around Rabbi Maimi. Taking a large white prayer shawl, the rabbi made a canopy, supported by his outstretched arms, to hold above himself and the children. As he looked upon these lambs, their faces shining with innocence, the rabbi felt that if heavenly aid were to be forthcoming, surely it would be on account of these very angels in their midst.

The assembled mass began a new lament. "If not for our sake, O Lord, then on account of our young babes who have never sinned." The rabbi watched intensely the faces of these children, their strained tender faces wrought with apprehension, as their mounted prayers ascended unto the Holy One of Israel.

Then the entire congregation intoned the words of the evening prayer.

This completed, Rabbi Maimi addressed his congregation. What could he say that would allay their fears? What hopes could he give them?

"If we have sinned, we have begged tonight the God of Israel for His forgiveness. And we hope that our prayers will be accepted. If we have erred, we ask for His divine correction. Yet we must blame not only ourselves for the calamity that has befallen us.

"The Edict accuses us of helping our Converso brothers to remain Jewish. That is our so-called crime. If this is why we are being expelled, then we need not fear. To help our brethren is not a crime; it is rather our God-given duty. It is our duty to bring our wayward Jewish brothers and sisters back to a knowledge of the ways of the Torah. If this threatened disaster is now upon us, it is not because we Jews have done wrong, but because the Christians have decided to commit evil.

"In this hour, the forces of darkness are gathered against us. Consumed with hatred of Jews, the Christians raise their hand against God's chosen, the holy people of Israel. Has not the prophet Isaiah said, 'No weapon that is formed against thee shall prosper, and every tongue that shall rise against thee in judgment thou shalt condemn.' Is it not so, my brothers and sisters? Truly it is not *we* who are being judged. Rather it is Spain that is being judged by enacting the Edict.

"But what does the Edict mean to us? Perhaps it is to remind us that our real place is elsewhere, that we have forgotten our destiny in Zion. The poet Yehuda Halevy once said, 'I am in the farthermost west, but my heart is in the east.' His heart was in the east. Rabbi Halevy longed for Zion, he longed for the Holy Land. Can we say the same? Do we still long for Zion, do we still yearn to see the Temple Mount in Jerusalem? Our roots in Spain, strong and deep as they may be, led us to falsely believe that we could regard this land as our home. We have erred. Because life was good to us in Spain, we came to forget the land of our fathers. We forgot the promised land of milk and honey. As we recite each year in Passover, so now this Edict reminds us where we belong . . . not in Spain . . . but in Zion . . . '*Next year in Jerusalem*!' "

The rabbi and the congregation returned to their prayers. As the night continued some worshippers went home to sleep, and by sunrise only a determined few were still present. Their eyes were red and bleary from hours of sleeplessness. Putting on their phylacteries, they finished their ritual morning prayers. Only then did they make their way home to rest.

Sarah Maimi waited for her husband at the doorstep of their home. Her mind was restless with worry. The thought that she would soon leave her home, leave Segovia, leave Spain, leave all that she had ever known troubled her. She waited anxiously for her husband, wanting to hear what he had to say. She knew that he would not hide anything from her. He would not give her a comforting sermon as he had given the congregation. He would tell her the truth, the cold hard truth, and nothing else. That was what she wanted to hear.

The rabbi arrived, weak from the fasting and prayer. He could barely keep his eyes open. Walking slowly to a cushion, he collapsed with a moan of relief. He was utterly exhausted.

"Simon, I know how tired you are after last night. The fast is still in effect, and so I cannot offer you either food or drink. Rest, my darling, we will speak after you have rested."

The rabbi opened his eyes slowly and looked deeply into her eyes. It was obvious that she too, tired as she was, wanted to speak.

"What is it, my beloved? Worried about the Edict?," asked the rabbi. Sarah Maimi nodded. She took a blanket and covered her husband. "Rest, my darling, you are tired. We will speak afterwards."

"We will talk now, Sarah. You want to hear about the Edict and what I think of it?"

"Yes, I do not want you to tell me what you told the congregation; I want you to tell me what you did not wish to tell them. I want to hear *all* the truth that you left out."

"All the truth?," the rabbi half-chuckled. "My dear, am I a prophet that I have knowledge of the future? What I know, you already know . . . at least from an official standpoint. Don Abraham Senior will be returning soon to Segovia, and he will surely give us more details. But if you ask me what I *feel* will happen, that perhaps I can tell you."

"Then, Simon, please tell me what you *feel* will happen," said Sarah.

The rabbi stroked his beard with his fingers and looked at his wife with a studious gaze, as if gauging how much of the truth she could bear. He sighed deeply once again, as if unsure how to best communicate his feelings.

"Sarah, let me tell you a story.

"About one hundred and fifty years ago, there was a Jewish official of the Castilian crown by the name of Don Samuel HaLevi. This Don Samuel was sent on a mission to a distant king somewhere in central Europe. The Jew presented himself to the foreign king as his mission required. The people, however, in the nearby village heard that there was a Jew in the fortress. These outraged Christian villagers, who had never seen a Jew before, came to the fortress and demanded that the king turn over the Jew to them. 'Our lord, we want to see the Jew, because we have heard that he is unlike any other human.' Of course, most of them still believed that Jews had horns and a tail.

"The king realized, however, that if he showed the Jew to the mob, the ruffians would kill him and stone him. So he warned them, 'Do you dare be so insolent as to presume that I do not know the evil intent in your hearts? Do you not ask for the Jew only because you intend to do him harm? Return, all of you, unto your homes. I will not bring out the Jew for you to see.'

"The villagers, upset at the king's refusal, returned to their homes.

The following day, however, the angry villagers returned to the fortress in even greater numbers. They demanded of the king once again, 'Where is the Jew that is with you? Bring him out that we may see him.'

The king came out suddenly a second time, and told the villagers, 'I beg of you, my subjects, not to do evil.' But the villagers paid him no heed, and the king was very upset that they would not listen to him.

"When Don Samuel HaLevi saw how taken aback the king was about being unable to control the mob of villagers, he was terrified for his life. Yet he had to do something. So Don Samuel came unto the king and told him thus, 'My king, go now unto the people and tell them that tomorrow you shall do as they request. Do not fear, I will advise you on all that you should do.'

"And the king went out again and told the villagers that tomorrow they would be able to see the Jew. Throughout the village that day, the people rejoiced. And they said one to another, 'Tomorrow we shall see a new type of creature, the devil-Jew. Tomorrow we shall see the creature that killed our Lord Jesus, and as the Jew did unto our Lord, so we shall do unto him.'

"So it was that Don Samuel HaLevi told the king to bring him an old goat from the field. The goat, he said, must be big, it must have a beard, two horns, and a tail. The king was surprised at this unusual request but did it anyway.

"The following day, all the people in the city came to the fortress. Everyone was there to see the creature called the Jew. Don Samuel advised the king thus, 'Tell the people now, behold, I will show you the Jew. Stand, all of you, in the midst of my courtyard below, and I will order the Jew to show his face through that window that you see above.' The crowd was happy to hear these words from the king, and they all gathered in the courtyard below.

"So this is what happened then: Don Samuel took a prayer shawl, a *tallit*, and wrapped it around the goat's head. Then he took the square box of the phylacteries, the *teffillin*, and put it on the goat's forehead. Afterwards, he took the goat to the window and thrust the goat's head through the window for all to see.

"The people in the courtyard were astonished at what they saw. They said to one another, 'Look! Look at him. The Jew's beard is like that of a goat. His ugly face is deformed and unlike that of any other human.' Upon seeing such a creature, the people went wild. They started cursing the Jew viciously: 'Come out! Come out, you bloody murdering Jew! You who have spilled the blood of our Lord, come out! Come out and die for your evil, you murderer!' The Christians were screaming for the Jew's blood, the old and the young, the women and the children alike. And the king, pretending that he had no choice, released the goat quickly into the crowd.

"The crowd grabbed the goat and began to tear it to pieces. They smashed its head with a large stone. Some kicked it. Others stabbed at it with knives and with axes. One after another threw stones at its deformed head, until the goat was buried under a heap of stones. And the outraged villagers, satisfied that they had done their Christian duty, now went peacefully each of them to their homes, and they left the king alone."

"Don Samuel HaLevi, of course, escaped. I hear that he used to tell the story of his experience many, many times. In any case, Sarah, you asked me what I felt was going to happen to us. I shall tell you.

"What is going to happen to us is what happened to Don Samuel HaLevi. This time the king will not be sending forth a goat. This time it is the real Jew who will be cast out into the hand of the angry mob. Sarah, I must tell you what I feel. I believe that it is but a short while before we too will be torn from limb to limb. That is what I *feel* will happen."

Sarah Maimi sat paralyzed. She stayed that way for some time, seemingly frozen in her chair, a cold numbness in her body, a dark emptiness in her soul. Finally, she sighed deeply, as if she had not breathed for ages, allowing herself to suck in the still air about her, allowing the truth in her husband's words to sink deeply into her consciousness. Now she understood what she had not understood before. She arose from her chair and slowly edged her way back to the bed. It was time for both of them to sleep.

Don Isaac Abravanel returned to Guadalajara with a single purpose: to meet with Rabbi Isaac Aboab, the head of the local *yeshiva*. Both Senior and he had agreed that Rabbi Aboab should be designated as the representative to Portugal. Abravanel wanted to meet with the rabbi, not only to discuss the Edict, but more importantly, to discuss how best to negotiate with the King of Portugal, João II. Abravanel intimately knew the King and the other high-ranking individuals at the Portuguese court, and it was important that he tell the rabbi what he knew about them. Because Don Isaac was himself in exile from Portugal, he knew he could not ask for refuge there. João II was not one to forget Abravanel's close ties with the now discredited Braganzas. Yet Don Isaac knew he could help others to enter the land he had once fled.

Wherever he went in Guadalajara, people followed him, demanding an explanation. Tugging at his shoulders and surrounding him, they wanted to know the reason for the disaster and what the future held for them, where they and their young ones were to go, when, by which routes, and by which means.

"What is going on, Don Isaac? Why do the King and Queen want to expel us? Why, Don Isaac, why?" Another shouted, "Don Isaac, is it really true? Are they really going to expel us . . . yes or no?"

A continuous flurry of questions, many of them unanswerable, were directed at him, and he did his best to answer all of them.

"Help us, Don Isaac, help us! Do not let them expel us."

Confronted by his panic-stricken brethren, Abravanel led them to the nearest synagogue, the *sinoga de los Toledanos*, where he knew Rabbi Aboab was. The queries continued en route, the people clinging to him as if he were their only beacon of light in a world now stricken with darkness. Through the narrow cobblestone streets they walked, with one despondent resident of the *judería* after another telling him their troubles. He knew them all by name. There was Jaco Soriano, '*el cojo*', 'the lame one', who hobbled next to him on his deformed leg; he was a poor and pathetic cripple who lived off the alms of the community. Don Isaac put his arm comfortingly around the man and slipped five maravedis secretly in his palm. "A thousand blessings on you, Don Isaac," the cripple smiled in toothless appreciation. Then there was Leonor Aben Arroyo who recently had donated several pounds of oil for the synagogue lamps. She was one who would not take no for an answer.

"I want to speak with you privately, Don Isaac. It is very important." Abravanel put her off gently. "Look about you, Señora Aben Arroyo, you see that there is no way I can do so at this moment. Allow me to invite you to my residence in the morning, and we shall talk then." The woman nodded in silent acknowledgment, and departed from the alleyway crowd. Another man tugged at his arm. It was Judah Creziente, the kindly sexton for the *sinoga mayor*, the largest of the four synagogues. "The rabbi wants you to come to our synagogue immediately . . . to explain about the Edict to our congregation. They are all waiting for you." Don Isaac told him that he would be there soon. "Good to see you again, Don Isaac," said the sexton, and he ran on down the street.

When Don Isaac Abravanel entered the *sinoga de los Toledanos*, people rose respectfully in his honor. One person chanted out loud, "Blessed be he who comes in the name of the Lord!" Rabbi Aboab, the saintly rabbi of this Toledan community, came up and greeted him warmly. Aboab, considered the greatest Talmudic scholar in all Spain, and known popularly as the *Gaon* or 'genius' of Castile, was old but still radiant with his majestic, long white beard and his schoolmaster's cloak. Rabbi Aboab had been the teacher of Abraham Zacuto, the astronomer, as well as of Don Isaac Abravanel. Aboab was a rabbi's rabbi, an encyclopedic scholar of the first rank. Abravanel shook hands with the rabbi and then addressed the congregation.

"My dear brothers and sisters, you know as well as I do what the Edict requires of us. Just as our ancestors centuries ago were forced to leave Egypt, so today we are being forced to leave Spain. As it was then, so it is now: a time of affliction, a time of trouble, a time of many questions. It is a time for us as Jews to show unity and strength. And yet it is a time where there is little that I can say that will comfort you.

"As the Edict came to us at Passover, there were many who continued to eat the *matza* and the bitter herbs after the holiday had ended. What more appropriate time than now can there be to eat the bread of affliction and the bitter herbs.

"As we prepare to leave, we must trust in the ways of the Lord. As God delivered us in times past from the hand of Pharoah in Egypt, so now He will rescue us from our Spanish persecutors, Ferdinand and Isabella. As we went from slavery in Egypt to freedom in the promised land of Israel, so now we will go forth from Castile in expectation of His ultimate salvation.

"We cannot look backward. The right to reside in this kingdom is nothing compared to our Jewish inheritance.

"There will be those who will be tempted to stay. These are the misguided ones who will betray us in their pursuit of comfort and convenience. But their material gains will be short-lived. The Old Christians will distrust and despise them, and the Inquisition will never let them know peace.

"In the final tabulation for these deserters, their losses shall far exceed their gains. What greater loss is there than to surrender one's very being? What is the price, the inner price, for cutting oneself off from one's people? What is the price for exchanging the truths of Torah for a life of falsehood and hypocrisy?

"The price, señores and señoras, is the destruction of your soul and lifelong confusion and despair. The price is not merely high. It is fatal.

"Let our lives then not be ones of regret. Let our souls rejoice that we chose the higher path at the peril of our lives. Let us tell our children and our children's children that when the tempest of evil came, we weathered the storm. Let us tell our children that, in this hour of greatest reckoning, we proved ourselves to be true children of Israel.

"Be strong and of good courage, children of Israel. As our ancestors wandered for forty years in the desert before they reached the promised land so, too, we shall wander to faraway lands — lands of promise, lands of peace and of freedom. That is where the God of Israel is taking us, to lands that are kinder and better than this one. Though there be trouble and sufferings ahead, there is redemption at the end of our journey. Though we may be afflicted, the God of Israel will save us and reward us for our faithfulness. Be strong and of good courage, children of Israel. God is testing us."

Don Isaac Abravanel stepped down from the podium. Despite Abravanel's comforting promises, there were still many questions unanswered. He tried to answer some of them in the open session that followed. The panic gave way to a matter-of-fact assessment of the situation: selling their properties, repaying and collecting debts, and disposing of Jewish sacred places such as the synagogue and the cemetery. Satisfied that things were now under control, Don Isaac went into a back room with Rabbi Aboab to talk about Portugal.

As Rabbi Aboab listened attentively, Abravanel described what he felt was the best way to approach the King of Portugal, João II.

"Rabbi Aboab, we are in urgent need of your services. A delegation must be sent to Portugal immediately. The King of Portugal must be persuaded to admit as many Jews as possible, preferably on a permanent basis. He must be made to believe that his acceptance of a large number of Spanish Jews is absolutely necessary to the welfare of his kingdom. The Jewish families selected for the delegation must be our very best: scholars, financiers, astronomers, physicians, trade merchants, and the like. You, *Gaon* Aboab, as the greatest Jewish scholar in all Spain, will lead this distinguished delegation."

"You do me great honor, Don Isaac," said Rabbi Aboab humbly. "I am a scholar, with little experience in court. Ordinarily I would not undertake such a mission, but because it is you who asks me, Don Isaac, and because the fate of our people depends on it, I must accept the task."

"I appreciate your acceptance," said Abravanel.

"Do you have a list ready?," asked Aboab.

Abravanel pulled out a piece of parchment and handed it to the *Gaon*. Rabbi Aboab studied the list with raised eyebrows when he saw the names of the official delegation.

"De la Cavallería . . . Bienveniste . . . Zacuto . . . As you say, our very best. A very impressive lot. They are all here, all except one. One person is missing."

"Who is that?," asked Abravanel curiously.

"Why you, Isaac, who else could it be?," said Aboab. "No such list could be complete without you."

Abravanel replied, "Rabbi, you know why I am not on that list."

"Yes, I know, Isaac. It is your lot to be doubly exiled."

Abravanel did not answer.

The *Gaon* rose from his chair. "There is much work to be done. We shall meet tomorrow morning, Don Isaac. Agreed?"

"Agreed," said Abravanel. They shook hands again, and Rabbi Aboab went back to the synagogue while Abravanel stepped outside into the street.

The multitude was waiting for him. A handful of street urchins circled around him. Wailing mothers with crying babes in arms, peddlers and burly merchants, tailors of all sizes — stood anxiously waiting for him in the street; most wanted to speak with him, others were content just to gaze at him or touch him to see if he was real.

"The sceptre has not departed from Judah!," shouted someone in the crowd. Obviously a rabbinic student. "The Lion of Judah lives! Long live Don Isaac!", came the follow-up cry. Abravanel continued to walk on. "Long live Don Isaac! Long live the Lion of Judah!," shouted others as they followed him.

Don Isaac went to the *sinoga mayor*, the main synagogue, as he had promised the sexton. There, too, he addressed the congregants, conferred with its rabbi, and conveyed his message of hope. From there, he walked on to the *sinoga de los Matutes*, the crowd trailing noisily behind him, again assuring one and all of God's ultimate redemption of his people. Don Isaac then decided to go home rather than to the *sinoga del Beit Midrash*, since the students of this synagogue had already heard him speak.

More people were waiting outside his villa. They were the proud poor of the city, those who could not beg in public, but knew that Don Isaac would help them in time of need, crisis or no crisis. Antonia Toletola, a widow of little means, came up to Abravanel.

"Don Isaac, Don Isaac . . . it is me, Antonia . . . Help us, me and my starving children." An orphaned child, blind in one eye, scarf around her head, ran up to Abravanel and tugged at his other arm. "Help us! Help us, Don Isaac. We know not what to do."

Hearing the commotion outside, Esther Abravanel opened the door. She carried a bag of maravedis. Without asking, she gave out handfuls of coins to those who were present. The poor, the widowed, the orphaned, the sick — all gathered around her. "Here, each of you, take some and return for more in the morning."

"Thank you, señora . . . for my starving children," said the grateful widow. Esther put her hand on the grieving woman's shoulder and said, "Come tomorrow. There will be more tomorrow." The orphan child, her one eye alight with appreciation, seized Esther's free hand and kissed it, "May the Lord protect you, señora, both you and Don Isaac." Others came in like manner, and Esther Abravanel gave generously to one and all.

"Thank you most kindly," one recipient said politely. "Many blessings on you and Don Isaac," said another. And Esther, sensing their dire need, would console them, saying to each of them, "God be with you," as she dispensed what she had into their eager palms.

As his wife aided the last of the people at their door, Don Isaac came up to her and hugged her affectionately. Esther put her hands around him and laid her head on his chest.

"I thought there would be no end, Isaac," she said, clutching the emptied bag.

Don Isaac sighed. "It is only the beginning. There will be much suffering before it is over."

Esther answered him. "I will be at your side always, my darling, to help you."

Abravanel backed away from his wife, a troubled look on his face. "How can I help them, Esther? They expect so much from me, and yet there is so little I can give."

Esther felt his pain too. "Isaac, wealth comes and wealth goes. Our fortune is only as valuable as the good that we can do with it. But you, Isaac, you more than anyone else, you are being asked to give more than all of us. Every one of these poor souls, in Guadalajara and elsewhere in Spain, depends on you. In this dark hour, in every Jewish home in the kingdom, people are praying that you and Don Abraham can somehow prevent the calamity. While we know this is not possible, it is still within your power to sustain their downcast spirits. You must give them hope.

Hope of better days to come. This you can give, Isaac, and this is surely what God Almighty expects from you."

Abravanel wrinkled his brow. "But has my leadership not been a failure? Did I not fail to see the omens of disaster? Why, my dear Esther? Why, I ask you? Why was I denied such vision?"

Abravanel covered his eyes with his hands. Esther took his hands gently away from his eyes. She came up close to him and kissed each one of his eyes. "No one could have foreseen this. No one is more pure and more selfless than you, Isaac. As you have been the protector of our people, so now you are being asked to be our Moses. It is you, Isaac, who is destined to lead us in this exodus from Spain."

"God's will be done," said Abravanel, placing his arm around her shoulder as they went inside.

Of all the enterprises Senior had undertaken as the supreme judge of Spanish Jewry, this was by far the most difficult. Indeed, it seemed overwhelming. The problems multiplied with each passing day, and there seemed to be no solution for them. Senior could do nothing; he did not want to return to Segovia to face his family or the members of the local community. It was far easier to tarry in Granada two or three days longer, to postpone facing the questions and hostility that waited for him when he did return.

Senior's prolonged stay came to the attention of the Queen, who summoned him to her chamber. But Senior ignored the royal summons, turning on the page who brought him the message, telling him that he wished to see no one, not even the Queen herself. Shutting himself up in his room, refusing to answer the Queen's commands, Senior isolated himself in his quarters.

The palace guards burst into his room. Grabbing him by the arms, the guards dragged Don Abraham Senior to the Queen. Senior offered no bodily resistance, but he did not go quietly.

"Unhand me, you knave. I said, unhand me!," he shouted, as the guard thrust him into the Queen's chamber.

"Enough," said a waiting Isabella. The guards released Senior.

"This is outrageous," said Don Abraham. "What is the meaning of all this?"

Isabella ordered him, "Step forward, Don Abraham."

Senior stood where he was. "I demand an explanation for this . . . this barbaric behavior. How dare you have me brought here like a common criminal. Have you not caused enough anguish?"

Isabella said, "It is all very simple, Don Abraham. I wish to make you a proposition."

An irate Senior answered her. "And I wish to tell *you* something, my Queen. From this day on, I want nothing to do with you. Is that clear?"

Isabella did not take offense, but said, "I am requesting that you and your son Meir remain in your official capacities as tax collectors for the crown. I am asking you to stay. We need you here in Castile, Don Abraham. We need you very much."

Senior asked, "And will we be allowed to remain as Jews?"

The Queen thought for a moment. At least, she thought to herself, the man was considering the possibility. "I cannot make an exemption for you, Don Abraham, nor for your family, as I have in the past."

Senior continued. "But you granted us such an exemption before . . . an exemption from wearing the distinctive Jewish badge, and exemption from the prohibition that Jews not be allowed to wear silk. You have done this before, my Queen. Why can you not do this again?"

Isabella said, "The situation is different now, Don Abraham. I cannot grant you this request. If you stay, it must be as a Christian, not as a Jew."

Senior spoke bitterly. "Then the answer to your question is no. The matter is settled. Is that all, my Queen?"

Isabella glared at Senior. She was unaccustomed to such impudence from her long-trusted adviser. But more than the slight of Senior's words, Isabella fretted over the promise that she had made Ferdinand, the promise that a knowledgeable Jewish tax-collector would remain. If she could not obtain Senior's compliance by persuasion, it was necessary for her to adopt stronger measures. She would not jeopardize her expulsion plans because of the intransigence of one man.

Isabella said firmly, "No! That is not all. You leave me no choice, Don Abraham. You will remain in Spain, you and your son-in-law, and you will convert even if I have to force baptism upon you. It has been done before and, if need be, I will do it again if that is what is required of me."

Senior was aghast. "You would convert me by force, my Queen, I, Don Abraham Senior, I who served you so long and so well. Is this the way you regard your faithful servant?"

Isabella said frankly, "There are compensations, Don Abraham. If you convert, nothing will be taken away from you. Indeed, I shall honor you with even more dignities and wealth."

"My Queen, where is your heart? Do you not see that I am a Jew and have been one for all the years of my life. How can you ask me in my old age to deny my very being . . . to deny my own people. After so many years of service to you and the King, how can you . . . how can you even think such a thing?"

Isabella was unsympathetic. "Because I need you. The crown needs you . . . it needs you and your son-in-law Meir's financial skills. I cannot let Castile be ruined financially."

Senior threw up his hands. "Then take someone else. Leave me and my family out of it."

Isabella spoke deliberately. "Let me tell you something and understand it well, Don Abraham Senior. The Jews of Spain are the property of the crown. You are my vassals, the least of my subjects. As I protect you, so I can destroy you . . . You and your son-in-law, Meir, will convert or I will unleash the rabble against all the Jewish communities. Do you understand? Your people will suffer if you disobey me. You decide who will suffer and who will not . . . Will it be you . . . or will it be the Jews of Spain?"

Senior was stunned by the Queen's words. Was the Queen truly going to bring devastation on the Jews of the kingdom because of his own obstinacy? There was no reason to doubt the sincerity of her threat, nor to doubt her willingness to carry it out.

"This . . . this is something unexpected. I must have time, my Queen, to give the matter some thought, to think about the consequences as you have presented them."

"One month, no more," said the Queen. "Your entire family in Segovia will be kept under surveillance by the Hermandad. Go, Don Abraham. You are dismissed."

Senior bowed respectfully and walked away slowly. His head spinning from disbelief, the Chief Judge of the Jewish community, asked to make the most fateful decision of his career, felt his knees buckle from a strange weakness that overtook him. Dazed and dumbfounded, fighting his weakness, Senior slowly edged his way back towards his room, a powerless bewildered being who knew not what to do.

Chapter 9

Rabbi Simon Maimi was visiting the sick members of his congregation. Going from one stone tenement to another, knocking on each door, the chief rabbi of Segovia made his rounds of the infirm, offering his kindly jovial presence and his words of comfort. A tale from the Aggadah, well wishes from friends, baskets of fruit and nuts — these were what Rabbi Maimi brought into the homes of the halt and the sick. But the Edict of Expulsion affected his flock even more than illness. The initial panic gave way to fear and despair, to an ache that festered in one's soul, producing sores from within as real as those which physical disease produced from without. It was these sores, sores of the soul, that Rabbi Maimi wished to treat with the spiritual liniments in his rabbinical armamentarium.

He knocked loudly on the door in front of him. "Señora Pardo, answer me. Are you there?"

The rabbi knocked on the door again. The door opened, and out came a small, thin woman with a broom in hand. It was Señora Pardo.

"Rabbi Maimi, what a surprise. *Buenos días*. Please, rabbi, come inside."

The rabbi walked into the house. Inside the bare white walls was an even more barren interior: a plain wooden table with three chairs, a fireplace, a few utensils, a candle on the wall, the bare necessities.

Gracia Pardo seemed far older than forty-five years: wrinkled and frail, since birth she had known only hardship. Born into poverty, plagued by illness in her childhood, she had married a cobbler in the hope of a favorable change in her fortune. Yet such was not to be. The two children she brought into the world she soon had to support on her own when her ailing husband died suddenly from gripping pains of the chest. Left to her own resources, with two hungry mouths to feed, she cleaned the homes of the well-to-do within the *judería*, barely making enough maravedis to sustain her and her family. As if her problems were not enough, her father became ill and moved in with them. Unable to pay her father's medical bills, she found herself struggling even further, having to work harder to make ends meet, yet feeling guilty about having to leave her father alone to earn a livelihood. Perpetual poverty and struggle seemed to be her lot in life. Yet she held her head high, enjoying the quiet dignity of the simple virtuous life that she led, and took pride in her two children as the sole joy of her existence. For the world as she knew it, she had a wise popular saying for practically everything. These sayings, *refranes* as they were called, were the distilled wisdom of the simple folk, harboring in the compactness of their phrase the accumulated kernels of Spanish homely wisdom. And Gracia Pardo used them freely to explain the harsh vicissitudes of her life. As she was wont to say, *"En lo que estamos bendigamos . . .* we are blessed with whatever we have."

The rabbi said, "Good to see you again, Señora Pardo. I hope all goes well with you and your children. How is your father? Your neighbor, Señora Halfon, gave me these fruits for your father, also some mint tea for him to drink as well."

"La agua de la vezina es melezina," Señora Pardo said, quoting a popular saying. 'The neighbor's water is medicine.'

They walked into the adjacent room where Gracia Pardo's father lay in bed on a straw mat, his head propped up with a bundle of clothes and rags, his body covered with a heavy quilt. They watched him sleep, his heavy breathing audible even at a distance.

Gracia said, "He is not doing well . . . poor father, he is so sick. So, so sick. Ever since my husband, of blessed memory, passed away, I have had to take care of him alone. It is hard for me. I am just a poor simple woman. I work cleaning houses, and get some aid from the local council, but it is never enough."

The rabbi said, "I will see what I can do about getting you additional assistance, Señora Pardo. About your father, what does the physician say is wrong with him?"

Gracia said, "He has a bad case of the dropsy."

The rabbi furrowed his brow in concern. "The dropsy, eh? Bad disease . . . very bad."

Gracia nodded her head in agreement. "And he mumbles day and night about the stones. Doesn't let any of us sleep."

The rabbi furrowed his brow further. "Stones, you say?," he asked curiously.

Gracia nodded again. As she did so, two children came running in. One was a young boy, perhaps seven years old, the other a girl of about fourteen who was chasing him playfully. The girl caught up with the boy and, amidst laughs, wrestled him to the floor.

"Children, behave yourselves!," shouted Señora Pardo. "Rabbi Maimi is here!"

The children, not having noticed the rabbi when they entered, quickly got up off the floor and dusted themselves. They stood still, uncomfortable in the presence of the community's chief rabbi.

"My children, Rebecca and Haim," said Gracia Pardo proudly.

The rabbi asked, "How old is the daughter?"

"Fourteen," answered the mother.

"Señora Pardo, now that the Edict has been announced, we, the rabbis, believe that every daughter of Israel who is more than twelve must be married before leaving Spain."

Gracia Pardo was taken aback. "Married? My only daughter? Rabbi Maimi, she is only a child!"

The rabbi was insistent. "I want no argument, Señora Pardo. The rabbis have decided this must be so."

"But, Rabbi . . .," said Gracia pleadingly, looking pitifully upon her daughter.

"For her protection, Señora," said the rabbi, looking into her tearful eyes.

"Surely you understand why, Señora Pardo . . . in case the two of you are separated, she needs a man to protect her."

Gracia Pardo's expression turned serious. "Yes, I suppose, yes, I see what you mean, rabbi. There could be more trouble ahead . . . all kinds of bad trouble."

The rabbi was relieved that she understood. "Perhaps, perhaps not. But we must prepare ourselves for the worst."

Gracia Pardo did not answer this time. She looked at her young daughter, Rebecca, only just become a woman, her breasts filling out. She conceded, "*Mi hija cazada, mi ansia dobada* . . . my daughter married, my worries doubled," wondering if she would have another mouth to feed.

A feeble high-pitched voice came from the adjacent room.

"Rabbi . . . Rabbi Maimi," the voice said weakly.

As the children ran outside again, Gracia led the rabbi into the room where her father Samuel Pardo was. As the rabbi entered the room, the elderly man slowly rolled to face his visitors. The ailing patient struggled to smile. His legs were swollen, as were the puffy regions about his eyes. He breathed heavily, wheezing slightly with each heave of his chest.

"Rabbi . . . Rabbi Maimi," he repeated.

The rabbi extended his hand along with his gift of fruits and mint tea. "Don Samuel, how good it is to see you again. Here are a few things from your neighbor, Señora Halfon, plus some *yerba buena*. Can I help you in any way, dear friend?"

The ailing Samuel lifted a finger with difficulty. His breath heavy and deep, with effort he managed to whisper, "The stones, rabbi . . . you must not forget the stones."

"Which stones do you mean, Don Samuel?," asked the rabbi as he drew closer. Samuel Pardo's eyes darted from side to side, terrified he was being misunderstood. "The tombstones, rabbi . . . the tombstones in the cemetery . . . the graves of our ancestors. They must be protected . . . the inscriptions on them, they must be copied." The man heaved mightily for air after such a long utterance and coughed up some pinkish frothy sputum.

Rabbi Maimi placed his hand comfortingly on the man's arm. "You know then," said the rabbi. "You know about the Edict."

Samuel Pardo nodded. Rabbi Maimi looked towards Gracia Pardo for confirmation. She, too, nodded. The sick old man knew.

The rabbi explained, "Arrangements are being made with local officials for the continued protection of our cemeteries. Rest, Don Samuel, the inscriptions will be copied . . . I assure you, all will be well. Please, now, drink some tea and get some rest."

"Thank you, rabbi . . . thank you," said the ailing Pardo.

The rabbi squeezed the man's arm warmly. The patient was exhausted by the effort of the conversation and began to cough fitfully. The man's dropsy was bad, thought Rabbi Maimi as he got up to leave.

Rabbi Maimi bade farewell to the señora of the house and continued on his rounds of the infirm. As he walked away from the Pardo residence, he heard the anxious mother caution her daughter, *"Antes que te cazes, mira lo que hazes . . .'* 'Before you marry, look at what you are doing.' "

Three weeks had passed. The representatives of Castilian and Aragonese Jewry gathered in Segovia for the general assembly convened by Don Abraham Senior and Don Isaac Abravanel. It was within the main synagogue that these people of distinction, learning, and rank were assembled. Castilian grandees and hidalgos, community rabbis from as far as Vitoria and Guipuzcoa, *yeshiva* heads from Toledo and Murcia, textile fabric plant managers from Huesca and Zaragoza, wine merchants from Rioja and Valmaseda, olive growers from Valencia, castle overseers from Maqueda and Escalona, financiers from Segovia and other cities of the kingdom, these and many more, had come to the impromptu council. Of the two hundred and sixteen *aljamas* in the kingdom, well over fifty were represented in the assembly.

Don Abraham Senior, *juez mayor* of the *aljamas*, looking haggard called the meeting to order. He welcomed the visitors who had come from near and far, and thanked them for their promptness in responding to his request. Senior described the unsuccessful efforts of Don Isaac Abravanel and himself to stave off the edict. After doing this and reiterating the terms of the Edict, Senior, his voice strained, admitted to those present, "Honored guests, it is I who have failed you. The King and the Queen, whom I once brought together in matrimony and whom I esteemed as the dearest of my friends and as the friends of the Jews of the kingdom, are our friends no longer. Barring a miracle, I am powerless, we are powerless to stop our rulers who seek to ruin us and banish us. Thus, it is my considered opinion as *juez mayor* that we make immediate arrangements to comply fully with the terms of the Edict of Expulsion."

The tough-talking textile manager from Huesca stood up, waving a fist in the air, "What? And let them throw us out like the vermin of the earth? Damn Ferdinand and Isabella . . . damn them to hell! Are we going to just sit here and let them get away with this?"

Senior answered him patiently, "Fighting is absolutely out of the question. Do you not remember what happened to the Moors? Do you not realize that any organized revolt on our part would be brutally crushed?"

The textile manager, his square face in a tight grimace, pointed accusingly at the Chief Judge. "You, Senior . . . you told us that they needed us."

Senior said, "Yes . . . I did say that. The rulers needed us as long as they were fighting the Moors. They needed us for money . . ."

The manager interrupted, "Ach, lots of it . . . for that damned campaign against the Moors. And what did it get us, eh? You tell me, Senior, what good was all that money that we gave them?"

Senior concurred, "Yes, they needed lots of money to continue the war. I put up much of it myself. In retrospect it now seems that they could not expel us earlier for fear that we would go to Granada to help the Moors. The war is over. The Moors have been beaten. Now, they feel, it is time to finish with the Jews once and for all."

The textile manager was irate. "In other words, Senior, we gave money to the wrong side. By giving money to those two bastards, Ferdinand and Isabella, we cut our own throats, is that it? And what were you, Senior, doing all this time? Playing your little courtier game with the King and Queen? Trying to win a few extra favors for yourself while the rest of us Jews, thinking that you were doing your duty to protect us, were being prepared for expulsion from Spain? I ask you, where were you, Senior? You, more than anyone, are the one who led us to believe that the King and Queen were our friends. You deceived us, Senior. You have failed us. And this Edict, as far as I am concerned, is the ultimate proof of your incompetence. You should have been replaced long ago, Senior, you selfish, pompous ass. What are you? Supreme Judge of the *aljamas*? *Rab de la Corte*? Chief accountant of the kingdom? Treasurer of the Hermandad? What else is there that your vanity has not pursued? I will tell you what you are, Don Abraham Senior. You are nothing, do you hear me, *nothing*! You are nothing, nothing, nothing!"

The textile manager continuing ranting, "Nothing, nothing," in total disruption of the session. Those in his immediate vicinity shouted him down. "Sit down!," said one grandee, "Sit down!," shouted another.

The textile manager, sensing the local hostility that he had provoked, made another grimace and sat down. A shaken Don Abraham Senior, who had stood silently at the podium while the textile manager had hurled his accusations, shook his head in disbelief and likewise sat down. The meeting continued.

A tall well-dressed individual, slightly bald, stood up. It was a vineyard owner from San Martin de Valdeiglesias, a small village west of Madrid. He spoke humbly, "But is it not possible to change the minds of the sovereigns, no? Talk . . . negotiate, offer them something to allow us to stay, no?"

Abravanel stood up to answer. "For the last month, we have struggled to influence the King and Queen until our voices grew hoarse. Even some of the great nobles helped us. We talked, we bargained, we pleaded. We tried and tried again, but to no avail. The Edict, my friends, I regretfully must admit, is irreversible."

Senior, seated at Abravanel's side, nodded his head sadly in agreement.

The vineyard owner said matter-of-factly, "Then we are finished."

Don Isaac Abravanel admitted, "At least here in Spain. Absolutely every single Jew must be out of Spain in three months."

A powerful grandee from Zaragoza shot out of his chair. "Three months time! That is not enough. Why were we not given some warning of all this?" The grandee, obviously accustomed to having his way, waited impatiently for an answer.

Abravanel replied, "The three-month deadline was not our doing. As long as Don Abraham Senior and I thought there was a chance of changing the mind of the King and Queen, we felt it would be unwise to alarm the community unnecessarily."

The grandee said, "But, even so, three months, that is not enough time to settle our business affairs. And besides, where are we to go?"

Don Isaac Abravanel answered, "In that regard, we have examined as many possibilities as time would allow us. Envoys have been sent to different countries, and we have received notice that some places will allow us to take refuge — some temporarily, some permanently."

"Where?," questioned the grandee.

Abravanel replied, "Only one country offered to take us without preconditions, and that country is the Turkish Ottoman Empire."

The merchant was taken aback. "Turkey? Surely you jest . . . the land of the Ottomans? Why, that is thousands of leagues away."

Don Isaac said, "It is a tolerant empire. The Ottoman rulers tolerate the presence of minorities such as ours. I have spoken with the Turkish emissary in Granada, and he has told me that the Sultan will accept us without reservation, and that all Jews will be allowed to settle peacefully in his kingdom."

A passionate rabbi from Zamora arose and spoke, "Need I remind you that Constantinople has fallen to the Turks! Yes, the eastern capital of Christendom fell to these mighty Ottomans just forty years ago. Surely as Christians are avowed enemies of us Jews, so, too, the Turks are the enemies of Christendom. My brothers, it is God's will that we should help these noble Ottomans in their glorious struggle against the Christians who never cease to do us harm. It is to the land of the Ottomans that we should go."

The grandee was unconvinced. Ignoring the rabbi's comment, he asked flatly, "What about France or England?"

Abravanel shook his head. "They refuse to accept any Jews. I should mention that the rulers of these countries expelled the Jews some time ago. England did it in 1290, France did it twice — in 1306 and 1394."

The rabbi from Zamora jumped up again. "Don Isaac, you did not state *why* they were expelled. It is a very important reason. The kings of France expelled the Jews only after they had confiscated all their properties. The Christians will do it to us here in Spain, my brothers, just as they robbed our brethren in France and England. Wherever Christians rule, there is hate for the Jew. They rob us, they kill us, they expel us. It is the same as ever. How many times must we be expelled before we will realize that there is no safety for us in a Christian land? How many times must they rob us before we come to our senses and realize that they mean us only harm, and not good? How many times?"

The mercurial rabbi from Zamora sat down. A strange but temporary silence filled the room, leaving the rabbi's questions unanswered.

Don Isaac Abravanel addressed the matter. "As there have been rulers that have been unkind to Jews, so, too, there have been Christian kings who have been good to us. I have known many good-hearted Christians in my lifetime as well, and I will not permit it to be said that all Christians are bad.

"Allow me, however, to return to the issue at hand. We had thought of requesting the kingdom of Navarre for temporary refuge and shelter. The community of Tudela submitted a petition on our behalf, but the request was turned down by the rulers. Thus Navarre is no longer under consideration as a place of refuge.

"The Italian states appear to present a good possibility. Indeed, it is likely that a substantial number of Jews will be allowed to settle there. There are altogether five territories: the kingdom of Naples, the Papal States, and the three northern city-states of Florence, Milan, and Venice. Negotiations with their representatives are still in progress. Finally, Genoese merchants operating here in Spain have agreed to accept letters of credit for those who intend to emigrate there. For those of you who are interested, we have brought a Genoese merchant tonight to discuss the practical aspects of obtaining a letter of credit, and he will speak to us later on this matter.

"Where else is there to go? Morocco is open to emigration, particularly through the port of Arcila, which is now under Portuguese control. From Arcila, it should be possible to go further inland to such cities as

Fez, where the local king is very hospitable to Jews. There are other cities, of course — Rabat, Casablanca, Marrakesh, to name a few, but I know relatively little of these places. On the basis of the various reports that I have received, Morocco appears to be a good place to settle. One final note: a major fleet of twenty ships will set sail from the Puerto de Santa Maria for the North African coast shortly; it will be heading in the general direction of Orán. Fleets are also being readied at Cartagena, Valencia, and other ports to transport the exiles to their points of destination.

"Now . . . that leaves Portugal. I should inform you that we sent a special delegation to the King of Portugal, João II, requesting that he permit as many Jews as possible to stay temporarily in his kingdom. Rather than disclose the results of these negotiations with the King, I will allow the head of the Castilian delegation, Rabbi Aboab, to speak. Señores, the *Gaon* of Castile, Rabbi Isaac Aboab."

The *Gaon*, his soft eyes looking out into the assembly, stood erect, his white fluffy beard extending halfway down his chest. "It has been my privilege to participate in these negotiations, thanks to Don Isaac Abravanel, who saw the important need to obtain the grace and good will of the King of Portugal. I am happy to report that this we have done, in part because of a special tribute of ducats to the King's private purse, in part because of the very favorable impression made upon him by the members of our delegation. Despite some reservations, the King has agreed to allow an unlimited number of Jews to enter the kingdom of Portugal, provided that certain conditions are met. I will now read these conditions to you.

'*One*. The Jews of Castile are to enter Portugal only by five predetermined sites, and they are: Arronches, Braganza, Castel-Rodrigo, Melgazo, and Olivenza.

Two. There will be an entrance fee of eight cruzados per Jewish head, to be paid in any of four designated places. Only children and certain craftsmen will be excepted . . . For those of you who are unfamiliar with Portuguese coinage, a Portuguese cruzado is equal in value to a Castilian ducat.

Three. Jews will be allowed to remain in Portugal for a time span of only eight months.

Four. Any Jew found in Portugal, who has not had his name registered in the royal official logbooks, or who has not left Portugal in the prescribed time, will be sold into slavery.

Five. King João II will arrange for a sufficient number of naval vessels to transport Jews to wherever they so desire, the expenses of such transport to be borne by the Jews themselves.

Six. Only six hundred Castilian families will be allowed to remain permanently in the kingdom of Portugal, this to be secured by payment to the King of a sum of sixty thousand cruzados, that is, one hundred cruzados per family.

Seven. Entry at the Portuguese frontier will be denied to any Jew who does not have a document from an official of his village or town which testifies to his freedom from pestilence.'

"These are the seven conditions which King João II has imposed." Rabbi Aboab sat down after reciting the conditions.

An Aragonese rabbi from Zaragoza, who had been busy taking notes, stood up and addressed the assembled representatives. "With all due respects to the *Gaon* of Castile, the Portuguese offer is not a solution at all. It allows Jews to enter Portugal only for a short period of time. By no means does it solve the basic problem of where we Jews will be allowed to settle permanently. Of the tens of thousands of Jews that will probably cross over into Portugal, only the rich will be allowed to settle there. Very few of us can afford to pay one hundred cruzados. As is always the case, the rich get the choice slices of meat, and the poor have to eat the droppings."

The textile manufacturer from Huesca, who had remained silent thus far, angrily came back to life again. "Who gave you Castilians the authority to speak on behalf of all the Jews of Aragon? You Castilians, with your fancy manners and your fancy speech, do you think that you are entitled to better treatment than the rest of us? Well, I will tell you what we of Aragon are going to do about this. We are sending *our own* delegation to the King of Portugal, and we will make *our own* arrangements for permanent settlement there."

The textile manufacturer, having said his say, sat down, arms angrily folded. The *Gaon* stood up, a distressed look on his face, obviously anxious to appease the Aragonese contingent. "It is not, nor has it ever been, our intention to exclude our brethren from the kingdom of Aragon from any negotiations with the King of Portugal. The six hundred families in question will be divided between the two kingdoms of Castile and Aragon on a fair and proportionate basis. I am deeply offended by the suggestion that I did not negotiate on behalf of all the Jews of Spain."

All eyes were upon the textile manufacturer, who continued to sit with his arms folded, a menacing frown on his face. Noticing the disapproving stares of everyone around him, the manufacturer bit his lip and apologized stiffly. "Rabbi, pardon me if I have offended you. With all due respect to you, *Gaon*, we in Aragon will still send our own official delegation." Then the textile manager sat down and returned to his arms folded position, oblivious to the resentful stares of those who sat next to him.

It was Rabbi Maimi from Segovia who took the floor next. "I am tired of hearing about these special arrangements being made for the rich. This is not what this meeting is for, señores. For God's sakes, rabbis and gentlemen, let us not waste this precious time on them.

"There are over one hundred thousand Jews who are about to be expelled — terrified men, women, and children who are in desperate need of our help and leadership. Most of the Jews have limited means, and very few of them will be able to pay the eight cruzados needed to cross over into Portugal, and even fewer will be able to afford the ship passage to North Africa or the Ottoman Empire. Let us stop squandering our time with the petty concerns of the rich and start to deal instead with the serious problems that threaten the very existence of our people."

A fierce applause broke out in the synagogue following Rabbi Maimi's impassioned statement. The mood of confrontation, of interregional resentment, was transformed into one of cooperation and concern. Rabbi Maimi spoke about the need to marry all unwed daughters of Israel above the age of twelve, so that all Jewish women in exile would have the benefit of protection of a male spouse. Don Isaac Abravanel, who conducted the rest of the meeting, stressed the need for the wealthy to distribute money among the poor to help them pay immigration fees, voyage costs, and related expenses. It was agreed further that the liquidation of community properties did not extend to synagogues and cemeteries which, as Jewish sacred places, should be turned over to local authorities for safekeeping. To illustrate this, the rabbi from Vitoria explained how the local *aljama* was planning to donate its ancient cemetery, the Campo de Judizmendi, to the city of Vitoria, the only condition being that the cemetery grounds be used for pasture only.

Then the Genoese agent spoke about the preparation of letters of credit, the fee charged for such a banking service, and the expected rate of exchange for other coinage. Other matters of communal importance were discussed. On and on it went into the late hours of the night, the assembled members thrashing out the details of their compliance with the Edict of Expulsion, rabbis and grandees coming together to formulate the master plan of their people's hurried evacuation and their own reluctant expatriation.

Esmeralda Funes, the matchmaker, had fat pink cheeks, a tiny nose, and a mop of brown hair. Opening the door to Gracia Pardo's austere home, she popped her head inside and looked curiously about.

"O Gracia . . . Gracia . . . where are you?," she bellowed.

"Where else, but on our knees?," came the reply from within. "Have you not heard? *La limpieza es media riqueza* . . . cleanliness is one half of being rich." Gracia and her daughter, Rebecca, both on their knees, were scrubbing the floor. "Ay, Esmeralda . . . you're looking good. Come in. Tell me, what brings you here?"

Esmeralda gesticulated with her hands. "Why, Gracia, do you pretend not to know why I am here? The rabbis have decreed that young women above the age of twelve must be married before they leave Spain. And I, the matchmaker, have come to do my duty."

Rebecca got up off the floor and wiped her hands on her apron. "Married? Oh, no! . . . *me* married?" She had a pleasant innocent look to her oval face.

Gracia said, "Yes, I heard about it. Rabbi Maimi told me so himself. But what about you, Esmeralda? Is it not yet time for you, too?"

Esmeralda put her hand to her heart and sighed. "Ay, were I but young again, I might have a chance . . . But, ay, as the saying goes, the shoemaker goes barefoot, and the matchmaker remains . . . well . . . you know. But let me tell you the good news: I have a match for your daughter!"

Swallowing wide-eyed, Rebecca asked, "A match for me? I'm only fourteen."

Esmeralda smiled widely. "Ay, but he is a jewel of a boy, a darling, heaven-sent for you, my sweet one. And he is so handsome!"

Gracia smirked. "And . . . and so costly, I am sure."

Rebecca blinked her eyes nervously. "He is handsome, you say."

With exaggerated emphasis, Esmeralda affirmed, "Oh, yes . . . very very handsome. Would I lie to you, darling?"

A sceptical Gracia Pardo questioned the matchmaker. "My daughter is so young. How old is this man?"

Evasively, Esmeralda answered, "Well, let us not get bogged down in details. Let us say, he is a trifle over fifteen."

"How old exactly?," asked Gracia firmly.

Esmeralda turned her eyes away. "He looks much younger than his age. Very handsome, I tell you."

More sternly than before, Gracia repeated herself, "How old?"

A mumbling Esmeralda hawed, "Well, really, all these little details . . . well, if you insist, he is . . . I believe . . . ah . . . fifteen . . . plus . . . ah . . . a mere three years."

Gracia said, "Eighteen then. So why didn't you say so?"

Esmeralda, clutching her hands to her breast, heaved her chest in relief.

The young Rebecca, the subject under discussion, blinked her curled eyelashes again. The gentle features of her face could not hide her curiosity about her potential groom-to-be. With excitement in her voice, she asked, "And you say he is handsome . . . and a dashing cavalier maybe?"

Esmeralda tucked in her chin. "Well . . . uh . . . yes, a cavalier of sorts . . . but he is a gentle man, a very gentle man."

Gracia asked, "What does he do?"

Esmeralda threw up her hands in the air. "Why so many questions all at one time? Do you know how many marriages I have to set up in the next two weeks? Really, I cannot keep all the details straight in my head."

Using the same stern voice as before, Gracia asked again, "What does he do?"

Esmeralda threw her hands up again. "All right, all right, I will tell you . . . he is a shoemaker, but a very fine shoemaker . . . one of the best in Segovia. He can make a good living wherever he goes.

Rebecca's shoulders and face sagged on hearing this. "A shoe-maker? . . . What kind of a cavalier is that?"

Gracia motioned to Rebecca, "Hush, daughter." Turning to Esmeralda, she asked quickly, "Tell me truly, Esmeralda, is it the son of Señor Abulafia? . . . Well, is it?"

Esmeralda, aware that the moment of truth had come, nodded her head slowly. Gracia raised her hands up to heaven and uttered a whoop of delight. She embraced Esmeralda appreciatively and then gave her daughter Rebecca a loving hug. Tears streaming down her eyes, she laughed happily, "Oh, Rebecca, is it not wonderful?"

The matchmaker could hardly believe her eyes. "So then . . . you are interested?"

Still hugging her daughter, Gracia wiped the tears of joy from her eyes. Turning her head towards Esmeralda, she said, "Bring the young man to us tonight for supper. The Abulafia family is a very good family. We agree to the match."

The *judería* was teeming with people. Hundreds from the City of Segovia and its environs streamed into the Jewish quarter in search of a bargain. Everyone heard that the Jews were leaving town, and all were aware that the residents of the Jewish quarter would have to sell most of their possessions as well as their houses. The rich Christians were eager to buy up local properties, and the poor ones were eager to find some bargains.

Every Jewish housekeeper had to make a hurried assessment of what could be taken and what could not, of what could be sold and what could only be thrown away. Thus it was in the Alhadeff residence. While Hacham Alhadeff and his son-in-law went to teach at the local Hebrew *yeshiva*, Morenica stayed at home to do what was needed. She had been told that the entire family would have only one cart to transport their belongings. Everything else would have to stay behind. It seemed an impossible task to put everything that they had on one single cart. Impossible, she kept saying to herself, it is impossible.

Morenica went systematically through their belongings. Dishes, pots, and pans were essential. So were candlesticks for the Sabbath. She picked two dresses for herself and put them aside; the rest she would simply have to do without. As for the men's items, she separated out the prayer shawls, phylacteries, the holy books used by her husband and her father. Some pantaloons, a few sleeveless tunics, and vests and undergarments for them, that was enough. Her few pieces of jewelry, she put away in a small square wooden box. She heard the baby cry in the next room. The crib for the baby, she suddenly realized, that would have to go as well.

She went to nurse the baby, now almost five months old. Taking the crying child into her arms, she loosened the top of her dress, giving him milk to suck from her engorged breasts. She thought of what the future held for them. Her father, the Hacham, insisted that all three, no, all four of them — how could he forget little Iziko? — yes, that all four of them emigrate to North Africa, preferably to someplace in Morocco. Their fluency in Arabic would be a distinct advantage there. Aaron, her husband, and the Hacham could both teach at a local Hebrew school, and little Iziko could grow up there and surely receive as good a Hebrew education as Segovia could have given him. All that they had in a Christian land, they could have just as well, if not better, in a Moslem land. She thought back to her memorable childhood days in Málaga when it was still under Moslem rule, and of how happy she had been there. It would be like that again, she thought to herself. Whether it was Spain or Morocco or wherever else they might end up, as long as she had Aaron and little Iziko and her father, she had everything that she needed in the world.

The child fell asleep in her arms. Morenica put the child back in the crib and continued with the disposal of the family's belongings. As the neighbors had done, she did also. All the household furniture items — tables and chairs and bookcases — were left out on the street for passers-by to see. On the outside table she placed linen, tablecloths, brooms, glazed jars and pottery, hoping to find a customer for them.

The narrow street was cluttered with furniture, household wares, artisan products, and the like. The tailor further down was clearing out his inventory; lavish pleated dresses, which she had never been able to afford, could now be purchased for four or five maravedis. Morenica would have loved to purchase such a fancy dress, but there was no place on the two-wheeled cart to put it. The shoemaker was doing the same, selling galoshes, leather shoes, short stockings reaching to the knees, and even a pair of that new style of French boots that extended halfway to the knees — all could be purchased for a pittance. Some members of the *judería* availed themselves of these slashed prices, and Morenica was tempted to join them. But she did not do so, preferring not to clutter her cart with unnecessary luxury items.

The tanneries in the lower portion of the *judería* had closed down their operation as had the wool-gatherers, leaving many animal hides and bundles of wool for the taking. Horses, which it was forbidden to take out of the country, were being sold by the wealthier members of the community to nobles who were not above passing up a bargain. Likewise, the saddle-makers of the quarter tried to rid themselves of the finely carved leather saddles on which they had been working. Goldsmiths and silversmiths were just as eager to sell their gilded ornaments and jewel pieces for a fraction of their true market value. So were weavers and tapestry-makers, whose embroidered rugs and unfinished tapestries hung from ropes strung across the street.

And everywhere, in front of every houshold, was the ubiquitous two-wheeled wooden cart, the carriages of transport lined up one next to each other, almost to the point of blocking free passage through the winding narrow streets. Filtering through the carts and the street clutter came the Christian residents of Segovia, sensing the desperation of the local Jews, knowing all too well that as the deadline stated by the Edict neared, the Jews would be forced to sell for even less and perhaps even give away what they had. The Christian buyers took their time, because it was to their advantage to wait until the last moment for the best prices.

Morenica's neighbor, Señora Josefina Matalon, paid her a visit. She was a kindly middle-aged woman, a mother of four herself, who felt it her duty to help the young mothers of the community. After Morenica's baby had been born, Señora Matalon came regularly to show the Hacham's daughter how to nurse and diaper the child. This day, however, she was much too caught up in the frenzied hubbub of the street to worry about toddler matters. Her husband, a goldsmith, was still busy next door trying to sell a pair of earrings, and she could not listen to the incessant haggling any longer.

Josefina Matalon covered her ears as she walked in, imitating the conversation outside. "Thirty maravedis! . . . No, three! . . . But sir, it is worth at least thirty! . . . three is all that I have! . . . Well, perhaps I can interest you in something less expensive! . . . No, that is what I want, and I can only pay you three maravedis, that is all! . . . But, sir, it is worth at least thirty! . . . Do you want to sell it to me or don't you want to sell it to me? Make up your mind! . . . But, sir, I am selling it to you for less than what it cost me. Very well, for three maravedis, as you say, señor . . . but it hurts me to do this."

Josefina uncovered her ears. "*Vaya*, Morenica, it hurts me more than it hurts him! Day by day, I see my husband Anton give away our choice gold and silver ornaments for a handful of maravedis. All these valuables, *así*, gone in an instant . . . and for what, for what, I ask you?"

Morenica shrugged her shoulders, not knowing how to answer Josefina. She let Señora Matalon continue to talk.

Pacing up and down the floor, Josefina remarked, "I cannot believe that this is all happening. For thirty years, we have lived peacefully in Segovia. And now, suddenly like this, for no good reason at all, we are being driven like animals out of our homes. And where do we go from here? Portugal, I guess. But even there, we shall not find a home. The king of Portugal will only allow us to stay for eight months. Then we must go elsewhere."

Morenica played with the infant's apron as she spoke. "But eight months . . . it is not much time. And what will you do there in Portugal,

I mean, without any money? You cannot take any gold or silver with you, and there will be guards at the border."

Josefina smiled mischievously. "My dear Morenica, did you think that we Jews of Segovia are going to allow the King and Queen to take our wealth? Everyone in this *judería* is thinking of ways to take out their wealth secretly. The rich ones are making arrangements with brigands in the mountains to smuggle out large quantities of gold and silver. Others have organized in secret bands to take out chestfuls of ducats across the Portuguese border by night, and they even have some Christians to help them. This I know for a fact. Every person I know is hiding ducats in all kinds of clever places. Some are hiding the gold coins in the covers of books, others in thick quilts, in leather belts and in the soles of their shoes. Others have burrowed special holes within the flat platform of their carts to create a secret compartment where they can hide their gold. Be clever, Morenica. We owe the King and the Queen nothing, and we owe Castile nothing. Do not leave anything behind, certainly not anything valuable, for them to use. And if all else fails, you can do what everyone else will be doing when we cross the border checkpoints."

Innocently, Morenica asked, "What?," a surprised look on her face. Josefina smacked her lips and looked again at Morenica with that sly mischievous look in her eye. "Why, Morenica, I thought you knew. Perhaps I had better tell you what most of us are going to be doing." Pulling a gold ducat out of her shirt pocket, Josefina took the coin and put it in her mouth. She winked at Morenica as she pretended to swallow the coin. "Now you know, Morenica . . . we are going to swallow our gold."

Opening wide her lovely brown eyes, Morenica knew it was something that she could never do.

The neighbor's husband, Anton Matalon, walked into the house. "Josefina, come over here! Señor Fernández, the city magistrate, is here. I think he wants to buy our house." Upon hearing this, Señora Matalon left in a hurry to join her husband. It was known that Señor Fernández was going about the *judería* buying up several homes.

Although the wealthy magistrate was no friend of the Jews, business considerations outweighed his hostility. The haughty official went from one tenement to the other inquiring whether the house was for sale. Without so much as the most elementary exhibition of cordiality, without any salutation or greeting whatsoever, the magistrate would introduce himself, state his business, and make his bid.

"Señor Matalon, for such a house in its present condition, I will make you an offer of three thousand maravedis."

Anton Matalon was outraged. "Fernández, you have done business with me for years. My house is easily worth thirty thousand maravedis or even more. How can you make me a preposterous offer of three thousand maravedis?"

The magistrate replied, "Do you have a better offer?"

The goldsmith Matalon stammered, "No, but . . . but really . . ."

"Three thousand maravedis is the offer," said Fernández, without the slightest trace of emotion.

The goldsmith looked at his wife Josefina, who shook her head to signal her disapproval of the offer. The goldsmith, who had already given away so much that day, likewise could not find it in his heart to give away his cherished home for such a trifling sum. He agreed with his wife. "No, Señor Fernández, not for three thousand maravedis."

As he started to back away, Fernández said, "You should take the offer while it stands."

Now it was Josefina's turn to be outraged. "Go to the devil, you thief."

Fernández, mildly amused by the remark, walked away to the next house, never once breaking his frigid mask.

Morenica watched the emotionless magistrate continue on to the next home. It was only a matter of time before he would pay the Alhadeff residence a visit. She did not have the courage, as Josefina did, to tell the man what she thought of him. In fact, she did not want to see him at all. She closed the door, wishing that he and his kind would simply go away.

It was a hectic week for Gracia Pardo. There were so many things to be done, and so little time to do them. The wedding nuptials of her daughter Rebecca with the shoemaker's son, Benito Abulafia, had been announced. But the announcement, which in ordinary times would have brought a deluge of well-wishes, scarcely attracted any attention. Indeed, all the young girls of the community above the age of twelve were being wed; and her daughter, however special Gracia thought her, was but one of many.

It was the custom in Spain to have daughters formally engaged at an early age. Usually, however, it took one to four years before the actual wedding took place. The Edict made everything different. Matchmakers and parents were busy finding suitable mates for their daughters, the sons of rabbis being the most highly sought grooms-to-be. Scribes worked day and night preparing the *Ketubot*, the wedding contracts, for the betrothed couples. And all these rushed preparations were compressed into a mere two weeks time.

The Pardo and Abulafia families had known each other for years. Yet when it was agreed upon by both sets of parents that their children should wed, the bride and groom were at a loss for words. Blushing in the face, an embarrassed Benito Abulafia had sat quietly through all the negotiations, saying scarcely a word, except to look up every now and then at his equally shy bride-to-be. Benito was strong and good looking and most of all, as the matchmaker stressed, he was a kind man. He was no scholarly son of a rabbi, nor was he a dashing cavalier. Yet he could be trusted to protect and care for the young Rebecca Pardo.

On the Sabbath preceding the wedding day, Benito Abulafia, along with the other *novios*, or engaged young men of the community, were called up during the synagogue service for the reading of the Torah. From the synagogue, people went their respective ways, many to a series of festive engagement celebrations in the homes of the brides, the *novias*. Friends and relatives came to the humble home of the Pardos, filling their house with joyful songs and romantic ballads. Gracia went from one visitor to the other — giving out sweet pastries, accepting their felicitations of '*En hora buena*!' and '*Mazal Tov*'!, making sure that her daughter got all the attention and kisses that she deserved.

On the day of her wedding, accompanied by her mother, Rebecca Pardo went to immerse herself in the ritual bath called the *mikveh*. There was a long line of young brides ahead of her waiting to do the same, and Rebecca patiently waited her turn. She immersed herself three times after having said the benediction. Rebecca was happy to be wedded in a state of purity and holiness. With her mother's assistance, she put on her borrowed white wedding dress and ornamented white headpiece. As she and her mother emerged from the ritual bath, a chorus of women greeted each bride-to-be with songs. Clapping hands, embracing the young brides as they came out of the ritual bath, the women wanted to make this wedding day a joyful one for these emerging daughters of Israel.

At the main synagogue, the line of young brides was equally long. Rebecca looked at the other girls about her, many of whom had been longtime childhood friends, as they excitedly waited their turn. All were dressed in white wedding dresses and had elaborate white headpieces. Worried mothers and talkative aunts made final adjustments to the headpieces and tightened the sleeves of their daughter's gowns. Hovering relatives made sure that everything was in proper order, creating all the while a continuous stream of feminine chatter that filled the synagogue street. Rebecca waved to one of her friends, a lively girl named Bella Bejarano, and her friend waved back. Excited to see Rebecca, Bella stepped out of line and came over to where Rebecca was standing. On the verge of exchanging wedding vows, they affectionately hugged each other, mingling their joys with their sorrows, their tears of parting mixed with smiles of temporary reunion.

Rebecca Pardo and her mother were finally allowed to enter the synagogue. Her brother Haim, the youngest in the family, also entered along with a small group of friends and family.

The synagogue was beautifullly decorated. Flower wreaths had been placed along the two main side walls as well as within large baskets that hung from the rafters. Long tapered candles burned brightly at the side walls, bringing out the full color of the roses, lilacs, and marigolds placed next to them. Next to the podium stood the *huppah*, the wedding canopy, likewise decorated with brightly-colored flowers, its silken roof supported by four ornately carved wooden poles. The synagogue interior seemed alive with color.

As the preceding party left by a side door, the Pardo family advanced toward the wedding canopy. Friends and family sat in the pews while Rebecca and her mother continued on. Rebecca walked slowly to the canopy, her soft lovely face barely visible through the lace veil. At her side walked her proud mother Gracia, unable to keep back her tears.

As the two approached the wedding canopy, a trio of musicians off to the side began to play a festive popular wedding tune, its plaintive melody the cue for Benito Abulafia and his parents to make their appearance from a separate entrance. They, too, proceeded toward the wedding canopy. Benito was wearing a maroon-colored embroidered sleeveless tunic on a white doublet having pleated sleeves and white stockings; his head was covered with a pointed tasseled hat. He looked utterly splendid.

Under the canopy stood Rabbi Maimi, the cantor, and Hacham Alhadeff, who were conducting the successive wedding ceremonies. They tried to make each service a memorable one for the young couples. They had watched these tender children, some barely twelve, some in their late teens, make their youthful commitment to the holy state of matrimony. A small unhappy minority came to the canopy only reluctantly, their sobbing protests to no avail as their parents forced them to be wed. With a few exceptions, though, the matchmaking had gone well. The Abulafia-Pardo match was, in Rabbi Maimi's estimation, a very good one.

"Is everything ready?," asked Rabbi Maimi solemnly.

Hacham Alhadeff answered, "Yes, everything is all here. The marriage contract has been signed by both parties."

A smiling Rabbi Maimi said, "Good. Let us begin."

Hacham Alhadeff, wearing his Moorish headdress and a long white cloak, read aloud the wedding contract defining the rights and duties of bride and groom. The cantor, silver goblet in hand, sang the *Kiddush*, the sanctification of the wine, and then passed the shining goblet on to Benito. The groom drank some wine and offered the goblet to Rebecca. Lifting her veil, she, too, drank some wine. It was then that Rabbi Maimi spoke.

"Welcome, my children, to this great day in your lives. You are both from good Jewish families, families that I have known for years. I have seen you grow up. I have seen you receive a fine education in the Holy Books of our people. I have seen the love and the care that your dear parents have brought you up with. And today, most of all, I see before me the seeds of a love that will always grow. Yes, I see such a love blossoming in your hearts, and I see such affection and tenderness already present in the glow of your eyes. Yes, Benito Abulafia, yes, Rebecca Pardo, yours is a love that heaven meant to be. During these difficult days, it is your love and concern for each other and for your Jewish brothers and sisters that will see you through the hard times ahead. Your love shall be your strength. Use it generously. It will be a source of your never-ending power. It will be a source of never-ending comfort to both of you. May the God of Israel protect you and your families wherever you may go. Yet wherever you may wander, be true to yourselves, and be true to the faith of your fathers and mothers.

"Both of you have read the marriage contract and have agreed to abide by its terms. It is good and well. Benito, do you have the ring?"

Benito nodded and pulled out a gold ring.

Rabbi Maimi instructed him to put the ring onto Rebecca's outstretched finger, and Benito did so. The rabbi told the groom, "Now, repeat after me . . . 'Behold, thou art sanctified unto me with this ring . . .'"

Benito repeated nervously, "Behold, thou art sanctified unto me with this ring . . ."

The rabbi continued, ". . . according to the laws of Moses and of Israel."

And Benito said, ". . . according to the laws of Moses and of Israel."

Rabbi Maimi smiled happily. "By the authority vested in me by the sovereign crown of Castile, and by the higher authority of the sacred laws of our Torah, I now pronounce you man and wife . . . Now, my children, in this moment of great joy, we must remember the destruction of our ancient Temple one thousand five hundred years ago and the dispersion of Jews throughout the world. We remind ourselves of our homelessness as a people. We must remember that our true home as a people is in the land of Israel and not in this land nor any other. By this tradition of the crushing of the wine glass, we are obligated to remember our past as we celebrate this wonderful happiness of the present."

The rabbi placed the wine glass on the floor. Benito raised his foot and crushed the wine glass with his heel.

"*Mazal Tov*! *Mazal Tov*!," came the hearty cheers from the pews.

Joined by the trio of musicians, the friends and family members broke out into spirited song, amidst hand-clapping and wild hugs and profuse well-wishes for the newlyweds. Gracia Pardo kissed her daughter and her new son-in-law, as did the parents of Benito. The groom, conscious that all eyes were on him, placed his arm inside that of his new bride and left for the side door, bringing along the entire group of happy celebrants, their songs and felicitations continuing unimpeded.

As the Abulafia-Pardo party left and the musicians stopped their playing, Rabbi Maimi signaled for the next couple and their families to step forward. It would be a long day, he thought to himself, the hardest part being that of finding something uniquely meaningful to say to each couple. As he composed in his mind what it was he would say to this next pair of newlyweds, he took small comfort in knowing that his opening statement to one and all would always be the same:

"Welcome, my children, to this great day in your lives . . ."

Chapter 10

The world of Don Abraham Senior was falling apart. His had been the most exalted activity permitted to Jews. Counselor and personal friend of King and Queen, spokesman for Spanish Jewry, chief tax farmer of Castile and Aragon, Senior had held this position for years and had become immensely rich and powerful in the process. Used to opulence and to the exercise of power, he could not see himself as anything other than a courtly grandee. The Edict, however, had changed all that.

Senior's world was falling apart. All that he had built was being destroyed. Fame, fortune, position, even respect — all of it was gone or would be gone by the time that the Edict's deadline came to pass. His fortune, estimated at one million ducats, would be reduced to a trifling one thousand ducats. What could he do with a thousand ducats? For a man of his station and habits, it was nothing more than survival money, a means to live out the rest of his years with the minimum of comforts. If he and his family moved to Portugal, it would cost him a hundred ducats to obtain permission to settle there permanently. That left nine hundred ducats. What could he do with nine hundred ducats? Buy a villa perhaps. But his son-in-law Rabbi Meir and Hanna also would need a place to live, so perhaps he would have to settle for an even more modest residence. He would have to learn Portuguese, unless he wanted to restrict his associations to Castilian-speaking exiles. He would have to live more humbly, live with outcasts in a strange land, live a life he had never known before. Meir could obtain a position in the Portuguese tax-farming system, much in the same way that Abravanel had come from

Portugal and worked with him in the Castilian tax order. Don Abraham had long wanted to retire totally from public service, but he wanted to do it voluntarily, not as a result of coercion. He was accustomed to having the final say on matters that affected his life. Now, it appeared he was on the verge of having no say at all.

His troubles were not of one kind only. Popular feeling was running high against Senior. There were many in the Jewish community who placed the blame for the Edict entirely upon him. He was repeatedly accused of gross negligence, of being the vain old man who had let the community down; it was Senior, it was said, who supposedly had been more protective of his own personal interests than the larger interests of Spanish Jewry; it was he, Senior, who should have given the Jews of the kingdom more time, more advance warning, of all that was to take place.

Yet, he was still the *juez mayor*, the Supreme Judge of all the *aljamas*, and he was not yet ready to abdicate his position because of ignorant grumbling. Nevertheless, by remaining in his position, Senior multiplied his troubles.

He was soon besieged by a deluge of personal requests for his intervention. Troubles were everywhere: In Segovia, as in the other *aljamas*, the evacuation was not proceeding in an orderly manner. The state royal council had issued orders that the local municipalities must arrange to pay the Jews all that was owed to them, and the Jews in turn were to repay their debts, if need be by the liquidation of their possessions. It all sounded fair and just, but local judges were all partial to the Christian participants in any legal dispute, particularly when the Christian owed money to the Jew. Thus it was that the judges, knowing that the Jews would soon be gone from the kingdom, paid no atttention to Jewish plaintiffs. Christian debts were freely annulled, many of them on flimsy charges of usury. In other instances, if it was known that a Jew owed money to a Christian, the Jew was often beaten until he parted with his choice possessions to settle the debt. Everywhere Jews were being beaten, financially as well as physically, and the injured parties came to Don Abraham Senior for his help. Senior was powerless, and claimed that civil cases were outside his jurisdiction.

Senior's troubles increased when it was announced that the King and Queen had decreed that the *aljamas* would have to pay the full taxes for the entire year. It was hard enough for the average Jew to pay off his debts, to sell what he had for practically nothing, but to be required to pay all taxes in advance was too much! Of course, Senior and his son-in-law Meir had to collect the annual taxes. When this was made public, Don Abraham Senior became the symbol of cooperation with the hated rulers.

While requests for his assistance poured into his office, the growing stack of these documents were a testimony of his impotence. Senior read the documents knowing that there was nothing he could do. True, some were indeed outside of his jurisdiction, but mainly it was his sudden loss of will to struggle. He no longer cared what became of him as an individual. And caring little for himself, he became less concerned with the plight of his brethren.

He looked at the first document. It described how the magistrate of Leon, Don Juan de Portugal, had committed several abuses against the local Jewish community. Apparently, the magistrate had demanded thirty thousand maravedis from the Jews simply because he promised to execute his obligations without delay. Furthermore, this Don Juan asked all Christians who had any demand against the Jews to come to him. When Christians came to Don Juan with a demand for repayment from a Jewish party, the magistrate made the debt payable the same day, so he could benefit from the forced execution of the debt. Even when Jews initiated the demand for repayment, the magistrate kept whatever money he desired from the execution of the debt for himself, and gave the Jew who had brought the demand whatever was left. The magistrate forbade Jews from reclaiming whatever was theirs and from complaining about it, or else they would suffer terrible consequences. Senior's friend, the corregidor of Segovia, was being sent to investigate these charges.

In other documents, Senior read how in certain villages, such as Gumiel de Izán and Gumiel de Mercado, Jews were prevented by the local authorities from selling their belongings. It was also forbidden for the villagers to buy any of the belongings, furniture, and other goods of the Jews. In the village of Amusco, one document attested, the same prohibition was applied and worse, guards had been placed at the homes of Jews so they could not leave their houses! A royal edict was issued protesting these practices, but what could Jews do if people refused to buy their belongings?

Most of the other documents dealt with the collection of debts. In many cities, the Jews were leaving the kingdom quickly, leaving their unpaid debts behind. In other instances, Jews destroyed their commercial properties, making them unusable by Christians. In Huesca and Zaragoza, the textile factories had been burned to the ground. There were reports of tanneries, munition factories, and other industrial plants being gutted of instruments and valuable supplies. Granaries, stock piles of wool, estates were being set on fire throughout the land. Unable to obtain good prices for their possessions, many Jews had proceeded to destroy everything they could not take with them.

Christians retaliated in other ways according to the documents. Christians who owed Jews money invented excuses to postpone payment of their debts, presumably to prolong these past the time when the Jews were to leave the kingdom. But Jews who owed money to Christians were being imprisoned or forcibly detained until all their debts were paid. A Rabbi Moses of the village of Carrion had been imprisoned because of failure to pay his debts. Another document contained complaints from the *aljama* of Fuenpudia about Jews being jailed who did not pay in advance all rents and revenues due over the next three-year period. There were many such documents, and Senior did not have time to read them all, much less to do anything about them.

Pushing the documents aside, Senior walked out into the garden. The Christian presence was there, too, in the form of the Hermandad guard who had been assigned to watch over Don Abraham Senior and his household. The air in the garden was crisp and cool, and Don Abraham pulled his velvet cloak tightly around him as he settled quietly onto one of the benches next to the pool. The gentle splashing of the water, the brightly colored flowers and foliage of his garden — all had a mildly soothing effect. But it was not enough; there was too much going on within Spain, within himself, that did not allow him any peace.

Don Abraham had not told anyone, not even his wife Fortuna, of the Queen's threat. If it pained him to consider Isabella's proposition, it pained him more to consider bringing up the matter within his family. Wishing to spare them hurt, he had kept the secret closely guarded within himself. Yet he could not keep it any longer from Fortuna nor from his son-in-law Meir Melamed. Time was running out. The month that Isabella had given him was almost over. Fortuna, crying inconsolably, was making preparations to leave; she deeply resented their sudden change in fortune. Meir's career was also over, and he was likewise making ready for departure. It was not fair to Meir that he had kept this information from him. After all, Meir was a trained rabbi. Most of all, the secret sapped Senior's will, affected his judgment, and undermined his health. Senior needed help with his problem before it was too late.

He decided to visit his old friends, Don Andrés Cabrera, governor of the Alcázar Castle, and his wife, Beatriz de la Bobadilla. Perhaps they could give him some useful advice. The guard went with him. At the Alcázar, Senior was received cordially, and his friends listened attentively to his complaints. They tried to be sympathetic about his overall situation. But when Don Abraham told them, that the Queen had threatened to destroy the Jews of the kingdom if he did not convert, La Bobadilla was incredulous.

Beatriz stammered, "I . . . I cannot believe the Queen would do such a thing, especially to an old friend. Surely the Queen was only making an idle threat. Surely, she simply wanted to pressure you to convert, but she would never carry out her threat."

The worldly Cabrera was not so sure. He had seen Isabella exert her will against any who resisted her plans. He had observed the severe measures she was willing to adopt to achieve those plans. He had seen Isabella establish the Inquisition, vanquish the Moors, and break the mind and body of all who stood in her way.

He argued, "If it is Isabella's intent to have you converted by force, Don Abraham, it is within her power to do so."

Beatriz objected, "Andrés, how can you say such a thing of our Queen? Do not forget that she is my dear friend, and that we do ill to ourselves by speaking ill of her."

Cabrera was unruffled. "My dear Beatriz, the question at hand is not my allegiance nor my affection for the Queen, but the one Don Abraham has raised. It is an honest question that he asks, and it is an honest answer that he expects from us. What we say to him may affect not only him, but also the lives of the many Jews that he represents. Is that not so, Don Abraham?"

A saddened Senior said, "Yes. It is so, Don Andrés."

Cabrera answered him. "Well then, Don Abraham, I shall tell you what, in my estimation, the Queen is most likely to do. If you resist, it is highly unlikely that she will use physical torture against an old friend . . ."

Cabrera paused, apparently wanting to choose his words carefully.

"However, she is obviously determined to bring you into the Christian fold, so that you may continue to serve her."

Senior concurred, "That is obviously her intent."

Cabrera continued, "Well then, if she is determined to bring you into the Christian fold, the Queen will do as she says."

"Andrés!" shouted Beatriz. "How dare you say such a terrible thing?" Beatriz was visibly angry and crossed her arms resentfully.

"Hear me out," said Cabrera, raising his hand as if asking for permission to speak. "The Queen, I repeat, will do as she says, but not to the extent of destroying *all* the Jews of the kingdom. Isabella most likely would allow a certain number of Jews to be killed, perhaps even an entire community, in order to make *you* and Meir convert to Christianity. If you resisted, she would have another *aljama* destroyed, and then another, until you relented. That is how important you and your son-in-law are to the Queen. If this were to take place, I am sure of one thing only, Don Abraham."

"What is that, Don Andrés?" said Senior, his face filled with worry.

Cabrera cleared his throat. "If this happened . . . the killings would start here in Segovia because you are here. Also, the Hermandad contingent and the men under my command would be instructed not to interfere in the killings. Of course, the King and Queen, being strong advocates of law and order, could never *officially* condone such killings . . . you must surely understand that, Don Abraham. It would have to be done under the guise of a spontaneous popular outbreak against the Jews, perhaps at the instigation of some fanatic such as that Dominican De la Peña. You remember him, do you not? Yes, a religiously inspired outbreak, which the royal forces of law and order were unable to contain in time. That would be the official explanation."

Senior arose from his chair and readied himself to leave.

"Don Abraham, where are you going?," asked Cabrera, concerned that he had overly distressed the aging courtier.

Senior said, "I am going home, Don Andrés. I thank you greatly for your extraordinary candor. From your words I have learned what I needed to know. Good day, Don Andrés, and good day to you too, Doña Beatriz."

And with that Don Abraham Senior stepped out of the room and promptly left the castle, the Hermandad guard escorting him as he did so.

Once outside the grounds of the Alcázar, Senior walked up to the edge of the cliff. He stood there in silence, hands behind his back, contemplating what he was about to do. The golden-orange sun in the west was setting in the mountainous distance, casting long sharp shadows in the valley below. Senior had seen a thousand such lovely sunsets in Segovia, yet none with the same significance as this one. As the sun sank, it was evident to Don Abraham that the sunset of his life was now upon him. Once he had dreamed of one last accomplishment as a Jewish courtier, an act that would close his career in glory. But his greatest accomplishment, the one in which he would most serve the needs of his threatened Jewish brethren, would go unrecognized. His last act as a Jewish courtier would be to ask for the ultimate exemption, the exemption from continued membership in his people. The act would be his greatest reward; it would also be his greatest punishment.

Senior knew that there would be accusations from his kinsmen that he had done this to preserve his wealth and station. There would be the vindictive judgment of those who would label him a traitor to this people. Yet there was no alternative, however painful and shameful it was. Senior, Chief Judge of the Jewish *aljamas*, would have to live with it for the rest of his life.

Senior left the cliff and walked back to his estate with a clear conscience, his decision firm. His sole concern was how to tell his wife, Fortuna, his son-in-law, Rabbi Meir, and his daughter of the heart-breaking decision that he had just made. In time, Don Abraham thought, in a week's time at the most, the entire Senior family, after much agonizing protest and argument, would also see the need to ask for the ultimate exemption.

Don Isaac was writing intently at his desk, quill pen in hand. During the last few weeks, he had used every spare moment to write his commentary on the Book of Kings. Despite a thousand interruptions, he found some time to interpret a single line or paragraph. Line by line, chapter by chapter, the commentary was taking shape as he had imagined it, a corpus of distilled scholarship penned in a spirit of interpretive piety. Yet his numerous tasks left little time for such literary undertakings.

First among his many personal matters was to settle his obligations as tax farmer for Don Iñigo López de Mendoza. Also unresolved were his tax obligations to the crown. A summary tabulation was being made of all debts, taxable and otherwise, payable to Abravanel by local individuals and town councils. Don Isaac owed debts to the crown that had been charged to him on the basis of the collected revenues during the past few years. He expected that some sort of exchange agreement could be worked out with the King and Queen to allow him to take out a certain number of gold ducats in return for the crown's assumption of the total debts payable to Abravanel.

As he was writing, a tax-farming aide appeared at the door. He was a young well-dressed man, about thirty years of age. "Good news, sir. I have collected from Alonso Gómez the six thousand maravedis that he owes you; and also from that clown Peral Pleno, I collected another one thousand and nine hundred maravedis . . . Now the bad news . . . I have not been able to locate Abraham Zarfaty or Ferran Altabet — perhaps they have left the country. Francisco Ximenes says he will pay you back in another week. Maybe he will, maybe he won't.

Abravanel said calmly, "Fine. That is enough. Do what you can. If I do not collect these debts and distribute the money among my own people, the crown will get it."

The messenger responded, "Yes, Don Isaac, I will do my best."

Abravanel waved him off, and the messenger departed.

Don Isaac continued to write as he recorded the community reaction to the pronouncement of the Edict, ". . . when the dreadful news reached the people, all mourned their fate. And wherever the edict was read, a grieving mournful spirit came amongst the Jews, a great trembling and lamentation that had not been seen since the time of the expulsion of our forefathers from their land in Judah. And one Jew would say to another: 'Let us be strong and of good courage on behalf of our faith and on behalf of God's Torah, holding our heads high with pride before the voice of the enemy who taunts us and maligns us. If they let us live, then live we shall. If they kill us, then we shall die. But we shall not transgress the sacred Covenant, nor shall our hearts retreat from the battle, but rather we shall venture forth in the name of the Lord our God . . .' "

There was a knock on the door. It was Esther with a cup of mint tea. As she laid the cup on his desk, she said, "Isaac, there is someone in the front who wants to speak with you."

"Very well, dearest. Send him in," said Don Isaac, sipping tea. As Esther went to get the visitor, Abravanel straightened out the scattered books and scrolls on his desk.

Luis de Santangel, the comptroller-general to Ferdinand and Isabella, appeared at the door. The man was tall and elegantly dressed. Luis de Santangel was a known converso of noble Aragonese lineage whose relatives had achieved notoriety for their Judaizing activities. A cousin of Luis by the same name had been burned at the stake for his participation in the assassination of the Inquisitor Pedro de Arbúes. Indeed, as many as fifteen relatives of the Santangel family had been tried and punished by the Inquisition. The present Luis would have fallen into the hands of the Holy Office had it not been for his long-standing friendship with Ferdinand. He had risen in the ranks of the

Aragonese court, first as a courtier, then as a tax collector of the royal treasury. Finally, he had been advanced to his present position as the *Escribano de Ración*, a position which gave him control over the King's private purse. Obviously a man of wealth in his own right, Santangel had been the one to secure the entire financing for the forthcoming voyage of Christopher Columbus, one of the financiers being his good friend Don Isaac himself. Despite the family's notoriety, Luis moved about freely, fearing no one. It was even rumored that Luis had secured protection from the Holy Office by paying a large sum to the King.

Don Isaac was happy to see his friend. "Luis de Santangel! What a surprise and what a pleasure!"

"The pleasure is mine, Don Isaac," said Santangel. "How is the family?"

Abravanel replied, "Doing as well as can be expected under the circumstances . . . none of us is happy about leaving. But what can you do? Yes, indeed, what can anyone do? Tell me, that young mariner Columbus, how is his project going?"

The comptroller-general laughed as he shook his head affirmatively. "That Columbus, he is an enterprising fellow. He has already assembled most of the seamen he needs. *Vaya*, he even has three men who were condemned to life imprisonment to ship with him. It seems they helped a condemned murderer escape, but Columbus was so desperate he was not too particular to take even these men."

"So when did he leave?"

Luis de Santangel cleared his throat. "He has not left. You are aware, Don Isaac, that in April of this year, the contracts between Columbus and the sovereigns were signed. The following month, the royal order was given that his fleet of three caravels be outfitted at the port of Palos and that it be made ready to sail within ten days time. Ten days is a very short time, but that is not the reason why they have not left."

"Then what, pray tell, is the reason?," a curious Abravanel inquired.

Santangel explained, "Torquemada is the reason. The Inquisitor began to get suspicious that so many Jews and Conversos were financing the expedition, and particularly when he discovered that you were involved. As a result, the Holy Office informed Columbus that he cannot sail from Palos until every single Jew has left Spain. That means that Columbus cannot leave before August 2."

Abravanel reciprocated the look. "Then Torquemada knows?"

Santangel's eyes widened slightly. "All that Torquemada knows is that Jews and Conversos are somehow behind this expedition; also that

Columbus is strangely vague about his origins, and that he mixes with individuals not to their liking. That is all he knows. Somehow the Inquisitor smells a Jewish plot in this expedition. He has a nose for us, you know. His grandmother was Jewish."

Abravanel shrugged his shoulders. "I suppose each one of us has distinct reasons for the expedition. Columbus wants to find his new trade route to the Indies and become an Admiral. You, Luis, want to make your investment pay off. And I . . ."

"Yes, what about you?," asked Santangel.

Abravanel smiled broadly, stroking his beard. "I suppose that I had Jewish interests in mind when I made the investment. If the island of Cipango is truly as close as Columbus claims, Jews could settle there, perhaps even flee there in times of persecution, as in our own day. But Torquemada has seen to it that all Jews will be out of Spain before the expedition begins. And even if Columbus discovers Cipango, it will be too late to do us any good. The world is over for us here in Spain, my friend, while this mariner goes off in search for another. Actually, I hoped that he might find remnants of the Ten Lost Tribes of Israel living in Asia . . . or perhaps even find the land of the Khazars."

"The Khazars? Who are they?," asked Santangel, mystified.

Abravanel explained. "The Khazars were an Asian people that converted to Judaism in the eighth century. According to correspondence of the Jewish vizier of Granada in the tenth century with the Khazar king, the kingdom of the Khazars was the only place where Jews had sovereignty over themselves. However, no one has heard from them for several hundred years. In any case, if such a Jewish-ruled kingdom did exist somewhere in Asia, and if contact through Columbus' voyage could be made with its ruler, it would make sense to divert the persecuted Jews of our day to such a domain. But this is all very hypothetical. For all I know, the kingdom of the Khazars may not exist anymore . . . But you did not come all this way to listen to me talk about Khazars and the Ten Lost Tribes of Israel. What is the real reason you came here, Luis? Problems with the fleet of ships you are organizing to take us away? Or is it something else?"

Abravanel stopped talking and took another sip of tea.

The tall Aragonese asked, "Don Isaac, have you heard about Senior?"

Don Isaac replied, "No, I haven't seen him the last few days. Why?"

Santangel took a deep breath. "He is converting to Christianity."

Abravanel bolted out of his chair, spilling the tea. "*WHAT*?!," he shouted, his voice choking with disbelief.

Santangel said, "The King and the Queen put great pressure on him and his son-in-law Meir to convert. They were afraid to lose their financial services and, from what I hear, they threatened to destroy the Jews of Spain if Senior and Meir Melamed did not convert."

An incredulous Abravanel buried his head in his hands. "Oh no . . . oh no . . . I cannot believe it . . . after all these years — Senior, Senior, Senior, how could you."

The Aragonese nobleman continued. "Senior and his family, including Rabbi Meir Melamed, will be baptized tomorrow in the Church of Santa Maria de Guadalupe. The godparents at the baptism ceremony will be the King and Queen. Cardinal Mendoza himself will perform the sacrament. They are making a really big thing out of the occasion."

Abravanel lifted his head and spoke, "Thinking it will lead other Jews to follow suit, eh? Oh, my God, who could have imagined such a thing?"

Santangel took another deep breath. "Isaac . . . I have something else to tell you."

Abravanel, a concerned look on his face, asked, "Yes . . . what is it?"

Santangel lifted and lowered his eyebrows, the frown flitting once again across his face. "Isaac, *you are next.*"

Abravanel's shoulders dropped upon hearing this.

Pausing for a moment, the Aragonese courtier continued, "After your words at the Alhambra, they want to break you just as they broke Senior. You must not let them. You must hire a bodyguard, perhaps several bodyguards, to protect you. If you go the way of Senior, Don Isaac, the Jews of Spain are finished. They will convert *en masse* if they see the chief rabbi, the great Don Isaac Abravanel, converting. You are their last hope."

The color returned to Don Isaac's face, and his eyes regained their look of vigor. "I understand, Luis. I understand. Thank you for coming to tell me. You have always been a friend at court that I can trust. Thank you, dear friend."

"I must take leave now, Don Isaac, I have endangered my position by such a disclosure," said Santangel. "Be careful. Protect yourself and your family . . . I have heard rumors of a plot to kidnap your grandchild. My advice to you is to get out of Spain as fast as you can."

Abravanel understood. "I will, Luis. I promise you. And I thank you once again for your time and consideration."

Don Isaac went up to Luis de Santangel and embraced him, knowing he would never see him again. As the Aragonese nobleman left, Don Isaac stood at the door contemplating his visitor's message. As time had run out for Senior and his family, so too time was running out for the Abravanels.

"Esther! Esther!," he shouted.

Esther came out of one of the rooms. "Yes, yes, what is it, Isaac?"

Abravanel told her. "We must prepare for departure immediately."

"But, Isaac, we are not scheduled to leave for another month."

"Then make other arrangements, Esther. I want all of us — you, me, our children and grandchildren, to leave within two weeks. We are taking a ship to Naples."

"But, Isaac, there is plenty of time . . . why the rush? Let us settle our affairs and *then* go."

"Please, Esther, do not argue with me. Just do what I say."

"Why, Isaac . . . I have never seen you talk to me this way. I feel something new has happened. Is it something that man said?"

"My dear, it is absolutely nothing to worry about. Just take care of these arrangements . . . please."

Esther studied his eyes. "Very well, Isaac . . . in two weeks from Valencia. Thus shall it be. Very little time, Isaac . . . but if you say so, I shall do it."

Esther went back into the room where she had come from. Abravanel wandered off in another direction to look for the house servant Alfonso. He found him in the garden potting flowers. Don Isaac instructed him, "Alfonso, find two Jewish guards, one to be stationed at each gate. Henceforth, no one is to enter our house without permission from me, do you understand?"

The servant answered, "Yes, Don Isaac, I shall do so right away."

Alfonso put aside the flowers, wiped his hands, and went to find the guards.

On returning to his study, Abravanel sat down again in his chair, stared at the books piled on his desk, and wondered if it was possible for him to continue writing. The notice of Senior's conversion was very disturbing. Yet he could not allow the mortifying events of the day to be a source of his discomposure. He knew that he had to stand steady in this time of tumult while others stumbled. Quieting his inner unrest, he knew that he had to go on, however great the hurdle, that somehow in the turbulence of the maelstrom, he had to make himself write, come what may. Opening his Bible to the Book of Kings, Abravanel took his plume in hand and continued the writing of his prophetic commentary.

A large group of gaily dressed people were in the plaza square in front of the cathedral in Guadalupe. Several nuns and priests were present, as were most of the local nobility. Counts and marquees, dressed in splendid silken outfits and tasseled pointed hats, came with their ladies. Knights on horses with flags of Castile and Aragon, the castle commanders from Coca and Guadamur, strolled back and forth in the plaza, honored to have been invited to the ceremony attended by the King and Queen. The excitement of the crowd had not yet subsided from the appearance a short while earlier of Don Ferdinand and Doña Isabella. The rulers had been greeted by the mayor of Guadalupe, the local aristocracy, high-placed officials, members of the church, and heads of local Hermandades.

The King and Queen had not left Granada since the beginning of the year. The rebellious Moors still sporadically resisted their Castilian overlords, and Ferdinand and Isabella had stayed behind at the Alhambra castle to ensure civil and administrative order. Nothing had been important enough for them to leave Granada until they received a message from Don Andrés Cabrera and his wife that Don Abraham Senior and his family were ready to convert to Christianity. The Chief Judge of the Jews, the *juez mayor*, was to become a Christian! That was cause for national celebration.

Putting other matters aside, Ferdinand and Isabella made ready to leave for the Castilian town of Guadalupe. At Senior's personal request, as communicated by Cabrera, the Chief Judge of the Jews did not want to be converted in a town or city containing Jews. Guadalupe was chosen because, since 1485, Jews had been forbidden to live in the town by order of Nuño de Arévalo, the local Inquisitor. The date set for Senior's baptism was June 15, 1492.

A horse-drawn carriage guarded by three Hermandad guards from Segovia led by Don Enrique Domínguez de Córdoba entered the square. Domínguez, famous as the archenemy of Conversos in Segovia, was bringing his greatest quarry, the Jew Don Abraham Senior, to the place where the mighty Hebrew would go down on his knees. Don Enrique Domínguez would thus finally receive the recognition that was his due. Domínguez slowed his horse, raising his gloved hand up in the air, halting the advance of the carriage and the two guards. Savoring the moment, Domínguez stood high in the saddle, making sure that all eyes were on him.

A youth from the crowd scrambled on the carriage, looked inside, and called loudly, "It is him! It's Senior and his family! They are here!"

The crowd burst into cheers. Domínguez doubled back towards the carriage and chased the youth away. Dismounting in a dignified manner, the Hermandad head went to the carriage and opened its door. Domínguez had delivered his man.

Six escorts armed with steel-tipped lances, accompanied by four nuns carrying crucifixes in their hands, made their way through the crowd to the carriage. There was a hush over the crowd.

A shamed Don Abraham Senior emerged with bowed head and downcast eyes. Senior was helped down by the escort, followed by Fortuna. Then his son-in-law Rabbi Meir Melamed appeared, nearly stumbling as he got out of the carriage; and finally Meir's wife came to join them.

Senior and his family were led through the crowd, a nun alongside each of them with crucifixes held high in the air. The escorts held back the crowd, which gave its enthusiastic approval of the goings-on, shouting 'Bravos', clapping, half-jeering, physically pressing upon the neophytes-to-be as they passed by.

Senior's family and their escort arrived at the foot of the cathedral steps. At the great doors of the church stood Cardinal Mendoza, a golden staff in one hand, a cross in the other. The Cardinal was flanked by priests from various religious orders.

Don Abraham Senior climbed the steps of the cathedral until he was face to face with the Cardinal. The two of them stood there in seeming confrontation, the one-time head of Spanish Jewry facing the primate of Christian Spain, staring into each other's eyes and saying nothing. The silence of the hushed crowd added to the tension. Then, in a sudden collapse of resistance, Senior went down on his knees in front of the Cardinal and proceeded to kiss the ring on the primate's hand.

A loud cheer burst forth from the crowd. The rest of the Senior family, heads bowed, stood in muted silence amidst the deafening roar of the multitude. Cardinal Mendoza raised his gold crucifix, and the crowd was silenced as before.

The Cardinal spoke, "Welcome, Don Abraham Senior. You and your family are to follow me." Then the Cardinal turned, his staff and cross held upright, and led the procession into the church. Senior rose from his kneeling position and was quickly joined by an escort guard and a nun. Together, the three followed the Cardinal into the cathedral of Guadalupe. Senior's family was accompanied in the same way into the church.

Altar boys waved censers with burning incense in front of Cardinal Mendoza, while Franciscan priests intoned a chant. Nobles and other dignitaries, seated in their pews, watched the procession advance towards the sacristy.

Waiting by the altar for the retinue were Ferdinand and Isabella, the godparents-to-be of Don Abraham. The Cardinal arrived first, followed by Senior.

Ferdinand came forward and embraced Senior, greeting him warmly, "Welcome, Don Abraham, to the fold of our Lord Jesus Christ." Senior ignored the feigned warmth, but nonetheless returned the embrace.

Isabella extended her hand to Senior, but Don Abraham ignored it. Isabella quickly motioned with her hand as if she had intended to do something else with it. She said cooly, "Yes, welcome, Don Abraham, and all of your family as well." Senior preferred not to answer. The singing stopped.

Cardinal Mendoza, sensing the tension in the encounter, said, "Let us proceed with the ceremony. Come this way, Don Abraham . . ."

Mendoza led the way to the nearby baptismal font. The Cardinal pointed to the white marble font and directed Senior to kneel and bow his head.

Senior hesitated, looking at the marble font, at Cardinal Mendoza, and then at his family. He saw Fortuna, stone-like, with a few tears on her cheeks. Meir had a blank stare on his face, his eyes glazed and distant. Meir's wife clung to him, her glance directed at the floor. Left to himself, Senior closed his tired eyes and meditated a short moment. Sighing deeply, he let his shoulders sag, mumbling silently to himself in Aramaic, "*Nidrena lo nidrei. U-shevuana lo shevuei.*" "Our vows are not vows, and our oaths are not oaths."

Slowly, ever so slowly, Senior went toward the font. He kneeled and positioned his head over it. The Cardinal, standing next to the kneeling figure of Senior, sprinkled the bowed head of the Jewish courtier with the baptismal waters while intoning, "I baptize thee in the name of the Father, the Son, and the Holy Ghost. And I christen thee, by which name you shall be called henceforth, Fernando Nuñez Coronel. Arise, Don Nuñez Coronel."

Don Fernando Nuñez Coronel rose. Don Abraham Senior was no more. The choir of priests broke out again in song, "*Gloria! Gloria!*

Gloria in Excelsis Deo!" The church bells pealed loudly, filling the air with their vibrations. Those in the pews joined in the *Gloria*; many left their seats to congratulate and welcome the new Christian to their midst. Coronel was besieged by well-wishers, from both the priesthood and the aristocracy. They vigorously shook his hand and embraced him. Don Nuñez Coronel looked bewildered, uncomprehending, because it was difficult to remain indifferent to such a massive and effusive display of apparently sincere goodwill. He nodded and smiled, accepting the many felicitations. He shook several extended hands, embraced a count, and even reciprocated the former hug of his godfather, King Ferdinand. He walked over to the Queen and extended his hand in an offer of friendly reconciliation. Don Fernando Nuñez Coronel, realizing he was no longer the same man, bowed respectfully in front of Isabella and kissed the hand of his Queen.

Chapter 11

Simon Maimi, chief rabbi of Segovia, was busy with last minute matters. The entire community was leaving, and like the others, Rabbi Maimi had sold his house for a trivial sum. He had already given away most of his belongings. As the rabbi of Segovia, however, Simon Maimi had an important duty to perform: he had to supervise packing the sacred scrolls.

In the now deserted synagogue, Rabbi Maimi watched two *yeshiva* students carefully remove the scrolls from the ark and place them in wooden crates. Each scroll was wrapped in a thick blanket, and then smaller pillows and blankets were inserted to prevent the scrolls from moving during transport. Then the gold and silver Torah ornaments were wrapped and placed in smaller packing cases.

Rabbi Maimi looked around the synagogue, its vast white-walled interior now an empty shell, its ceiling rafters now become the wooden tombstone of a defunct community. Only a few days earlier the synagogue had seen its last Sabbath, resonated to its last Hebrew prayers and chants. In his service, Rabbi Maimi had tried to strengthen the weak and fortify the faithful with parting words of comfort. Now as it was time for him to go, he felt the building's stillness within himself. He felt a sense of loss, a loss not only of his community, but also of a centuries-old Sephardic tradition. It was to be a tradition no longer to be seen in Spain.

In the corner, Rabbi Maimi saw a *yeshiva* student studying by the light from a nearby window. He walked quietly over to the student and looked over his shoulder to see what he was studying. The student, named Yosef Almosnino, was of frail constitution, yet he had an intelligence and zeal to learn that was unequaled by any of his classmates. The rabbi found his answer. "*Maseket Toharot*, . . . the laws of purity and cleanliness. Laws of joy and health. You have studied them well, Yosef. You know the laws of our Talmud better than anyone else in the *yeshiva*."

The student looked up and replied, "I will devote my life to its study, Rabbi Maimi . . . if the Holy One, Blessed be He, grants me life and understanding."

Rabbi Maimi put his hand on the youth's shoulder. "Yosef, you are the pride of our *yeshiva*. I expect great things of you. You will be a light to our people and lead them in the paths of righteousness and sacred learning."

The student added, "I hope I will be worthy, Rabbi . . . I . . ."

Rabbi Maimi kept his hand on the young man's shoulders. "I have no fear of that. But now, my son, it is time to pack your belongings and books and even your Talmud . . . and leave this land where we are not wanted. It is time, Yosef."

Yosef closed the book. "Yes, rabbi, I shall start getting ready." The rabbi patted him gently on the back. Carrying the hefty volume, Yosef went to settle his affairs.

The rabbi, seeing that the packing of the scrolls was completed, had the *yeshiva* students carefully carry the loaded crates onto the mule-drawn carts. Once this was done, the students covered the crates with a thick quilt to provide a final layer of protection to the sacred scrolls.

Rabbi Maimi returned to the synagogue. He looked around one last time to see if anything had been forgotten. The prayer books, the eternal lamp, and the Torah scrolls had all been packed and readied for transport. The inside was now empty and he could not stay there any more. Using an iron key, the rabbi locked the entrance door securely. He walked down the path that led away from the synagogue, knowing that it would soon be converted into a church by the Inquisition. There was no need for him to look back.

Rabbi Maimi stepped out onto the street, where there was frantic activity. Scores of people were loading their belongings onto carts, donkeys, and wagons; others carried their belongings on their backs. The rabbi continued walking down the street, when he saw that a barefoot street urchin was following.

The child asked playfully, "Rabbi Maimi, Rabbi Maimi! Where are you going?"

The rabbi turned around to face the child. "Oh, close by . . . shouldn't you be with your parents?"

The urchin replied, "Haven't got any."

The rabbi said, "Then you wait here in this place for me. You understand?"

"But, rabbi," the orphan said, "you're going the wrong way." The urchin pointed in the opposite direction. "The boats, the road to Cartagena is this way."

The rabbi bent down and spoke gently but firmly to the orphan. "You wait for me right here, child. Trust me. I will be back soon."

The orphan stayed as the rabbi continued on his way. Fearing that he would be left behind, the youngster reminded the rabbi. "But hurry, rabbi. Everyone is leaving. Hurry, or we will miss the boat."

The orphan watched with disappointment as Rabbi Maimi headed in the direction of the cemetery.

The portly rabbi headed for the *Fonsario*, the ancient cemetery of the Jewish community of Segovia. Rabbi Maimi left the city walls via the San Andrés gate and carefully walked down the steep slope towards the large caves of the 'Hill of the Pits,' to the tombs of the community. Crossing the tiny bridge that spanned the river Clamores, he came upon the opening that led to the limestone bedrock of the cemetery. He saw several people there, most of them women, clutching at tombstones and wailing over the graves of their deceased relatives. Their sobbing cries echoed through the cavern. Rabbi Maimi placed a candle next to one of the stones and began to copy the Hebrew inscription on it. He had work to do.

Gracia Pardo, her daughter Rebecca, and son-in-law Benito were attempting to place their ailing grandfather on the back of a hay-filled wagon. The mule-drawn wagon was already full with leather bags, sacks, bundles of clothing and food. The grandfather, Samuel, swollen with dropsy, was resisting.

"Please, leave me here to die," he pleaded, gasping for air.

Gracia was insistent. "No, Father, we all go together. All of us go, or we do not go at all."

The elderly Samuel struggled to breathe. "Leave me here, please . . . no more. I say, no more. Leave me alone . . . I don't want to go . . . No . . . please, no, please leave me here."

Despite his moanings, they lifted him on the hay-covered portion of the cart.

"There! That does it," said Gracia, relieved that this was over. "He will be more comfortable now. Anything else inside?"

Rebecca blurted, "The brazier! I forgot the brazier. I left it at the fireplace."

Benito said, "I will get it, *querida*," and went inside the house to get the brazier.

While her son-in-law was inside, Gracia sighed heavily, "Good. Very good."

Rebecca asked, "What is it, mama?"

Gracia explained, a nostalgic look in her eye, "Your husband . . . he is a good man, like your father of blessed memory."

"I don't want to go!," said the grandfather. "Let me be, for God's sake!"

No one paid any attention to his groans.

Benito returned with the brazier and placed it on the wagon heap. The grandfather, he noted, looked very ill and continued to be short of breath.

Gracia slowly walked up to the door of her humble tenement and took off the *mezuzah* from the door post. She reached into her pocket, pulled out a large iron key, and locked the door securely. She walked back to the wagon and handed the key to her son-in-law.

"Benito, my son, this has always been the key to our house for as long as I remember. Although it is no longer ours, still we have many beautiful memories of the time that we spent here, especially when my husband, God rest his soul, was still alive. Anyhow, I do not know how to say this but, being as you are the new man in the family, I want you to have this key. I want you to keep it and treasure it and save it for your children and your children's children. Let it be a reminder to all the generations that come after us of what we once had in Spain."

Benito gripped the key tightly in his hand and hugged his mother-in-law comfortingly. Gracia began to cry, as did her daughter Rebecca. They clung to Benito, bemoaning their plight in having to forever leave their abode, however humble it might have been, for some place, God knows only where, someplace far away in some distant land, someplace that they would never be able to call home.

The nearsighted goldsmith, Anton Matalon, and his wife Josefina were packed. With the help of some Christian friends, Anton had been able to smuggle out the major gold pieces in his jewelry collection, as well as a substantial number of gold ducats. It had been agreed upon that he would meet his helpers on the other side of the Portuguese border, where they would split the smuggled wealth, fifty-fifty. Anton had been very careful to engage only Christians he knew well. They were for the most part apprentices, who saw a chance to make some money. It was beneficial to both sides, as Anton and Josefina would save at least half their assets, rather than lose it all according to the Edict. There was always that risk that the Christian smuggler would take the gold and disappear, but they were held in check by promises of more gold from other exiles and the realization that someone might tell the local Hermandad of their illegal activities if they tried any double-dealing.

Yet Anton and Josefina had not been able to dispose of all their belongings. They had not been able to sell their house at the price that they wanted. Up until the very last moment, Anton had been busy selling his trinkets and baubles, making a few maravedis here and there, exchanging them in turn for gold ducats. With four children to support, they needed to take out as many gold ducats as they possibly could. As the day of departure was upon them, it became imperative to dispose of the few gold ducats in their possession.

Josefina spat out the first coin she tried to swallow. "I can't, Anton, I can't swallow the coin."

Furrowing his eyebrows, Anton beseeched her. "But you must, my love! You must do it . . . if not for me, then for the children. Come on now . . . we have got to do this. I swallow some, and you swallow some too. It is our only hope."

"*But I can't!*," said Josefina, shaking her head.

Anton pleaded. "Do it for me, *querida*, sweetheart, my darling, my precious, my jewel . . . please do it for me, my one and only . . ."

Josefina heaved her chest. "All right, I will try again," she said, staring once again at the ducat, studying its size and shape. Looking at her husband, she said jestfully, "But do you love me?"

The goldsmith lifted his hand and blew her a kiss. "Like the sweetest flower of Córdoba . . ."

Josefina closed her eyes and put the ducat on her tongue. Holding her breath, she tried to swallow the coin but gagged on it. She spat out the coin again as her terrified husband looked on. She took another deep breath and put the coin back in her mouth. This time, she gulped loudly, her face contorted frightfully into a grimace, her eyes stretched wide open in a gasping look of horror. Then, as her gagging ceased, she took a cautious breath of air. Nothing happened. A flicker of a smile came upon her face as she turned her head towards her husband for approval.

Anton understood immediately. Beaming radiantly, he yelled, "Ay, Portugal, here we come!"

Emboldened by her success, Josefina swallowed another ducat, and then another, until she had swallowed a total of twenty such gold coins. It was enough for one day. Proud of her accomplishment, and with an occasional clanking sound in her belly, she sauntered off to tell Morenica and her other neighbors that she was almost worth her weight in gold.

Anton was very proud of his wife. He knew that he would have to do the same very shortly. But first, he had to sell the house.

Many Jews in the *judería*, had sold their homes to Converso families in Segovia, while others had simply accepted what the calculating magistrate had offered them. Either way, you ended up selling your house for far less than it was worth. Fernández, the magistrate, had at least made him an offer of three thousand maravedis, this being equal to eight ducats. Eight ducats was eight ducats, gold was gold, and it was better to have this than nothing at all.

Making his way out of the *judería* , Anton Matalon managed to find the residential estate of the magistrate of Segovia.

Admitted by the servant and escorted into the reception room, he was greeted coldly by the magistrate Fernández. "Yes, what is it, Matalon?"

"Well, Señor Fernández, it is about my house. A few days ago, you were kind enough to make me an offer of three thousand maravedis. If you would be so kind as to make that same offer again, I am willing to sell it to you for such a low price."

"That offer was made ten days ago, Jew," the magistrate said nastily. "I will offer you only three hundred maravedis for your house."

"Three hundred maravedis!," said Anton unbelievingly. "Why, that is less than one ducat!"

"Three hundred maravedis. Take it or leave it . . . Jew," said Fernández in the same insulting tone of voice.

The goldsmith's face turned red with anger. "Three hundred maravedis! You cheat, you think I'm going to sell you my house for three hundred maravedis! I tell you to your face, Fernández, you are a cheat. You are a thief. And you know what, you make me want to vomit. Let the Crown take my property, for all I care . . . but damn you, Fernández, you . . . you will never have my house, so help me God!"

Fernández snorted and called his servant. "Get this Jewish excrement out of my house, and do not let any more of these vermin into my house."

"*Sí, señor*," said the servant, who grabbed Anton suddenly and thrust him out the door.

Anton landed on the hard ground outside. He picked himself up slowly and dusted himself off. Still a little wobbly from the incident, he slowly regained his composure. As Anton stepped off the magistrate's property, he looked towards the house and spat in that direction. He could not wait to leave Segovia.

The goldsmith continued walking back to the *judería* and its beehive of departing bustle. As he approached the Jewish quarter, Señor Matalon stopped to rest against a wooden post, resting his head on his forearm. He cursed Fernández and cursed himself for having gone to see him. As he stood there, a woman approached him cautiously. It was Señora Anita Gonzalez, an elderly Christian lady whom he had once helped.

Before Ferdinand and Isabella had established the Inquisition and confined all Jews to the Jewish quarter, Jews and Christians had befriended one another. Christians were not afraid of exchanging gifts with Jews, nor were they hesitant about attending Jewish ceremonies. In those days, it was customary for the Jews to bring gifts to Christians during Christmas, and for the Christians to send to Jews fruits, eggs, and other items during Passover. On Jewish festivals, Jews would give alms to the poor, Jews or Christians. And Señora Gonzalez, whose family was hungry one Christmas, received six capons, partridges, and fruits from the Matalón family. She never forgot it.

Tapping him on the shoulder, the elderly lady inquired anxiously, "Señor Matalon, are you feeling all right?"

The goldsmith was startled. "Señora Gonzalez, what are you doing here?"

The lady replied, "I was looking for you in the *judería* , señor. I heard you were going away. You've been so kind to me and my family . . . and I'll never see you and your family again. Well . . . I just thought that I might bring you a little something you could use . . . a loaf of freshly cooked sponge bread. It is not much, but it is very good. I baked it myself."

Accepting the loaf, the puzzled goldsmith looked at the lady with a curious wry smile. "Señora Gonzalez . . . you did this for me and my family?"

The lady remarked, "Yes . . . you and your wife have always been so kind to our family, and we've never had the means to repay you. So I thought . . . well, just maybe, I could help you yet a little bit.

Matalon smelled the sponge bread's delicious aroma. "Sponge bread, eh? So this is my departing gift from Spain, eh? . . . *mi pan de España* . . . Señora Gonzalez, come with me. I have one more thing to give you." The goldsmith pulled out a parchment deed from his vest. "This . . . this is the deed of ownership to my house." Anton wrote quickly on the deed and signed his name in a flourish. "I now transfer my house, through this deed, into your hands and with my seal." The goldsmith pressed hard with his seal on the parchment wax, indenting it with the mark of legal validity.

Señora Gonzalez was overwhelmed. "Oh, no, señor . . . how can you do such a thing? *Ay, Dios mío* . . . Oh no, Señor."

The goldsmith placed the deed into her hands. "There it is, Señora Gonzalez, there is nothing to argue about. The house is yours to keep and enjoy. It is obviously worth no more than a loaf of bread."

"But Señor Matalon, this is too much," she protested.

Anton Matalon would have it no other way. "Take good care of it, Señora, and thank you most kindly for the sponge bread. *Adios, Señora.*" Carrying the loaf of bread, he waved goodbye to her as he walked away.

The astonished lady, her hands trembling from the document in her hands, stood in place, watching her benefactor return to the *judería*. As before, she knew that she would never be able to repay the gift. With great affection, she again waved goodbye to the man who had rewarded her kindness with an even greater kindness. Never having had a house of her own, she could not thank such a man enough. She wished him well, this Señor Matalon that she would never see again.

"Ay, señor," she said, "*Vaya con Dios.* May God be with you."

The orphan was watching four children playing a game of blind man's buff in the street. One child was blindfolded in the center, while the others tried to touch him. The object was for the blindfolded child to grab whoever tried to touch him. It looked like fun, so the orphan went over to join them. As they played, the children were careful to go to one side whenever a cart went by.

The entire street was teeming with crickety two-wheeled carts, loaded with the belongings of the departing Jews. Struggling with the heavy loads, the donkeys brayed loudly as they were prodded and whipped into motion.

Ships were ready for the Jews in the port of Cartagena. Seeking an Arabic-speaking country, the Hacham and Morenica decided to immigrate to the land of the Moors and to use Cartagena as their point of departure. Gracia Pardo and her family also intended to take a vessel from Cartagena, but they wanted to go to the land of the Ottoman Turks. The community of Segovia was split in two halves, one half planned to leave by sea, the other half to cross into Portugal. To help the poor with traveling expenses, all the wealthy members of the community contributed generous amounts of money.

Benito and Rebecca Abulafia were ready to leave, but Gracia Pardo rushed to her friend Morenica's house to give her a last parting kiss and hug, and likewise bade farewell to Hacham Alhadeff. They wished each other well, asking for God's protection along the way, wishing each other a safe journey on the road to Cartagena. Then Gracia rushed back to the cart and got on. They were on their way. As the four set out, a commotion arose at the entrance gate of the Jewish quarter.

Two Dominican priests, one the Inquisitor Diego Lucero, and four guards, suddenly appeared in the street. The priests carried crosses high above their heads, which alarmed any Jews crossing their path. Other Jews who were farther away went back into their homes to seek cover. Those Jews who could not get away scrambled underneath their wagons.

The group of children quickly disbanded their game. A panic-stricken pregnant woman came by quickly, gathered two of the children by the hand, and pulled them inside a nearby house. The blindfolded child was left feeling blindly in the air for his now departed playmates; miraculously, a young teenage girl seemed to come out of nowhere and jerked the child to safety. The orphan was left standing alone, because he was the only one who had no house to hide in. The orphan stayed behind the edge of a large building where, safely out of sight, he could watch the action.

Two of Lucero's men pounded upon the door of a Jewish merchant. As the men beat upon the door with their fists, the priest held his crucifix high in the air and proclaimed, "Convert and be saved, my children. Be baptized in the name of the Lord Jesus Christ. Accept and all shall be forgiven." Lucero's men pounded on the door to no avail.

Gracia Pardo and her family moved slowly in their wagon. Her son-in-law Benito whipped the donkey harder, but the animal could not go any quicker. As they approached the entrance gate of the Jewish quarter, they saw people running in all directions. Gracia felt something was wrong, so she stopped the wagon. Holding onto the reins, a puzzled Benito wondered what was going on.

The Inquisitor spotted the Pardo wagon and ordered, "Stop the wagon!" Lucero's men left the door and ran towards the wagon.

Gracia Pardo screamed as she saw Lucero and his men approach. "Help us, someone! Help us! *HELP!*", she screamed again and again, but the men surrounded the wagon quickly so that no one could get away. Lucero came up behind his men, saying, "Stop and listen to the word of Christ risen." Now Rebecca also screamed in terror, joining her mother with pleas for help.

Lucero thrust the cross into Benito's face. "Convert and be baptized in the name of the Lord. Accept and all shall be forgiven."

Benito backed away from the crucifix. "Get out of our way. I said, get out of our way."

Lucero's men moved in closer. One held the donkey, while another reached for Benito, who still held the reins. Benito shook him off. Gracia's and Rebecca's screams filled the street when it looked like Benito would be dragged away.

The orphan came out of his hiding place and ran down the street looking for help. There was no one to be seen. He banged on one door, then another, asking for help, but no one answered. He ran frantically down the street, then turned around and raced breathlessly toward the San Andrés Gate. Out of the city walls he went, his tiny legs churning up a small cloud of dust as he sped down the rock-strewn slope that led towards the cemetery. He crossed the bridge and went past the river Clamores, until he arrived at the *Fonsario*.

Inside the cemetery, Rabbi Maimi was writing down the last of the Hebrew inscriptions on the tombstones. Crouched by a tombstone, he read Hebrew inscriptions by candlelight, "Here lies the son of Nissim Ben Reubeni, a child perfect in understanding of the Bible, with sweetness of soul, beloved of his parents, may the Holy One, Blessed be He, grant him eternal peace and comfort." The rabbi went on to the next tombstone and placed the candle next to it. He was about to continue writing when he saw the child, panting heavily, standing at his side.

The rabbi said, "I thought I told you to wait for me until I came back."

Still breathless and barely able to speak, the child stammered, "Rabbi . . . Rabbi . . . you must come . . . now . . . hurry."

The rabbi was firm. "I told you before that there is enough time to get to the boats. Now go back and wait for me."

The orphan shook his head, and managed to say, "No . . . Rabbi . . . you must come now. The priests . . . they are in the *judería*."

Rabbi Maimi got up. "Priests in the *judería*? So why didn't you say so, child?"

The rabbi bolted out of the cemetery, and he and the child hurried up the slope. The rabbi struggled to place one leg swiftly after another, banishing the rising pain in his aching muscles, finding the extra strength to keep going. They had to get back immediately. He knew what had happened in Teruel — was it happening here too? In Teruel, shortly after the Edict of Expulsion had been announced, the local Franciscan priests had carried on an intense door-to-door campaign to convert the Jews. Rabbi Yose, the rabbi of Teruel, had been locked in his home while the priests did their work. When it was all over, over a hundred Jews had been converted to Christianity. Was it happening in Segovia as well? Rabbi Maimi hoped not. Another Teruel was, God forbid, the last thing Segovia needed.

Gracia pleaded with the Inquisitor and the other assailants, "Please, leave us alone. The King and Queen promised us protection. It says so in the Edict."

Benito threatened with his whip. "Get away, all of you."

One assailant reached for Benito, but Benito lashed out with his whip and lashed the man's angry face. Touching his face and seeing the blood on his hand, the assailant said, "You dirty Jew, I'll get you. Don't think you're going to get away with this. Come on, let's grab this Jewish dog."

The other attackers joined their bloodied comrade and tried to help him pull Benito off the wagon, but Benito used his whip to keep them off. He was not going to go down without a fight.

As the two guards fought Benito, Lucero climbed on the back of the wagon and pulled the blanket off the ailing grandfather. The Inquisitor declared, "Convert and be baptized in the name of the Lord. Accept the Holy Spirit in your heart."

Gracia turned around to see what was going on in the back of the wagon. She tried to push Lucero away, but could not. "Get away from him you, you . . . monster. He is dying. Leave him alone!"

Rebecca screamed when she saw one of the assailants get a solid grip on Benito's boot and start to pull him slowly off the wagon. With one hand, Benito clung to the wagon and with the other, he tried to fight off his attackers.

Lucero bent over the sickly Samuel Pardo and thrust a crucifix between his half-shut eyes. The Inquisitor shook the decrepit Samuel fiercely, hoping to arouse him somehow to consciousness. "Old man, I am offering you eternal life. Believe in our Lord and all will be forgiven."

There was no response from the grandfather.

Suddenly, Gracia swung at the Inquisitor with her bag and struck him solidly on the head. Half-dazed by the blow, Lucero sat on the hay. Again Gracia swung ferociously, but Lucero dodged and backed away to avoid being struck again.

Getting off the wagon, Lucero saw Rabbi Maimi leading a band of angry men carrying hammers, sickles, and knives. Screaming wildly, the enraged defenders of the *judería* were getting closer by the moment. It was time to get out.

The assailants pulled Benito off the carriage, beating him with their fists and kicking him in the stomach. The men would have gone on beating him, but the avenging band forced them to beat a retreat. One guard said to the other, "Come on, let's get out of here."

Lucero and his men fled when they saw they were in danger.

Rabbi Maimi and his men arrived at the wagon. While some of the men pursued Lucero and his guards, the rabbi helped Benito off the ground. Benito said, "I will be all right, Rabbi. Just a few bruises, nothing more."

Rebecca came down off the wagon and tenderly applied her kerchief to the bruised areas on Benito's face. Gracia Pardo checked to see that her father was no worse. "We will be all right, Rabbi," said Gracia, "Just badly shaken up."

The rabbi addressed the crowd. "Everyone, get ready to leave this city. Pack your things and load your carts. All of us . . . we are leaving together within the hour!"

The armed men dispersed to their homes. People came from underneath their carts, opened their doors, and joined the rest of the traffic on the main street. The bustle of the Jewish quarter returned, even if only to endure for its last hour.

Carts were loaded at a frantic pace. In front of every household, people were piling their belongings on the carts. The hour of departure was nearly upon them.

Hacham Alhadeff was loading some Hebrew books on his cart. But Morenica had already stuffed the cart's few remaining spaces with small bundles of food. Refusing to give up, the Hacham managed to force the books between some bundles. Morenica came out of the house carrying her baby, and she was helped on the cart by her husband Aaron. The child wailed loudly, and she rocked the infant in her arms till he was quiet again. Because there was only room for two passengers on the front seat of the cart, the Hacham and Aaron agreed that they would alternate riding and walking on the long road ahead to Cartagena.

The Hacham stood proudly next to Morenica and his grandson, ready to walk by their side. He was stronger now, much stronger than when he had first come to Segovia, and he was ready to leave. Aaron took the whip in his hand and snapped the mule with the cord. "*Vamos!*," Aaron shouted. The mule brayed and moved forward, pulling the cart behind it. They were off.

As Morenica passed by the Matalon residence, she waved to Josefina. "*Caminos buenos*! Good roads!," shouted Morenica to her departing neighbors. "*Caminos de leche y miel*!", replied Josefina. "Roads of milk and honey!" With their friends now past, the Matalons gathered their four children together, putting the younger ones on the back of the cart and allowing the older ones to walk alongside. It was time to leave for Portugal. Anton drove his crickety cart into position behind that of the Alhadeffs, wishing to stay neighbors as long as possible.

Other people were leaving. Esmeralda Funes, the matchmaker, having no cart of her own, was walking, as were many others with limited means. The community council had arranged for a certain number of carts to be dispensed to the needy, but families with children came first, and Esmeralda Funes was alone. Carrying her bag on her shoulder, the matchmaker of Segovia set out on the journey. She watched the couples she had brought together pass by, turning down temporary rides from those she had helped, knowing that she would have to go it alone on foot as she already did in life. Superstitious by nature and a firm believer in the powers of the occult, she placed an amulet around her neck, hoping that this would ward off the *evil eye*, demons, and disease.

A young Jewish saddler on horseback saw the orphan in front of him. Bending over sideways, the saddler tapped the orphan on the shoulder and lifted him up on the back of the horse. The orphan boy, his face awash with a beaming smile, was spirited away as the horse clip-clopped down the street.

The wealthier residents, merchants and traders for the most part, assembled on horseback at the entrance to the Jewish quarter and waited anxiously for Rabbi Maimi to give them the signal to begin the procession. Everyone had expected that Don Abraham Senior would lead the community procession out of Segovia, but Don Abraham had disgraced the community by his conversion. What Senior had done was unforgiveable, and his name was not mentioned by anyone.

Rabbi Maimi finally appeared, telling the merchants which streets the procession would take out of Segovia. Going from one cart to another, the rabbi told the departing congregants what to do. When he came to the Pardo wagon, he said, "Now everyone listen to me . . . I want you to sing to show the Christians that our spirit is not broken. We shall all sing, '*Ein K'Eloheinu*' in Castilian . . . You heard me . . . *SING!*"

Urged on by the rabbi, Gracia started to sing the popular liturgical chant, at first half-heartedly, then loudly. Others joined her. Rebecca went to the back of the wagon, checked to see how her sickly grandfather was doing, and pulled out a tambourine from one of the bags. Along with Benito, she began to sing the song of the procession.

'*Non como muestro Dio, non como muestro Señor,*
'*Non como muestro Rey, non como muestro Salvador.*'

('There is none like our God, there is none like our Lord,
There is none like our King, there is none like our Savior.')

The procession began, with the noble merchants on horseback leading the way. One by one, the carts rolled by, their wooden wheels clattering on the cobblestone surface. The Pardo wagon led the way, this honor granted to them by virtue of their being recent victims of Christian attack.

Rabbi Maimi then went to the Alhadeff wagon and urged Morenica and Aaron, "Sing, my children, sing unto the Lord for his everlasting grace. Sing in the name of Heaven. SING! Sing as you never have before!"

The procession continued through the gate of the Jewish quarter and onto the street called the Calle del Sol, which led away from the *judería*. Curious onlookers lined the streets as the Jews made their coordinated exit. Others watched the procession from their windows.

A rousing song rose from the street's motley caravan of people, wagons, mules, and whatnot as it made its way to the center of town. Undaunted, the Spanish Jews sang,

'*Quien como muestro Dio, quien como muestro Señor,*
Quien como muestro Rey, quien como muestro Salvador?'

('Who is like unto our God, who is like unto our Lord,
Who is like unto our King, who is like unto our Savior?')

Young Jewish men and women danced in the street, playing timbrels and tambourines in order to make the people happy. And the tireless Rabbi Maimi kept on encouraging them to sing at full intensity, never allowing them to rest for a moment while they were still in the city. Swept up in his own enthusiasm, the rabbi went from one family to the other, saying, "On to the promised land! For just as God took us out of Egypt with a strong hand and an outstretched arm, thus shall he take us out today — with miracles and wonders! Sing, children of Israel! Sing unto the Lord!"

The singing grew in ardor and in strength, and to the singing and the timbrels and tambourines was added the penetrating high-pitched sound of the *shofar* or ram's horn.

An old bearded Jew, bent over by the heavy burden of the belongings on his back, advanced slowly step by step, but then stumbled forwards. Slowly he picked himself up and walked on, his head borne high, as he sang with fervor with the rest of his kinsmen,

'*Loaremos a muestro Dio, loaremos a muestro Señor,*
Loaremos a muestro Rey, loaremos a muestro Salvador.'

('We shall praise our God, we shall praise our Lord,
We shall praise our King, we shall praise our Savior.')

The procession spilled onto the Calle Real, the main thoroughfare of Segovia, and the chanting continuing unabated. There was taunting and jeering from many of the Christians who watched, and priests along the way invited the Jews to accept baptism, but the Jews paid them no heed.

Rabbi Maimi and several rabbinical students took out the Torah scrolls and adorned them with the silver and gold ornaments. Singing as they went, the rabbi and his students jumped happily up and down with the Torah, kissed the sacred scrolls, and raised the Torah in the air for all to see. In a spirit of rejoicing, they ran between the carts and cried, "For it is a tree of life unto those who hold it, and its supporters are filled with happiness." Using the familiar Hebrew refrain, they went one cart to another, encouraging all to kiss the scrolls.

Rabbi Maimi came to a sick woman on a stretcher; he danced around her with his students, and lowering the scroll, he allowed her to touch the Torah with her feeble hand. The sick woman slowly brought the hand that had touched the holy Torah of God to her lips and kissed it. "May you have complete health!," the rabbi wished her, as he continued on joyfully down the street. He wanted everyone — old, young, sick, and healthy — to keep the love and joy of Torah with them as they left the land of their birth. The chanting continued.

'*Bendicho muestro Dio, bendicho muestro Señor,*
Bendicho muestro Rey, bendicho muestro Salvador.'

('Blessed is our God, blessed is our Lord,
Blessed is our King, blessed is our Savior.')

Thus the Jews of Segovia left Castile: rich and poor, old and young, rabbis and rascals, nobles and orphans, men and women of all walks and stations. As they marched past the aqueduct, their chanting was heard everywhere. The song was their parting answer to those who would have them abandon the ways of their fathers. As the Jews rejected the ways of Edom, so too they affirmed their abiding faith in the one God of Israel. Forcefully, unequivocally, they proclaimed to the world:

'*Tú el muestro Dio, tú el muestro Señor,*
Tú el muestro Rey, tú el muestro Salvador.'

('You are our God, you are our Lord,
You are our King, you are our Savior.')

The Maimis and the Matalons, the Alhadeffs and the Pardos, the matchmaker Funes, and the other Jewish families of Segovia left their homes, trusting the Lord to help them in the days to come. Whatever tribulations they might endure in exile, they knew that at the journey's end, however arduous and convoluted it might be, awaited the Holy One, Blessed be He, who in His infinite love would finally bring redemption to the saving remnant of Israel. Surely this time the Messiah, the Redeemer of Israel, was on his way to rescue them from the hand of their Christian oppressors. Surely this time, the Jews so believed, evil would not triumph, God's elect would be rescued in their moment of ultimate peril, the oppressors would be punished, and the children of Israel would be miraculously delivered unto safety in the land beyond. Buoyed by such rabbinical exhortations, the Jews of Segovia took heart and commenced their exodus from the land of *Sefarad*.

What was taking place in Segovia was not unique. There were two hundred and sixteen Jewish communities throughout the kingdom, and all were being dismembered and disgorged just as the Segovian community was.

The roads leading to the ports and to Portugal were filled with refugees. The exiles from Castile, Extremadura, and Leon entered Portugal by way of Braganza and Miranda, passing on the way through the cities of Benavente, Zamora and Ciudad-Rodrigo. Ten thousand souls marched through Badajoz on their way to Helves. Another fifteen thousand entered Portugal by way of Valencia de Alcántara to Maruán and then on to the official entry point of Arronches. The Jews of the Basque regions sailed from the northern coastal port of Laredo. Those from Navarre had to traverse the village of Rioja. The ports of Valencia and Barcelona were the points of departure for the exiles from the kingdom of Aragon and Catalonia, some setting sail for Italy, others heading for the land of the Moors, with still others continuing on to the far end of the Mediterranean on their way to the empire of the Ottoman Turks. At the southern end of Spain, the ports of Cartagena, Cádiz, Málaga and Santa María were teeming with Castilian exiles, who hailed from cities as far as Segovia, Toledo, and Guadalajara. All told, one hundred and fifty thousand homeless souls fled the country in great haste. Nearly half of them entered the neighboring kingdom of Portugal; the others went across the sea in search of yet another homeland.

As the exiles reached the Portuguese border, many told of having been attacked and robbed on the way. Others complained about tavern owners who refused to allow them to stay for the night or to sell them any food. And the avaricious guards at the border towns added insult to injury by requiring each Jew to pay an exit tax of several maravedis.

When the Segovian exiles reached the Castilian border, the Matalons, like everyone else, had to wait their turn at the end of a long line of people, animals, and carts that led to the makeshift *aduana*, or customs office. They saw screaming children and angry adults, women in labor, black-scarved women in mourning, others falling and stumbling from the arduous trek that they had made — all united in their refusal to be left behind in the God-forsaken country of Spain. Braying mules and donkeys, clucking hens in wooden coops, dogs barking at stray sheep, and cows mooing in the barren pasture were all part of the cacophony of noise that filled the countryside. After half a day's wait in the increasing heat of the noonday sun, it was the Matalon's turn to have their cart and belongings examined.

The guards were very thorough. Each was examined from head to toe — mouth, ears, and nose, pockets, and the insides of shoes and hats. Carts were unloaded and inspected piece by piece. Leather water gourds and pottery were shaken for possible coins; quilts were unfolded and palpated for hidden items. Books were opened and flipped upside down. All clothing, cloaks and blouses, were meticulously explored. Loaves of bread and pastry items were sliced down the middle to see if they contained any objects of value. After such intense scrutiny, the Matalons were told they could pass into Portugal — provided they paid the guard twelve maravedis for his services. Anton, wishing no argument with the man, paid the requested amount to the guard. It was the least of his worries.

When they crossed over into Portugal, Anton and Josefina looked at each other with sly looks in their eyes, and as the Castilian customs office disappeared from sight, they broke into laughter. Josefina patted her stomach victoriously, and Anton did the same, whooping with delight. "We did it! We fooled them, by God, yes we did!" Their ducats had been well hidden, and the dumb Castilian guard had missed them. Anton stopped the cart suddenly: he had almost forgotten to make his oath of departure. He stepped down from the cart and turned to face Spain, vowing, "Spain . . . land of my fathers and yet not of my fathers, mine and yet not mine. By the heavens above, I swear on this very day that I shall never set foot on your soil even if all is returned to me. I swear it, so help me God!"

With that, Anton climbed back on the cart, a happy smile returning to his face. He cracked the whip energetically above the mule's head, and shouted for the world to hear, "Aya! Portugal, here we come!"

Others from Segovia passed into Portugal, as well. At Castel Rodrigo, Rabbi Maimi saw his friend from Salamanca, the astronomer Abraham Zacuto. Impatiently, without indulging himself in introductory pleasantries, the blunt Zacuto asked, "Rabbi Maimi, what is this I hear of Don Abraham Senior? Is it true what people say, that he became a Christian?"

Rabbi Maimi shrugged his shoulders. "To the great shame of all our people, yes, it is true. Please, Don Zacuto, it is a subject which I do not care to discuss."

But Zacuto pursued the subject. "Senior and his son-in-law Rabbi Melamed both changed their names. What names do they go by as Christians?"

"Don Abraham Senior is now named Fernando Nuñez Coronel, and Rabbi Meir Melamed was christened as Fernán Pérez Coronel."

Zacuto shouted excitedly, "That is it! That is it!"

"What is?," asked Rabbi Maimi.

Zacuto exclaimed, "Pérez Coronel!"

Rabbi Maimi still was puzzled. "Yes, so what?"

Zacuto exclaimed. "Pérez Coronel, ha! So *that* is the name that Rabbi Melamed took, eh? Ha! What a clever name. It says it all. Don't you see? Melamed and Senior, they fooled them. They fooled the King and the Queen."

"What do you mean, Don Zacuto? Explain yourself," inquired the perplexed Rabbi.

Zacuto took a deep breath. "Very well. Take Pérez Coronel, Melamed's new name. Break it into syllables. Pé-rez Co-ro-nel. But that is not how Rabbi Melamed wants us to read it. The syllables must be grouped thus: '*Pe-rez-co ron-el*.' Tell me, rabbi, what does '*perezco*' mean in Castilian?"

"Why, it means 'I die'," said Rabbi Maimi.

"And what does '*ron-el*' mean in Hebrew?," asked Zacuto.

"Singing unto God," answered the rabbi, a flash of understanding emerging on his face.

Zacuto clapped his hands. "Pérez Coronel is '*perezco ron-el*'. Melamed wanted to tell us that he was dying as he was being baptized. In his adopted Christian name, he encoded his message to us: 'I die singing unto God.' "

"That is an amazing deduction," said Rabbi Maimi, his mouth open wide with admiration. "But what about Don Abraham Senior?"

"The same holds true for him," said Zacuto. "Nuñez Coronel should be read '*no niz-cor ron-el*' which means 'we shall no longer remember singing unto God'. Or if one eliminates the Castilian '*no*', one is left with the Hebrew expression '*niz-cor ron-el*' which means 'We shall remember singing unto God.' Either way, it appears that Senior was trying to tell us something."

"Quite possibly, Don Zacuto, you may be correct. But, it does not lessen the awful shame and humiliation that the entire Jewish community felt when Senior converted."

Zacuto interrupted him. "On the contrary, Rabbi Maimi. If Senior was indeed forced to convert, then we are not humiliated, and the so-called Christian triumph is nothing more than a sham. Furthermore, if my explanation is correct, Don Abraham Senior and Rabbi Meir Melamed left us a clear message of their faith at the time of their christening."

"Are you going to Lisbon?," asked the rabbi, anxious to discuss other matters with this extraordinary scientist.

Zacuto replied, "Yes. I have been invited to be the court astronomer for King João II."

Rabbi Maimi said, "You would do me great honor by allowing me to join you on your way to Lisbon."

"The honor is mine," answered Zacuto politely. "All Spain knows of the great Rabbi Maimi of Segovia. I merely hope that I will not prove to be uninteresting company on subjects that the great rabbi wishes to talk about."

"Of that, Professor Zacuto, I have no fear," chuckled Rabbi Maimi, as the two continued their lively discussion on the road to Lisbon.

The port of Cartagena was bustling with activity. The wave of Castilian exiles had brought thousands to the teeming Iberian shore, all of them weary from their wanderings, their spirits depressed by the ordered expulsion. But the sight of twenty caravels in the harbor gave them new hope and strength.

Sitting on a plank near the main quay, Hacham Alhadeff and his son-in-law Aaron rubbed their sore feet. Though they had taken turns riding on the cart, each had walked half the distance from Segovia to Cartagena. Relieved that the strenuous journey on foot was now over, they basked in the warm Andalusian sun and relaxed as they waited their turn to board one of their ships.

Those ahead of them were going through customs. Esmeralda Funes was berating the guard who had the audacity to pocket the two ducats she had hidden in her hair bun. The matchmaker howled hysterically at such a loss, her shrieks and yells being heard by everyone in the port.

The guard, unable to control this wild and fitfully sobbing lady, and not wishing to bring attention to himself, thrust the money back into her hand and angrily pushed her on the boat. Observing this scene at a distance, the Hacham and Aaron chuckled at the matchmaker's resourcefulness.

They watched others from Segovia board the waiting vessels. Gracia and Haim Pardo, Rebecca and Benito Abulafia were among those who embarked on one of the ships. Gracia's father, Samuel Pardo, had died on the road between Segovia and Aranjuez, and the Hacham had assisted with the burial and the recitation of the *Kaddish* prayers for the dead. Arriving in Cartagena in deep mourning, the spirits of the Pardo family were lightened by the prospects of a better life ahead. The Pardos waved goodbye to the Hacham and to other friends as their ship left the harbor, its white sails flung wide to catch the wind. Other exiles did likewise, the departure of each vessel becoming an occasion for final salutations and well-wishes.

Soon it was time for Hacham Alhadeff, Aaron, Morenica and their child to board ship. Proceeding through customs, they found themselves on the wooden deck of an old smelly cargo ship, its dark underside covered by pitch, its exterior a dark wooden grey. The passengers wandered about aimlessly, going up and down the stairs leading to their quarters.

Finally all was ready. The wooden gangplank was lifted and the anchor hoisted. Sailors took their positions and loosened the thick ropes on the sails. A large square sail opened on the main mast, a leathery rippling sound caused by the stretching of its canvas. Then foremast and mizzen mast and top sails were spread to catch the harbor wind. Slowly, amidst creaking and swaying, the vessel began to recede from the harbor. On the lower deck, the chest-high rails were lined with the exiles who made their final goodbyes to those on the shore. As the ship began to pick up speed, it steadily left the harbor area. As the refugees looked back, they saw all of Cartagena and its surrounding hills, taking their last look at the Spanish earth that they were leaving behind.

At the rails, Morenica caught the fresh sea breeze in her face, but protected her child from the ocean spray with a blanket. As Aaron came up to her side and put his arm around her, Morenica was moved to say, "Aaron, what have we Jews done that we should have to suffer so? Why has God made our lot so bitter time after time, driving us from one land to the other? Is there no end to this . . . to having no place where we Jews can live in peace?"

Aaron thought about this and said, "There will be a day, Morenica . . . yes, I know it . . . a day will come when we Jews will have a country to call our own."

Morenica sighed deeply as she closed her eyes in a moment of reflection. She kissed her child, little Iziko, and clutched the infant ever tighter. She sighed again and said softly to Aaron, "I am going to put the child down to sleep."

Hacham Alhadeff wandered on the lower deck and came on a small group of *yeshiva* students huddling around their rabbi, a wizened white-haired man of seventy. The rabbi opened a Hebrew book and read from the Talmudic tractate of Avot, "Hillel said — Be of the disciples of Aaron, one that loves peace, that loves mankind and brings them closer to Torah . . . And he used to say: If I am not for myself, who is for me? And when I am only for myself, then what am I? And if not now, when?"

The Hacham, glad to have stumbled on an impromptu Talmudic learning session, listened to the ancient words of wisdom. The recited words of the ancient sages tinkled in his scholarly ears as an enthralling melody from afar, the wisdom song of the People of the Book whose sweet melody only scholarship could elucidate from the sacred writ. His delight could be no greater when, in the midst of the Talmudic session, he heard his daughter singing a lullaby to little Iziko, his grandson and scholarly sage-to-be. Against the background of golden words of scripture and the soft rush of ocean breeze, he could hear his daughter lovingly sing her blessed song of sleep:

"Durme, durme, mi hermosa doncella,
Durme, durme, sin ansia y dolor
Durme, durme, sin ansia y dolor."

It was joyous sweetness to his ears.

PART III:

EXPULSION: 1492

Chapter 12

As the ship bearing the Alhadeffs heaved its way across the Mediterranean and through the Gibraltar Strait, the hills of northwest Africa came into view. There the sea crashed against the rocky reefs and sprayed foam against the hills. The creaky ship kept its distance from the restless shore as it headed southwards towards Arcila, the Portuguese foothold on the Moorish coast. Steadily, the vessel bobbed its way down the coast, attracting a host of sea gulls in its wake as it neared the end of its week-long journey.

Along with the other passengers on the deck, Hacham Alhadeff carefully watched the coastline, studying the outline of its hills and crags with keen attention. Here at last, he thought to himself, in this harsh and barren land of the Moors he would finally find a resting place, a home for his family. His sense of homecoming was not unique. Others aboard ship felt this way, too. They had different reasons for coming to Morocco. A few Andalusian-born Jews came because they knew Arabic; others, because they distrusted settling in a Christian land. One passenger had a distant relative in Marrakesh; another had heard that the King of Fez treated Jews kindly; still another was a munitions expert from Toledo who wanted to teach the Moors how to manufacture arms. Whatever their motives, all agreed that with God's blessing, the new life in Morocco would be a good one.

Hacham Alhadeff listened to every passenger's tale: of where they were when they had first heard of the Edict of Expulsion, of how their community had reacted to the terrible pronouncement, of conversionary attempts by zealous missionaries, of unscrupulous judges and

232

magistrates, of harrassment and beatings, of sales of vineyards for a donkey, of despoilment of their homes and belongings to liquidate their debts. All these accounts became the daily fare of conversation aboard ship, making the passage of time aboard the crowded vessel far more bearable. The Hacham had his own story to tell from the early days in Córdoba to the recent ones in Segovia. One of the passengers, a wealthy courtier named Don Isaac Ben Zamora from Badajoz was arrogant and aloof. If he had a story to tell, he was not interested in sharing it with the others, and consequently he was ignored by the Hacham and other passengers. The humble rabbi of Murcia, on the other hand, gave Talmudic sessions on shipdeck and told legends about the ancient sages. Among the rabbi's audience was the Hacham himself, always eager to hear a well-told tale or a fresh scriptural interpretation by an insightful rabbi. The exchange of stories and the mixture of different people made for an interesting voyage.

"Arcila! Arcila!," shouted one passenger as he sprinted down the deck. As the ship veered suddenly towards the coast, the passengers rushed to the rails to get their first glimpse of the port. Against the background of the Moroccan hills, the fortified town of Arcila came into view. It had battlement towers and high protective walls. "Arcila," whispered the Hacham unto himself, as he set his eyes on the quiet white-walled town that was to be his gateway to the Moorish heartland.

Morenica came up alongside him with little Iziko in her arms. "Oh, Father, is it not wonderful? We have made it to Morocco. Now all will be well," she said assuringly.

"Blessed be the Holy One who has given us safe journey to this land of Ishmael," intoned the Hacham seriously.

The town of Arcila, the ancient Carthaginian Zilis, had been taken in 1471 by the Portuguese King Alfonso during his military expedition to North Africa. It was known to the Hacham as the place where the Portuguese had taken two hundred and fifty Jews as prisoners and made them slaves. Indeed, no less a person than the great Don Isaac Abravanel had arranged for their ransom. The Hacham, himself a ransomed Málaga Jew, knew what that meant. Arcila, like Málaga, evoked unpleasant memories from his past. Were the Portuguese in Arcila the same ones who had enslaved his kinsmen? If so, he could not suppress the thought, his daughter's statement notwithstanding, that all was not yet well.

When the shipload of exiles did disembark and went through the Portuguese inspection station, the governor of the town, the Count of

Borba, had little sympathy for the empty-handed Spanish exiles. Borba had given strict orders to his guards to collect a token entry fee; they were also to search for hidden weapons that could be used by the Moors against the Portuguese. The guards, however, were more interested in pocketing the valuables than in looking for weapons. Familiar with these unstated rules of the border, the Hacham slipped a thirty-piece silver maravedi into the guard's palm. While pretending to look elsewhere, the guard glanced at the silver coin in his palm, nodded, and signaled to his comrades to allow the Alhadeffs and their cart to pass through without being checked.

Now all was well, thought the Hacham, as they emerged from the Portuguese inspection station to the world of the Moors. They hardly had stepped out of the station when they were besieged by a swarm of Berber camel-drivers.

"I take you to Fez!," shouted a swarthy Berber, pressing his face into the Hacham's.

Another bearded camel-driver, not to be undone, tugged at the Hacham's arm and echoed the same offer. "I take you! I, Abdul, I take you to Fez for one hundred *oukiyoot*!," the second Berber offered in broken Castilian.

Other would-be guides came from the nearby encampment and added their voices to the babble, imploring the new arrivals to take them as their escort on the road to Fez. "I have mule! I have donkey!," shouted one in the back who leaped frantically up and down to catch the newcomers' attention.

Faced with all these unsavory characters, the Hacham realized that his choice of a guide would be a matter of luck. Searching for the most civil-looking fellow, the Hacham picked out the Berber guide called Abdul.

The guide was short and thin, with a stubble of beard, a beak of a nose, and a pair of deep-set black eyes. His snarled turban and caftan were grey from the dust and grime of the road.

Abdul wasted no time. He haggled with the Hacham until they settled on a price. Then, Abdul instructed some youths to hitch the Alhadeff cart to one of the mules, while he hurried back to the Portuguese inspection station to get more clients for the caravan in the making.

Meanwhile, as the Hacham waited he looked around. A few camels hitched to a nearby palm tree were resting on their stomachs. Morenica took little Iziko close to one of the sprawled beasts, the chomping movements of its gaping mouth never ceasing for a moment. Holding tightly to his mother, Iziko half hid behind her as Morenica approached even closer. "You see, little Iziko? Camel . . . camel," she said, pointing to the animal. The camel, as if conscious of being the focus of attention, suddenly twisted its long curved neck in their direction, the froth in its mouth nearly thrust into their alarmed faces. Little Iziko, clutching his mother even tighter, burst into tears and Morenica pulled the child away from the animal and withdrew from the camel's presence. "There, there, little Iziko, everything will be all right," she said kissing and soothing the frightened child. Her comforting words had effect as the sobs of the child finally diminished into an irregular whimper.

As the Hacham looked toward the ocean, he could see incoming ships slowly breaking over the horizon, their masts piercing the cloudless, brilliant blue sky. As the ships came closer, the multitude of teeming refugees could be seen. The ships, as the endless waves that bore them, came one after another in a steady discharge of human flotsam.

To where were all these exiles going?, the Hacham asked himself. Surely not all to the city of Fez. Some were bound for the interior cities of Marrakesh and Mekhnez. Others would remain at the port of entry such as at Larache under Portuguese control, or perhaps at the coastal towns of Salé-Rabat and Tangier.

From a distance, the Hacham saw the haughty Ben Zamora together with a prominent Portuguese official — perhaps the Count of Borba. Of course, Ben Zamora would have smuggled gold out of Spain to line the pockets of the Portuguese for the privilege of settling in Arcila or in nearby Aspe. It was ever so, thought the Hacham.

Abdul's caravan consisted of fifteen exiles, four camels, and five mules. The carts were attached to the mules, with the extra baggage heaped on the camel's backs. Everyone, of course, was expected to walk.

Finally, all was ready. Under Abdul's direction, the caravan moved toward the soft sands of the Moroccan coast. Heading southwards towards El Araish, the Berber guide led them through a narrow coastal strip bounded on the left by steep mountains and on the right by the ocean. They walked this way for several leagues, slowed occasionally by a mule stuck in the sand. Refreshed by the ocean spray blowing in them, they made their way on the narrow strip of beach.

The members of the caravan introduced themselves to each other along the way. The Hacham presented his own family to the three other families in the traveling party. They met the craftsmen Efrain Medigo, his wife Joya, and their two teenage daughters, all hailing from Maqueda. A humble native of Ciudad Real, Menahem Lerma by name, introduced his wife Estrella and their three children. Finally, there was a childless middle-aged couple, Tomás and Amelia Tarica, who were weavers by trade.

Despite the heat of the mid-day sun, the journey was eased by the conversations along the way. Efrain Medigo told of the fortress of Maqueda and of the important role the Jews had played in its economy and defense. The women spoke of their lives, their regional styles of cooking, and their children. Morenica, a proud mother now, held up a shy giggling little Iziko, the babe of the caravan, to the doting attention and playful endearments of the other women.

By nightfall the caravan reached the port of El Araish on the left bank of the River Kus, and there, just outside the city, the travelers rested in a large goat-skin tent, husbanding their strength for the arduous journey ahead. Abdul roasted a quarter of mutton, slicing it carefully and dividing it among the travelers. The camel drivers sang hymns in their lilting, musical tongue, and a feeling of campfire warmth pervaded the group. The Hacham listened carefully to the Arabic words as he dined on some plucked figs and dates. By the gentle crackling of the fire and the soft hush of ocean waves nearby, the exhausted Hacham dozed off, mindful of the pleasant sounds around him.

They were off before sunrise. Into the interior of the Moorish heartland they went, winding their way through well-worn dusty paths lined with brush, birch trees, and clumps of huge stones. They hiked past villages of mud and stone huts whose inhabitants went about their business ignoring the caravan. Black-robed women with veiled faces, balancing large urns on their heads, could be seen. Goats and sheep grazed in the countryside, shepherded by young children who wore rag headdresses and waved wooden staffs as the caravan passed by.

As the sun rose higher in the sky, the heat of day became more pronounced. The soft cool breeze of the coast gave way to the hot, dry wind of the inner plain. Parched, the travellers' spirits sunk as their strength waned. Morenica could not carry little Iziko for long by herself, as she gave the child to Aaron and to the Hacham to carry by turns. Jugs of water were passed between the wayfarers, each one satisfying their thirst with noisy gulps and swallows from the upturned jug, followed by a feast-like sigh of satisfaction as they wiped their wetted lips.

Despite pleas to stop, Abdul relentlessly kept the caravan moving.

"Can no stop. No good. Can no stop," he would say to those requesting frequent pauses, his arms flailing in the air to support his point. Before mid-day, however, Abdul did relent and allowed the caravan members to pause at an isolated oasis. Drinking and basking in the shade of leafy palm trees, they bathed their aching feet in the spring that fed the oasis. After eating dried fruits and sweetmeats and filling their water jugs, the travellers were instructed to be on their feet again.

"We go!," said Abdul, once again the taskmaster. "We go to Fez!"

With soreness of muscle, the trekkers got up slowly and followed in the footsteps of their tireless guide. "We see Fez mountains tonight," promised Abdul, to encourage the weary group.

Onward they marched toward the hot plain of the Sebú. An hour's journey brought them to the raised banks of the tortuous Sebú River, whose meandering course went from the Atlas mountains to the Atlantic. The river was the halfway point between El Araish and Fez.

Following Abdul onto the muddy banks and down to the river edge below, the travellers boarded barges to cross to the opposite shore. The two aides remained behind with the mules, crossing on the next barge.

Shaking the mud off their shoes, the exiles continued to follow the hard-driving Berber guide to Fez. Abdul, as if unhappy with his progress thus far, quickened the pace, whipping the mules with his stick. The overloaded animals, struggling to satisfy their task-master's oner-ous demands, darted forwards in frightened spurts. The exhausted exiles complained to Abdul to slow down. But the Berber paid them no heed, impelled as he was by some obvious sense of urgency.

Sweat poured in rivulets down the Hacham's face. His failing muscles shrieked with pain upon taking every single step. The color gone from his face, he told Aaron that he was feeling weak, and he asked to be relieved of having to carry little Iziko. This was getting to be too much for him, he admitted, as it was surely for the others about him.

"What is the matter with Abdul?," the Hacham asked.

"He is a crazed Moor," answered Efrain Medigo behind him. "*Loco!*"

Stumbling and falling, they covered more ground. More frightened of being left behind than anything else, each exile somehow found the strength to pick themselves up from the dust and to continue. Wilting from the heat, the sweat pouring down their dropping faces, their muscles in sheer agony, the exiles kept up the grueling pace dictated by the mad Moor.

Suddenly, a huge mountain gorge opened up enclosed by sharp, almost perpendicular mountains. At the bases of the mountains were palm trees, flowering shrubs, and tall oaks.

"Here we rest!," said Abdul in a commanding tone of voice.

The exhausted exiles collapsed on the sides of the road. Gasping for air, the worn-out exiles could hardly move a muscle, much less their bodies, as they moaned feebly on the ground. Subdued by their own exertion, they emitted faint-sounded cries, as if giving voice to their total bodily enfeeblement. They rested utterly.

It was Aaron who noticed it first. Abdul was nowhere to be seen. Slowly raising himself up, Aaron looked around to be certain that he was not imagining things.

"Where is Abdul?," he asked worriedly.

The Hacham sat up with difficulty and looked around. He, too, could not see Abdul. Others in the group also became conscious that the mad Moor was missing but they were too weak to search for the guide.

"Perhaps he is looking for wild figs and berries," said Morenica reassuringly. "Do not worry, Aaron, my love. Fez is but a short distance away."

Aaron half-shook his head in agreement, a worried look still on his face.

Suddenly, shrieks shook the still air in the gorge. A swarm of wild Berbers surrounded them from both sides. Atop their horses, the swarthy tribesmen came screaming wildly, their scimitars swishing in the air. They looked ferocious. Their cruel coal-black eyes added to their frightful aspect, as did their stubby unkempt beards and rotting yellowed teeth. Covered with dirt from head to toe, with a look of savage malice in their eyes, the Berbers struck fear in everyone.

The Berbers attacked with such speed that there was no time for anyone to run and hide. Quickly jumping off their horses, the Moors assaulted the men first, there being at least three Moors to each of the male exiles.

The Hacham was incapable of much physical resistance, as he was thrown rudely onto the ground by two of them. The Moors pinned his shoulders and roughly jerked his arms behind his back, causing the Hacham to scream in pain. Straddling his back, they tied a rope around the Hacham's wrists and ankles. Then they left him helpless, on his stomach. The Hacham spit the dirt out of his mouth and rolled over to see what was happening to the others. He could not believe his eyes.

The other men were also being tied up, the women screaming hysterically. Efrain Medigo, the craftsman from Maqueda, was being pounded into submission by the fist-blows of three Moors. Aaron, arms tied behind his back, writhed ineffectually as he tried to free himself. The other two adult males, too weak to offer any resistance, were tied up the same way.

Once the men were subdued, the Berber chieftain let out a brutish yell of triumph. Handing his sword to an aide, he went to the captured Jewish women. With his soldiers holding the struggling females, the chieftain examined them one by one. He lifted the chin of one of the adolescent Altabet daughters, casting his lecherous black eyes on her innocent face.

"She is but a child, señor," pleaded Joya Medigo in Castilian that meant nothing to the Moor. "My daughter, she is but a child. In the name of God, I beg of you to have mercy on us."

The eleven-year-old girl screamed when he pawed her breastless chest. The chieftain bared his filthy teeth and angrily cast her aside and went on to examine the girl's sister. Both were too young for him, and their mother was of no interest as well. As he passed the middle-aged women, he felt their breasts, inducing stark terror on their pallid faces. Amelia Tarica fainted at being touched thus.

The chieftain came to Morenica. She said nothing, but her eyes revealed her inner fright. The Berber touched her soft cheek and looked at her. Morenica moved her head away.

"Don't touch me, you mountain savage!," she said in Arabic.

The words infuriated the Berber. "This one!," he shouted to his men.

Two Berbers suddenly grabbed Morenica, one for each arm; two others grabbed her legs. Morenica screamed. It was a loud piercing cry that ripped into the hearts of both the Hacham and Aaron who looked on helplessly. Morenica, suspended in the air by the four Moors as they moved her to an open area, struggled valiantly. Kicking with her feet, trying to bite the hands of her assailants, thrashing her head wildly, she tried desperately to free herself. But it was no use. Her four captors held her limbs firmly. They moved her to a level grassy area and put her down. Fearful of what might happen, Morenica cried for help.

"Aaron! Aaron! Help me, Aaron! Aaron, where are you?," she shouted.

The Berber chieftain stood over her squirming body. He said in Arabic, "A mountain savage, eh?"

The Hacham called out. "In the name of Allah, in the name of Mohammed the Prophet, I beseech you to leave my daughter alone. She is a mother. Please, kind sir, in the name of Allah, do her no harm."

The chieftain made a signal to his men. One of the Moors came over and kicked the Hacham in the face.

"Silence, Jew," said the Moor.

Blood ran briskly down the Hacham's face from his swollen nose, but he did not stop pleading. "In the name of Allah . . ."

To put a stop to this, the Moor kicked the Hacham viciously in the eye, causing a flash of white to utterly fill his field of vision. All he could see was white. The white was everywhere — white figures, white outlines - everything was white. "I can't see, I can't see," the Hacham said, as the blood continued to pour down his face.

With his arms and legs tied, Aaron could see what was about to happen. He rolled himself in the dirt towards the Berber chieftain, shouting angrily as he went. "Leave her alone, you Arab pig! Leave her alone!"

The Berber chieftain, amused by the dust roll of this would-be defender, asked for his dagger. He stopped Aaron's roll with his outstretched leg. The Berber bent over, grabbed the screaming Aaron by his hair, and slit his throat. The blood spurted from Aaron's neck in a pulsating fountain of red blood.

Morenica's dress was slit down the middle, baring her engorged breasts and private parts.

Morenica screamed. "No, please, no, no, no, no . . ."

The Berber chieftain, hovering over her with a gloating lecherous look, lifted his tunic to reveal his uncovered genitals. Descending upon Morenica, he fondled her breasts, kissing one nipple after the other. His aides spread open her legs. He slid into her, ravishing her with his member, as she cried out for help. The help never came.

The Hacham, his vision slowly returning to him, could see clearly out of one eye only. He would have preferred being blind than to witness what his one good eye could now see. His nude daughter was being violated by the Berber. The panting Moor plunged into his daughter time and again. It seemed as if Morenica's dishonor was endless. It was a degradation that no father's eye could look upon; it was a disgrace that no father's love could lessen. Mortified, the Hacham could not bear to watch further. He closed his eyes to the torment.

Finally the panting stopped. The Hacham quickly opened his eyes as the Moor, having had his fill, withdrew from his moaning daughter. Morenica lay there limp and nearly lifeless, her lovely face smitten with shame and tears. The chieftain, flushed with satisfaction, ordered his men to do as they pleased with the other women.

The Berbers went wild, throwing the women to the ground and stripping them. The tribesmen raped them in front of their spouses and children, committing one outrage after another. Even the two adolescent girls were not spared from brutish attack as they, too, were despoiled by the Berbers. The women's screams, their sobs and their tearful pleas, were to no avail as each was violated repeatedly by a succession of rapacious Moors. When the Moors finished, the assaulted women were left naked sobbing on the hard ground.

Daughter sought out mother, their vile disgrace the same, their tears mingling on the Moroccan earth. A few of the women crawled to their clothes and covered their bodily shame. Others, weeping, could not move at all.

The Berbers took everything: their honor, their mules, and their belongings. They left the Jewish men with the clothing on their backs; the dishonored women had nothing but the shreds ripped from their bodies. Climbing on their horses, the Berbers left howling like wolves, their blood-curdling screams echoing in the gorge. They rode away into the distance, emitting frequent cries and yells which became progressively more faint as they disappeared from sight. At last they were gone.

A disgraced Morenica, her face drenched with tears, rolled on her side and reached for the tatters of her torn dress. She sat up, and covered her breasts and private parts. Then she saw what had happened to Aaron. She screamed frightfully. Crawling on her hands and knees, she dragged her body over to Aaron's.

"Aaron, my love. Aaron, my sweet one," she stammered between sobs as she kissed his pale lifeless lips, staining her chest and clothes with the blood of her beloved. She clung to him, holding his limp head in her arms, showering him with kisses, not wanting to let him go. "Aaron! Aaron, my love!," she yelled hysterically, her body and soul overwhelmed by what had overtaken them. Her body had been defiled, her husband had been slain — could there be any loss greater than this? She screamed again. This time her scream became a shrieking lament that she could not stop, an endless harrowing scream of unmitigated agony.

A crying Joya Medigo went to untie the men. But the men could not look at their wives in the eye. Ashamed at their own impotence, they had watched helplessly while their women were violated. Men and women, Efrain and Joya Medigo and their two daughters, Menahem and Estrella Lerma, Tomás and Amelia Tarica — all shared a common shame. The sobbing of the families continued.

After he had been untied, the Hacham picked up little Iziko. The child had been crying in the bushes nearby. With the child in his arms, the Hacham walked over to Morenica. She wept inconsolably over her husband's body. The Hacham, at a loss for words of comfort, knelt down next to her and placed his hand on his daughter's shoulder. Morenica turned towards him and buried her head in her father's chest. Holding his daughter with one arm and Iziko with the other, the Hacham patted her soothingly on the back. Morenica then took little Iziko and clutched the child tightly to her chest. She felt Aaron's presence in the flesh of the child. She kissed little Iziko, kissing all of him, kissing the Aaron that was within him. Then a strange sound was heard, and Morenica stopped her kissing. She looked in the direction of the sound, and in her eyes was a new terror.

The Berbers were coming back! Morenica screamed wildly and thrust the child back into the Hacham's arms. Half-clothed, Morenica got up shakily on her weak legs and tried to run. She stumbled on the irregular surface, almost falling, struggling to keep her balance. The other women in the group also began to scream as the Moorish horsemen roared back towards them. They, too, with their husbands, ran for the cover of the nearby trees. The panic was everywhere.

The Berbers burst anew into the camp. The Berber chieftain rode at their head and drove his horse in pursuit of the fleeing Morenica. Coming up behind her on his galloping steed, he grabbed her by the hair, snapping her head backwards. As the horse continued on, Morenica was dragged with the animal, the sharp rocks of the ravine cutting sharp gashes in her feet, her half-nude body being flung every which way.

The Berber stopped his steed. Holding Morenica's hair, he jumped off the horse and threw her to the ground. Encountering no further resistance, he pulled out his dagger and plunged it into Morenica's chest. Again and again, he drove the dagger deep into her heart, drenching its blade with her blood. He did this until every breath and movement disappeared from her once lovely body. The radiant flower of Al-Andalus, Batya Alhadeff, otherwise known as Morenica, was no more.

The murderous chieftain arose from his victim and wiped the bloodied blade clean on Morenica's torn tunic. Then, with a primitive whoop of conquest, he climbed back on his horse and was ready to gallop away.

A sobbing Hacham Alhadeff, carrying little Iziko in his arms, went up to the Berber. The Hacham's voice choked as he tried to speak. "Why? . . . Why, oh cruel one! Why . . . Why did you have to do such a cruel thing?"

The Berber snarled angrily, "Because the young Jewess has received my seed. She could become pregnant and bear my son. My child would then be a Jew, Allah forbid! . . . Now you, old Jew, get out of my way before I kill you too!"

The Berber kicked his horse and sped away. Almost as quickly as he had come, the Berber marauder rode away with his men back into the plain.

The Hacham ran after the Berber chieftain screaming, "Murderer! Murderer! Murderer!" With crazed abandon and holding tightly to little Iziko, he ran into the vast arid plain after his daughter's killer. Leaving the camp behind him, he was possessed by a blinding desire for revenge. His heart shattered, his mind senseless with rage, the Hacham ranted uncontrollably at the perpetrator of this vile deed. Yet, even in this surge of searing hate, even as he felt the futility of his vengeful notions, he wandered on into the plain with grandchild in arms. The plain was a great empty void, its interior as barren as his own.

He was gripped with grief. Tears, endless tears, welled in his blood-shot eyes and poured down his checks. With the silent plain to witness, he screamed uncontrollably into the void. Yet no scream, no outcry, no flood of tears could give adequate vent to his anguish.

"Why, dear God?," the Hacham asked. "Why have you done this to the innocent?"

Night fell. For hours the Hacham walked on, refusing to stop even when his legs buckled under him. Picking himself and little Iziko off the ground, he drove on, far from Morenica's and Aaron's agonies. He thought of returning to the gorge to bury his loved ones, but he was now lost. It would have to wait for morning. Finally he could go no further. He collapsed on the ground.

Iziko cried for food. But it was the cry of Morenica that he heard. He could still hear her heart-rending cries, her unheeded pleas for deliverance. He could still see the horror in her face when the Moor defiled her body. He could still see the Moor driving the dagger into her chest. The awful memory of Morenica's dishonor and of her death kept him from sleep.

He could make no sense of it. What sense was there to Morenica's slaughter? What sense was there to a true daughter of Israel having her life ended in satisfying the bestial lust of some mountain savage? Was it for this that he had raised her? Was it for this that he said his prayers? How could he affirm, 'Blessed be the Judge of Truth', when there was no justice? He could see no truth in Morenica's or Aaron's deaths. Where was the God of justice, where was the God of truth? Doubts began to form in his mind. If he continued to doubt, the religious principles that had guided his life would be meaningless. Yet he could not suppress the doubts either.

Night became day, and the Moroccan sun rose in the eastern sky, casting its rays onto the central plain. The Hacham and little Iziko found themselves bathed in its brilliance. It became hotter as the morning progressed, the fiery orb scorching the land and its lost trespassers.

Both the Hacham and Iziko were thirsty. Neither had had anything to drink since the previous day. Their mouths and skin were dry and parched. Having lost his sense of direction, the Hacham tried to find shade from the mid-day sun. But there was none. There were occasional small bushes, but nothing so much as a palm tree against which to rest and bask in its slender shadow.

Iziko's cry became weaker, his breathing shallow and rapid. The child's tender skin was very hot, and his pulse rapid. The Hacham covered the child with his garment to protect it from the sun.

As mid-afternoon approached, the Hacham felt Iziko's tiny body was on fire. The child's skin was scorching hot, and his eyes sunk in their sockets. The child was listless and unresponsive. It was obvious that he badly needed water.

The Hacham fell to the ground. It was no use. He could walk no more. He was now more concerned with his unresponsive grandchild. Lying on his side, the Hacham covered his motionless grandchild with part of his tunic. With his hand, he tried to fan Iziko's flushed face. But this too was without effect.

The stifling heat continued unabated, and the Hacham fainted. How long he and the child had been lying there he was not sure.

When he finally awoke, he saw the child was ashen-colored and still warm to the touch. He jabbed it, but it did not move. The child was not breathing. Little Iziko, the flesh of his flesh, was dead. The Hacham placed his head on little Iziko's body and sobbed fitfully. His loss was now total.

Slowly lifting himself back on his knees, he raised his arms limply towards heaven and spoke out loud. "Lord of the heavens, you have done much to give me cause to abandon your Law. But it is certain that, though it be against the will of those who dwell on high, a Jew I am, and a Jew I shall remain, even if all that you have brought upon me, or will yet still bring upon me, shall count for nothing."

The Hacham slowly took a handful of dirt and began to cover his dead grandchild. "Blessed be the Judge of Truth," he intoned. He thought about what he had just said. Where was justice, where was truth? It seemed to the Hacham that the greatest injustice of all was that he was still alive.

Chapter 13

His mind was whirling. Strange and grotesque faces pressed up to his, and then the bulging eyes retreated into a canvas of moving color. When he looked up, he saw a spiraling funnel converging to a point high in his tent. Tent? Where was he, the Hacham wondered. The hovering visages swung through the mist of the mysterious funnel, seemingly unaffected by its circular flow. The eyes scrutinized him once again. A tent with eyes? No, that was not it.

Muted voices could now be heard over the soft hum of the funnel. Dislocated voices, floating faces, writhing hands, a world of dismemberment. And where was he? Was he but a pair of eyes likewise adrift in a chaotic space? The voices became stronger, clearer.

"He's coming around." The eyes teamed with a scarved face. Had he seen that face before? The eyes looked warm and kind.

"Hacham Alhadeff, it's Amelia Tarica . . . you know, from the caravan." The face had a name. He struggled to speak, ". . . Amelia," the word came out as a painful whisper.

"Drink this, Hacham. You have been delirious for days." It was warm liquid. He drank more, feeling better with each sip.

"Amelia Tarica . . .," he said softly, understandingly. "Where am I?"

"You are on the outskirts of Fez," answered Amelia.

Hacham Alhadeff closed his eyes as if comforted. Then, he opened them in disbelief as a terrifying bolt of consciousness hit him, rousing him to full wakefulness and a remembrance of the recent past. In a moment of horror, his face twisted with agony, he voiced his greatest fear, "Oh my God . . . I am alive".

Over the next few days, the bedridden Hacham grew stronger as a result of Amelia Tarica's gentle ministrations. She too had shared in the misery of the hapless caravan, and she had the good sense not to bring back memories which they preferred to forget. Yet the Hacham could not forget, was not allowed to forget. He was bound by tradition to mourn for seven days, to recite the sanctification for the dead, to sit on overturned couches with a disrobed head. Yet the prohibitions of mourning lost their usual significance. The forbidden activities — not to leave your house, not to conduct business, not to bathe, not to cut your hair, not to wash your clothes — were not possible anyway. He wore sackcloth and ashes as much from necessity as from religious duty.

"We were worried about you, Hacham. When we found you in the desert, you were like a dried grape. You were so hot to the touch that we thought you were dead. But we gave you water to drink and something to eat, and you revived. With the help of the Holy One, blessed be He, we brought you here to Fez to recover. And so you have. You are much better now."

"I owe my life to you, Señora Tarica, may God shine his grace upon thee."

"Thank my husband. He is the one who found you and brought you here."

"You said we were close to Fez. Does that mean we are not in the city of Fez itself?"

Amelia sighed. "Yes, that is so. The King of Fez does not allow the exiles from Spain inside the city walls. There are certain Jews of Fez who live in the Jewish quarter called a *mellah*. In the *mellah*, they organized a committee to help the exiles. Every day, the Jews of Fez bring out food and clothes for our brothers and sisters but it is never enough. There are too many of us, and too few of them."

"How bad is it?", asked the Hacham who thus far had not ventured outside the tent.

"Very bad. The Jews from the *mellah* are very good. They do their best to help us. Each morning a group of men and women bring food and water to the camp. And the last time the caravan came, fights broke out among those in the camp. Starving men, women, and children fell over each other in a wild scramble for food. You should have seen it, Hacham. But things are better now. The men from the *mellah* use force to make sure that the food distribution is orderly. They have to. Everyone now has to stand in line to receive a ration of food."

"And how is it that there is extra food for a sick person like myself?"

"*Bueno*, I am one of the lucky ones, if you want to call it that. I was asked by one of the ladies from Fez to help distribute the food. Every day, I make sure that there is some food set aside for the sick ones."

Before the Hacham could thank his nurse a second time, a tall, swarthy, middle-aged man entered the low-roofed straw dwelling. From the fine garments that he wore, it was evident that he was a person of high social station. Jacob Ohana, as he was called, introduced himself graciously to Amelia and to the Hacham. Dressed in a bright-colored tunic, he offered a hearty welcome in Arabic, his bright brown eyes shining with friendship. He tried talking to Amelia in Arabic, but she did not understand. The Hacham, who spoke Arabic fluently, listened to the warm greetings brought by this representative from the Jewish quarter of Fez. The man was a merchant, highly esteemed in the community, who tried to help the Jews in the camp. He said the King of Fez would open the doors of the city to the newcomers soon. The *mellah* had synagogues, houses of learning, it had ritual bath houses, and of course, his gold-buckle shop. But first . . . patience!

The Hacham answered in Arabic. "We accept your hospitality, kind sir, even though our patience has been sorely tried."

"You speak like us. You are one of us," said Ohana.

"No, I was born in Spain, in the city of Málaga."

Ohana seemed disappointed. "So then you are a *megorash*."

"Pardon me, sir, but what was that word you used? A *megor* . . .?"

"A *megorash* . . . you know, someone like yourself, an exile from Spain. It comes from the Hebrew word *gerush* which means 'expulsion.' "

"A *megorash*," the Hacham echoed.

Ohana added, "And I am a *toshav*, a native Moroccan Jew. We have lived in Fez for many years, maybe seven hundred or a thousand years. But we feel strong ties with our brothers and sisters in Spain. When they are in trouble, we help them; when we are in trouble, they help us. Some of our scholars studied in Spain, like our great rabbi, Rabbi Ibn Danan. But now that Spain no longer wants the Jews, the *megorashim* came here to Fez. Also Rabbi Danan has come from Granada to Fez. But the *megorashim* are too many for us. The *mellah* is too small for so many people. We try to help you, but you are too many. You understand?"

"I have heard many praises for the great Rabbi Ibn Danan. And may the good deeds of the Jews of Fez be incribed in the Book of Life forever! But tell me this, what has become of the King of Fez? Why does he not honor the invitation that he extended to us to settle in this land?"

Ohana raised his hands in a motion of despair. "The King . . . ah yes, the King. He is a good king. He wants to help. But even he can only do so much. The Moslems, they do not want so many Jews in Fez, and the King listens to the Moslems, not to us. The Moslems in the city are afraid the Jews will drive up the cost of food and housing. For them, there are already too many Jews in Fez, so they make the King keep all the *megorashim* outside the city walls."

"Tell me how many Jews live in the mellah?"

"About one thousand families."

"And how many families, of *megorashim* are there here in the camp?"

"More than five thousand families."

Hacham Alhadeff tried to get up off the mat. "Five thousand? What do you say? It can not be! So many?"

Amelia nodded her head in agreement. "Oh yes, Hacham, *at least* fifteen thousand Jews in the camp. Some say twenty thousand. Many stay. But others, when they come here and see how bad it is, they keep on going. They go to other places, Turkey, Naples maybe. The situation keeps getting worse day by day."

"I must see this with my own eyes. Help me, please."

Amelia and Ohana supported the Hacham and cautiously led him to the entrance.

The vista that he beheld was overwhelming. "Oh my God, oh my God", he uttered in gasps. In front of him was a vast plain covered by a swarm of barely animated human skeletons, their bony frames barely supporting their layers of discolored flesh. Sunken eyeballs and sunken cheeks, thin limbs, scaphoid bellies were seen everywhere that one looked. There were thousands of these wasted cachectic creatures wandering in and out of a multitude of straw huts. All had the same uncaring look on their shrunken faces. All were *megorashim*. Ohana was right. He was one of *them*.

In the distance were the walls of the New City of Fez, its minarets and towers glistening in the blazing Moroccan sun. Camels undulated their way toward an arched gate with several militiamen.

Ohana pointed to the gate. "That is the *Bab-el-Gisa* gate. Nearby is the ancient Jewish cemetery, the *gisa* as it is called. In fact, you can see the tombstones of the cemetery from here."

The Hacham turned his gaze back to the camp. "The Jews of Fez have their cemetery. We are creating ours."

Ohana was silenced by the Hacham's words. Wails and groans came from every direction. Those newly arrived still had some strength to spare, but they wailed the loudest with the pains of hunger. The Hacham seemed utterly perplexed. What was this morbid spectre? Was this the final wasting of his people, the dry bones described by the prophet Ezekiel? The desolate arid plain seemed like a gaseous fire-breathing oven, in contrast to the encompassing mountains in the far distance, their peaks cool and inviting. Beads of sweat trickled down his forehead as much from the baking heat as from the unnerving sight that his eyes now beheld. A sobbing mother clung tearfully to a dead babe in her arms. And what of his babe, his precious one, his lovely Morenica?

A starved young boy no more than ten years old walked slowly past him. And the child's eyes, had he not seen them before? Phrases of the *Kaddish*, the prayer for the sanctification of the dead, emanated from every makeshift hovel. A choirsong, a dirge, a death song. And he, Hacham Isaac Alhadeff, among the walking dead! Its choirmaster! Old men, old fools like himself, clutching yet still to the life that was not life. And the heavy, hot wind from the south bringing its cover of fine, powdery sand upon one and all ailing things, laying down the many layers of dust upon that which was to be their graveyard. The boy's eyes, eyes from his dream, haunting him in the daylight! *Iziko's eyes*, dismembered, remembered. He wrenched himself away from his hallucination. He retreated into the safety of the straw enclosure, withdrew from the outside world, becoming an exile to the reality of the senses, becoming a *megorash* like the rest of them.

As weeks passed, nothing seemed to change. Jewish representatives from the *mellah*, and spokesmen from the camp outside the city, visited the palace daily, urging the King and his ministers to allow the Spanish Jews to settle within the walls of the capital city. All such pleadings fell on deaf ears, and the Jews outside the city stayed where they were.

Hacham Alhadeff stayed where he was, limiting the scope of his existence to that which his self-appointed nurse Amelia Tarica allowed him, struggling to hold on to the vestiges of his sanity. He was content to watch Amelia stand for hours underneath the fiery Moroccan sun. He counted the number of times that she scooped out the thin soup from the large clay pots and poured it into each shakily extended bowl.

Amelia Tarica often found herself face to face with a starving mother who would glance downwards at her assigned ration, then look pleadingly with hollow eyes at Amelia for a larger portion. Amelia, unable to turn the woman away, would pour out an extra helping. The starving woman, head bowed, and in a hushed voice, would say *"Gracias,"* and then wander off. Amelia would then take it upon herself to deliver bowls of soup to those who were too weak to stand in line. She went from one straw hut to the other, bringing nourishment to the weak and the infirm. More than food, she brought herself — her smile, her concern, her words of comfort.

She met many of the exiles. They came from all over Spain, some by way of Portugal, others directly to the land of the Moors. All had terrible stories to relate.

Amelia told the Hacham a tale that she had heard from one of the heart-stricken mothers. A large ship of Gentiles anchored in the port city of Saleh-Rabat for provisions. The captain went ashore and called out to the hungry Jewish children of the city, giving each a generous chunk of bread. When the children saw the bread, they told the good news to all the other children in the city. The following day about a hundred and fifty young Jewish boys presented themselves to the captain, who said he would give them bread to their heart's content if they came aboard his ship. As soon as the boys were aboard, the captain sailed away. When this became known in the Jewish camp, the mothers of the young boys ran to the shore, screaming and yelling, yet there was no one who could help them. Their wailing did not prevent their lovely children from being kidnapped in order to be sold in some distant country. What was hunger compared to such a loss?

The situation in the camp had a telling effect on Amelia. Each evening she went to see Hacham Alhadeff to tell him the news or rumors she'd heard in the camp.

Then, one Friday noon, a wild-eyed child ran through the camp shouting, "Fire!"

"Fire in the camp!", the child screamed, "Fire!"

Amelia understood, as did the other occupants of the straw hut. The dry bones seemed to come to life as they jerkily moved towards the entrance, animated as they were by the unwelcome prospect of being roasted alive. Amelia looked outside and came back for the Hacham.

The blaze, which had originated in one hut, had spread quickly to the nearby straw huts, its sparks carried by the shifting gusts of wind. People emerged from their straw homes only to see their makeshift lodgings serve as crackling timber for the devouring fire. The screams were everywhere. Panic-stricken boys and girls, men and women trampled over anyone in their path, the look of terror on their faces.

Fiery arches leaped through the air, igniting one straw hovel after another, creating a scorching wall of fire that marched across the camp. Clouds of black smoke rose in the darkening sky.

Amelia helped the Hacham to the entrance. The Hacham was unperturbed by the pandemonium without.

" 'For I have brought the sun at noon and darkened the land in the brightness of day'. . . Is that not what the prophet Ezekiel says, Amelia?"

Amelia placed her arms around the Hacham and tried to steer him in the right direction. "Come, Hacham Alhadeff. Come, or we will die."

The Hacham stayed where he was.

The roaring flames leaped further into the sky. The exiles continued to pour forth from the camp by the thousands. The Hacham continued to talk to himself, "The prophet Ezekiel said all this. 'A third of the people shall be burned in the fire in the middle of the city, when the days of the siege are finished. And a third, you shall kill with the sword round about her. And a third, you shall scatter to the wind, and I will draw a sword after them.' Is that not so, Amelia Tarica? Is that not what is happening to the *megorashim*? Is it not God's anger that we now see with our eyes?"

Amelia raised her voice. "This is no time for philosophy, Hacham." She tugged on the Hacham's arm but, weak as he was, he refused to budge.

"Punishment. Punishment from God . . .," Alhadeff rambled on, his eyes dazed and distant.

Amelia spoke, panic rising in her voice. "Punishment for what?"

Now it was the Hacham's turn to shrug his shoulders. "I do not know. Only the Holy One of Israel, blessed be He, knows."

Amelia said, "The fire in the camp . . . it is an accident of nature. Now let us get out of here."

The Hacham was surprised by such a rational explanation. "An accident of nature? Perhaps . . . perhaps not. I think not. God is the cause of all things."

Amelia was at the end of her patience. "Hacham, I cannot stay here and yet I cannot force you to go. You may want to die, but I do not. This is the last time. Are you coming with me or not?"

"Punishment from the heavens . . .," the Hacham intoned.

Exasperated, Amelia threw up her hands and joined the mad rush for safety.

Coughing from the smoke, Amelia struggled to catch her breath as she stumbled on her way toward the periphery of the camp. As she did so, she took note of a couple who had tarried to watch their makeshift home being consumed by the flames.

"My books!," shouted a distressed rabbi. The woman next to him yelled. "All that I have in the world, my clothes, my blankets, everything — gone! Gone! Gone!"

Amelia made it to the edge of the camp, her lungs gasping for air. Victims of the fire were all about her. On the ground next to her was a youth with the skin on his arms and chest burned raw from the flames. Another woman was screaming hysterically, her hair and clothes afire. One man knocked her to the ground and covered her head and body until the flames were extinguished. But the woman wanted to return to the fire; she yelled at the top of her lungs, "*Mi hijo*! My son, Ruben! My son, he is still in the camp!" She tried to push her way back toward the fire, but Amelia and others held her back. She twisted and struggled to get free. "My son!," she screamed, as she tried to fight off those who stood in her way. "My son! For the love of God, save him! My son! . . . Ruben! Ruben!," she uttered with ripping anguish as she sensed the growing futility of the situation. "Ruben, *hijo mío*! Ruben! Ruben! Ruben!" Then the tormented woman fainted in the arms of those who restrained her.

Meanwhile, the numbers of people who were burned were increasing. All ages were affected. Many had white-red burns on their arms and legs. Others had disfiguring sores and vesicles on their swollen faces, the flames having burned off all eyebrows and eyelashes. In their fits of coughing, the gasping victims brought up blackened phlegm from the carbon smoke still in their lungs.

As the fire raged on, Amelia saw an elderly man enclosed by a ring of fire. The man stood petrified as the fire engulfed him, flames leaping high about him into the air. Amelia screamed for help. In response to her plea, she recognized the familiar face of Jacob Ohana among the rescue workers. "Help him! Help him!," she cried, pointing to the victim. Without hesitation, Ohana plunged into the thick smoke, covering his mouth and nose with a handkerchief. The smoke and fire were intense. Tongues of flame lashed out from every direction.

Ohana called out to the solitary figure. "This way, old man! This way!"

Yet the old man stayed where he was, mumbling to himself. Ohana had no choice. He had to rush in to save the old man. He dashed into the ring of fire, zig zagging his way through the flames.

"Morenica! Iziko!," shouted the sickly old man in the midst of the fire. There was a crazed happy look on the man's face, and his darting wild eyes seemed fixated upon some compelling vision in the distance. "I see them in the fire! I see Morenica! I see little Iziko!," he said happily to his rescuer.

Ohana recognized Hacham Alhadeff immediately. The merchant shouted to get Alhadeff's attention. "Hacham! Come with me! Hurry!"

The Hacham did not move. His glazed eyes shone with a new contentment as he continued to speak to his loved ones. "Morenica, Iziko, Aaron, O precious ones . . ."

Ohana saw that the Hacham was delirious, so he carried the unresisting Hacham on his shoulders and rushed once again through the flames. Panting for air in the oppressive heat, his eyes smarting from the smoke, he charged through the wall of flame shortly before it devoured them both.

Ohana carried the Hacham to safety. The scrawny scholar, oblivious to all that was taking place about him, was laid down alongside the other victims.

"Morenica, my sweet one! Come back to me," the Hacham shouted with his arms raised, a glorious smile on his shrunken face.

Amelia came to aid the Hacham.

"The Hacham! It's Hacham Alhadeff!," she shouted.

"I know," said Ohana. "He is delirious."

Amelia brought some water for the Hacham to drink.

"Drink," she said. "Drink!"

The elderly scholar sipped slowly from the cup, the water flowing into and around his quivering lips. With his mouth full of water, the Hacham suddenly blurted out, "Morenica! Iziko! Aaron! I see them! I see them!"

The Hacham tried to get up to run back to the fire while Amelia tried to hold him down.

She cried out, "Help! Help over here!"

Two men helped her hold the Hacham down. The Hacham twisted his head towards the fire. "Morenica, Iziko! Aaron! I see them! Look! Over there! I see them over there! They're over there! Don't you see them? Morenica! Iziko!" Amelia saw nothing. Neither did anyone else.

"He has gone mad," said one of the men who had come to her aid.

Amelia nodded sadly, acknowledging the truth of the statement. The Hacham, her sweet teacher, had gone mad. The whole world, she thought had gone mad. Nothing made sense any more. In this non-sensical world, where beasts ruled the earth and innocents suffered and where nature added ravages of its own, it was becoming more difficult to keep one's sanity. How long would it be before she, too, would cry out as he did?

Amelia vowed to bring the Hacham back to health, back to sanity. However much she might give up on the world, she could not give up on herself and the ones that she loved. She would never give up on the Hacham until he was well again. Never.

The devastation wrought by the fire was staggering. More than two thousand of the straw huts had gone up in the flames, leaving thousands of exiles without a roof over their heads. Eighteen people had been burned alive, and another eighty victims had died within the next few days. All had horrible burns on their bodies. All the food reserves in the camp, all personal valuables, all books — all had gone up in smoke.

The camp was a flat expanse of charred earth. All that was left were scattered patches of black ash marking the sites of former straw homes.

The survivors, some sobbing from loss of family, others bemoaning their loss of fortune, walked about in a daze. Without food in their stomachs, without a roof over their heads, without even a coin to buy a slice of bread, they had no resources to call upon except themselves. Even their will to survive was weakening.

With their bare hands, the Spanish Jews dug holes in the ground within which to sleep. In vain, thousands scavenged the parched fields for plants to eat. However, because of the aridity of the land, very few edible roots could be found. Some exiles, who had been particularly careful not to violate the prohibitions of the Sabbath day, crawled on all fours and used only their teeth with which to strip away the edible portions off the plants, consoling themselves that they had not ripped it out by hand.

But neither the local vegetation, nor the charitable offerings from the mellah could sustain so many. While hundreds were dying of hunger, the survivors were too weak to bury them. Desperate, the exiles resorted to extreme measures to hasten an end to their suffering.

One poor woman, unable to feed her starving child, took a stone and smashed the child's head with it until the child expired. Having done this, she then took the stone and struck herself on the head until she too expired.

Many Jews went to the city walls and sold their sons into slavery for a piece of bread. Others went to the city gates hoping somehow to slip into the city. Many succeeded. Once inside the city, the hungry Jews scaled courtyard walls to pluck oranges and figs from trees. Others prowled the streets and tried to snatch food from local vendors. Some Jews wound their way to the *mellah*, where they demanded food from their kinsmen. Although it was forbidden by Islamic law for any Jew to enter a mosque, some of the exiles strayed into the sacred Moslem shrines and begged for alms. Many others converted to Islam rather than starve to death.

When all seemed lost, the King of Fez, Muhammed es-Sheikh, reversed his policy and decreed that any Spanish Jew who wished to settle in the city of Fez could do so. This was the turning point. The exiles in the camp praised the Holy One of Israel for listening to their pleas for mercy and forgiveness.

Every Friday, the King donated hundreds of gold coins to sustain the poor Jews who had been dying in the marketplaces or starving in the camp. Because the *mellah* was narrow and could not accommodate the many exiles, the King commanded that it be enlarged. A cadre of soldiers chopped down thousands of trees on the outskirts of Fez in order to build hundreds of small wooden two-level homes for the exiles.

The extended area of the *mellah* was regarded as a blessed site; indeed, the exiles named it *Emek Berachah*, the Valley of Blessing, for the Holy One of Israel had blessed them there. Planning for the future, they planted new fruit-bearing trees of every possible variety. As they thanked the Lord, they also remembered the King of Fez for his many acts of kindness.

*   *   *   *   *

When it became known that the King of Fez had admitted the Jews to his city, many Jews from Arcila made plans to leave for Fez as well. Before their departure, however, the ruthless Count of Borba tried to convert them. The Jews ignored the Catholic priests, and Borba, outraged by their stubbornness, ordered all Jews to leave Arcila immediately. Further, the ships carrying them had to leave the port within two days.

While Borba ordered all adult Jews out, he decreed that all children under eighteen must stay behind in Arcila . . . as Christians, no doubt. The wails of parents were heard throughout the night as the fateful decision had to be made. Many parents, unable to bear being separated from their children, accepted the Christian religion on the following day. Many others, however, said: "We shall love the Lord our God with all our hearts and with all our souls and with all our might, and we must be ready to sacrifice our lives, yea, even our very children if that is what is required of us."Wishing to remain Jews, these stalwart Israelites resolved to leave Arcila and their young loved ones behind.

Borba was astounded as well as angered by the tenacity of the Jews. His anger at such obstinence provoked him to new levels of inhumanity. He stripped those Jews who wanted to leave Arcila by sea of all their possessions as well as their children. Prior to the Jews' departure, the ships' captains were instructed to take their time with the Jews and to have no pity on them. The Jews were not to be allowed back on land until much time had passed. And so, indeed, it was done.

The Portuguese captains wandered aimlessly at sea with their human chattel. They fed thick sweet drinks laden with honey to their passengers to induce diarrhea, hoping that this would cause the prompt release of whatever coins or jewels were walled up within the bowels of the Hebrews. As the ships never reached any port, the apprehensive Jews became aware that they were going nowhere. Many became ill aboard ship, some even died. The famished Jews pleaded with the captains to cast them off wherever the captains wished, wherever it might be, just so that they would be buried someplace on dry land, just so that their carcasses would not be flung like refuse to feed the fishes of the sea. The Portuguese captains, as heartless as Borba himself, turned a deaf ear to their pleas. The captains tortured the Jewish passengers, leaving them with just enough life to endure the last of their trials.

The final blow came after harrowing weeks at sea. The captains brought the Spanish exiles back to the port of Arcila, where Borba was waiting for them. The exiles screamed mightily unto the Lord, praying for a miracle. None was forthcoming. As soon as they stepped ashore, Borba ordered the Catholic priests to bring the wandering Jews into the Christian fold. The priests, using hyssop dipped in holy water, helped to commit this most unholy of deeds. Some Jews, who resisted conversion to Christianity, were killed by Borba to speed the conversion of the rest. When all this was done, Borba was satisfied: there were no more Jews in Arcila.

Chapter 14

Life aboard the ship was awful. There were no cabins or bunks, and all the passengers had to sleep on the crowded deck on rolled blankets and makeshift chairs, tightly pressed against one another, wherever the smallest space was available.

The rough weather made many sick. Benito spent most of the time leaning over the rail vomiting. "Ay, I am sick," he would say to his month-old bride, Rebecca. "Ay, I am so sick." The fourteen-year-old Rebecca would look sympathetically at her husband, but she could offer little help.

They were all hungry and cold. Gracia and her son Haim shivered underneath a cold wet blanket. Their clothes were always wet, as much from the slosh below as from the spray above. Many passengers coughed, and Gracia prayed that none of her children would become ill. "How much longer, Mama?," asked little Haim, "When will we arrive in Genoa?"

Gracia was not sure how much longer it would be. To put her child at ease, she said confidently, "Soon, Haim. Just a few more days."

Haim pulled the wet blanket tighter about him. "I hate this ship. I can't wait to get off it. And I hate the sea, too. The sea is for seabirds, not people."

"Wait patiently, Haim," Gracia said, "When we get to Genoa, you will be the first to get a good hot meat pie."

"A meat *pastelico*, Mama? Ay, I can taste it now," Haim said, smacking his lips. "Can I have two?"

"You can have two meat *pastelicos*, Haim Pardo, if you behave yourself," Gracia said sternly.

Haim rubbed his stomach and rested his head on her shoulder.

It was not often that the Pardos, poor as they had been, ate meat dishes. Two meat pies, two *pasteles*, all for himself! Since they left Segovia, all he had eaten were cold melons, olives, and oranges. He fell asleep at his mother's side, dreaming of a hot meal, dreaming of the two meat pies that would soon be his. It was reason enough to sleep well this night, even if his stomach growled every now and then.

Before dawn Gracia was rudely awakened when someone pulled the blanket off her. She opened her eyes and saw a sailor standing in front of her, with his knife pointed right between her eyes. Gracia sat still with fright. A terrified Haim did likewise.

The sailor said, "Get up."

Gracia did as she was told. She got up slowly, making sure she made no sudden movement to provoke the sailor. Rubbing his eyes, Haim looked again at the knife to be sure this was not a dream. The knife was real. Holding on to his mother's dress, he got up with her, his heart pounding with fear, as he too wondered what was going on.

"To the main deck!," the blade-carrying sailor commanded. He pushed them forward. Gracia and Haim were led to the main deck. All the ship's fifty passengers had been huddled in one central area, with Benito and Rebecca already among them. A tremulous and tearful Rebecca clasped her mother in tight embrace and would not let her go.

"Mother, they're going to kill us!," Rebecca whispered into her ear.

"Who told you such nonsense, child," answered Gracia.

"Just look around you, Mama, and you will see the answer."

Gracia Pardo looked around. The Genoese sailors, swords in one hand and knives in the other, looked mean and threatening. Gracia's face was grim as she looked back at her daughter. Rebecca was right.

The Genoese captain of the ship stood above them in the top deck. Dressed in a red-buttoned coat, wearing black French-style boots and a curved plumed hat, the bearded captain spoke in a loud voice, "You Jews have been banished from Spain for a reason. The reason is simple. Your ancestors killed our Lord Jesus Christ, and it is written that Jews must forever suffer for what they did to our Lord. And, on this occasion, when God has seen fit to deliver you Christ-killers into my hands, I will do unto you as you did unto our Lord."

One of the exiles, a handsome merchant from Ocaña, shouted out, "It would be wickedness to do such a thing, sir, because you would be spilling innocent blood. Yes, you would be committing a mortal sin against your Lord, for which you as a Christian would never be forgiven."

The captain huffed angrily. "Why . . . I only intend to avenge the blood of Jesus that you Jews spilled."

The outspoken merchant replied, "Is it not said in your Christian religion that Jesus forgave us all with his blood, to redeem mankind? And if Jesus forgave us, will you not forgive us? If you spill our blood, your Lord Jesus Christ will hold you responsible for this sin. Consider my words, captain, for they are the words that Christ will judge you by on Judgment Day."

The Genoese captain felt he had to say something to save face with his men. "You accursed Jew, do not think that your clever way with words will save you from the punishment that is your due. I will spare your lives. I will not spill your blood, but just as God Almighty has seen fit to punish you Jews by making you wander from one land to the other, so I shall make you wander yet one step more. Yes, you Jew-devils, I will cast you all on some God-forsaken island where the foot of man never treads!"

The captain drew his sword and ran down the steps to the lower main deck. Confronting the Ocaña merchant face-to-face, the captain ordered his men. "Strip him!"

The outspoken Jewish merchant said nothing as the sailors took off his clothes piece by piece. Within a matter of moments, the merchant was totally nude. Ashamed and humiliated, he shivered in the cold, covering his private parts with his hands, as all eyes were upon him.

The captain placed his sword in the man's genital area and flicked away the merchant's hands. He placed the top of the sword underneath the shaft of the man's circumcised penis and raised it slowly. With raised eyebrows, the captain pretended to curiously examine the object in front of him. "Pardon me, sir," he said with feigned seriousness, "I am no great student of human anatomy, but it seems to me as if something is missing."

The sailors laughed uproariously. The merchant stood deathly still as the captain continued to lift and lower the man's penis with the sword. The captain did this for some time, prolonging his joke for the pleasure of his crew. Finally, tired of this sport, the captain went back to the top deck.

Brandishing his sword in the air, the captain bellowed at the passengers, "All right, you Jewish swine. I am tired of playing games. Every one of you, listen to me. Take off your clothes at once. Otherwise we will strip you by force."

The people on deck obeyed the captain's order, though not without hesitation. They began to take off their clothes, dropping their garments on the deck. An elderly woman, cowering in shame, stripped down to her undergarments, but could go no further. Pointing his sword at the old woman, the captain shouted, "Take *all* your clothes off, you old Jewish bitch."

The woman, trembling, could not bring herself to do so. At the captain's signal, four sailors quickly jumped upon her and tore the undergarments off her body. The old woman, her nakedness bared, cried with closed eyes, her public shame too much for her to witness.

An aroused Benito was angry and ready to fight. He had fought off the attackers in Segovia. Could he not do it here as well? How could he allow himself to stand by while his wife and mother-in-law were stripped naked? Had he not married Rebecca to protect her? What kind of man would not keep Rebecca from shame? He was ready for combat to preserve his wife's honor, even if it cost him his life.

Gracia read his mind. "Benito," she said threateningly to her son-in-law. "Do as they say."

Benito asked, "But how can we? What about our honor? What about my wife's honor and your honor?"

Gracia replied sharply, "Honor? Who can afford honor at this moment? We are Jews, not Spaniards. Our goal is to survive, even at the cost of our honor. Benito, I want you to strip just as everyone else is doing. You, too, Rebecca. *Mejor la verguenza que la venganza.*"

Benito shook his head and said, "No, mama. I will not let Rebecca strip."

"Strip, I said!," shouted Gracia as she slapped Benito on the cheek. "Strip! . . . before your honor gets us all killed!"

Benito was shaken by Gracia's slap and looked to Rebecca for some sign of support.

Rebecca said, "We will do as Mama says." She quickly began to take off her blouse. "As you say, Mama," he said weakly to Gracia, as he, too, began to undress.

A short while later, everyone was nude. A dispirited Benito put his arm around his shamefaced wife, holding her close to him as they stood exposed. Likewise, Gracia stood hunched over, vainly attempting to cover her private parts from the stare of her son and the other passengers.

"Close your eyes, Haim," Gracia told her son. And Haim would pretend to do so, closing his eyes into narrow slits so that he could barely see the unclothed people around him. His curiosity in such matters got the better of him, and he peeked at the others. "Close your eyes, Haim," Gracia repeated, but her son, even with only slits to see with, had already seen too much.

The fifty passengers stood disrobed in the center of the main deck, shivering in the morning cold and huddling against one another, their heads bowed, and eyes lowered. No one wanted to see his neighbor's shame.

The sailors gawked at the unclothed passengers, eyeing them as if they were a group of herded animals that were being readied for the kill. They seemed ready to devour all flesh, especially the womanly flesh, that was within their immediate grasp. All that they needed was the signal from the captain to fall upon the passengers.

Three sailors picked up the clothing from the deck — tunics, sandals, blankets, headdresses, blouses, dresses of all kinds — and placed them in a heap to one side. They searched the garments for valuables, gold coins, and jewels. Over one hundred gold ducats and an odd assortment of jewels were found, much to the captain's delight.

As the ship neared a rocky island, the captain had the Ocaña merchant brought to him.

"See that island?," said the captain. The naked merchant nodded, saying nothing.

"That is an island where the foot of man never treads," the captain said mockingly. "And that, Jew, is where devils like you belong."

The Genoese captain grabbed the merchant by the hair. With the asistance of two other men, he cast the Ocaña merchant overboard. A loud splash was heard as the merchant hit the water. The captain laughed heartily at this, and his men likewise joined him in laughter.

"Throw them all overboard!," he lustily ordered his men.

Lunging at the men and women, the sailors threw the passengers over the rails. An unresisting Benito was flipped over the rails and landed on his back as he struck the water. Three sailors grabbed Gracia; two of them grabbed her arms, and the third grabbed her knees, swinging her back and forth and then flinging her overboard. She flew head first through the air, screaming as she plummeted towards the sea, finally crashing against its surface with a loud splash. The sailors whooped it up, taking delight in the flight of their human projectiles, judging their efforts both by the trajectory effected as well as by the loudness of the ensuing splash. Slapping their thighs, patting their associates on the back, the sailors seemed to greatly enjoy the new sport. When the last passenger was thrown overboard, the captain called out to those bobbing below in the water, "And all of you, remember me for the good Christian I am. Not one drop of your impure blood has been spilled. I say not one drop! You ingrate Jews, aren't you going to thank me? Ha, ha, ha, ha!" The captain and his crew crowed with laughter.

As the ship pulled away, the exiles struggled in the cold chest- high water. Most were able to tread the water somehow. Others, realizing that they could touch the ground below with their feet, edged their way slowly towards shore. A few elderly individuals, flailing frantically with their arms so as to avoid going under, were lent a helping hand. Step by step, aiding one another, the discarded passengers made their way to the rocky shore.

As they emerged from the water, they were once again conscious of their nakedness. Everyone had an overpowering sense of shame and could not look at themselves or one another. Climbing over rocks and running into bushes, they dispersed quickly. Some crouched down low to keep from being seen. Others kept on running till they had found a suitable hiding place. Shame drove them apart as they pursued their own place of self-concealment.

Benito led the way. Holding Rebecca's hand, he dashed inland, making sure that he did not lose sight of Gracia and Haim who trailed behind. In a short while, Benito found a secluded area underneath a clump of boulders.

"Here is a good hiding place," he indicated to Rebecca and Gracia. "Stay here while I look around."

"I will go with you," said Rebecca, covering her breasts with one arm and her private parts with the other.

"You stay here until I come back," said Benito firmly as he ran off again.

Rebecca returned to the narrow area underneath the boulders. She sat down alongisde Gracia, their backs pressed against the cold rocks. Rebecca placed her arms around her mother and hugged her tightly. Both of them began to cry, and the salty tears that fell on their cheeks were indistinguishable from the sea water that still covered their bodies. Shuddering in each other's arms, caressing each other's soggy stringy hair, the mother and daughter gave vent to the shame that had befallen them. Haim, his eyes closed from as much an extinguished bodily curiosity as from a developing sense of shame, likewise wiped the tears off his face.

What Benito saw was a rocky island. A few patches of vegetation struggled through the rocks, but the sharp crags made the going difficult. Further inland, where the isle rose to a high peaked summit, Benito noticed more green, and he had notions of heading in that direction. In this initial search, however, he preferred not to stray too far away from the area where he had left Rebecca and her family.

A short while later, in an area close to shore, Benito came upon an area of reeds and scrawny trees. As he neared this cluster of foliage, he noticed that the trees surrounded an irregular pool of water. One of the other passengers had preceded him and was about to drink some of the water.

"Is it sweet water?," asked Benito

The man jumped up and scrambled away to the rocks. Benito was upset that he had frightened the man, but he could not worry about everyone, shame or no shame. He had a family to protect and to care for, and that was uppermost in his mind. His mother-in-law had been right, survival was foremost. Honor was not the only thing that mattered.

Benito tasted the pool water. It was fresh.

"*Agua dulce*!," Sweet water!," Benito shouted.

"Sweet water!" The elderly man nodded his head but stayed behind the boulder. Benito understood, and he decided to withdraw from the pool to allow others to use it. As he did so, he noticed animal tracks on the soft ground leading to the water. The island has wildlife on it, Benito concluded. Benito tore Rebecca some leaves and branches off the trees, pulled up some of the slender reeds, and headed back. Maybe he had no food, but at least he could now cover their shame. When he returned, they all covered themselves with the leafy branches.

"I will find food," said Benito, "just as I found the pool of sweet water."

Soon he went to look for food, this time accompanied by young Haim. The two hunters walked down to the shore, hoping to find some helpless animal. Picking up rocks from the seashore, they would take aim at the seagulls and throw rocks at them. But except for an occasional near miss, the missiles were way off target.

They found deep pits, half-full with stagnant water like Benito had found earlier. Further inland, they found a tall tree with nuts. Benito picked up one, cracked it open, and ate it. Haim then climbed the tree and shook the branches so the nuts would fall to the ground. Together, they gathered the nuts that fell until their arms were full.

"Look, Benito! A squirrel!," Haim said excitedly. The squirrel stood at a distance, nibbling on a nut, its tail raised upwards. It regarded the intruders between noisy chomps, moving its tiny jaws and cheeks with nervous rapidity.

Benito put his nuts down slowly and reached for a rock. The animal stood still but when Benito raised his arm, the squirrel ran away into the open area. Benito threw the rock at the fleeing squirrel, but missed the target. The squirrel darted elusively among the rocks, in seeming mastery of the intricacies of all the local nooks and crannies, until it vanished from sight among the rocks. Benito, sensing the futility of further pursuit, gave up on the squirrel. It would have to wait for another day. Benito signaled to Haim, and they returned to their family with the nuts.

They dined on nuts . . . in the 'Abulafia mansion,' as Benito called their hiding place.

"Rocks for a bed, nuts for a meal," mused Rebecca. "As if our poverty was not enough, God has seen fit to bring us down even lower, so that we are no better than the wild dogs of the field. We have no clothes to wear, and we have hardly any food to eat. We were poor in Segovia but, dear God, *never* like this. How much lower can we get, Mama? In the name of Heaven, I ask you, why is God doing this to us?"

Gracia answered her with a saying. "*Cada mal se tiene que acabar.* 'Every bad thing must end sometime.' Even this, my daughter, bad as it is, will pass. Remember what I am about to tell you, and remember it well: *Para todo hay remedio, menos para la muerte.* 'There is a remedy for everything, except for death itself.'"

Accepting her mother's explanation, Rebecca stopped complaining. She continued cracking the nuts with her teeth until a dry bitterness filled her mouth. "I need some water," said Rebecca.

"Me too," said Haim.

"Very well," said Benito. "Let us all go to the water-hole together."

They waited until dark to go. The new moon barely gave off enough light to find one's way through the dimly lit jumble of rocks. At the water-hole, they found themselves among a host of naked creatures who, likewise welcoming the darkness, had come out of their hiding places.

Softly whispering to one another, the shadowy creatures came and went, drinking the water, exchanging few words with a fellow being of the night and then disappearing once again into the engulfing blackness. Benito watched these activities with concern. It was obvious that something had to be done, or they would all soon die from cold and hunger. A few leaves were no protection and it was too late to start a fire. Tomorrow he would look for flint, gather some dry wood, and try to get a fire going. Yet Benito knew that no one else would come close to the fire if they were still naked. Of that he was sure. Carefully, he approached a figure in the darkness.

"You, señor, please do not run away. I am Benito Abulafia. I want to help you."

The figure stood up, "I am listening. Speak."

Benito spoke. "Get branches from the big tree next to the pool. Cover yourself below with the leaves and branches, and you can use the center part of each branch as a kind of string. Do you understand me?"

The figure spoke. "Yes, I understand. Tomorrow morning I will do as you say. Is there anything else?"

Benito paused. "Yes, tell everyone you meet what I told you. It is very important. Also, there is a nut tree further down on the seashore that you can use for food. Go eastward to find it, in the direction of the rising sun. That is all."

"Thank you most kindly," said the voice in the darkness. "Will I see you again?"

Benito said, "Tomorrow night, we can meet here after sunset. Bring others with you if you can. We need to work together if we are to survive."

With that, Benito and his family returned to their hiding place. He slept with Rebecca in his arms. They huddled against one another, sharing the warmth of their bodies against the cold of the night. Gracia and Haim also pressed themselves tightly against the married twosome, adding their body heat to the family huddle.

After a cold and damp night, Benito awoke at sunrise. He shook off the aching muscle stiffness and set about trying to start a fire. He spent half the morning rubbing rocks against one another, trying to get a fire going. Finally he succeeded. Cupping his hands over its first flames to protect it from the wind, he felt the fire grow stronger as he added larger pieces of wood. He was jubilant.

"I've done it!," he shouted joyfully. "Fire! I've done it!"

Rebecca came over and hugged him. "Ay, Benito you are wonderful."

"We shoemakers know a thing or two, eh?" said Benito with evident pride.

Gracia said, "What did I tell you, Rebecca? Didn't I tell you to marry an Abulafia?"

Rebecca kissed her husband. "Yes, I am so happy I did. Benito is the man I always wanted. Who needs a cavalier?"

Benito smiled and hugged her.

The rising smoke attracted the other exiles. Emerging from their hiding places, some scantily clad, others not at all, the exiles could stand the cold no longer. Hungering for warmth as much as food, the shivering castaways sought out the fire's warmth.

Benito invited them all. "Come. Join us. Make yourselves warm," he shouted.

Those with branches to cover their private parts came forward to warm themselves by the heat of the Abulafia fire. Those who were still nude, however, preferred to shiver at a safe distance.

Benito went after them. He caught up with two couples and their five children and taught them how to use the branches to cover themselves. Then he brought them back to the fire. Soon a second fire was started a short distance away. By mid-afternoon, there were fifteen of them gathered around the two fires, exchanging stories and expressing thanks to Benito and to God Almighty, happy still to be among the living.

Benito, the maker of fire, became their leader. He directed the women to the nut tree and had them gather more nuts. Other women went in search of the remaining exiles, only one-third of whom had thus far been located, while the men went to search for other food.

Benito took three men with him, one of them the Ocaña merchant whose timely words aboard ship had saved their lives. Haim came along too. The neophyte hunters were armed with nothing more than a few small rocks. While they did see an occasional rabbit or squirrel, they were unable to catch anything and although they returned to camp empty-handed, they remained hopeful that the next day would yield some food.

The camp had grown to twenty-five half-clad hungry exiles. The children, who had not eaten well for days, cried incessantly. Benito worried about how to feed so many mouths. He knew they could not exist for long on a diet of only nuts. It was necessary to find more food, any kind of food. Benito started a third fire and thought about what to do next. He decided to go further inland, which meant they would have to climb the sharp-ridged mountain that was at the center of the island. Its steep slopes seemed more promising than elsewhere.

On the morning of the third day, Benito and Haim joined three others to begin the trek. They followed the winding central ravine leading to the foot of the mountain, walking along its sharp edge, checking along the way for fruit or nut-bearing trees. Halfway to the mountain, Haim found a pomegranate tree. He cracked the pomegranate open and put the fruit to his mouth. He chewed on its crimson-colored seeds and spit out its pulp, smearing his face with the reddish juice of the berry. Others did the same.

At the foot of the mountain, Benito looked up. It was a harsh rough-hewn mountain, the ravine below being the irregular continuation of a huge cliff that loomed above. Benito studied the cliff and noticed dark recessed areas about half-way up.

"Caves!," he said, pointing to the cavernous areas in question. The Ocaña merchant came up alongside him. "You are right. Those are caves. The question is: Are they natural or man-made?"

"We shall soon find out," said Benito, as he started to climb the mountain. "Perhaps this island is inhabited. There may have been others before us who may have been stranded also."

"Wait!," said the cautious merchant. "If it is not man-made, it could be a nest for eagles. We could find eggs there. And if we do find eggs, we may need to fight off the mother eagle. We need something to fight with — a stick maybe. If we break off some branches, we will have some sort of weapon."

Benito agreed, and every man, including Haim, soon had a wooden stick in his hand. It was better than nothing.

They ascended the mountain, making their way along the spiraling ledge that led to the overhanging cliff. On one side of the precipice was the near-vertical wall of the escarpment. On the other was the open airy expanse of the island. Benito stayed as far away from the edge of the projecting ridge as possible, because he felt giddy from the high altitude. He kept his eyes fixed on the narrow strip in front of him, watching every step, closing off from view in his mind's eye the vacuous space to his left.

They arrived at the caves. But still there was no sign of life. Everyone was ready, sticks in hand, as they followed Benito into the dark caverns.

Something rustled within. "What was that?," asked Benito to those behind him, a trace of fear in his voice. It was very dark inside.

"There is something inside," said the Ocaña merchant. "I suggest that we get out of here."

More rustling sounds took place, followed by what sounded like a series of hurrying footsteps.

"I am getting out of here," said the Ocaña merchant who retreated back towards the cave entrance.

Benito was angry. "Come back here!"

The footsteps came closer and closer. Benito also began to retreat. "Everyone back!," he shouted.

It was too late. The lion pounced upon Benito. It ripped into him with its claws, emitting a mighty roar that shook the cavern. Benito was thrown back, his arm cut deep. He scrambled back towards the entrance, holding the stick in front of him, trying to keep the lion at bay. The lion, undeterred by the stick, lunged at Benito again. Its claws tore into his chest, flaying his skin with the razors in its paws. Benito fell, and the lion pounced on him, its jaws wide open as it went for Benito's neck. Benito tried to fight the lion off, but the animal was too strong. Its powerful teeth tore out a chunk of flesh from Benito's throat, and then it tore out another, mangling and dismembering his body. Benito was torn limb from limb by the lion and by its cubs which also joined in the feasting upon such an easy kill.

The others ran for their lives, with the middle-aged Ocaña merchant leading the way. But a second lion shot forth out of the cave and blocked their escape. The fleet-footed lion cornered one of the hunters and lunged at him. The terrified man jumped off the cliff. Screaming as he fell, he plunged into the ravine two hundred feet below.

The Ocaña merchant and Haim Pardo ran down the narrow ledge. Behind them was the other member of the group who, overweight and slow, struggled to keep up. As Haim and the merchant ran, they heard a frightening roar from behind them. Haim looked back to see the lion leaping at the fat one behind and knocking him to the ground. The exile was on his back, trying to stave off the animal with futile shoves and pushes. The lion drove its teeth into the man's flailing arms and gouged out a hole in the man's forearm. As the lion clawed him viciously, lacerating the man's face and arms with its paws, the exile struggled to extricate himself. Rolling with the lion, he slipped from its grasp and threw himself over the cliff, his body crashing on one sharp ledge and then bouncing off another, ultimately ending up as a gnarled and deformed heap of muscle and bone at the ravine's bottom. The lion looked down into the ravine, angry that his prey had eluded him. It gave off a vicious roar and bounded off in pursuit of the others.

Then, the lion came after them! The Ocaña merchant pushed Haim forward, racing down the ledge. They could hear the bounding footsteps of the animal behind them. It was catching up with them! Haim's heart pounded rapidly, the blood spurted through his head, his lungs shrieked from breathlessness, as he whipped his legs even faster.

"Fast! Faster!," shouted the Ocaña merchant behind him, also breathless, as the animal kept gaining ground on them. Faster and faster Haim ran. About half-way down the ledge, the exhausted Ocaña merchant knew that he could run no further. It was no use. Gasping for air, the merchant shouted out to Haim, "Run, child, run! Warn the others! Warn the others!"

With that, the Ocaña merchant spun around to face the charging animal. He raised his stick in the air and held it horizontally between his two arms. The lion came around the corner, its teeth bared in a vicious snarl. Leaping high into the air, it was suspended for a deadly instant, and then crashed headlong into the merchant. The Ocaña man fell onto the ground, trying to hold off the animal as long as he could.

Haim did not look back. He kept on running, numbed by fear. He ran as fast as his legs would carry him. He ran down the ledge, down the winding course of the ravine, down towards the campsite. With every stride, he felt the lion closing in, reaching out with its huge paw and pulling him down, ripping out his flesh with its jaws, swallowing him whole.

Haim reached the campsite. He stumbled to the ground, his lungs ready to explode, his legs no longer capable of supporting him. He had reached his destination, and it was enough. He could collapse.

"Lions! Lions!," he said between heaving breaths. "Lions! Lions! We ran into a lions' den!"

Rebecca ran up to her brother and shook him by the shoulders. "What about Benito? What happened to Benito?"

Haim began to cry. "Benito . . . the lions killed him . . . and the others too. I . . . I am the only one who got away."

Rebecca could not believe her ears. "What? Benito . . . dead?"

Haim breathlessly nodded in silence.

Rebecca screamed. She was not alone. The other women in the camp whose husbands were killed, joined her in her wailing. Gracia put her arms around her widowed fourteen-year-old daughter, consoling her as best she could, knowing that no proverb could help their misfortune. Disaster was disaster, death was death, and there was no way around it. *Para todo hay remedio, menos para la muerte*, she had once said. 'There is a remedy for everything, except for death itself.'

Someone shouted, "The lions! The lions are coming!"

Now it was everyone who screamed. There was panic, with everyone fleeing every which way.

Haim, still short of breath, got off the ground and climbed to the top of a boulder. A short distance away, he spotted two lions and three cubs approaching the camps, their sleek bodies crouched low, the two huge adult cats stealthily leading the way.

"To the sea! To the sea!," Haim shouted out for all to hear. "Everyone to the sea!"

Haim jumped down from the boulder. Quickly he told his mother and weeping sister Rebecca, "Quick! Follow me!"

"Let the lions take me," whined Rebecca as Gracia and Haim tried to push her toward the shore. "Let them eat me! I don't want to live any more!" Rebecca, overwrought with grief and tears, refused to move. "Let me die, Mama."

Gracia slapped her daughter's face. She slapped her again. "Now listen to me. You are going to live! And you are going to run when I tell you to run. Now . . . RUN!"

Temporarily shaken, Rebecca recovered her wits. As if roused to consciousness from a bad dream, she awoke only to find herself in yet another. Taking hold of her mother's arm, taking hold of herself, Rebecca ran as she was told.

The three of them ran as fast as they could. Rebecca tripped and fell. Lingering in the dirt for a moment, she heard a blood-curdling roar behind them. A terrified Rebecca, lifting herself up in an instant upon hearing such a frightful noise, continued to run where she had left off, this time without so much as a stumble, as she sensed the nearness of the approaching menace behind her.

They reached the shore and splashed their way into the sea, kicking their way through the waves of foam. Other exiles had also found the water, the count of bodies in the water growing quickly to twenty or so. Yet at least that many exiles remained stranded on land. There was no way of telling whether they would be safe or not, whether they would be able to escape from the beasts of the field.

Screams were heard from afar, then stopped, only to be followed by new screams and roars, and then the silence would return again. Only the soft sound of the lapping waves, as they crashed and receded from the rocky shore in rushes of foam, offered to fill the acoustic void. There was an uneasy silence among the exiles at the death of their fellows; it was a silence from the knowledge that the death could have been their own.

The instruments of the carnage emerged on the shore. The two lions came down to the water's edge, growling and snarling as they went. They bounded on all fours down the full length of the visible shore, taking note of their quarry immersed in the waters of the sea.

One of the lions tested the water in front of Gracia and her family. Gracia held her breath as the animal came closer. It waded out into the water, and was soon up to its neck in water, its head bobbing with each wave. Rebecca and Haim each held onto their mother, all three petrified from fear, as they watched the animal use its hairy limbs to paddle its way toward them.

"O my God, O my God," said Gracia in disbelief.

"Mama, it's coming!," screamed Rebecca, her panic returning.

With presence of mind , Haim said, "Let's get back."

The three of them began to retreat into the deeper water as the lion came closer. Further and further back they went, until the water reached Haim's neck. Finally, they could go no further. Neither could the lion, which, seeing its potential victims were in too deep, reversed itself and swam back to shore.

The Pardos sighed with relief and made their way back to a safer depth, all the while keeping a close eye on the lions.

The lions paced up and down the seashore, first in one direction, then the next. The animals prowled the coastline waiting for the first foolhardy person to abandon the safety of the water. The lion cubs frolicked on the shore, playing at times with the incoming waves and intermittently chewing on the carcass of some unrecognizable man or woman. After an hour of pacing to-and-fro, the adult lions decided to rest. They lay down on their stomachs, basking in the sunshine, flipping their tails back and forth in the air. At other times, they would playfully paw their youngsters with a friendly parental growl, all the while waiting calmly for the sea to deliver their victims up to them.

None of the exiles left the water. However cold it might be, however much they shivered, however hungry or thirsty, no one dared to step on shore. Better to die of hunger than to be some animal's feast, better to die of thirst in the water than to be torn apart on the land. Gracia was prepared to outwait the lions, knowing that under no circumstance would she step on shore as long as the lions were there.

All day the lions waited. By evening the lions had tired of the wait and returned to their cave in the interior of the island. When the lions had gone, the exiles made their way cautiously back onto the shore. They looked around for any lingering presence of the lions, but they could find none. Their amphibian existence was over, at least until the following morning when the lions were sure to return. The exiles from Spain were back where they started, cold and naked, hungry and tired. Without a homeland to flee to, without even a home to provide them with minimal warmth and shelter, the abandoned Spanish Jews could not even claim this God-forsaken island as their own, having had to rudely discover that their only secure abode was in the frigid waters of a shifting sea.

This went on for five days. During the day the exiles would take to the sea to avoid the roving lions. By night, when the lions returned to their lair, the exiles would regain the shore, and drink and eat what they could find. Their stomachs aching from hunger, Haim and Rebecca found some clams in the sand and ate them. Gracia was at first unable to eat the clams because they were ritually forbidden. But when a terrible weakness and dizziness came upon her, she relented. Gracia's feet grew swollen from hours in the water, and Rebecca's were so tender the skin between her toes began to bleed. All were sick and hungry, naked, and coughing from the cold. As others fell by the wayside, succumbing either to the ruthless elements or to the waiting beasts, the Pardos were content to have survived one day at a time, wondering if the next day would be their last.

On the fifth day, they sighted a ship. Yelling wildly and waving their arms frantically, they tried to attract the attention of the ship. Their cries met with success. A small boat left the ship and came toward them. The sailor was astonished to see a dozen nude people in the water. For the exiles the sailor was nothing less than their salvation.

The sailor reported to the captain about the exiles' suffering, and the captain, an old Italian mariner by the name of Enrico Panzarella, was very distressed. Moved by a spirit of compassion, he ordered that the exiles be brought to the ship immediately.

It was a pitiful sight to see these pale, naked, and moribund beings being brought aboard ship. So wretched did they look, the legs of some swollen to the size of their waists, that they seemed utterly unredeemable from their misery. Captain Panzarella was ashamed that one of his own countrymen should have behaved in so barbaric a manner. He felt it his Christian duty to right the outrage as quickly as possible.

The captain had an old sail torn into pieces to be used a makeshift garments for the exiles. To the women, he gave shirts to wear; to all he gave food and drink. Anxious that they be promptly placed in the custody of their coreligionists, he set sail for the nearest Italian port with a Jewish community.

Gracia Pardo, thankful to God that she and her children were still alive, put her arms around Rebecca and Haim and kissed them both, hoping that their trial of suffering had finally come to an end.

Chapter 15

"Pirates! Pirates!," shouted the captain of the Venetian galleon that bore Esmeralda Funes. "All hands on deck! Prepare to do battle!," the captain ordered his men. The crew members scurried about the deck, rigging the rope on the sails, positioning and fastening the iron cannons into place, bringing all arms to the deck. As the pirate fleet drew nearer, iron balls were piled in heaps next to the cannons. Sailors strapped swords to their waists, while others took to the bridge ready to unload their muskets on the brigands of the high seas. As the lead pirate ship drew alongside, the skull-and-dagger flag waving high on its main mast, it became apparent to the crew that their adversary was none other than Fragoso, *le corsaire terrible*, the most dreaded pirate of the Mediterranean!

Fragoso's ship arrived with a blistering cannonade. Half the broadside of the Venetian ship exploded from the impact of the cannon balls, with sailors and wood flying in different directions. The one Italian cannon that worked was directed against the hull of the opposing ship, causing damage to its wooden exterior and to the pirates who manned it. The battle raged on. The air was filled with smoke, and the Venetian galleon shook with each blow it took. Its hull was splintered badly from the relentless attack; its main sail was gaping with holes, and caught on fire from one of the many blazes that broke out aboard ship.

The pirates were winning. When the last Venetian cannon was silenced, the corsair ship pulled up alongside. The pirates stormed the deck of the Italian vessel. Swinging their cutlases with vengeful fury, they chopped the Venetians to pieces.

Esmeralda Funes hardly knew what was happening. She and the other Jewish passengers had been ordered below deck as soon as the pirates' ships had been sighted. All of them — men, women, and children — had been crammed into the dark confines of the brig, lying one atop the other, as the battle began.

It was frightful. With each hit that the Italian vessel took, the huddled exiles were thrown from one side to the other. Screaming people fell on top of one another.

Esmeralda was relieved when it was all over. She could not wait to be free of the oppressive weight of the sweaty bodies all around her. All she wanted was to get out of this lightless hole.

Someone opened the door to the brig, letting the bright light in. Esemralda squinted and put her hands up to shield her eyes. What she saw was a bare-chested, scar-faced man holding a steel cutlass in his right hand, its blade still dripping with the blood of Venetian mariners.

People began to scream.

"Silence!," yelled the pirate, raising his cutlass threateningly into the air. The exiles in the brig stopped screaming. The pirate continued to hold the cutlass high in the air.

"Out! . . . One by one!," the gravel-voiced pirate ordered.

The exiles came out one by one as he commanded. Their arms were tied behind their backs. After her arms were tied, Esmeralda was given a vicious shove forwards. She climbed up the sloping ladder to the main deck.

The deck was still smouldering from the fires. The slain Venetian sailors were strewn across its floor, one lifeless corpse after another steeped in its own puddle of blood. Esmeralda stepped over one dead Venetian after another. She thought she was going to faint. Looking away from a headless sailor, Esmeralda grasped the ship's rail for support.

At the rail, Esmeralda observed the male exiles being transferred from the Venetian to the pirate ship. The ships were connected by hooks and ropes, and several wide planks were placed between the two ships to serve as a walkway. Esmeralda watched the prisoners walk the gang-planks. Once aboard the pirate ship, the men were quickly taken below and disappeared from sight.

Esmeralda asked the scar-faced pirate behind her, "The men, why did you take them on your ship?"

The pirate replied, "To be sold as slaves. We sell Jews for good price. You too."

At the statement of these last two words, the pirate roared with laughter. An incredulous Esmeralda stopped walking and turned around to confront this contemptible seafaring savage. The pirate was not intimidated. With a soft nudge of his cutlass, he poked Esmeralda in the chest, causing her impulse of resistance to dissolve as quickly as it had formed. A startled Esmeralda jumped back as the blade tip scratched her chest. Quickly getting back in line with the others, she did not even dare to look back at this half-naked ruffian, whose cackling howls of laughter continued unabated. Animals! Beasts!, she thought to herself as she trembled with fright. The devil with them! Her unvoiced epithets notwithstanding, she was not inclined to openly manifest any further noncompliance. The spirited Esmeralda Funes, the matchmaker who took a mischievous pride in being no man's subordinate, had become as tame as a lamb.

Fragoso, the pirate captain, boarded the Venetian vessel. Of medium build, he had an olive-complexioned face with a huge curved nose underneath which sprouted a bushy thick moustache. When Fragoso came on deck, he ordered the pirates to seize the captives. With one hand, each pirate grabbed a woman's hair and, with the other hand, held a knife at her throat. Esmeralda stood speechless and unmoving as the sharp steel of the blade touched her neck. She was terrified.

Fragoso carefully appraised the young and old. He twirled his moustache with a sinister type of motion, as if he were scheming some devilish foul play upon these captured women. Finally, he tired of his walking and he spoke.

"You Jews, I know you take much gold out from Spain. I know you have gold. If you give me your gold, your lives will be spared. Otherwise . . ."

One half-sobbing woman told the pirate behind her that she had gold in her shoes, and when the pirate pulled the woman's shoes off, he found three gold ducats. The pirate shouted gleefully at this discovery, and Fragoso indicated his approval with a nod.

Next, a white-haired woman, shaking uncontrollably, confessed that she had a few gold coins in her headdress. The pirate jerked the head-dress off, and five ducats and three gemstones fell on the wooden deck.

The pirate captain examined the gemstones and placed them with the other gold coins. He twirled his busy moustache with seeming contentment as the roaming pirate continued to search the other captives.

Going from one woman to the other, the pirates searched pockets, bags, hairpieces, and clothing. The woman next to Esmeralda, stifling her screams for fear of losing her life, was searched from head to toe. Her hairbun was opened, her mouth and teeth inspected, and then the pirate took a knife, slashing the front of her dress. Continuing the search, the pirate reached into her armpits, felt around her breasts and waist, and finally spread open her legs. He put his hand on her crotch and quickly thrust it inside. The woman screamed, and the man jerked his hand out.

"Nothing!," he shouted out to his captain.

"Nothing?," Fragoso said in apparent astonishment. After a slight pause, he said, "From behind!"

The pirate positioned himself from behind. He exposed the woman's buttocks and spread the cheeks far apart, hoping that something might fall out. Nothing came out.

"Nothing!," the search pirate said angrily, a tone of finality in his voice.

Fragoso was furious. He came over to the woman and slapped her viciously across the face.

"Nothing? You have nothing, you Jewish dog?" He slapped her again and again. "You have nothing?" Fragoso thrashed her face mercilessly. Viciously he grabbed her hair and jerked her head back.

"Did you swallow your gold?," Fragoso asked, his face almost pressed into hers.

Frightened almost out of her wits, the woman shook her head rapidly. She lowered her eyes and stammered, "No . . . I do not have any gold."

Fragoso studied her response and let go of her hair. He immediately summoned some men. Five pirates came to his side. Fragoso continued to stare at the woman in front of him, watching her carefully, and then turned to his men, ordering, "Open her up!"

The pirates grabbed the woman and slit her throat. Choking on her own blood, the woman sputtered and struggled helplessly, and then went limp.

One pirate, a foul-looking, one-eyed fellow dressed in putrid rags, a black patch over his bad eye, attended to the butchery. The pirate proceeded to open the woman's abdomen with his dagger. Through the vertical incision, the pirate reached in with his bare hands and pulled out the woman's guts. Spreading the slimy innards on the deck, the raggedy, one-eyed pirate went through them inch by inch. Placing one hand in front of the other, the pirate squeezed each segment of intestine in his search for hidden coins. When the pirate found a suspicious area of gut, he made an incision down its length and let the fecal material spill out onto his hands. With his hands smeared with excrement, the pirate shouted as he pulled something out from the coil of tissue.

"I found something! I found something!," the one-eyed pirate shouted as he held an object up to view.

Another pirate ran up to him with a pail of water and poured water over the object. It was indeed a gold ducat.

Delighted, Fragoso slapped his thigh. He had been right after all. He signaled to his men to continue with the disembowelment.

The woman's stomach and intestine were ripped out, sliced open, and explored for other coins. Two more gold ducats were found, much to Fragoso's pleasure.

The woman's carcass was flipped over on its stomach, or rather what was left of it. The evisceration was still not finished. The pirate drove the dagger into the woman's rectum and sliced it apart. Reaching into her rectum with his bare hand, he probed there as well, but found nothing. Then, what was left of the mutilated woman — the neck and face drenched with blood, the abdominal cavity converted into a smelly excavation of excreta and chopped flesh — was dragged to the side of the boat and thrown overboard.

Esmeralda was next. She had watched with horror and disbelief as the pirates had cut the woman next to her into pieces.

Fearing she might suffer a similar fate, Esmeralda said, "I have two gold ducats in my hairbun, and a thirty-piece maravedi in my pocket. That is all I have, señor, nothing more."

Nevertheless, the pirate checked her out from head to toe and subjected her to the same humiliating exam as all the other women. Finding what Esmeralda said he would, he then left her for the next woman. Esmeralda, ashamed but still alive, sighed deeply with relief.

The searches continued, and the confiscated gold was placed at Fragoso's feet. Three women down the line, another woman was found who had nothing. She pleaded with the pirates.

"Please, señores, I have nothing to declare. I beg of you not to hurt me, for my children's sake if not for my own. Please señores, I have not a maravedi to my name . . . Please, please do not hurt me." Ignoring her pleas, the pirates eviscerated her as they did the other women who had no gold to give them.

After the searches, some of the pirates took five women to the rear of the ship. Esmeralda wondered what was going on. Soon horrible screams were heard coming from the women. It was clear to all that now they were going to be raped as well. This was too much!

Esmeralda, hot-tempered and outraged, struck the scar-faced pirate in the face. Surprised, he momentarily lost his grip on his blade, and it slashed across her shoulder. Esmeralda twisted away from him and broke free.

Following Esmeralda's lead, others tried to break free. Most did not succeed, for the pirates slashed the throats of those who dared to offer resistance. One by one, the women slumped onto the deck, their life-blood pouring out of them.

Only one other woman besides Esmeralda had been able to escape by running to the rail and throwing herself overboard. Esmeralda tried to do the same, but a pirate stood between her and the rail. Esmeralda reversed direction and ran to the opposite side. One pirate lunged for her, but missed. Another pirate tried to grab her arm, but she was able to shake him off. She climbed onto the siderail and looked back. The scar-faced pirate was almost on top of her!

Esmeralda jumped. The pirate lunged over the rail and tightly grabbed one of her ankles. Esmeralda was suspended in mid-air by the pirate who, holding firmly on to her ankle, began to pull her slowly upwards. Esmeralda looked down at the water below her, and then at her captor. Summoning all her strengh, Esmeralda kicked with her free leg, and struck the pirate in the face. The pirate screamed and let go.

Esmeralda fell head first into the water. Down, down she sank — and then surfaced again. Her head bobbing in and out of the water, she tried to catch a few breaths of air. Mostly she caught salt water which she spat out in mouthfuls. She looked up one last time and saw the angry pirate berate her with his raspy voice. It was enough. She no longer tried to stay afloat. She allowed herself to go under, allowing the abyss of the ocean to swallow her up, to once and for all consume her as she had vowed that no man ever would.

Chapter 16

It was a time of mourning: *Tisha b'Av*, the ninth of Av, was the traditional day for remembering the destruction of the ancient Temples in Jerusalem and the dispersion of the Jews. Don Isaac Abravanel, barely a week out at sea, noted the pattern of history: this day was to witness a third exile for the people of Israel. It was a new exile within the larger exile of the Diaspora. The Jews of Spain, the educated Sephardim of Castile and Aragon, who had for centuries held positions of power and importance, were now to suffer the same fate of their downtrodden Ashkenazic kinsmen. Scattered to the four winds, their place in the land of *Sefarad* was no more. It was indeed a time to mourn.

It seemed appropriate to observe *Tisha b'Av* aboard the ship of exile. Neither food and water, nor leather shoes were permitted on this day. Don Isaac Abravanel, along with the other exiles, lay on the floor of the deck for the recitation of the Book of Lamentations. This was followed by the hushed chanting of gloomy dirges called *Kinot* and by the reading of the curses in the twenty-sixth chapter of the Book of Leviticus. The sadness of the verses were made more poignant by the events of the day, which seemed to fulfill the scriptural prophecies of woe and misfortune.

In Spain, it had been the custom to extinguish the candles after the conclusion of the evening *Tisha b'Av* service. Gathered around Don Isaac Abravanel, as he held up a brightly lit candle, the congregation prepared for the ritual.

Abravanel said, "This year is the year 5252. It is one thousand, four hundred, and twenty two years since the destruction of our Holy Temple. For that length of time, God has seen fit to punish us with exile for our sins and to scatter us amongst the nations of the earth. Although our ancestors were the first to suffer the burden of exile, we, too, share in the historic punishment. Yet, if we are faithful to the ways of the Torah, if we keep His divine commandments in the fulness thereof, then our reward shall be our redemption, and the black curse of the exile shall be lifted. As we extinguish the light of the candle, we remember the darkness that has overtaken Israel, we remember the brightness that was once ours, and we cherish the hope that the light of a redeemed Israel shall one day return to illumine all the corners of the earth."

Don Isaac blew out the candle. Darkness came. Within the human huddle, the blackness of their history had been encapsulated in the flame become no flame. Each passenger then returned to his family, as did Abravanel.

In the cool blackness of night, the ship pitched and heaved as it continued on its way, bearing its cargo to a land that did not yet await it, plunging on into the blackness of night upon this blackest of days.

No European port wanted the Jews. The vessel bearing Don Isaac Abravanel and his first family stopped at Marseilles. By order of the municipal council, Jews could settle in Marseilles only if they paid substantial bribes. Abravanel remembered how much the shipowners of Marseilles charged to transport the exiles to Italy or Turkey; he remembered the destruction of the Jewish community in Marseilles seven years ago. Few aboard ship tried to settle there, and Don Isaac Abravanel was not one of them.

Nor did Genoa want the Jews. To this northern Italian seaport came one crowded vessel after another, but the Genoese did not welcome them. The ancient Genoese law prohibiting Jewish travelers from staying there more than three days was strictly enforced. While the ships could be refitted, no Jew was allowed in the city. Some were permitted to stay on the nearby mole, a small island cut off from the rest of the city. But those who did stay there died either from illness or the cold.

No republic or duchy in all northern Italy allowed Jews to settle in their territory. The four republics of Venice, Florence, Lucca, and Siena, and the four duchies of Milan, Ferrara, Modena, and Savoy — all refused. Nor would the papal states accept a significant number of Jews.

Naples was the one exception. As the ship entered the bay of Naples, Abravanel could see the islands of Ischia and Capri. As the ship moved further into the bay, the city of Naples came into view, its shore lined with towns and villages. The city was terraced, with white stuccoed houses rising in successive levels from the harbor to the fortress castle at the top.

The exiles disembarked at the main quay, relieved their journey was over. Cartfuls of belongings were unloaded on the main quay and identified by their owners. An aide from the local Jewish community showed them to temporary quarters in the eastern part of the city.

Some members of the local Jewish community prepared a celebration to honor the famed Don Isaac Abravanel. Rabbi Isaac Arama, a scholar from Calatayud, headed the delegation. He toasted Don Isaac, "Blessed be he who comes in the name of the Lord! Welcome to Naples, Don Isaac Abravanel, you and all of your family. We are honored indeed that the House of Abravanel, renowned throughout the Jewish world for its leadership and wisdom, will plant its foundation in our very midst. May your presence be a signal blessing unto us all. May you and all Israel enjoy divine favor, much study of Torah, health of body and soul, and material well-being. May the riches of your wisdom enrich us all, and may the Holy One of Israel, blessed be He, see fit to grant us speedy salvation in the days to come."

"Amen!," said Don Isaac, together with the others in the room. Abravanel embraced the Aragonese rabbi and thanked him for his toast. "My house is your house, distinguished rabbi, as it is for all those who are here. As it was in Spain, so it shall be here — a house of learning, a house for rich and poor, a house that will be open to all Israel."

Rabbi Arama took Don Isaac by the arm and introduced him to the other people present — Jewish exiles who, like themselves, had come from Castile, Aragon, Valencia, and other parts of Spain. Some had come to Naples as early as August 14, 1492 aboard nine poorly outfitted caravels. The exiles, half-starved and riddled with disease, were grateful to Don Ferrante, King of Naples, who permitted them to settle in his land.

Everyone talked in glowing terms of the King, some declaring him to be a 'savior of mercy', others pronouncing him to be a 'prince of justice and righteousness.' Who was this Don Ferrante to whom all the exiles, Abravanel included, felt a profound sense of debt and gratitude? Rabbi Arama explained, "Ferrante, the King of Naples, is the illegitimate son of King Alfonso V of Aragon. The Aragonese line has ruled Naples and Sicily since 1443. Before, it was ruled by the Anjous, who still lay claim to the crown of Naples. The present King of Spain, Ferdinand of

Aragon, is the nephew of Alfonso V. Ferdinand believes he rather than Ferrante is the rightful ruler of Naples.

"But, Ferrante rules with an iron hand. Ferrante has already crushed rebellions of his feudal barons with ruthless force. He is sixty-nine years of age, and neither his barons, the Anjous, or the Aragonese have been able to dethrone him. His victory over the Turks at Otranto eleven years ago increased his power even more.

"Yet for all his power, the man is a patron of the arts. 'Old Ferrante' greatly enjoys the company of learned men. His chancellor, Giovanni Pontano, is an Aristotelian rationalist. I am sure both the King and Pontano will want to meet you, Don Isaac."

Abravanel still was not satisfied. "I suppose, Rabbi Arama, that my basic question is: Why? Why did Ferrante allow thousands of Jews to enter the kingdom?"

Arama's smile coming to his lips, the rabbi answered slyly, "I shall let the King and his ministers tell you why."

"What do you mean?," asked Abravanel.

Rabbi Arama smiled again. "You see, Don Isaac, your great reputation has preceded you. All Naples is aware that the chief rabbi of Spain has settled here. For us that would have been enough. But besides being the rabbi, you were chief financial adviser to the Portuguese king, as well as a royal tax-farmer in Castile. Yes, yes, we know all about you. Your qualifications have also come to the attention of the King of Naples. Through one of his agents the King has asked me to extend to you a personal invitation to visit him within the week at Castel Nuovo."

Abravanel sighed. "I am deeply honored, rabbi. Allow me to say this. My service to kings and other great nobles has availed me but little. I should have learned my lesson in a small town called Segura de la Orden. The lesson is simple: The study of Torah, and not the management of royal finances should be my main pursuit in life. What shall I say of the Portuguese King João II who, after my honorable service in his behalf, accused me of conspiracy and sought to have me killed? What shall I say of Ferdinand and Isabella, whom I aided with years of wise counsel and financial assistance, yet who in the end saw fit to have my people and me expelled from their kingdom? Why should I serve yet a third worldly master and neglect the service of the King of Kings, the Holy One of Israel, blessed be He? Why should I submit myself to the potential treachery and perfidy of yet another secular ruler? Nay, Rabbi Arama, let me spend these last few years of my life in peaceful contemplation of the holy scriptures. What little time I have left I wish to spend in writing a commentary on the Book of Kings."

Rabbi Arama listened attentively. "Don Isaac, the exclusive pursuit of Torah is an ideal which we scholars all pursue, but necessities must come first. The situation with Ferrante is unstable. There is pestilence in our quarter, and many exiles are pouring into the city. We have no adequate food or housing for them, nor do we have anyone to lead us in this crisis.

"The local rabbis cannot represent us at court. One Jacob Provenzal has even condemned the study of medicine and all secular learning. Ferrante and his councillors will not listen to anyone like that. Some of the exiles from Spain tried to serve as temporary spokesmen for the exile community, but not with much success. I am no court rabbi. I do not know how to deal with kings and ministers. I speak little Latin and no Italian. Don Isaac, I ask you to intercede on behalf of all the exiles in Naples. We need someone with experience in court, someone capable of unifying our people, indeed, someone like yourself to lead us."

"Rabbi Arama, your words do me far more honor than I deserve. I could not prevent our expulsion from Spain — how can you expect me to be of any help here?"

Rabbi Arama answered, "Whatever misfortunes our people have experienced, they have not been caused by anyone's failings. That much all of us know. If you are called again to duty, you cannot refuse to serve your people."

Abravanel spoke softly, "I will be at the Castle Nuovo within the week, Rabbi. But I will need your help. I have just arrived in Naples, and there is much I do not know. Will you help me?"

Rabbi Arama answered, "Of course, I will do all I can to help you."

Within three days, Don Isaac Abravanel presented himself at the Castel Nuovo. In the courts of Italy it was customary for each new ambassador to present his credentials, and to show his skill in oratory in a formal address. As he was led from vestibule to courtyard and finally to the royal chamber, Don Isaac was ready to address the court in the language of scholarly discourse.

As he stood before the King, Don Isaac Abravanel addressed him in perfect Latin. "To King Ferrante I, ruler of the Two Sicilies, King of Naples, arbiter of Italy, guarantor of peace and prosperity in his domains, dispenser of justice, protector of the oppressed, and most generous patron of the arts, I, Don Isaac Abravanel of the royal House of David, do hereby present myself to your Majesty as the newest of your most loyal subjects, honored to be called unto your royal presence, honored to serve the 'prince of righteousness' whose charitable renown is on the lips of every child of Israel. Yet no lips can sufficiently extol the virtues of your Majesty, one who deserves to be counted among the 'Righteous of the Gentiles.' A fountain of praises daily flows from my Hebrew kinsmen. The praises are the waters of love that pour from their grateful hearts to you. I offer you only a small drop of their affections, boundless and uncontainable as they are . . ."

Abravanel continued with his lavish oration, praising the noble-mindedness and wisdom of the monarch in permitting Spanish Jews to settle in such large numbers in the kingdom of Naples. Emphasizing the practical consequences of such a decision, Don Isaac lauded the industry of his peple, elaborated on their skills as artisans and crafts-men, and noted that Jewish merchants would stimulate commerce and trade. As dyers and weavers or as erudite translators of Graeco-Arabic scientific and philosophical texts, the Jewish exiles from Spain con-stituted an asset to the Neapolitan crown. Physicians versed in Arabic medicine; mathematicians, astronomers, philosophers and religious leaders — all would enhance the reputation of Naples as a center of learning. Material prosperity, he argued, would increase from the labor and ingenuity of the artisans and merchants, and the brilliance of the court would be augmented by the new arrivals. Abravanel also added a few words about the financial expertise he could contribute:

". . . and were it to please your Majesty to request my assistance in matters affecting the financial sphere, be it on the tax-roll of Foggia or on the annual revenues of the crown, I would deem it a privilege to serve in such a capacity."

His oration concluded, Abravanel bowed respectfully. The King, a slender taut-faced man in a cloak of purple velvet, broke into a warm smile. "Welcome to my kingdom, Don Isaac Abravanel. May you and your people prosper in it. May it become in time a place that your people can regard as their home by virtue of choice, rather than by the pressure of necessity. I shall let you speak now to my chancellor, Pontano, who is as eager to secure your participation in the Academy as I am that you serve in our treasury department."

The presentation had obviously been a success. The King introduced Don Isaac to his counselor Diome de Carafa and to the enthusiastic chancellor Giovanni Pontano. Then the King and his aides led Don Isaac to the royal library in the eastern wing of the Castel Nuovo.

The royal library of the Academy was one of the wonders of Naples. It contained thousands of manuscripts and books in many subjects. The enlightened rulers of Naples — Frederick, Charles I of Anjou, Robert of Anjou, Alfonso I, and now Ferrante — actively encouraged the translation of the classic texts of antiquity into Latin. Many of these ancient works, preserved by the Arabs when Europe was in decline, were translated by Jewish scholars from Arabic, through Hebrew, into Latin. The shelves of the royal library were lined with these translations.

Ferrante took a book from the shelf. "Don Isaac, look at this: *Liber posteriorum analiticorum Aristotelis: cum magnos commentaries Auverroys*: Aristotle's 'Posterior Analytics' with the commentary by the great Arab philosopher Averroes. It was translated into Latin by none other than our Jewish court physician, Abraham de Balmes. I commissioned the work, which was completed ten years ago. Do you know this work?"

Abravanel nodded. "Yes, your Majesty. I am familiar with it."

Ferrante smiled approvingly. "With the possible exception of the Vatican library, our own is the finest of its kind in the entire peninsula. I take great pride in it."

Abravanel said, "You can indeed be proud, your Majesty. Truly, any lover of learning must admire this impressive collection of human knowledge."

They made their way through the library. There were Latin treatises on every conceivable subject — philosophy, the healing arts, astronomy, theology, and more. At one end was the section containing works in Hebrew. There they paused.

Don Isaac chose a Hebrew book at random; it was the *Sefer HaKabbala* by Ibn David. He thumbed through its pages. The collection contained classic works by Saadia Gaon, Halevy, Maimonides, Crescas, Albo, and Duran. Talmudic tractates, anthologies of Hebrew poetry by the great hymn master Ibn Gabirol, and the Biblical commentaries of Ibn Ezra were to be found on the shelves as well.

Pontano explained, "You understand, Don Isaac, we are gathering all the learning of the ancients. Although it is the Greek philosophers that interest us most, we also want to learn something of Hebraic lore. The court of Naples has supported Hebraic studies for some time now, and we intend to continue our leadership in this sphere. In the court of Florence, Pico della Mirandola, one of the great scholars of our day, has become an enthusiastic advocate of Jewish Kabbalistic mystical lore. Pico claims that the secrets of philosophy, even the great truths of our

Christian religion, can be revealed from studying the Kabbala. Whether Pico is right or not is not the point that I wish to make. My point is that, whether it be in Florence or Padua or Milan, everyone of note is studying Hebrew. Cardinals and counts, ladies and bankers, scholars and diplomats, everyone has the notion that one must know Hebrew in order to be a cultured individual. Aha! You see, Don Isaac, I am willing to wager that you had no idea that you would have such fine company here in Naples!"

Abravanel put the book back. It, as well as everything else, was seemingly falling into place. Pontano was right. There was no need to wager. Don Isaac had no idea of the extent of the intellectual curiosity in Naples. How fine a feeling it was to be respected in Naples for what one knew, rather than to be detested in Spain for what one was. How fine it was not to be forced to wear a distinguishing badge, how fine it was to be able to reside wherever one so desired. How fine it was to be a whole person again! His wife, Esther, had already praised the physical beauty of Naples. Now it was his turn to praise the generous and noble-hearted character of the Neopolitans themselves. Napoli, Napoli! What finer city could there be?

Judah was waiting when Don Isaac returned. "Father, we have a problem."

A look of consternation appeared on Abravanel's face. "Yes, what is it, Judah?"

"Rabbi Arama took me to the quarter where there is pestilence. It is very serious. You had better come and see for yourself."

"Judah, how can I help? You are the physician, you have knowledge concerning such matters. I would be of no help to you, son."

"I think you had better come, Father."

"Very well, Judah. Lead the way."

Soon they were at the makeshift infirmary. It was a high- ceilinged building, white walls crumbling from decay but able to accommodate the scores of victims lying on the floor. So weak had the illness made them, that the merest exertion was beyond them. Large buckets filled with human excrement were everywhere. The nauseating smell of expelled feces filtered through the window. As Don Isaac looked inside, he took note of a particular female patient who had been placed atop a wooden platform with a large hole in its center. The diarrhea gushed profusely out of the pallid woman, as water being poured forth freely from a pail, all her bodily fluids seemingly being discharged in a rush into the underlying container.

"It is the cholera," explained Judah. "It is a terrible disease, and I can do nothing for the sufferers. Most of them will die. Some who have not been stricken so severely may survive. The question is what are we to do about the community?

"The infirmary is in the center of the Jewish quarter, and the disease is spreading rapidly within our community. If it is not brought under control soon, everyone will get it."

Don Isaac asked, "What do you advise us to do, Judah?"

"First, all who come down with the sickness must be isolated. Part of the problem is some patients are cared for at home. This spreads the pestilence. Anyone who comes down with the cholera must be moved to the infirmary immediately. But the infirmary will soon be inadequate for our needs. It looks bad, Father. It may be too late to save the community."

Don Isaac was thoughtful. "I understand why you brought me here. If this pestilence is not controlled, Ferrante may use it against us. Indeed, it could result in the expulsion of all Jews from Naples."

Judah nodded his head in agreement. He repeated, "It looks bad, Father. Ferrante had every new arrival checked for evidence of contagion . . . and now this happens. He will be very angry."

Don Isaac said firmly, "Judah, I am placing you in charge. Talk with the other physicians in town. Get their approval of your recommendations, and submit your proposal to the local council no later than tomorrow. I will take responsibility to convince the local rabbis and other leaders on the community council. Something must be done about this immediately."

Having said this, Don Isaac walked into the infirmary.

Judah shouted, "Wait! Father, do not go in there!"

Don Isaac walked toward the pallid woman he had seen through the window. The woman had a smelly stained sheet over her shrunken body; her cheeks were pinched inwards, creating the effect of two symmetric concavities. The eyes were dim and distant, without an evident point of focus. The eyes looked at him, through him.

Judah came up to Don Isaac's side. "Father, have you gone mad? We cannot afford to lose you too. You are too important to get sick. Please, Father, listen to me and leave the infirmary."

Don Isaac looked tenderly at the patient and said, "Let me be, Judah. Allow me a few moments with this poor, unfortunate woman. Allow me to fulfill my duty to those who are sick and dying. *They* are the ones who need me most."

Judah reasoned with his father, "Would you endanger the leadership of our community for the comfort of a dying woman? Your words will not save her."

Don Isaac looked sadly at his son. "Yes, Judah, that is true . . . and neither will your medicine."

Chastened, Judah said, "I spoke out of turn, Father. Forgive me. I should know better."

One of the nurses came up to Don Isaac and ordered, "Señor, you have no permission to enter this building. You must leave this moment!"

Judah spoke up. "Leah, he is with me. This is my father, Don Isaac Abravanel."

The nurse's face turned red with embarrassment. "Don . . . Don Isaac, please . . . please forgive me. I had no idea it was you, señor."

Abravanel raised his hand. "It is I who must apologize, nurse Leah. I am the one in error here, not you. It is I who must ask for forgiveness."

Nurse Leah answered, "Don Isaac, please, I shall trouble you no further."

Don Isaac thought he heard a voice behind him. He turned around to face the patient whose glazed eyes were now open. With a faint voice, she cried out, "Don . . . Don . . . Don Isaac Abravanel."

Abravanel crouched down next to her, for she spoke in a whisper, "You are Don Isaac Abravanel?"

Abravanel nodded.

"The great eagle of our people," she said. "Our great eagle has come to visit me."

"What is your name, my child?," asked Don Isaac softly.

"I am Mira Beton. I come from Tarragona in the north."

"And your family? Are they with you here in Naples?"

"My husband, may God rest his soul, died of the pestilence a week ago. We had a boy and a girl. The girl, she is ten, she is still alive, thanks be to God."

Suddenly there was the sound of gushing fluid, and the woman winced. There was an uneasy silence as the woman noisily discharged herself.

"I am sorry, Don Isaac. I cannot control myself."

Don Isaac said, "Mira, what about your son? You did not tell me about him."

Mira smiled weakly again. "I will tell you. We sailed from Tarragona. The sailors, who were Genoese, were evil and cruel. When they took us out to sea, they took our food away. They would give us food only if we gave them all the gold coins we had. We gave them our gold. We gave them everything we had. Still they would not give us food. But they did not believe that we had given them all our gold. They thought we had more. So they kept us at sea for weeks, going nowhere. All of us were starving. We thought we were going to die. Some did. Then the pestilence broke out aboard ship, and the Genoese sailors took us to a port. They threw us out in the territory of Genoa, I remember they let us enter a city — I forget its name. They put us in the city square. My son, he was a lad of twelve, he was very hungry like we were. The Christian priests . . ."

Mira stopped once again as the fluids poured forth from her depleted body. Her voice was weakening. She tried to speak again, but her voice broke.

Don Isaac said calmly, "Take your time, Mira. There is no need to rush."

Mira took a deep breath again. ". . . the Christians, they came to the city square. They had a cross in one hand and a piece of bread in the other. The priests told the children, 'If you will worship the cross, you will receive bread.' My son, he was hungry. He was weak. He could not take it any longer. He took their bread and he allowed himself to be baptized. My son, I am so ashamed to say it, he is a Christian."

Mira closed her sorrowed eyes.

Don Isaac got up to leave. "Mira, may God grant you a speedy recovery, health of body and health of soul. If there is any way we can help you, please let us know."

Mira lifted her limp hand slowly. She struggled to speak again, "Don Isaac . . . I know . . . I know that I am going to die. My daughter, she has no one but me. She is staying with friends. If . . . If I die . . ."

Don Isaac said, "Be assured that the community will take care of her, Mira. I personally will see that she is taken care of . . ."

Mira spoke faintly, "If I die, Don Isaac . . . what about me?"

Abravanel answered, "All Israel has a share in the world to come, Mira. As a faithful daughter of Israel, you have nothing to fear."

Mira started to cry softly. "Rabbi, before I die . . . give me your blessing."

As Don Isaac Abravanel gently put his hand on the woman's fore-head, she slowly closed her eyes. He, too, closed his eyes, wishing to give his words special meaning. "May God regard you as Sarah, Rivka, Rachel, and Leah. May God bless you and protect you. May He shine His countenance unto thee and grant thee peace."

Don Isaac lifted his hand. The ailing woman had found peace. Don Isaac's blessing was answered: Mira suffered no more. This was enough for him, as he now prepared to leave.

In the days to come, Don Isaac was to hear the personal accounts from many of the exiles. At meetings held at his home or Rabbi Arama's, or indeed at the synagogue after services, people would come up to him and tell their harrowing tales.

There was the tale of Judah Hayyat, a Spanish rabbi:

"My name is Judah Hayyat. When I lived in Spain, I loved to pursue the sweetness and light of wisdom. Indeed my heart was inclined to seek out and explore Torah wherever it could be found. I went from one place to another, gathering knowledge here and there, until I learned what I now know. And I do believe that the merit I gained from my quest enabled me to withstand the awful trials that befell me during the expulsion from Spain. What I have to say is too horrible for the ears of gentle souls. So, I will not tell about everything, but only some of it, praise the lord.

"My family and I went from Spain to Portugal when the evil decree was announced. Then all of us, along with two hundred and fifty other souls, took a boat from Lisbon, in the kingdom of Portugal. It was in the middle of winter when we set out. And the Holy One of Israel, blessed be He, did not allow us to escape from the punishment that He had ordained for us. This was why they were not willing to receive us anywhere. 'Stay away from us, unclean ones,' was what we heard everywhere. We were forty days at sea, wandering from one place to another, with little bread to eat and with water in short supply.

"At the end of this time, our ship was overtaken by a Basque vessel from the region of Biscay. The sailors took us captive, robbed us of our money, and brought us to the city of Málaga, in southern Spain. In port we were forced to stay aboard ship against our will. We were not allowed to disembark on the mainland, nor were we allowed to set sail from there. It was also decreed that we were not to be given either bread or water or any other type of food or provision until we converted. This continued for five days. During this time, the priests and the city dignitaries would come to the ship and say unto us, 'How long will you continue to refuse to accept Jesus? He who wants life, he who wants Jesus, come down and be baptized, have your fill of food and drink and live.' On the fourth day, more than a hundred souls left the ship, because they could not stand the hunger and the thirst any longer. Those of us who were still left aboard ship were very few. We prepared our souls for death, and we said unto one another, 'Better to die in the hands of the Lord than to live amongst the wicked.' Then my dear and beloved wife, may God rest her pure soul, died of thirst and hunger. So did many others, young men and young girls, old men and women, all told fifty souls perished. I, too, was on the verge of death. Many were those aboard ship who fainted and remained unconscious. Others, too weak to stand up, crawled slowly on their stomachs. Pain, a terrible ripping pain, a pain that no one should ever know, was in my stomach. It was terrible. Our parched throats were dry, our voices weak and hoarse, yet with what little strength we had, we cried out unto the Lord from our straits and He answered us in His fullness.

"On the sixth day, our trial was over, as God heard our prayers and turned our affliction into a time of plenty. From that day on, we were brought all kinds of food to eat. Still, however, we were forced to stay on the ship for an additional two months against our will until they finally let us go to whatever place we desired.

"From Málaga, we traveled to the Barbary lands of the kingdom of Fez in the land of Ishmael. What the hail spared was eaten by the locusts. Nor did I find peace and tranquility there. And it happened I chanced on a party of four Andalusia Arabs who had likewise been expelled from Spain. They beat me so, it caused me much pain. They took the clothes from my back and threw me in a pit with snakes and scorpions. Finally, they decided that I should die by stoning. But they said if I would become a Moslem, then I would hold an important office in their religion. Yet I, Judah Hayyat, remained faithful to the Holy One and to His chosen. And God, in whom I placed my trust, did not forsake me when for forty days and forty nights I was lowered into this pit of darkness. I had very little bread and only a small ration of water. Hungry and thirsty and naked, my stomach seemed to cling to the ground as I crawled on it day after day after day. While I was thus bereft of everything, the Holy One of Israel awakened the spirit of my Jewish brothers in Sharshan who came to redeem me. In return for my ransom, I gave them the almost two hundred books that I still had with me.

"From Sharshan, I went to the city of Fez, but the famine there was so great we had to eat the grass and plants in the field. I went to work as a grinder in the house of two Moslems. For one day's work with the sweat of my brow and the toil of my hands, I received a small piece of bread that was not fit for dogs to eat. At night, my stomach still knew the pangs of hunger. When it was cold at night, I had nothing to cover myself with. Indeed, because we had no houses to dwell in, we used to dig holes and sleep in them. After further misfortunes and troubles, which I prefer not to tell of, I finally reached the kingdom of Naples. Here the people took compassion on me. They clothed me and fed me, may God bless their sacred work! If my soul has been strong as stone, if I have been able to withstand such hardships, it is because my quest for Torah wisdom is just. It is this, with God's help, that made me hold to the Torah while others faltered.

"That, Don Isaac, is my story."

Not all Jews were well received by their kinsmen. Don Isaac heard of some Jews who had been impelled by the famine and hostility they met with in Genoa to go on to Rome. The Jews living in Rome met to discuss how to deal with their exiled brethren. Fearing a threat to their live- lihoods, they resolved not to integrate the newcomers in their midst. Immediately, these Jews gathered a thousand crowns to bribe Pope Alexander VI, so he would not permit the exiles to settle in his territory. But the Pope, upon being apprised of the purpose of this present, was said to have remarked, "This is something new, because I have always heard that it is the custom of the Jews to succor and help one another, and here we have these Jews that behave so cruelly." For this reason, the Pope decreed that the resident Jews of Rome should be likewise expelled and no longer allowed to dwell in Papal territory. Astonished by this response, the Jews of Rome quickly raised an additional two thousand crowns, which they submitted as a gift to the Pope. This was not only to enable them to remain in Rome, but also so that Spanish Jewish exiles would be allowed to enter. Thus it was that the exiles were finally allowed to settle in the Papal states.

Of the nine thousand Jewish refugees that sought refuge in the kingdom of Naples, not all came from mainland Spain. The islands of Sicily and Sardinia, ruled by the Spanish Kingdom of Aragon, also were affected by the expulsion decree.

The Edict dispersed the Jewish communities of Sicily after having a continuous presence on the island for nearly fifteen hundred years. Sicilian Jews were poor artisans for the most part, eeking out their existence under increasingly restrictive regulations. Often they were forced to do menial jobs such as clearing the city streets of mud and garbage, acting as executioners, and digging canal ditches. Jewish communities existed in Palermo, which was the largest, having about five thousand inhabitants, as well as in Messina, Nicosia, Sciacca, and other towns of note, together totaling more than thirty five thousand souls. In fact, Sicily had the greatest concentration of Jews in the Italian peninsula.

When the Edict was announced in Sicily, all Jewish private and communal property was sequestered. The confiscation of goods extended even to the tools of the Jewish craftsmen, which made them unable to engage in their occupations. As in Spain, creditors could bring claims against the liquidated value of the confiscated Jewish properties; furthermore, the community was obligated to reimburse the crown for the loss in revenues entailed by the expulsion. A plea was submitted to King Ferdinand by members of the Privy Council that much economic harm would result from the expulsion order; furthermore, conditions in Sicily were quite different from Spain because there were no Conversos there for existing Jews to influence. Hence, the argument advanced in the Edict that Jews undermined the faith of newly converted Christians, while perhaps true in Spain, was most certainly not true in Sicily. Indeed, the Jews of Sicily were good law-abiding citizens whose departure would cause irreparable loss to the kingdom. But the Edict was made to stand, and the Jews were ordered to leave.

The poorer Jews were allowed to take with them only the clothes on their backs, a wool blanket, an old mattress, some food, and no more than three *tari* for ship fare. The wealthier Jews could take out six *tari*. All Jews were forbidden to take their best clothes out of the country, nor were they allowed to take out their *tallit* prayer shawls. After a thorough and humiliating search, the destitute Jews of Sicily were finally allowed to leave.

Those who arrived in Naples had their share of horror stories to relate. On the Sicilian island itself, one of the feudal barons, a certain baron of Ciminna, imprisoned the Jews on his estate and refused to give them any food. The viceroy intervened and managed to save a few, but many had already died of starvation. The baron of Cammarata, it was reported, had done likewise. En route to Gallipoli, a vessel full of

Sicilian exiles had been overtaken by Italian sailors, and all the passengers had been slaughtered.

Sharing a common origin and language, the Jews of Sicily naturally tended to band together for prayer purposes in Naples, preferring to be with their former island kinsmen than with the culturally alien Castilians. From the island of Sardinia to Naples came a smaller contingent, because most of the Sardinian Jews had fled to North Africa or Turkey.

Shipload after shipload of exiles arrived in Naples after having seen or been subjected to murder, drowning, hunger, rape or disease. Some, it was reported, had been stripped and left on an abandoned island. Others had been captured and sold as slaves in the markets of Genoa. Even at Naples the Jews arriving on ships were threatened with slavery if the local Jewish community did not ransom them. The local Jews tried to raise the required sum, but could not. Angry, sailors took the abducted Jews to the mountains to be sold as slaves.

Don Isaac heard the tale of a cantor named Joseph Sibhon. Joseph had a son and two daughters, one named Gloria and the other Palomba. The captain who was transporting them to Italy fell in love with Palomba and threatened to kill her if she resisted his advances. Appalled at the choice, Palomba's mother threw her daughters and herself overboard. The sailors aboard ship jumped after them and brought them back to the ship. Palomba was ultimately seduced against her will. When the Jewish passengers disembarked at Naples, the captain refused to let Palomba leave. She was forced to stay with him as his mistress. Thus, Joseph Sibhon would often quote Jonah 1:15, "They have taken the *palomba*, my dove, and cast her into the sea."

Another fate befell an elderly woman named Rosa Barokas. She, her husband, and two daughters sought refuge in Morocco, where Moors killed her husband, violated her daughters, and tore out their insides in search of gold. Having lost all her loved ones, Rosa could no longer bear to live. She took some sewing scissors and began to dig her own grave. Having done this, she lowered herself into it and refused to eat or drink anything. She died shortly afterwards, in the empty loneliness of her grave. May the God of Israel have mercy upon her departed soul!

Some exiles were cast off on an island close to Provence, where the local inhabitants refused to give them any bread. One of the exiles named Leon Franco saw that his ailing father and son were wasting away from hunger so he begged the natives for bread. But no one would give him any. Hungry and desperate, Leon could no longer bear to see his father in such agony. With great reluctance and with tears streaming down his eyes, he took his five-year old son and sold him to a local baker in exchange for a few loaves of bread. A tearful Leon rushed to his father with the loaves in his arms, but his father was already dead! Leon tore his clothes in accordance with Jewish custom and then he ran back to the baker to retrieve his son. When the baker refused to return the child, Leon broke into heart-rending screams. Tormented by his double loss, Leon Franco could never forgive himself. Don Isaac remembered well this Señor Franco who was always so grief-stricken. It was not only the sad tale of Señor Franco that he remembered, but the odd fact that Leon never ate a single morsel of bread.

The accounts that the exiles told were horrifying. Everywhere it was the same. Exiled and unredeemed, hounded and humiliated, sick and starving, the half-dead survivors poured into the shining bay of Naples, hoping that a new and a better life awaited them.

The respite that the new arrivals enjoyed was short-lived, however, for cholera broke out in full force among the community. Rapidly extending beyond the confines of the makeshift infirmary, the pestilence spread throughout the entire Jewish quarter despite the precautions Judah took. Day after day, week after week, the plague grew in intensity and virulence, its victimized men and women dying by the hundreds. As Judah tended to the sick, Don Isaac went to inform the King of the seriousness of the problem.

When Don Isaac completed his report of the pestilence in the Jewish quarter, Ferrante closed his eyes in thought. Don Isaac tried to guess what the King was thinking: it could not be good.

Ferrante finally spoke, "I am most distressed by this, Don Isaac." "I understand, your Majesty. We are all distressed, but our physicians are doing all they can to bring it under control."

Ferrante breathed heavily, his nostrils flared in anger. He spoke again, "It is imperative, Don Isaac, that this be kept secret! If the people of Naples find out about the pestilence, there will be panic; the townspeople will hate you for bringing pestilence. I know my people. They will want all Jews out of Naples. Therefore, I advise you to bury your dead at night so that no one will know the full extent of the disease. Otherwise, hundreds of people will come to the castle demanding to know why I admitted the accursed, pestilence-ridden Jews to my kingdom."

"Of course, your Majesty," answered Don Isaac, "None outside the Jewish quarter will hear of the disease." But Don Isaac did not know how to keep news of the plague from spreading. Even more worrisome was how long the King would remain a friend of the Jews. Don Isaac no longer trusted kings, and had good reason to be suspicious of Ferrante.

The secret burial teams were formed. Groups of volunteers worked long hours into the night as they dug hundreds of graves in specially designated plots of land. Still other volunteers went with carts from one house to the other to collect the dead bodies. When the foul-smelling corpses were dragged out of the houses and put on the carts, the fetid odor of death was everywhere. Sometimes the disease felled entire families with a single stroke. The wasted bodies wrapped in sheets were stacked one atop the other. Carts of death could be heard all night long wheeling corpses to their final resting place. Mourners trailed the carts to the fresh graves, offering prayers for the deceased. Many of the mourners already noted within themselves the first signs of the dreaded disease, wondering if their offered prayers could just as well be meant for themselves. The disease spared none. Even the volunteers who collected the bodies succumbed to the scourge, their courage no match for the contagion. Soon it was impossible to recruit anyone for this work.

Victims of the disease increased every month. Don Isaac Abravanel watched helplessly as the pestilence consumed all in its path. The epidemic struck down thousands — the young daughters of Israel, good and bad, saints and sinners, strong and weak, making a mockery of the principle that virtue is rewarded. Everyone kept away from strangers, suspecting one and all of being carriers of the deadly malady. The epidemic of fear and suspicion raged through the community with the same speed as the pestilence itself. Synagogue attendance fell sharply, as many people no longer wished to come together. Others fled to the hills to hide in caves or under rocks. Wandering aimlessly through the countryside, they shaved their heads and beards, thinking this might be of some hygienic benefit.

Anyone afflicted with the earliest signs of the cholera wandered about town in sackcloth and ashes. These skeleton-like zombies stumbled from one street corner to the other. They screamed hysterically, they cursed, they moaned, they uttered inanities. Fluids gushed out of then and onto the city streets. Nearby pedestrians ran from them to avoid the slightest encounter with these carriers of the disease.

It was no secret anymore. All knew there was raging pestilence in the city; all knew the Jews had brought it. The dead bodies on the street were proof of that. So were the infested carcasses thrown into courtyards and fields, bodies piled in tangled heaps of grotesque arms and legs. Not just Jews, but Christians, too, were dying . . . dying by the thousands. Within six months of the arrival of the Jews, it was estimated that more than twenty thousand people died as a result of the hideous pestilence. It was no longer a specifically Jewish problem. It was a Christian problem, too.

While the pestilence raged, Don Isaac Abravanel made his daily visits to Castel Nuovo to discuss financial matters with the King's counselors, Pontano and Carafa. But it was apparent that the counselors had experienced a change of heart towards him, a change brought on by the pestilence. Pontano and Carafa were decidedly cool. While he was able to discuss problems of state with them, he no longer felt they were friends. Were Pontano and Carafa advising Ferrante to reconsider his decision to admit the Jews? Were they telling him it was a tragic mistake, an unbelievable miscalculation? Were they telling him it was time to rid the kingdom of the Jews? Abravanel feared it was only a matter of time before what had occurred in Spain would repeat itself in Naples.

The plague devastated the community in spirit as much as in body. Everywhere the exiles fled, calamity struck them down. Wherever they went, whatever they did, however much they prayed — it made no difference. All was in vain, all was lost! A plague of disbelief feeding on the widespread sense of despair spread throughout the Jewish camp of Naples.

One old man, who had lost his wife and four children, accosted Don Isaac and asked, "What has happened to our God? Does not the Holy One of Israel see the immensity of our suffering? Why does He not send His Messiah to provide us with the salvation that we so desperately need?"

A young weaver interrupted, "You fool, do you not realize by now that the Messiah will never come? It is an illusion. There is no Messiah. No son of Jesse will ever come to save us. It is an illusion!"

Don Isaac was furious. "You little worm, how dare you blaspheme against God's Anointed? The words of our holy prophets and saintly rabbis all assure us of the ultimate redemption of our people. If the Messiah has not yet appeared, it is because of faithless people like you who are utterly beyond redemption. Who are you, who, by your unkind words, increase the suffering of the bereaved? Know this well, you faithless vessel of dishonor to our people, you will not be among those who merit salvation, not on this day nor on the day when the chariot of the Redeemer finally appears!"

The weaver was temporarily silenced, walking angrily away. But he turned around and warned, "I repeat what I said: there is no Messiah. And what is more, there is no God either. All is as I have said . . . an illusion, nothing more. Nothing will save us. Not the Torah, not Jesus Christ, nothing will save us. Nothing!"

Don Isaac ordered, "Leave our presence, you believer in nothingness! All that emanates from nothing is worth nothing, as are the words that sputter from your lying lips. Detach yourself from our beloved illusion, and fill instead the void in your soul with your principles of emptiness. Leave our presence, you fool, I command thee!"

After the weaver left, Don Isaac explained to the elderly refugee the eternal principles of salvation and the conditions under which the Messiah would ultimately come. The explanation calmed the lonely exile, and he thanked Don Isaac profusely for his time and patience. But Abravanel felt somehow dissatisfied with himself. Such one-to-one encounters, however individually helpful and well-intentioned they were, could not deal with the larger problem of the spiritual malaise that afflicted his people. Many who had been strong in faith were beginning to doubt; those of weaker faith were completely rejecting the religion of their fathers. Don Isaac sensed the need for a systematic statement about the Messianic prophecies, a convincing statement that would sustain the discomfited flock of Israel against their tribulations. Had it not been foretold by the prophets of Israel that the redemption of the Jewish people would come in a time of cataclysmic destruction and misery? Was this not the era that had been foretold, an era that would witness the appearance of the long-awaited Messiah? Surely it was so, he answered himself. This was the era! As the fortunes of Israel were at its lowest ebb, so too it would be the time when the Redeemer would rescue Israel. It was a time to rejoice! Hear, O Israel, the Messiah was coming!

Abravanel had been working on two books, one a commentary on the Jewish Prophets, the other a penetrating philosophical defense of Maimonides' Thirteen Principles, the *Rosh Amanah*. Now he would have to investigate all Messianic passages in Biblical and Talmudic texts. The prophetic portions must be reinterpreted and extrapolated to correlate with present events. Now was the time to alert the people to the good tidings. The Messiah was coming!

The people of Naples were fed up with the Jews. They were tired of the excuses the King made. They were angry, angry at the countless promises of a cure, angry that their families had died, angry that the Jews had introduced the disease into their city. They wanted the Jews out of Naples.

The people were not alone. The ministers, Pontano and Carafa, were on the people's side and were urging the King to expel the Jews. All the citizens of Naples, except for the Jews, were clamoring for the expulsion of this pestilential race.

Abravanel was aware of the anti-Jewish feelings. He could not fault the local townspeople for wanting to rid themselves of the apparent source of the contagion. He could understand how the Gentiles had suffered, how they too had lost precious sons and lovely daughters and beloved fathers and mothers. Yes, he could understand their anger, he could understand their fierce hatred of the Jews. But even so, Don Isaac asked himself, would the expulsion of the Jews from Naples put an end to their suffering? Would it bring an end to the epidemic? The answer was no, because the pestilence was now as widespread among the Christians as it was among the Jews. If the King truly wished to eradicate the disease, he would have to rid the kingdom of as many Christian subjects as there were Jews. And anyway, where would the Jews go? To an abandoned island or to some desolate, uninhabited area in the kingdom?

No sea captain would permit pestilence-infected passengers on board, however much the Jews offered to pay. No country, not even the liberal-minded Turks, would accept the sickly Jews and risk introducing the pestilence into the Ottoman Empire. Except for the kingdom of Naples, no country in Europe had wanted the Spanish Jews when they were healthy, and obviously much less so now when they were sick. Naples was stuck with the Jews. But the real question for Abravanel was not what the townspeople felt, but how long it would take before the King shared their animosity.

An angry delegation of local nobles and merchants presented itself to the King. Their spokesman, a baron by the name of Gino Carinola, was irate. In an indignant tone of voice, the baron shouted, "Don Ferrante, what have you done to Naples and its people? Why have you brought these Jews to afflict us and our children with the pestilence? Is it not clear what you must do? What, in the name of heaven, are you waiting for? Act now, our King! Throw the Jews out lest we all die because of them!"

Hardly had the baron finished his statement when Ferrante's stern face clouded over. Eyes ablaze with fury, his nostrils flaring, and with a cruel look on his face, the King came down toward the insolent baron. It was the 'old Ferrante' come back to life, the Ferrante that had smashed the rebel barons, the Ferrante who had smitten the Turks, the Ferrante with whom no king nor army wanted to tangle. It was this feared Ferrante that the baron had roused to anger.

Ferrante, looking at the baron, addressed him. "Baron Carinola, since you have decided to throw the Jews out of my kingdom, it appears you see yourself as wiser than the present king. Perhaps you feel you should be King yourself. Is that not so, Baron Carinola? Are you here because you want the Jews out, or is it because you want me out?"

The baron bowed his head. His voice was now soft and supplicating. The baron said, "No, our King, I meant no such thing . . . I merely wanted to suggest that the Jews . . ."

Ferrante blasted him away. "You dare criticize my judgment? You want the Jews out? Very well, Baron, take my crown and make yourself King. *You* rule and I will serve you. What are you waiting for? . . . Take my crown!"

Ferrante held out the jeweled crown. The trembling baron did not reach for it. The wary baron, who was not a novice at court, knew full well that this was a trap. If Carinola so much as lifted a finger for the crown, if he so much as expressed the slightest interest in displacing Ferrante, it meant certain death for the baron and his supporters. Shaking his head the baron quickly backed away. He wanted no part of this. He did not want his action to be misinterpreted as a developing plot to overthrow the King.

The memory of his uncle, the Count of Carinola, came back to him. He remembered how his other uncles, the Count of Sarna, and the Count of Policastro, all rebel barons, had been put to death by Ferrante. He remembered how they were dragged through the street of Naples, choked to death in the plaza and then beheaded. He remembered that he was a Carinola.

The baron, his hands trembling, went down on his knees. "O my King, I am your most loyal servant. Neither in my deed nor in my thoughts have I contemplated that anyone but yourself, your Majesty, should rule over the kingdom of Naples. Forgive my rashness of speech, beloved King. Accept my plea for your bountiful forgiveness so that I may still enjoy the goodness of your support. Allow me once again to

bask in your royal presence. O my King forgive me, your most loyal
servant, for my rashness of speech."

The King put the crown back on his head, and grudgingly said,
"You are forgiven, Baron Carinola." Having finished with the baron, the
King turned around to face the other city dignitaries. They, too, went
down on their knees, tendering their unconditional support to the King
and to his royal policies. Everyone in the court — Pontano, Carafa,
Abravanel — knew the crisis was passed. Ferrante had done it again.
The resistance movement had been broken, and its leaders had been
made to go down on their knees. The Jews would stay.

Abravanel could only marvel at the King's resolution to keep the Jews
of his kingdom. Simple logic dictated that the treatment of a contagion
required the elimination of its source. But, the King had done otherwise.
Perhaps, Don Isaac surmised, the King felt that his long-term interests
would be ill served by the expulsion of the Jews, that it was better to
suffer the short-term consequences of one miscalculation than to
compound it with another error. In any case, Don Isaac felt that the
King merited his title, 'prince of righteousness'.

In the days ahead, Ferrante was to prove his steadfastness to the Jews.
As the pestilence raged on, the King took radical measures to bring it
under control. He caused a large infirmary to be constructed outside the
city to house the afflicted. The facility was equipped with beds, supplies,
medications, and bandages. The King ordered an entire corps of physicians to do all in their power to bring the dreaded disease to a halt.

In addition, Ferrante closed all the roads to and from Naples so
no one could leave or enter the city. Armed guards patrolled the
roads, interrogating and searching all travelers and making sure no
one escaped. This measure only increased the hatred of the citizens
of Naples for the Jews. Viewing the Jews as mortal enemies, they cried
out, "The Jews have come to bring our past sins to remembrance, and
they have returned to destroy us and our sons!" Fearing for their lives
and those of their children, the Gentile citizens did their utmost to
avoid contact with Jews. Any Jew caught trespassing in a pre-
dominantly Christian neighborhood was stoned and insulted. "Jews
out of Naples! Jews out of Naples! Get out of our city before you kill us
all, you Jewish dogs!"

Many of the still healthy Jews tried to leave for Turkey. The ones who
left early succeeded. Those who left later were not so fortunate. The
pestilence broke out aboard their ship, extending to the sailors. When

this happened the enraged sailors plundered the Jews and threw them all overboard. This effectively put an end to emigration to Turkey.

After the pestilence began to subside, famine came to the land. To the cries of those being borne away by the tide of the pestilence were added the woeful screams of hunger. "Bread, bread, bread," was on everyone's lips, the famished souls hungering for any type of food. The local Jewish community attended to many of the hungry, giving them food as well as water. But the available food provisions were not enough, and many Jews were in danger of dying from starvation. When the King was informed by Don Isaac of the community's plight, Ferrante was greatly disturbed. He ordered the royal storehouses and granaries be used to feed the Jews, so no one would starve in his kingdom.

Time and again, Ferrante proved himself a true and loyal friend of the Jews of the kingdom. He was a 'savior of mercy' and a 'prince of righteousness', a dispenser of exalted justice to his subjects one and all, Jews and Christians alike.

Don Isaac worked tirelessly on behalf of the King. Going back and forth between the Castel Nuovo and his villa, it seemed that he was once again in two worlds: the secular royal court and the religious world of Jewish learning. Statesman and scholar, counselor and Biblical commentator, Don Isaac, through the breadth of his learning and the acumen of this political instincts, was able to combine both. Throughout the course of the pestilence and the ensuing famine, the King used Don Isaac as an official emissary of the state to cities such as Florence and Pisa. Abravanel was admired wherever he went, making his name worthy of mention alongside the illustrious luminaries of the land. He did all willingly for the benefit and greater glory of his King, Don Ferrante of Naples.

Nor was he the only one in the family attracting attention. His son Judah, apart from his growing reputation as a physician, was also acquiring a name for himself among the thinkers of the day. Indeed, Judah had made such a favorable impression on Pico della Mirandola, one of the most important humanists in Florence, that Pico urged him to undertake a philosophical inquiry into the harmony of the heavens. Judah started work on this subject, and the insightful book he wrote, *De Coeli Harmoni*, was the result.

Don Isaac's wife Esther organized a group of women to supervise the distribution of food to the hungry during the famine. While this work took up all her time, it gave her much personal satisfaction.

Disorder was giving way to order, the pestilence was subsiding, the worst of the famine was over. While there was still hatred of the Jews, there were no major outbreaks of violence. There was good reason to believe that the worst was now past and that better days were sure to come as long as Ferrante was in control.

On leaving Castel Nuovo one day, Don Isaac noticed that a ship from Portugal was anchored at the quay. He watched as the haggard passengers disembarked, gathered their belongings, and slowly made their way up the ramp. Among the passengers, Don Isaac thought that he spotted a familiar face. It was Judah's nurse, the one who had secretly taken Don Isaac's one-year old grandson to Portugal! Don Isaac's heart was filled with happiness at the thought of holding his grandson again after so many months of waiting. Overjoyed he ran down the ramp to the unsuspecting nurse and shouted out his happy greeting.

"Nurse Perla, how good it is to see you. Welcome to Naples!"

The nurse turned around to see her welcomer. Her eyes opened wide with fright and she instantly dropped her bundle. Covering her face with her hands, she hunched over in shame.

"Don Isaac, please . . . forgive me. I could not help it!"

Don Isaac's elation turned to puzzlement. "Help what?," he asked uneasily.

The nurse began to cry. "Don Isaac, forgive me. I tried . . . tried to stop them."

The nurse cried fitfully, her body shaking from her sobs. Don Isaac put his arms comfortingly on the woman's shoulders. What had happened? He was almost afraid to ask. Had something happened to his grandson? Was little Isaac sick or perhaps, God forbid, dead? He had to know.

"Nurse Perla, please, I beg of you, tell me what happened. I must know."

The nurse backed away from Don Isaac. She uncovered her sorrowful face.

"Don Isaac, how can I tell you this? How can I tell you what will only bring pain into your heart? Believe me, believe me when I tell you it was not my fault. I protected him, I cared for him, I fed him from my very breasts."

"My grandson, Perla, . . . is he dead?"

The nurse shook her head. "No, Don Isaac . . . he is not dead. Your grandson lives."

Don Isaac was relieved. "Then, is he ill perhaps? Is his life in danger?"

The nurse shook her head again. "No. Your grandson is completely healthy."

Don Isaac was very confused now. "Perla, then what is the matter? Tell me, for God's sake!"

The nurse sighed deeply, wiped a tear from her eyes and lowered her head. "The King of Portugal . . . he somehow found out that your grandson was hiding with me in Portugal. The King sent soldiers to our hiding place. They took the child from me and . . ."

A crest-fallen Don Isaac said, "Yes, and . . .?"

The nurse closed her eyes and said, ". . . and they baptized the child and converted him to Christianity!"

Don Isaac Abravanel felt a dagger slice through his heart. He felt as if his entire being was being torn asunder. His legs became wobbly, his vision blurry, his head faint. Half-dazed, he reached up for his tunic and tore it apart so as to mark his clothing with the rent that he felt within his soul.

Don Isaac staggered away from the nurse. "Believe me, Don Isaac, I tried to stop them . . ." the nurse repeated, but her words fell upon ears that had now become deaf to all but the shouts of pain from within. A staggering Don Isaac Abravanel half-stumbled up the ramp, his body lurching with each step, his soul tumbling wildly in its own ethereal space.

The great eagle was wounded. He felt his strength ebbing away. He needed some place to rest where those who believed in the unbreak-ability of the great eagle would not see their leader falter. He needed to be alone.

Everything was a blur — trees, buildings, faces, streets. Ill- defined figures came and went, familiar faces became shadowy apparitions. A film of unreality clouded his vision as he trudged to the outskirts of Naples.

Several hours later he scaled Mount Vesuvius. It was a strenuous climb, leaving his breath heavy and his legs sore from the steep ascent. Perching on the crater's rim, he looked for new insight. What did the expulsion from Spain signify? Why was there so much wanton destruc-tion, so much suffering of innocents, so much unexplained misery? Why did the Holy One of Israel allow evildoers to take his grandchild? His faith was shaken. He sensed that the solutions somehow could be ascertained if he would but search scripture, search himself, for the key that would unlock the dilemma. The search, the struggle within himself, for himself, unearthed the vast storehouse of memories of the past. A swirl of learned information, all of it involuntarily recalled streamed through the fore of his consciousness — ancient philosophical arguments, scriptural expositions, wild speculations, Talmudic riddles — all floating loosely in the unsettled sea of his mind. The more that he tried to find answers in religious commentaries, the more he questioned. Yet for all his hours of sound searching, for all his hours of grappling with the questions that he had raised, he could find no better answers than those which had served him well in the past. The path to a solution lay in the re-affirmation of his simple faith, in the guiding principles of his life. If his questions could not all be answered, that was no reason to discount what he already knew was true. Therefore he again decided to undertake a thorough examination of the Messianic texts. This path would shed light on the great mystery of national redemption. As sure as he was of what he must now do, he was more sure of the forthcoming rebirth of the Jewish people.

He looked around. From the pit of the crater came a twisting column of smoke which was the only sign that the volcano was still alive.

Yet Vesuvius, with all its fire and smoke, could not fume forever. Its fiery wrath one day had to subside, its base of cinder and hardened lava in time had to give way to the encroachments of life. Flowers were growing on the periphery of the crater rim, the patches of vegetation driving their sustenance from the matter of decomposed lava. Even here on Vesuvius, where life had once been totally obliterated, new life had amazingly sprung up from the remaining ashes. As the outburst of Spanish Christian hatred had destroyed Jewish life in the Iberian peninsula, so too the Spanish Jews would similarly spring up from the ashes of their shattered communities. They too would find a way to reconstitute themselves as a people.

Don Isaac Abravanel picked a yellow flower and began his descent from Vesuvius. He had no graven stone tablets to show his people. All he had was a flower, born of the cooling lava of his pain, a flower plucked from the heights when his soul had been in its uttermost depths. This secret of rebirth from on high would be his, and he would pass it on to his people.

Chapter 17

Abraham Zacuto walked as fast as he could. He left his office at the Lisbon nautical academy when he received the message *"Donde la niña estuvo, el moro canta sin sombra."* 'Where the child was, the Moor sings without a shadow.' While Zacuto understood what it meant, he had a premonition of bad things to come. Leaving his maps and instruments with the other clutter on his desk, he put on his heavy cloak and set out toward the harbor.

Zacuto was by nature a problem solver: Talmudic riddles, predicting eclipses, even cryptic messages from an affable Moor. But the problems were insignificant compared to Israel's difficulties. Ever since the expulsion, so many things had happened, some evidently for the better, most clearly for the worse.

On the better side, Zacuto was royal astronomer to the court of King João II. The Portuguese mariners all used his improved copper astrolabe in their voyages around the southern cape of Africa to find a new route to the Indies. This and the mariners' frequent use of his astronomical tables were sources of much satisfaction. His name was known to many, but his name was not the one that was foremost on everyone's lips. It was Christopher Columbus who was the talk of Lisbon, when he sailed into the harbor on March 8, 1493, proclaiming himself to be the new Admiral of the Ocean Sea! Columbus claimed to have discovered a westerly route to the Indies. The news devastated Zacuto. It also staggered those Portuguese mariners focusing their attention on the route around Africa.

Zacuto had first doubted the reports, but then decided to investigate the matter himself. The evidence was overwhelming. Indeed, Zacuto had never seen anything like it before. Indians! These strange bronze-skinned natives that Columbus brought back from the Indies babbled away in a strange tongue. What odd ways they had, what utterly different plants they cultivated and ate! Zacuto was shaken. He could not wait to speak with Columbus and his crew about the strange new world and uncharted seas to the west. He had so many questions to ask the daring voyagers. Everyone was pressing around the proud Genoese captain.

Columbus, his ruddy face beaming, spotted him in the crowd. "Professor Zacuto!"

Zacuto pushed his way toward him.

Columbus heartily shook Zacuto's hand. "Professor, how good it is to see you. You heard that I discovered the westerly route to the Indies? I have done what all the world, including you, Professor, said was impossible. I proved all of you wrong."

"My congratulations, Captain."

"Wrong again, Professor. My title is now admiral, Admiral of the Ocean Sea. Yes, and I am to be Viceroy and Governor of all the lands that I have discovered."

"I congratulate you, Admiral. I admit you have discovered something of great significance."

"I have discovered the Indies," Columbus said firmly.

Zacuto rubbed his beard. "Admiral Columbus, will I have the honor of your illustrious company during your visit to Lisbon?"

Columbus shook his head. "That is not possible. I will be in Lisbon only long enough to outfit our caravel. At this moment, I am on my way to see the King of Portugal at a monastery about thirty miles inland. He requested that I present myself to him. The fool turned me down twice when I sought a sponsor for this voyage. I cannot wait to see his face when he realizes what he passed up. He, too, was wrong."

"We were all wrong, Admiral," Zacuto admitted in humble acknowledgement of his error. "What can I say in my defense? I, the Talavera Commission, the King of Portugal, we were all wrong. But, Admiral, if I may change the subject," Zacuto cleared his throat. "Did you perchance . . . uh . . . make use of my copper astrolabe?"

"All the time," Columbus said.

Now it was Zacuto's turn to beam with pride. Columbus' reply was answer enough for him. Columbus' ship tarried in Lisbon harbor for five days only, and then set forth for Spain. A new world had been opened up by the bold young Genoese mariner. Abraham Zacuto contented himself with his own nautical contribution to Columbus' pioneer voyage across the sea.

As he continued to walk down toward the harbor, Zacuto recalled his many losses of the past year. And now the cryptic message from the Moor — what does it mean? *"Donde la niña estuvo"*. "Where the child was" must refer to *la niña*, that is the Niña, Columbus' ship. That points to the harbor where the Niña had been. And what about *"sin sombra"*? What does that mean? When does the sun not cast a shadow? Why, at noontime, of course. And *el Moro*, the Moor, who was he? Who else but the *Arraby Mor*, the newly appointed chief rabbi of Portugal, Rabbi Simon Maimi!

What was the chief rabbi's message all about? Did it relate to King João II's declaration allowing the exiles to stay in Portugal no longer than eight months? Was that it? While 600 of the Jewish families were allowed to settle in Portugal permanently, if each family paid 100 cruzados, other Jews either had to leave Portugal or risk being sold into slavery.

Zacuto was one of the fortunate 600, as was Rabbi Maimi. They were allowed to remain in Portugal because of their learning, with the expenses of their permanent settlement being borne by the wealthier members of the community. But they were still sensitive to the miseries their brethren suffered. Zacuto and Maimi, who had become close friends in the intervening months, often met to discuss these community matters.

Most important was to see that the departure of the close to 60 thousand Jewish exiles from Portugal was safe and orderly. While many of the exiles left on one of the 120 ships the King of Portugal provided for that purpose, most ended up wherever the Portuguese vessels chanced to be headed. Many Sephardim never reached their destination; many died of thirst and hunger at sea; others were cast on uninhabited shores to fend for themselves. Some even disembarked at the Portuguese fortress in Arcila, only to find themselves in the clutches of the merciless Count of Borba.

Rabbi Maimi spent much of his day ransoming Jews who were reduced to slavery. Thousands of poor Jews, unable to pay the entrance fee, crossed the border illegally into Portugal, and King João II was angered at this. The King sent his police after the aliens who tried to deceive him. Altogether, during the past eight months, 15 thousand Jews were forced into servitude. Because the resources of the Jewish community were strained to their limits, only ten thousand could be redeemed. To make matters worse, a pestilence had broken out in Lisbon, and the King's ministers were blaming the Jews. These same ministers were also urging the King not to permit the Spanish Jews to stay beyond their allotted eight months.

Problems, problems, problems. Abraham Zacuto, master problem-solver, felt at times that he could not solve any of them.

"The round-up has begun."

Those were Rabbi Maimi's opening words to Zacuto. The chief rabbi of Portugal stood in the harbor, his once jovial face now grey with worry, his eyes blood-shot from lack of sleep.

"When did it start?," asked Zacuto.

"This morning. Guards are going from house to house in the Jewish quarter of Lisbon, dragging men, women, and children out of their homes. I saw it with my own eyes. I tried to stop the guards, but they shoved me aside, saying, "King's orders, King's orders!""

"Damn the King," said an astonished Zacuto. "May his name be blotted out!"

Rabbi Maimi shook his head. "It was awful. I stood there unable to do anything. I saw iron chains placed around their hands and feet and heard them cry out to me to save them. And I could do nothing, Abraham. I stood there and did nothing while . . . while my brothers and sisters, pleading for my help, were taken away into servitude."

Zacuto said, "But you will be able to redeem them."

Rabbi Maimi shook his head. "No, not this time. This time, those who have been here longer than eight months and did not pay the 100 cruzados will become the property of the King . . . they will become unredeemable slaves."

"Oh my God! I had no idea," blurted Zacuto.

"The King's orders, they told me . . . the King's orders. What could I do, Abraham? Tell me, what could I do? Nothing."

Zacuto began to pace up and down, his head bobbing up and down. "We could ask for an audience with the King. We could ask for an extension of time before the enslavement condition is enforced."

Maimi answered him, "I already tried that. The King refuses to see me."

Zacuto twirled his beard. "Then try again, chief rabbi. The King has his price. Perhaps he can be convinced to adopt more lenient measures. Surely no harm can come from a second attempt."

"We will get nothing from this King," the chief rabbi insisted. "I know his type. He is no different from Ferdinand and Isabella. They are all the same . . . cold, heartless rulers to the core. They want us only as long as they need us. When we have outlived our usefulness, they want to be rid of us . . . as in Spain. You know what happened to the Jews who stayed behind in Spain past the three month deadline?"

"No," said Zacuto.

Rabbi Maimi continued. "Any Jews who stayed behind in Spain were burned at the stake. Some tried to save themselves by offering to become Christians. But no, even that did not help. It was past the deadline. As Ferdinand and Isabella promised, Jews who stayed in Spain were burned. Why should we believe King João is any different?"

Zacuto shrugged his shoulders. "Perhaps he is not, but it is important to try again. Maybe we should form a delegation to go to the King. What do you say?"

Rabbi Maimi sighed gently. "A delegation . . . how often I heard Don Abraham Senior say those very same words. I have become to the Jews of Portugal what Don Abraham was to the Jews of Spain. He was a disappointment to us all. Will I be one too? A delegation, you say, Don Abraham Zacuto? What can I say to you? What can I do except try again . . . and again . . . and again."

Zacuto placed his hand on the chief rabbi's shoulder. "Come, come, chief rabbi, let us see how well you sing. Follow me."

"Where to?," asked Rabbi Maimi.

Zacuto shook his head and smiled.

"Na, na, na. Now it is my turn to be secretive. But do not worry, my errant Moor. I shall be your guide. Trust that this deviser of astrolabes does not often lose his way."

Josefina Matalon dashed frantically through the narrow streets of Lisbon. Her heart raced and the blood pulsated in her temples. Her heaving lungs, unable to gather enough air, seemed ready to explode at any moment. With flailing arms she charged through the crowded street, knocking down whoever was in her path, screaming frantically as she went.

They had taken Anton and her two oldest boys, and she was devastated. Anton! Her boys, Yosi and Jaime! How she loved them! How, how, how, she asked herself between sobs, how can this happen to me, how can this be? "O God, help me", she cried, "Help me, dear God, help me, help me please."

Startled bystanders watched the mad woman lurch on. It was clear she was possessed. "Help me, help me, dear God," she raved on as she continued to run down the street, "Help me."

The chains on Anton Matalon's wrists caused no great pain. The mortification that he felt was not for himself, but for his two sons who had thick ropes around their tiny necks, and whose hands were bound behind their backs. What had they, mere children, done to deserve this? Did they deserve to be treated as common criminals merely because they remained in Portugal? Surely, if anyone was to blame, it was he, the master of the house, who should be punished. But not, God forbid, Yosi and Jaime. It was his fault that the tales of atrocities committed convinced him to tarry in Portugal past the eight-month period allowed by the King. He, alone, should be punished.

He turned to the lead guard.

"Pardon me, sir. Please let my children go. Take me instead. Do anything you want with me. But leave my children alone."

The guard ignored him. In one hand the guard held his sword, and with the other he held the chains that bound Anton's wrists. The guard turned his head to one side and spat in Anton's direction.

Anton winced and looked back. His sons dragged their feet behind him. Yosi, a dark-eyed lad of nine, stared at him with a bewildered, frightened look and Jaime, little Jaime, only seven years old, was crying. "It hurts, father," he whimpered as he tugged at the rope around his neck. "It hurts . . . it hurts so much. Tell them to take it off."

"I know it hurts, son," said Anton. "Very soon, they will be taking it off. You will see, they will take it off soon."

"When?," asked little Jaime, trusting his father.

"Soon," replied Anton emphatically, "Very soon."

"How soon?" This time it was Yosi's turn to ask.

The lead guard spat again in Anton's direction.

"Very soon."

"And where is Mama?," asked little Jaime.

Anton said unconvincingly, "Do not worry, Jaime. Mama will be with us soon. You will see."

Another lie. Anton waited for the guard to spit. But this time, the Portuguese officer held back. Anton's answer troubled him less than the child's question. Where indeed was his wife Josefina? Where did she go when the four of them had been attacked by the guards?

It all happened so quickly. Anton, his wife, and two sons were selling trinkets to passers-by. Business was going well that morning. The Lusitanian women liked his Spanish baubles, rings, and brooches. And then, suddenly, the attack came. It took no more than a moment or two for the guards to overwhelm them. He struggled, but he knew it was pointless resistance. Only Josefina, behind the vending table, was able to escape. Somehow she managed to break free from the one guard who chased her.

Josefina probably ran home to their two other children who had been left under the care of a Jewish nurse. Would the Portuguese take children of five and three also? What threat could they possibly be to the King of Portugal? Anton did not have any answers, not to the child's question, not to the ones that he raised in his own mind.

As Anton and his sons walked down the streets of Portugal, tradesmen and artisans stared at them. Walking with his head bowed, unable to look at passers-by, a heartsick Anton Matalon could not forgive himself for his mistake.

An hour of walking brought them to the outskirts of the city. Goatherds could be seen on the dirt-filled roads, leading their goats from pasture to the local slaughterhouse. Itinerant peddlers followed with their pack-ridden mules, the overburdened beasts plodding down the worn trails. Added to this braying traffic were the slowly moving huddles of bound Spanish Jews, similarly driven by their Portuguese captors like so much animal kine.

Anton and his two sons were directed to the prison gates. Along with the other Jews, they stood quietly, waiting to be led into prison.

"Come next to me, children," Anton whispered unto his two sons as he crouched down. He gave Yosi and little Jaime each a tender kiss.

"Papa, what are they going to do to us?"

Anton did not answer. Instead, he planted another long kiss on Jaime's cheek, hoping to calm his son's rising fears. What could he tell the child? What lie could he invent this time?

"Papa, you are crying," said little Jaime. He had never seen his father cry before. And now, tears welled in Jaime's eyes at seeing his father cry. The two began to weep, hands tied behind their backs, neither able to wipe the tears of the other.

"Papa, don't cry," said Jaime. "I will be all right. Don't worry. Mama is doing fine. Right, Yosi? Is that not true, Yosi?"

"Of course, she is," said Yosi emphatically. "Of course, Mama is fine. There is no need to cry, papa. Mama, she is fine. You'll see, Papa. Soon we'll all be together again, won't we?"

"Of course, Yosi, Jaime, of course, you are both right. Soon, very soon we will all be together again."

The three neared the end of the line. A short distance away, Anton could see a stiff-looking Portuguese official, flanked by armed guards, sitting at a wooden table. Anton had seen the guards leading the prisoners away in different directions.

"Now, Yosi, Jaime, listen to me. You let me do the talking. Do you understand? I will do the talking."

His sons nodded their heads in silent agreement as they came before the official.

Glancing at them, the official squinted at the document in front of him and readied his pen for writing.

"State your name, your age, your place of birth, and the number of members in your family."

"Anton Matalon is my name. I am thirty-eight years old. I am a native of Segovia, Castile."

"And how many children do you have?"

Anton hesitated.

"Only two. This is Yosi on my right. This other one is Jaime."

The scribe scribbled away. Anton glared at Jaime and Yosi.

The scribe looked up, his eyes testing Anton's. "Only two?"

Anton said calmly, "Only two."

"And their ages?"

"Yosi is nine, Jaime seven."

Pointing with his pen, the scribe said, "You go to the left with the guard, Señor Matalon. The children will go to the right."

"I want my children to go with me."

The scribe spoke with authority. "You will do as you are told, Señor Matalon."

Anton shot back. "And you, señor, you go to the devil! My children stay with me!"

The scribe made an angry face and signaled to the guards. Three men quickly grabbed Anton. Two of them pinned his arms, while another wrapped an arm tightly around his neck. They began to take him away.

Yosi cried out. "Leave my father alone! Leave him alone!"

The nine-year old tried to come to his father's rescue, but a guard held him back by the rope around his neck.

"Papa! Papa!," sobbed little Jaime. "Papa! Papa!"

Anton was overpowered. In the commotion he could say nothing to the parting cries of his children. The arm around his neck was choking him. He gasped for air. His lungs ached. His resistance vanished with the loss of his airway, and he was shoved toward the prison. Unable to continue further, he stumbled and fell at the prison entrance, but the guards shoved him through the door. Lying on the stone floor, he had hardly caught his breath when one of the guards kicked him viciously. The other guards joined in the booting of the Jew, smashing their hard leather boots into the flesh of their victim. He felt flashes of pain rip through his body. Anton was dragged down the winding staircase, scraping his knees and ankles raw. At the bottom of the stairs, the guards flung him into his cell of dust and straw. The exile from Segovia now ached all over.

They were not through with him yet. A few moments later, they dragged him from his cell to a nearby chamber, its dark and dreary interior filled with smoke. Although Anton could offer little resistance, the guards took no chances. They forced the goldmsith on the floor and held him firmly.

Out of the corner of his eye, Anton could see a blazing furnace, its flames spewing smoke in the room. A bare-chested hairy behemoth of a man stoked the fire, raking the coals with an iron rod. The fire sputtered and hissed with each stroke of the iron rod. The half-nude giant turned towards Anton, sweat glistening on his chest; the rod in his hand was now a white-hot branding iron.

Anton screamed in terror. The arms around him tightened so Anton could not move. Someone ripped open Anton's shirt. The white-hot iron came closer and closer. The brand on the rod's tip was the crown of Portugal. Anton screamed again as the smoking rod was pressed into his chest. Bolts of unbearable pain tore through him as the branding iron seared his flesh! Time stood still, a moment became an infinity of pain.

The rod was withdrawn, as were the arms that had held him. All that was left was the stabbing pain in his chest, the smoke now coming from his own roasted flesh. Anton wished that the rod had gone through him, yes, through his heart. He wanted a quick end to this terrible misery. Anything was better than this cruel indignity of being branded a slave of the Portuguese crown!

Josefina ran as fast as she could. She wanted to get home before the guards and to get out of this dreadful city while there was still time. She would take her two other children somewhere, somewhere far away from Lisbon, somewhere where the guards could not find them. Jaime! Yosi! Anton! The loves of her life, snatched from her in a moment. All three gone. What was she to do, she, alone, a woman, without Anton, without her two beloved sons? She continued to run down one street after another, her eyes red with anguish.

She stumbled on a large crowd gathered in front of the church of St. Martinho. Josefina heard the animated murmurs of the crowd. Could it be that what they were saying was true? She put a halt to her mad dash, wiped the tears from her eyes, and frantically looked about. Hope sprang anew in her heaving breast. It was he! It was the King, Don João II! Surely there was some hope left if she could sway the Christian heart of the Portuguese King. Surely the King had room in his heart to grant her sorrowful pleas. Fate, perhaps God Almighty, had made their paths cross. Now it was up to her to make the King listen to her. She pushed her way through the crowd until she was at the front of the wall of onlookers. Her chest heaving with every breath, she was ready to receive the King.

The King of Portugal rode his horse into the area between the church and the royal palace. Alongside him was his entourage of mounted dignitaries and armed foot-soldiers. At the head of the stately procession was a group of pious-looking young men bearing the miracle-working statue of St. Maria of Belem. They were followed by three frocked priests, silver crosses dangling at their waists, heads bowed in religious devotion. As the priests and the saintly image passed by, people in the crowd respectfully made the sign of the cross. All eyes, however, were focused on the King who made his way toward the church. Josefina began to tremble with anxiety as the procession moved toward her. She could not wait any longer; she must tell her story to the King.

When the King drew up alongside of her, Josefina burst through the crowd. The King's guards were taken by surprise as she threw herself at the King's feet. Josefina passionately entreated the sovereign, "Your Majesty! I beg of you to hear me out. I am a Jewish woman. Your guards took my children. Please, your Majesty, in the name of God Almighty, do not take them from me. Please, your Majesty, I beg of you, have mercy on my innocent babes."

The King made an angry face. "Out of my presence, woman!"

Guards quickly ran to Josefina and grabbed her. Trying to free herself, she shouted, "Your Majesty, in the name of heaven, in the name of God, I beg of you not to take all my children. Leave me something. Let me have but one child, the youngest child. That is all I ask of you . . . one child, nothing more. Your Majesty, I beg of you!"

The King was irritated even further. "Take her out of my presence!"

The guards began to beat Josefina. One punched her in the jaw, snapping her head to the right. Other pounding blows to the head and body followed in full view of the watchful King and spectators.

The King raised his arm to stop the beating. He exclaimed, "Leave her alone, for she is like the bitch who cries because her young whelps have been taken away from her."

Leaving Josefina sobbing on the ground, the King spurred his horse and continued on his way to receive the holy sacraments.

Josefina's wretched face was smeared with blood and tears as two royal guards led her away. She could barely talk. "I . . . I have two children at home. What will become of them if you take me?

A guard answered, "You are going to jail, you Jewish bitch, and nowhere else."

Josefina was crest-fallen. She had to find a way to see her two youngest children, cost what it may. Time was running out.

She whispered to the guards. "Listen, my husband is a goldsmith. We have much gold hidden at home. Much gold . . . gold coins, gold jewelry. It is yours if you let me see my children again. I have more than thirty gold pieces that you can divide up between yourselves. You can have it all, every last piece of gold . . . but you must allow me to have a few last moments with my children, alone, before you take me to jail."

The two guards looked at each other. One guard nodded his head, and the other did too. It was a deal. "Very well," said one guard cagily. "But just a few moments."

"Just a few moments," concurred Josefina with a deep sigh of maternal relief, "alone with my children." She was ready to trade these last few moments with her two youngest children in exchange for all her valuables.

Josefina said, "I realize that the King has sent you to gather our sons and daughters, and that you have your duty to perform. As I stand before you, I know what it is that you have to do. I will not stand in your way. I will obey you fully as I have every intention of obeying the King."

"That is wise," answered a guard. "It is good that you accept the decree of the King. In this manner, though you will be made slaves, you and your children will also be made to accept the Christian religion. This will be good for you. Christ will console you in your new life ahead."

Josefina remained silent, then spoke again. "Christ, you say, will console me and my children . . . in our new life ahead?"

The guard said, "I am sure of it."

Josefina said nothing and looked straight ahead, shoulders slumped, her unhappy eyes lowered and fixed into position.

"God's will be done," she muttered to herself.

The guard, with whom she had conversed, answered her with an unspoken nod of approval.

They arrived at the Matalon home. Josefina stood at the doorway, saying to the guards, "I will be with you shortly. Give me but a few precious moments to be with my children, and then you can do with us as you will."

"Go . . . hurry up," said the guard.

Immediately upon entering the house, she bade the housekeeper, an elderly Portuguese Jewish woman of sixty, to take her leave. The old lady stepped outside and was the immediate subject of interrogation by the two guards. The elderly woman, a native-born Portuguese Jew, was exempt from the King's decree and had nothing to fear. The guards, hearing her speak perfect Portuguese, had no choice but to let her go.

Josefina closed the door behind her and locked it from inside. She took a deep breath; it was time for a hard decision. Going to the kitchen she pulled out a butcher knife and examined the blade for nicks. The knife was perfect. It was fit to perform ritual slaughter.

Hiding the knife behind her back, she went to her children. One, three-year old Rachel, was playing with a doll; the other, five-year old Leah, was sleeping in a corner.

Rachel turned her head and smiled when her mother entered the room, happy to see her mother again. The child's big brown eyes went back to the doll that she held close to her chest.

Josefina crept up behind her youngest child and smoothed Rachel's curly hair. She kissed Rachel tenderly on the cheek and hugged her. Tears streamed down her face as she embraced her child for the last time. Josefina pressed her right hand over the child's mouth. Quickly she thrust the child's head back against her chest and kept it there. The child tried to scream, but only muffled sounds came out. With her left hand, Josefina used the butcher knife to slash the child's throat in one quick motion. Blood spurted out of the child's neck in jets of red, drenching them both. The child went limp in her mother's arms. Josefina kissed the child, "O my sweet one, it was meant to be that we should sanctify the name of the Holy God of Israel. Forgive me, my child, but I could not allow the Christians to bring you up in their religion. If you are to be taken from my bosom, it is only to the bosom of the Holy One of Israel that you shall go. Farewell, little Rachel, love of my loves."

Josefina laid the child down to eternal rest.

"Mama, Mama, don't hurt me."

It was Leah. She was awake, Josefina realized. How much had the child seen? Josefina stood up, the butcher knife dripping with the blood of her babe. She hid the knife quickly behind her back.

"Mama, Mama, are you going to hurt me?," asked Leah, terrified beyond measure.

Leah jumped out of bed and tried to escape. Josefina moved swiftly to block the doorway. Leah moved back, then frantically scrambled all over the room knocking over furniture. When she tripped and stumbled, Josefina pounced on top of her. She sat on the child's chest, her knees immobilizing the child's arms. With one hand, she pulled aside the child's hair to expose Leah's tiny neck. Once again, the butcher knife did its deadly work, cutting a deep gash in the soft neck of its second victim.

Josefina bent over and kissed her sweet Leah on the cheek, saying, "O my darling, your hurt is now over, as mine is just beginning. Fly away, my little one. I have set you free from a fate worse than death itself. Let your soul fly, let it soar unto the heavens to join the sacred martyrs of our people. There, in the presence of the Holy One of Israel, we shall live once again, reunited with one another, reunited with the one true God of the universe."

Josefina stood up, with fresh tears streaming down her face, the thick drops of blood dripping from the hem of her dress. She opened a window and thrust her head out to call to the guards. "Why do you just stand there, you two? Have you not come to carry my beloved children away? Come, you two. Come and drink your fill of Jewish blood. Come and take what your hearts really desire." Then slamming the window shut, Josefina held the butcher knife with both hands and drove it into the pit of her stomach. She fell on her knees and plunged the knife deep into her chest. She plunged into darkness, putting an end to the life that she no longer wanted to live. In the altar of her home, the sacrificer had become one with the sacrificed.

Anton Matalon ached all over. Could all this be happening to him? First he was branded in the flesh; then he was beaten in prison. Now, his mind, too, was being reduced to submission. He was becoming a slave. It began with the branding iron to subdue his flesh, and now they were after his mind.

Along with other prison inmates, Anton was put on a galley ship, made to strip to the waist, and chained to the oars. The sting of the lash soon caused the prisoners to bring the massive ship into motion. While the coxswain barked out the rhythm, the oars sliced through the water and came out again, ready for another cycle.

Anton felt the blisters forming on the palms of his hands. Sweat poured down his brow and oozed from every pore on his chest. He groaned as the sore muscles on his back and shoulders cried out for rest. Yet there was no rest, as the coxswain drove them on. Those who weakened and fell behind in their rhythm were the first to feel the lash. When a prisoner showed stripes of blood on his back, the others knew he would not make it.

Anton rowed on, his new existence as a galley slave just beginning. He looked about him at those who were to share his new life of bondage. They were men like himself, men with wives and children, men who had been torn from their loved ones. What had become of his own loved ones? What had become of his dear Josefina, and of Yosi and Jaime and Rachel and little Leah? Would he ever see them again? How many years was he to be chained to these oars paddling the high seas, holding on to memories of a life that was never to be his again?

Nor were the children spared. The Portuguese ruler decreed that all such slave children, from three to ten years of age, were to be exiled like hardened criminals to the newly discovered island of Sao Tomé off the west African coast. It was one of the *Islas Perdidas*, the "Lost Islands", reportedly inhabited only by serpents and lizards, and to which hardened criminals were exiled as part of their punishment.

Three hundred Jewish children were transported to their African destination aboard ships commanded by Alvaro de Caminha. The voyage was made more difficult by a lack of food and water and unsanitary conditions. In the hot cramped quarters below, children cried for their parents. Hungry and thirsty, miserably seasick and vomiting one on another, they found no comfort in their common fate and were equally unprepared to survive unaided on the tropical island of Sao Tomé. Unable to care for themselves, much less for one another, these dispossessed children hardly seemed fit to play the role of island colonizers.

The children were allowed to disembark. Yosi and Jaime Matalon splashed through the warm, shallow equatorial waters, toward the island. Ahead of them loomed the lush green island of Sao Tomé, its mountains brushing against the bright African sky. Tall palm trees lined the sea shore, their elongated branches swaying slowly in the soft heated wind. Yosi and Jaime felt relieved at being able to leave the joyless ship. Wading through the water, they lingered in the foamy surf as it licked at their feet.

The children on shore joined in the general frolic. Some kicked at the sand; others rushed back into the water and, with arms flailing away in waist-high water, splashed each other in the face. It was a moment of pure childish merriment. But it was to be no more than a moment.

The Portuguese captain, Caminha, drew near in a rowboat. "Silence! Everyone, listen to me . . . I said, everyone listen to me! Silence! Everyone get on shore . . . and stay there in one group. You heard me . . . on shore! . . . Now!"

Yosi turned to his brother. "Run, Jaime, run!"

Yosi began to run, and so did Jaime. Other children did likewise. But some, especially the younger children, did as they were told. Captain Caminha and his men jumped out of their rowboat, climbed ashore, and chased anyone they could catch. Those who were too slow or indecisive were caught.

The two Matalon brothers did not stop. They were runaway slaves now — fugitives, criminals. Slashing through the dense tropical forest of the island, they moved in the direction of the mountainous interior. In the distance, they could still hear the shouts of their pursuers, and they ran harder still, pushing the overhanging thick ferns out of the way ahead of them. They treaded upon a jungle carpet of fallen leaves. Giant kapok trees, their massive tangled roots sprouting from the ground, spread their fibrous tendrils skyward and outwards through the forest like some verdant uncoiling medusa. Tapering palms overrun with decaying moss let slivers of light penetrate to the floor of the tropical forest. Clumps of ferns, the silvery drops of water condensing on their fronds, lined the base of every tree. Exotic brightly-colored birds flitted through the air, creating a peculiar medley of high-pitched calls and jabbering shrieks.

"A serpent!" Yosi cried out as he suddenly stopped his forward motion. A huge boa constrictor, its cylindrical body slimy and undulating, slithered its way in the leafy crosspath ahead of him. Yosi grabbed hold of Jaime and prevented his little brother from going any further.

"Hold still," said Yosi, as the serpent glided past them and disappeared. Yosi looked both ways and let out a long sigh of relief.

"Did you see that, Yosi?"

"Of course I saw it."

"Did you see how big it was?"

"Of course it's big. It's a serpent."

Jaime began to cry. "Yosi, I'm scared. I want Papa."

Yosi tried to console his brother. "Look, Jaime, don't cry now. You think I'm not scared? Listen, I'm scared . . . real scared."

Jaime asked, "Don't you wish Papa was here?"

"Sure I do," answered Yosi. "Sure I do . . . just like you. Just don't cry."

"I cry because I'm scared."

"I know, I know . . . just don't cry."

"All right, Yosi. You go first."

Yosi nodded his head and looked both ways. The serpent was gone. It was time to move on.

"Come on. Let's go."

The dense vegetation of the island surrounded them. Tramping through the thick underbrush, they looked for a good place to hide. Captain Caminha was coming after them, and they had to find a place where they would be safe. They came onto a buzzing and hovering swarm of mosquitoes. The pesky insects pricked their shoulders, only to incur a rapid slap of the skin, the slap being almost as bad as the prick.

"Aaaah! Aaaah! Help!"

They stopped slapping themselves. What was that? Suddenly they heard a scream in the distance. From where had it come? Silence again. Yosi and Jaime looked at each other, the fright in their eyes showing. Yosi put a finger to his mouth and signaled for Jaime to get down low. Crouching, they wondered who screamed for help. It had been a child's voice. Caminha, was he around? Or could it be the serpent? Or some other beast of the jungle? They waited. Nothing . . . no more screams. Then, they rose cautiously from their hiding position. With Yosi leading the way, they looked around for some telltale sign of a struggle. An undefined danger seemed to be lurking in the bushes, waiting for them to make a fatal move. Their eyes and ears were attentive to everything about them.

They came to a river. The murky water rolled slowly past them, making its steady indolent way down from the mountains upstream. The muddy banks were overgrown with a wall of reeds and thick-stemmed fronds which extended into the river itself. Yosi and Jaime looked up and down to be sure it was safe. Noticing a clearing by the river's edge, they decided to head for it.

"I am thirsty, Yosi. Aren't you?"

"Yes. Let's go get some water to drink."

They waded into the river and drank their fill.

Yosi said, "Aah, that tastes good."

Something suddenly bit Jaime's leg. Jaime was terrified as he struggled to remain above water. He stammered. "Yo-Yosi!"

A giant crocodile surfaced with its jaws clenched around Jaime's leg and pulled Jaime down with him. Jaime tried to free his leg, but could not. The reptile's tail slashed viciously through the air, twisting and turning its tough scaly body. Little Jaime was dragged through the water. He reached out for his big brother to help him. "Yosi!," he cried. "Yosi!" Yosi tried to grab Jaime's arm, but he was beyond reach. Now it was Yosi's turn to cry out. "Jaime!"

Jaime went under. While Yosi saw signs of his brother's struggle, he could do nothing. Then Jaime reemerged, his arms flailing wildly, his mouth gulping for air. As quickly as he had surfaced, he was drawn back by the crocodile into the waters below. Bubbles, a swirl of water, and then suddenly he saw Jaime's outstretched arm! The arm disappeared, only to be followed by the huge crocodile thrashing and drowning its victim into submission. More bubbles, more agitated swirls of river water ensued. Yosi watched with disbelief as the bubbles and swirls subsided, and the river returned to its undisturbed flow.

"Jaime! Jaime!," he cried out. He began to back out of the lizard-infested waters.

As he started for the riverbank, he could not believe what he saw blocking his way. Three giant lizards were waiting for him! The dragon beasts slid on their underbellies into the water, propelling themselves forwards with their webbed limbs and a powerful swish of their tail. Yosi backed away from them, and then ran for the riverbank. Kicking his knees high, he felt the lizards' jaws snapping at his feet. One missed, thank God!, then another missed. He was out of the water! Suddenly he lost his footing on the loose mud of the riverbank. He fell to the ground, and a lizard fell on top of him. Another lizard clamped its powerful jaws around his calf. Yosi clawed with his hands on the muddy bank, all to no avail. "Ay no!," he shouted as he was dragged into the water.

They were his last words.

PART IV:
1497: SECOND EDICT, SECOND CHANCE

Chapter 18

It was Isabella, the fanatic queen of Castile, who had brought all the calamities on the Jews. It was she who was to blame for the continuing sufferings of his people, thought Abraham Zacuto.

On the death of King João II, João's cousin Manuel, the Duke of Beja, became the ruler of Portugal. Initially, King Manuel's rule seemed to bode well for the Jews. The ruler ordered that the enslaved Jews were to be set free and their liberties restored. Furthermore, he ordered that the Jewish children, who had been deported to the island of Sao Tomé were to be brought back to Portugal. Unfortunately, most of the children had already perished on the island, most of them being devoured by the crocodiles, the rest dying from lack of food and adequate shelter.

Manuel's early kindness toward the Jews was short lived, however. His desire to marry Isabella, the eldest daughter of Ferdinand and Isabella, led to harsher legislation. This Spanish princess, bearing her mother's name, had previously married Don Alonso, heir to the Portuguese crown in 1490. But Alonso had died shortly thereafter when he was thrown rudely from his horse, and the young widowed Isabella returned to Castile. Manuel submitted a proposal of marriage for Isabella to the court of Castile. The stern Queen would accept the marriage on two conditions: a mutual defense pact in the event of invasion by France and the expulsion within one month of all individuals of Jewish ancestry who had been condemned by the Inquisition and who had sought refuge in Portugal. While Manuel's representative at the Castilian court initially resisted the precondition, the

326

Spanish Queen and her daughter were adamant. His passion greater than his principles, Manuel was forced to relent so that arrangements could proceed for the wedding.

But even this was not enough. King Ferdinand and Queen Isabella further demanded of their future son-in-law that he expel all Jews in the kingdom of Portugal; their daughter, Princess Isabella, also made it clear that she had no intention of having a husband who showed favor and succor towards such a detestable people. The terms of marriage were made utterly simple to the prospective groom: King Manuel had to choose between the princess or the Jews.

King Manuel chose the princess. Despite the strong reservations of Manuel's council about the expulsion, the Portuguese King would not permit any objections to prevent the marriage. On December 4, 1496, Manuel signed the edict ordering all Jews to leave the kingdom within ten months. Thus, even the native Portuguese Jews who had lived in the Lusitanian kingdom for centuries were to be expelled. All Jews who stayed beyond October 31, 1497 were to be put to death and their properties confiscated. The Jews would be allowed to leave the country with all their belongings, and their safe transport to North Africa would be arranged by the crown.

Some Jews left as soon as the edict was announced in that cold December. Others tarried, preferring to make their exit during the milder climate of the spring. There was no indication that this would proceed any differently from the expulsion from Spain. There was no need to rush. Zacuto, one of the recognized leaders of the community, also bided his time.

In the spring, the King declared that no one could secure a ship to exit from Portugal except with the approval of the crown. The pace of departure suddenly quickened as the gates began to close, with the apprehensive Jews paying large sums of money to leave the country. Only the very rich were able to do so in time, mainly because they were able to bribe the officials at court to authorize their departure. And then the King shut the doors completely.

A short while later, ships were forbidden to transport Jews from Portugal. Sailors who took Jews out of Portugal would be hung unless they had been authorized by a royal judge or counselor.

Abraham Zacuto never dreamed he would have difficulties leaving Portugal. So when the court astronomer contacted his Portuguese friends at the maritime academy, he could not understand why they pretended not to know him. Vasco da Gama shook his head and threw up his arms. "If only you had come to see me two weeks earlier, Don Abraham, I might have been able to help you. But now, Don Abraham? Now?"

Everywhere he went, from the famed Da Gama to the lowliest captain, the answer was the same. Regrets, apologies, excuses. No friend of his wanted to risk his neck to save a Jew. Friends? What friends? Surely it was Zacuto's turn to shake his head.

From various sources, Zacuto heard that the King was planning to have all the Jews of the kingdom converted. Fearful of losing the talents and assets of the Jews, King Manuel was ready to use severe measures to keep them. Reportedly, members of the King's royal council, and even high-ranking members of the Lisbon archdiocese, informed the King that baptisms achieved by force were invalid in the eyes of the Catholic Church. The King was unmoved by these arguments. "In Christian devotion, I am not lacking. It is my will that is and ever will be the law of Portugal. If I so declare, so shall it be done."

The King's will was done. The royal council was dissolved, and shortly thereafter, a new proclamation was made throughout the kingdom. The proclamation was issued around Passover time, just as had the Edict in Spain, and stipulated that all Jewish children under fourteen years of age were to be taken away from parents who refused baptism and were to be dispersed throughout the cities and towns of the kingdom to be brought up as Christians.

On the first night of Passover, when the angel of death had in the distant past slain the first-born of Israel's Egyptian tormentors, so it now seemed that the children of this tormented Israelite generation would themselves experience the angel's consuming wrath. Zacuto remembered the night well. On the first night of Passover, it was the Christians who assumed the role of the angel of death. It was their night to pass over the homes of the huddled Hebrews. But this time there was no lintel marked with blood to keep the angel away. This time there was no Moses to rescue them. This time a reincarnated Pharoah was about to avenge himself. The bread of affliction became transmuted into affliction itself, the bitter herbs into bitterness, the four cups of wine were left untouched. "How is this night different from all other nights?" children asked on this night of nights. Though it seemed different from all other nights, the distinction between the exodus of old and the one at hand was lost in commemoration, and the night of the Passover became a painful reenactment of the past which it remembered.

The Jewish quarters of Portugal were swollen with the cries of mothers whose babes were snatched from their arms, as were their other children, who could not be saved with their torrent of tears and desperate pleas. Some resorted to subterfuge, others to pointless resistance, but the ruthless sheriffs of the Portuguese crown took them away.

Zacuto was witness to this and more. He saw parents, clothed in the black of mourning, accompany their children to the church for baptism, calling to God Almighty that they wished to die in the law of Moses. He heard of distraught mothers who killed their own children, by strangling or by drowning or whatever other means they could think of, to avoid profanation of their religion and submission to the faith of their persecutor. Certain Portuguese Christians, he had heard, were so moved by the heart-rending cries of the Jewish fathers and mothers that, at great risk to their lives, they hid many Jewish children in their homes.

When October arrived, it meant that the ten-month deadline would soon be upon them. The King ordered all Jews of the kingdom to assemble in Lisbon to prepare for their departure from Portugal by the vessels he had summoned. In response to the King's command, some twenty thousand Jews came to Lisbon and were confined in the corraled area known as Os Estãos. Abraham Zacuto and Rabbi Maimi were among those in the corral.

As soon as the Jews were assembled, they were told to become Christians, thereby doing out of their own free will what they otherwise would be made to do by force. Children of parents who had thus far eluded the royal dictates were forcibly torn from their parents' arms. Still the Jews paid no heed to the persuasive efforts of their captors.

The King, perceiving that stronger measures were required, ordered all Jewish men and women up to the age of twenty-five to be brought to the baptismal font. These young Jewish men and women fought furiously; they were dragged by their legs and arms to nearby churches where the priests were ready to sprinkle baptismal water on their heads. Others, shouting angry epithets against the Christian religion, so provoked their attackers that they were pulled by their hair and beards to the churches.

The attackers returned to Os Estãos to inform the parents that their children had been duly converted and, as a result, had been given Christian names. The christened young men and women were to be given to the custody of Old Christians to be brought up in the precepts of their new faith. But, any parents who converted would have their children returned. They would be free men and women in Portugal and would not be required to pay the taxes assessed by the King. Despite these enticements, the Jews stood firm and refused to be converted. Then the King ordered that the Jews should be denied bread and water for three days, hoping to facilitate their conversion.

Rabbi Maimi was deeply concerned. While confident that the Jews walled up in Os Estãos could withstand the hardships, the approaching October 31 deadline worried the rabbi. After the deadline the King could make all the Jews in Os Estãos his slaves. Rabbi Maimi summoned other prominent Jewish leaders to join him in a last-chance representation to the King. Among these were Don Abraham Zacuto, Rabbi Abraham Saba, Rabbi Jacob Luel, and three others.

It was Rabbi Maimi who spoke first at the imperial palace.

"Our dear King Manuel, protector of Portugal and all its domains, majestic ruler of Lusitania, we come here as your most humble and devoted servants, eager to learn what it is we must do to regain your royal favor. The events of the day indicate that we have incurred your displeasure, although the cause of your ire is not clear to us. Far be it from us, or from any of the Jewish subjects we represent, to seek the anger of our protector. If it be within our power to do so, we will be the first to fulfill your wish as our very command and so remove the cause of our present discomfiture."

King Manuel said, "Rabbi Maimi, it is within your power alone to spare the Jews of Portugal much suffering. Yes, if you will but listen to what I say to you as your King."

"Speak, my King, all of us are listening with open ears and eager hearts."

The King spoke. "Join us. Become Christians. I will reward each of you handsomely, most handsomely, if you will take the sacred road to baptism. If you, Rabbi Maimi, lead the way, the other Jews will follow. Of this I am sure. If you wish to gain my favor, then this is what you must do."

Rabbi Maimi spoke calmly. "Your Majesty, respectful as I am of your request, however right and well intended it may appear from your perspective, nonetheless I and those with me are beholden to One greater than yourself, to none other than God Almighty, the Holy One of Israel, blessed be He, to whose holy Torah we have committed our lives and our souls. Therefore, I must inform you that, though we do not wish to offend you, it is not within our power to do as you say."

The King looked sternly at Zacuto. "And you, Don Abraham? You do not wish to stay on with us as court astronomer?"

"Not if it means my soul, your Majesty."

"You Jews have souls, do you?," the King snorted in contempt.

"You evidently think so," answered an incensed Rabbi Saba, "insofar as you spend so much of your time devising ways to take them away from us."

Rabbi Maimi raised his hand to silence Rabbi Saba. This was no time to irritate the King.

"Rabbi Saba, I command you to hold your tongue during the rest of these proceedings. You will say no more."

Rabbi Maimi continued, "Your Majesty, if I may be so bold as to remind you of the December 1496 decree which states that you will provide the Jews of your kingdom with vessels of transport to take them safely out of the country, along with all of their belongings. Forgive this most humble servant, your Majesty, for asking this question, yet, if I may be so bold to ask, are the ships being readied for our evacuation prior to the deadline at this month's end?"

"There are no ships being readied," answered the King.

"No ships, your Majesty?"

"You heard correctly, *Arraby Mor.* No ships."

"But, your Majesty, if there are no ships, we cannot leave Portugal before the deadline, and the edict states that all Jews who stay behind will be put to death."

"Yes, that is true, for all those who remain Jews . . ."

"Your Majesty, I am afraid that I do not understand."

"And I am not afraid that you do understand, *Arraby Mor.* I tell it to your face: there will be no more Jews in the kingdom by the end of October. At my command, all Jews will be baptized in the faith of Christ before month's end."

"Your Majesty, surely you cannot mean to do so. It is against the common law of Portugal which you are sworn to uphold."

"I am the law, *Arraby Mor.*"

"But, your Majesty, is it not true that a conversion by force is invalid in the Christian religion? Even in Spain, we were given the option of baptism or exile. Never were we threatened in Spain with violence to effect our conversion. My Spanish coreligionists all chose the path of exile, with many of us thinking ourselves fortunate that we had found a temporary refuge in Portugal. Will you behave in a manner that does injustice to your name and to your religion? Will you, as a faithful Christian, not abide by your word, as you solemnly pledged in the original edict of expulsion, to allow us the option of baptism or exile?"

"Rabbi Maimi, you will find out soon enough what options are indeed left to you. Guards, take this Jew and all those with him to the prison chambers below."

As Rabbi Maimi and his delegation were thrown into the dungeons, the King ordered that all the Jews in Os Estãos should be denied bread and water.

Some Jews converted at this point, seeing a chance to save themselves as well as to reclaim their abducted children. Most, however, could not be induced to do so, much to the displeasure of the King.

Seeing the failure of these milder measures, Manuel gave orders for all remaining Jews to be converted by force. Many were dragged in chains and thrown into the dark dungeons of the royal prison until they saw the light of Christianity. Others were pushed to nearby churches, where they were unwillingly baptized into a faith they abhorred. And so it was done to the thousands of Jews that gathered within the precinct of Os Estãos.

Many of the children of Israel, seeing that there were none who remained unchristened, consulted with one another and proceeded to sanctify the Holy Name. As they were thrust into the churches, many Jews decided to smash the idols of their putative saviors, bringing upon themselves death by burning. This was the martyr's death that the Jews were seeking, a death by which to sanctify the Holy Name.

When King Manuel realized that Jews had found a way to kill themselves, he ordered that any who spoke against the Christian God should not be punished on account of what they were presently being made to suffer. The Jews in turn, realizing that nothing they said or did would be sufficient reason to provoke a punishment by death, hurled themselves from the roofs of the buildings in Os Estãos, falling to their deaths. Others choked themselves or slew one another. Although some Israelites were able to save themselves by such measures, the great mass of Jews were forcibly brought into the Christian fold. These Jewish converts were to be the cause of Portugal's future Converso problem.

Into the dungeons they were cast, scholars and rabbis all, into what Abraham Zacuto described as the netherworld of the Christians, into their dungeons of spiritual eclipse.

Zacuto thought that his pains were endless. Fiendish devices were applied to his arms and legs, racking the bones of his body with harrowing pains. But *what* pains! Pains that made the pounding blood stand still in your temples, agonizing pains that gripped you from head to toe, pains that made you wish you were dead! The pitiless guards did with him as they willed, pummelling him with their fists until his face was swollen to a hideous purple mask. His arms and legs were covered with welts that ached at the slightest touch. All the while he was reminded that all such torture would stop as soon as he accepted the Christian religion. Abraham Zacuto, tormented as he might be, refused. He drew strength and comfort from those, such as the saintly Rabbi Maimi, who with perfect faith could endure every torture of the flesh and of the soul. He, Abraham Zacuto, would strive to do the same.

What these demons did not do to poor Rabbi Maimi! The diabolical guards struck the rabbi with all their might; they beat him with stones; they flayed him with whips; they gagged and choked him; they racked his extremities, until his body was discolored and screaming with pain. Each day he was beaten to a state of unconsciousness. At the end of each day, the limp body of the rabbi was returned to its dreary cell, bloodied and bruised. The soul of Rabbi Maimi came back each night to hearten and strengthen the other rabbis. Abraham Zacuto drew near to the man who had been his dearest friend for five years and found that he needed his friend more than ever. The court astronomer put a blanket under Rabbi Maimi's head and waited patiently for the chief rabbi of Portugal to wake up.

"Rabbi Maimi," he whispered softly. A dark discoloration surrounded the rabbi's left eye; about his nostrils were clots of dark red blood, which made him breathe heavily with a flutter of swollen lips. Rabbi Maimi woke, his eyes still closed, and began his morning prayers.

"I thank thee, living and everlasting King, that thou hast mercifully returned my soul unto me; thy faithfulness in thy servant is great . . ."

Zacuto whispered in his ear. "It is I, Zacuto. Can I get you something?"

Rabbi Maimi thought for a moment. "My *tefillin* and *tallit* . . ." Get them for me, please, Don Abraham."

Zacuto did as the chief rabbi requested. He brought the *tallit*, the tasselled prayer-shawl, and placed it around the rabbi's shoulders. Then he took the *tefillin*, the leather phylacteries, and bound them to the rabbi's blood-stained forehead and right arm.

Rabbi Maimi said weakly, "It is said, Don Abraham, that whoever has *tefillin* on his head and arms and a *tallit* about his shoulders is strengthened against sinning. I pray to Almighty God that I should not sin against His holy Torah and His commandments. I pray to Almighty God for strength and sustenance."

Zacuto muttered, "It is we, not you, who are the weak ones. It is we who are in danger of sinning."

The chief rabbi added, "We are all in danger of sinning, but we may also cause others to sin. If we are weak, our sins, the sins of the few, can become the sins of the many. We must all be strong and of good courage. We must all be ready to sanctify the Holy Name, at the cost of our very lives, if that is the divine will.

Zacuto nodded in agreement. He observed the chief rabbi's recitation of the morning prayers. As the rabbi in front of him was fortified, so, too, was Zacuto. The others in the group, aware of the greater sufferings of the venerable chief rabbi, likewise took strength from the man's example. The seven members of the delegation clung to the Torah and its commandments, fired in their resistance by the perfect example of Rabbi Maimi.

King Manuel was incensed at the obstinance of the Jewish leaders. He ordered the seven to be brought to a nearby church to be forcibly converted. But the seven, though weak in body, were fierce in spirit. And they proclaimed loudly that they wanted nothing to do with the gods of the Gentiles whose gods were not gods and whose truths were not truths. Rabbi Abraham Saba, now unrestrained by the chief rabbi, spoke disdainfully of the Christian religion and smashed the icons in the church. Even Rabbi Maimi, who ordinarily sought to avoid confrontations, spoke out as an angry lion against the King of Portugal and against the Christian religion. The priests in the church were so outraged by the actions and words of the Jews that they urged the King to have them executed.

But the King did not intend to kill the chief rabbi nor his colleagues. The ruler still believed that if the leading Jews of Portugal could be brought to the baptismal font, all the Jews who were converted would be strengthened in their newly adopted faith and the still unconverted Jews would be convinced to convert. Thus he ordered that the seven Jews should not be put to death.

Instead, the Jewish leaders were returned to the castle prison and placed in huge pits. Mud was poured in the pits until it reached their necks. The hole of mud and slime was their new home. Zacuto detested the cold, wet, foul matter on his skin. Worse yet, he detested moving about in his own excreted bodily fluids which mixed freely with the sludge. The foul odor of the pits coupled with weakness from insufficient food and water made it worse, but the seven did not budge. A Catholic priest came down to the malodorous subterranean pits, holding his breath, sprayed them with holy water to effect their conversion. Weak as they were, Zacuto and the rabbis were able to laugh at the priest. Seeing that he was wasting his time, the priest rushed away from the noxious pit area.

When the pits had not had the desired effect, King Manuel had the Jewish leaders washed down and brought to him once again. This time the King promised them rewards.

"Friends, I am willing to give you all that your hearts desire, provided that you listen to me and become Christians. If you, Rabbi Maimi, will do this, I will give you a position higher than all the ministers in this court. And as for the rest of you, I promise to give you high-ranking positions within the kingdom. All this and more!"

The King signaled to his aides to bring in the chests full of gold and silver coins. "Do you see this gold and this silver? This is yours to keep if you will listen to me, this and all the other good things my land has to offer. All I ask of you is that you inform your people that I, the King, mean well for you and that I care for you in wanting you to become Christians. Do this for me, and you shall have all that I have just promised."

It was Rabbi Maimi who spoke out. "Your promises, O King, are as worthless as the original promises that you made to us. You promised to provide us with protection and safe transport to the land of our choosing. You did neither, which means you are a man without honor, a man whose word is not to be trusted. As a liar, you are not worthy to deal in negotiations with men of our caliber. As a King, you are unfit to rule over the beasts of the earth, much less over men and women. And as a practicing Christian, you have given us the best possible reason for not wanting to join the ranks of those such as yourself."

The King was furious. "You insolent Jew! I should have you killed for what you just said!"

The chief rabbi shot back. "Kill me then. I do not fear your threats. If you still harbor the illusion that we can be made to profane our holy Torah, if you think that your dungeons and your guards will make us exchange our religion for yours, then you are indeed a greater fool than I imagined."

The King rose from his chair. "You have gone too far this time, Rabbi. This time your words will cost you dearly . . . You fool, you could have had everything! Take him away to the dungeon!"

With those words, Rabbi Maimi and his comrades were brought back to the dreary depths of the prison. They expected that Rabbi Maimi's answer would bring new punishments for each one of them. Within a matter of hours, the dreaded punishment came. But even the courageous chief rabbi was unprepared for this.

"Sarah!," said a startled Rabbi Maimi as he saw his wife in front of him. "What are you doing here, beloved?"

"Simon! Oh, no!," she gasped, clasping her hands to her horrified face. In her mind she could not connect the battered and bloodied figure standing in front of her with her husband.

"Do not cry, beloved. It is a time for thankfulness. I thank God Almighty that, despite all they did to me, I have not forsaken my people, nor have I swerved from His commandments. I have chosen the way of faithfulness. Strike me though they may, they shall not succeed in weaning me unto falsehood. As I have treasured His Holy Torah always in my heart, as I have delighted in the Law and loved its precepts all the days of my life, so too I shall not depart from the sacred testimonies in these last of my breaths."

Sarah Maimi started to cry, but then caught herself. Her voice broke as she spoke, "Oh, Simon, when I saw you a moment ago, I felt faint. My heart melted at seeing you this way. But your words give me strength. I now realize my eyes deceived me. In the bruised vessel of my husband, I failed to see the pious soul of one who is infinitely greater than his enemies. I see the spirit of that great man, ever kind and pure, whom I have always loved. I see you, Simon Maimi, my beloved, my husband, who is sanctified unto me by all the holy laws of Moses that we hold dear. I see you, Simon Maimi, and I love you . . . I love you more than ever before."

"Sarah, my sweet one, you give me comfort in my affliction. Your words are as balm on my wounds and as sweet honey on my lips. They strengthen my soul. You were beloved unto me on our wedding day, and the passage of time has only served to deepen my affection for you. I too, Sarah, love you more than ever before. We have tasted great joys and endured many hardships. Now we are being asked to endure suffering again. As I once told the couples I married when we were about to leave Segovia, our love is our strength. It is a source of our never-ending power. With our love, however difficult the trial might be, we must be true to ourselves and to the faith of our ancestors."

"Simon . . .," said Sarah, hesitating to speak further, but forcing herself to speak. "Simon, our daughters and grandchildren . . ."

The chief rabbi spoke, "Yes, how are they, Sarah? How are they taking all this?"

"Simon . . .," said Sarah, her voice suddenly subdued and toneless, "The King brought us all here. Our daughters Nehama and Luna, and our sons-in-law, even all our grandchildren, we are all here in the prison."

The chief rabbi closed his eyes, as if gathering strength from meditation.

"I am sorry, Simon. I did not know how to tell you."

Rabbi Maimi opened his sorrow-laden eyes again. "My trial is not yet over, Sarah."

His wife added, "And mine has yet to begin. The guards told me to tell you that if you did not convert, they would torture me and the children. Simon, tell me, what must I do?"

Rabbi Maimi spoke assuringly, "You will do what every daughter and woman in Israel is expected to do. You will be strong and of good courage. Though your life and that of your children be in the shadow of death, you will stand firm in the faith of our fathers. Trust in the Lord God of Israel and His saving power. Make unto Him a freewill offering of your flesh. Incline your soul unto Him to receive His holy light so that we may together proclaim His glorious mercy forever and ever. Sarah, do you not see? All our lives have been but a preparation leading to this final chapter in our earthly existence. Crown your life of virtue and piety with an act of limitless devotion, and earn for yourself a goodly place in the world to come. Sanctify the name of the Holy One of Israel, blessed be He, if and when your time should come. That, my dear Sarah, is what you must do."

Sarah nodded her head in silent understanding. After a reflective moment, she came up to her husband and tenderly kissed him on his bruised forehead. "Farewell, beloved. You know how much I love you."

The chief rabbi reciprocated the kiss. "Farewell, dear Sarah. May the Lord God shine His countenance upon thee and give thee peace."

While they were still facing each other, Sarah called out, "Guard, we are ready."

A Portuguese guard came out to the cell area. "You are ready to convert, both of you?"

"Never! So help us God!," was Sarah's instant reply.

Sarah Maimi was chained to the rack and tortured in the chief rabbi's presence. Every evil contraption known to man was applied to her, provoking her to agony, as her husband helplessly looked on. As she was being tortured, the guards would turn to Rabbi Maimi and ask if he wanted to convert. The answer, as always, was an emphatic "no." The torture was then allowed to continue. Sarah's arms were alternately stretched and squeezed; hot coals were applied to her exposed flesh; her head was beaten, this and more; yet all was without effect. Sarah Maimi was steadfast in her faith, alongside her husband. The guards, realizing she was as tough and inflexible as the chief rabbi himself, decided to kill her. Rabbi Maimi was asked one last time if he was willing to change his faith. The answer was again "no." Sarah Maimi was then pinned on the rack, and a sword was driven through her heart. She expired quickly, the blood gushing freely from her chest. Her body was then removed from the rack and placed at the feet of a sobbing Rabbi Maimi.

But the chief rabbi hardly had time to weep over the loss of his wife. Anguish overtook him as his two daughters and sons-in-law were dragged into the dungeon. Before Rabbi Maimi's eyes, they were beaten and savagely tortured just as his wife had been. One by one, they were slaughtered and placed alongside him in a ring of his own flesh and blood. Finally, his grandchildren were subjected to the vicious blows of the jailers, and they too were murdered. The tiny limp corpses of the children were thrown atop the mound of death. Rabbi Simon Maimi was all alone, his soul overwhelmed with grief.

His sufferings were not yet over. Along with the other rabbis and scholars, Rabbi Maimi was removed from the prison and, in full public view, was pulled by his feet into the central courtyard. A rope, attached to the tail of a horse, was wound about his wrists. As the animal was whipped into motion, the chief rabbi fell forward. The horse galloped through the prison gates, carrying with it the torso of Simon Maimi, and flung its human burden against the cobblestone rocks. Each stone etched its mark on his bruised face and gouged out strips of flesh from his chest. Dangling uncontrollably from a rope, he twisted and turned endlessly as he was dragged through the filthy slime-filled streets of Lisbon. Slithering across a muddy intersection, Rabbi Maimi was hurled into a signpost. The brutal impact of the collison broke his ribs, and he lost consciousness. The limp discolored creature, its shredded skin covered with blood and dirt, was brought next to the corral of Os Estãos.

The few Jews still in Os Estãos were dumbfounded by what had befallen their beloved chief rabbi. A strange and profound silence overtook them — louder than the loudest scream, it testified to their unspeakable misfortune. They crawled to the edge of the corral and remained there motionless.

The prison guards made the horse go round and round, with the eyes of the Jews following its motion. The saintly bloodied figure was steadily ground into the dirt, his corpus of flesh and bone leaving a well-grooved circular trail in the earth underneath. Then, no longer able to bear witness, the doleful eyes looked away.

The guards placed the mangled body of Rabbi Maimi within a pillory in the area facing Os Estãos. Then they brought the other six Jewish leaders to the pillory. At first, none of the other leaders recognized the creature whose head and hands protruded through the holes of the structure. And then understanding came in a jarring flash.

An incredulous Abraham Zacuto, his head twisting to get a better look at their leader, screamed in disbelief. "Aaaya! Rabbi Maimi, is that you? Can you hear me? Rabbi . . . Rabbi Maimi? Can you hear us? Answer us if you can. It is I, Zacuto."

The bloodstained creature did not answer, nor did it breathe or move. Zacuto screamed at the guards, "What have you done, you savages of Christ? What has this man done to you that you beat him so? Why, why, in God's name, why? Tell me, you god-forsaken murderers! Tell me of your love that is not love. Yes, tell me of your god that is no god. Yes, tell me all your lies so I can laugh in your face. Because next to me is a man that lived and died as no other. Yet he lives within all of us. From him and from you, we have learned that Christianity is not the answer, but rather is the root and cause of our suffering. Come, you Christian hypocrites, tell us why you beat him out of love."

The guards laughed in the distance at the rantings of Zacuto. Zacuto tried uselessly to free himself from the wooden pillory. Rabbi Saba next to him offered a prayer for the dead. "Zacuto, calm yourself. All of you, join me in honoring our beloved teacher who in his death, as in his saintly life, led us down the paths of truth and righteousness. Happy is he who is upright in the ways of Torah, who walks in the law of the Lord. Happy is he who keeps the sacred testimonies and is faithful to the Holy One of Israel with his whole heart and soul. Did not the Psalmist say that God's anger is but for a moment, and that His favor is for a lifetime? Let us weep for the night, but salvation shall await us in the morning. My brothers, repeat after me. *Yitgadal veyitkadash . . .*"

The corraled Jews of Os Estãos listened to the laments of the *Kadish* dirge. It was Rabbi Saba who gave the eulogy:

"The wise and pious God-fearing Rabbi Maimi has been taken from us. There was no evil in him all of his days. He was a true disciple of Aaron, one who loved people and pursued peace. All of us have seen how the hand of Esau was lifted up and how it mightily struggled to snatch away his soul. Yet the soul of the *Arraby Mor* could not be delivered over unto the will of his adversaries. His soul, unable to bear false witness against itself, shall now be as a bundle of life with the Lord our God."

Zacuto added, "He gave us strength to withstand our trial and taught us that the sins of the few can become the sins of the many. We are fortunate that this righteous man, this *tzadik*, this saint for all ages, has been the lamp unto our feet. In the appointed hour of our death, he has caused our faces to shine with the gladness of salvation. Though our bodies languish with affliction, he has given us a foretaste of the waters of deliverance. We shall take refuge in the Lord, and glorify Him, as long as we breathe in the presence of the living."

As night came, three hunched figures crept into the pillory area. Sneaking past the guards, whispering softly, they came to the wooden structure and cut off the lock on the main beam.

"Who are you? What are you doing?", asked Zacuto.

A muted voice in the dark answered. "Silence. We are taking the body of the *Arraby Mor* to be buried in a secret location according to Jewish law."

"Take him, and leave him not to his oppressors," answered Zacuto softly. Rabbi Maimi's lifeless body was carefully lifted out of the pillory and wrapped in a quilt. Zacuto overheard the whispers. One spoke of taking the body to a nearby cave or vault, another of how to elude the guards at the nearby corral. Moments passed. The muted voices became silent again. Carrying the blanketed figure, the three faded quietly into the darkness of the night.

In the pillory at Os Estãos, the leaders were pinioned for seven days and seven nights, with only crumbs of bread to eat and handfuls of water to drink. Zacuto was fading; his dry, parched mouth was raw, his eyes dim. His flaccid extremities were thinned down to the point that he could almost slip his hands out of the pillory hole. If he could only lose his head, all would be well! Madness would be a welcome release. Weak as he was, he could still sense what was happening about him. Two of his pilloried companions died from starvation and thirst.

"May the memory of their saintly souls . . .", Zacuto slowly formed the thought, ". . . be enshrined forever."

The King then ordered the remaining four scholars, including Zacuto, to be placed in a ship without food or water. The ship, without oars or sails, would be cast into the sea to wander aimlessly. At the port,

Abraham Zacuto was asked one last time to convert. He answered, "You fools, do you think that I would exchange eternal life for an extra hour on this earth? Would I exchange my best clothes and garments for those that are shabby and torn? Nay, it is better to die than to live." The port officials, sensing the scholars' readiness to die, spoke no more. Following the King's command, Zacuto and the other rabbis were taken to the middle of the sea and left there to die.

Zacuto found it ironic that he, a student of the sea, should find his final rest in such unchosen waters. He, deviser of the copper astrolabe, was left stranded in an unnavigable ship. He, the famed compiler of astronomical tables, could now look upon the heavens no longer as objects of curiosity, but as muted witnesses to the end of his days.

But it was not to be. A wayward eastern wind blew the ship into the path of a Moorish vessel. The four enfeebled survivors were hauled aboard and taken to the nearby shores of Morocco. Given food and water, their strength was restored as was their faith in the wondrous workings of the Lord. Later, when they arrived in Fez, they were hailed by one and all in a tumultous welcome. The elders of the city, the rich and the poor, all came to honor the famed four survivors.

The days of Abraham Zacuto were not yet at an end. Soon the one-time court astronomer would find himself in Tunisia, working on his book of Hebrew genealogies, the *Sefer Yuhasin*, a scholarly endeavor which had occupied his attention for the past few years. It would be his token of repayment unto the Lord of all existence for His gracious kindness. For those scholars who came after him, it would be his navigational guide to the sea of human characters that populated the Bible and Talmud.

Chapter 19

For Gracia Pardo it was the beginning of the redemption. The Ottoman Empire welcomed her and her children, Rebecca and Haim. Indeed, it welcomed all the harassed and oppressed members of her people. A friendly new world opened up to the persecuted Spanish exiles, many of them as destitute and ill as they had been five years ago. Here in the land of the Turks, all the cities of the empire were open to Jewish settlement. There were no distinguishing badges, no restrictions on travel, no confining ghettoes, no Inquisition, no popular malice, no limitations on their religion. Even the Sultan himself, Bayezid II, had proclaimed the death punishment to anyone who mistreated the Jews or did them harm. When the Sultan heard about the skills and talents of the Jewish refugees, he said, "The King of Spain is a fool because he impoverishes his kingdom and enriches mine."

Gracia Pardo had much to be thankful for. She and her children were brought to Salonica through the intervention of the noble Italian, Captain Panzarella, who rescued them from the forsaken island of lions. The local community of Salonica showed its appreciation by holding a feast in honor of the Italian mariner, after which the captain and his crew respectfully took their leave.

The assistance that Gracia received from the local community was equally welcome. Gracia and her two children were given food and shelter. Everywhere she went, from one terraced house to the other, or even as she walked to the outlying sea walls of the city and its fortified towers, she could feel the mutual concern for the welfare of one's fellow Jews. It was one Jew helping another, those already established welcoming the newcomers and inviting them into their homes, brothers and sisters in Israel united by their common love for their dispersed brethren. Most helpful was Rabbi Moses Capsali, chief rabbi of Constantinople, who organized the relief effort on behalf of the incoming exiles. He went from city to city, from Salonica to Edirne and to Izmir and other places, alerting the existing communities to their responsibilities. She heard that in Istanbul, where the chief rabbi lived, there were already more than forty synagogues and she wondered what it would be like to live in the bustling metropolis of the Ottoman Turkish Empire.

She was happy to be in Salonica now. There were only a few thousand Jews when she arrived in the city, most of them Yiddish-speaking Ashkenazim from the north along with several hundred Romaniot and Catalan Jews. But this was all changed. All ports of call in the Mediterranean knew that Salonica welcomed the scattered exiles from Spain. In response to this, the exiles came first in a trickle, then in progressive waves swelling the streets of Salonica with the sonorous dialects of Iberia.

The exiles came from all over. There were the stubborn and traditionalist Aragonese Jews, withdrawn and insular. There were Jews from Mallorca, Navarre, Sicily, and Portugal. Of the energetic and hardworking Catalans, successful in any business enterprise, it was said, '*Los catalanes de las piedras sacan panes*'. 'The Catalans make bread out of stones.' The humble Jews of Galicia, most of them unlettered peasants, accustomed to performing menial tasks in Spain, continued to do the same. Then there were the Jews of Castile, proud and educated, experienced in finance and scholarship. So important was the Castilian presence that their dialect became the vernacular within a few years. Castilian Jews dominated the community, became the heads of rabbinical seminaries, assumed positions of leadership, and directed the developing commercial forces that were to make Salonica into a major trade center. Gracia Pardo, being a Castilian, although a poor one at that, nonetheless took pride in being a member of the dominant group in Salonica.

Even the few hundred Turkish families that lived in the high city were overshadowed by the newly arrived Spanish Jews. Turks, Armenians, Greeks — all took second place to the Israelites who now predominated in this ancient Macedonian city. Salonica became a Jewish city or, as the popular saying would soon have it, it had become a mother-city in Israel.

Everywhere Gracia Pardo went, she heard the language of Castile. At weddings and festive occasions, she heard the sweet songs and romanzas of Segovia, strummed on a mandolin. In business and pleasure, with strangers and with friends, she always conversed in her native tongue, forgetting at times that she was no longer in Spain. Even the local Turks and Greeks were beginning to use the language. Here in the outskirts of the Ottoman Empire, far away from Spain, they created their own Jewish version of Spanish life. They kept the customs, the songs, the ballads, even the language of Old Spain but without any of its Christian trappings. It was a new and better life here in the Ottoman Turkish Empire, a life which they would fashion to their inner callings and sentiments.

Rebecca, her widowed daughter, was making a good living embroidering the fancy cloaks and capes of her Castilian customers. Time had lessened the intense sorrow of her daughter's grief. Rebecca did not forget Benito, God bless his soul, but she no longer rejected the prospect of remarriage. Haim, her little one, was little no longer. A strapping twelve-year old, he made himself useful on the docks, helping the stevedores load and unload the ships that came to call at port. Even she, Gracia Pardo, found intermittent work cleaning the homes of the wealthy. She was happy with her lot in life which, though small, was secure. The Castilian proverb said it all. *En lo que estamos, bendigamos.* 'What we have, we shall bless.'

And to Gracia Pardo, being free to live as a Jew in Salonica was the most blessed lot of all.

*   *   *   *   *

It was a mystery to Hacham Alhadeff why he had survived when the others had perished. Why had he been spared?, he asked himself time and again. Why had his loved ones been ravished by the beasts of the earth, while he had been rescued not once, but twice, from the grip of the angel of death? On the desert sands of Morocco, had he not been brought back to life by a passing caravan of Jewish exiles? In the fiery blaze at Fez, had he not escaped a death by burning thanks to the bravery of the Moroccan merchant, Ohana? Had he not been nurtured back to health as a result of the tender ministrations of the caring Amelia Tarica?

In all these efforts to save him, Hacham Alhadeff saw the mysterious workings of the Holy One of Israel. He was alive for a purpose, a reason, a sacred calling that still eluded him. With each passing day, the urge to elucidate the mystery of the purpose of his earthly existence grew stronger. During moments of prayer and thoughtful solitude, he searched frantically within himself for the answer that never came. At other times, he would walk the streets of Fez accosting rabbis, hoping that they might guide him to enlightenment.

The inklings of an answer came to the Hacham from a blind Moroccan rabbi who was no stranger to life's sufferings. The eyes of this wizened old rabbi, seeing nothing, somehow saw the Hacham's torment, saw where the key to the mystery was concealed.

"My son," the sightless rabbi said, "the secret which you seek is disclosed only to the wise ones who know the secrets of the Zohar. It is they who give all their mind and all their being to the contemplation of the Divine Presence, seeking the illumination and radiance of the All-Hidden Holy One. Pure of spirit, righteous in their ways, these lovers of the Torah have gathered in the land of Israel in a place called Safad. Together, they have learned the secret of separating the soul from the body. They have learned how to ascend unto the celestial spheres and the firmaments. They have learned how to penetrate into the Palace of Love which sits amidst a vast rock in a most secret and highly placed firmament. And there, in this Palace of Love, are kept the treasured souls of those loved by the Holy One of Israel, blessed be He. There in this Palace of Love, should you be deemed worthy to enter it, there and only there shall you find the answers that you seek."

The blind rabbi said no more. Pounding the walking stick ahead of him, he disappeared in the din of the *mellah*, his truth half-disclosed, the Hacham's inner sight half-restored.

The Hacham found half of his answer. He decided to emigrate to the holy land of Israel and to join the mystical ranks of those who contemplated the Divine in the Galilean city of Safad. Thanking all who had restored him to health, the Hacham bade farewell to his dear friends in Fez.

Sailing to Egypt, he stopped over in Cairo for a few days to enjoy the company of the growing community of Spanish Jewish exiles who had settled there. He continued his eastward journey on an old Turkish vessel that was headed for the port city of Jaffa. When he disembarked from the ship a few days later, he prostrated himself and kissed the hallowed earth of his ancestral homeland. In a strange way, he felt very much at home.

Safad was a city perched high in the mountains of the upper Galilee. Its air was cool and thin. Above the city hovered silvery puffs of glistening clouds that allowed shafts of light to stream down to the grassy slopes below. To the south were the soft blue waters of the sea of Galilee. And within Safad itself, the orange-hued stone tenements harbored a vibrant Sephardi population which saddled up and down its muddy streets. The newcomers traded in cheese, oil, honey, and spices. Using wool from the Merino sheep that the exiles had brought with them from Spain, they manufactured cloths and garments.

Yet the real business of this mountain city was the Kabbala, the mystical lore of the Jews, which was cultivated in all its eight synagogues. Hacham Alhadeff joined the pious sages of Safad in donning the silken prayer shawls and phylacteries, learning to pray as they did, sometimes in isolation, often at night amidst a multitude of brightly lit candles. He learned the names of the ten *Sefirot*. He meditated upon the many names of the Holy One and the secrets they conveyed. He received special instruction about divine illumination and how the soul could free itself from the body. As he mastered the secret wisdom, he felt a growing sense of moral perfection — the love of one's neighbors, the conquest of the evil impulse, the true comprehension of the inner meaning of the commandments of the Torah, the path offered by the love of God.

Dressed always in white, Hacham Alhadeff began his self-purification by eating and drinking little. He felt his soul gain strength as his body weakened. Day by day, his concentration intensified as he grew stronger in Kabbalah, purer in thought, and happier in spirit. 'Happy are they who walk in the way of truth', he repeated unto himself. By others he was told, quoting the Zohar, "To God there is no joy save in the souls of the righteous. Only the souls of the righteous here on earth can stir the love of the community of Israel for God." And, as the daily prayer of the *Shema* enjoined him to do, he loved God 'with all his heart and all his soul and all his might.' Days evolved into months, and Hacham Alhadeff evolved into a rarefied being which spent its days in a trance-like state of ecstatic contemplation, a being become an alien to its own body.

And then the Hacham knew his body no more. It was on the eve after the Sabbath when it happened. He felt his body leave him or, rather, his soul disengage itself from his body. He was a free spirit, finally and utterly.

His filmy wisp of a self hovered over its flesh and blood counterpart, contemplating that static vessel which no longer held him captive. In an instant he ascended through the unresisting roof, taking note of the patch-roofed homes of a sleeping Safad. In a slow rising twist, he spiraled his way through the overhanging moon-drenched clouds. Higher and higher he went, beyond the vapors of the earth, unto the celestial spheres in all their radiant glory.

Guided upwards by some unseen force, his soul sailed through a region of connected pearls, all the shiny orbs rotating on their axes behind a shimmering translucent veil. Comprehension came to him: the lower treasury of souls unblemished by sin, souls deserving of ascent unto the first firmament.

He levitated above this region, gliding like a buoyant bubble borne by the winds of heaven. Above him was stretched a raiment of undulating liquid gold, each wave quivering in the light that shone from above. His spirit unfurled, he sailed effortlessly through the glittering sheet-like expanse into the next higher level.

Pulsating celestial spheres, intermittently emanating a distinct bluish-white brilliance, towards the soft stream of radiant light from above. Another thought: carrier forms achieving geometric perfection, altering their form as the souls bound within them achieved a perfect understanding of the workings of the Holy One, blessed be He.

A vast transparent rock-like structure separated the highest firmament from those below. Beyond the last firmament was the ever-present brilliance, the inexhaustible fountain of light, the creator of all beings, the radiance of all radiances, the Holy One of Israel, formless and limitless, attended to by the ministrations of a host of angels moving to and fro along spoke-like beams of light that emerged from the blinding central emanation.

Off to the side stood a magnificent structure in the uppermost mists of the seventh heaven, its pillars dazzling white. The Palace of Love! Here the treasures of the king of kings were kept, here the love of the Holy One was dispensed to the blessed souls who graced its sacred precinct. The soul of Hacham Alhadeff drifted to its new heavenly home, his soul gathered unto the presence of the Holy One amidst the holiest of his people.

Basking in the divine effulgence, his soul beheld yet another nearby presence. Morenica and little Iziko and Aaron, they were all with him! He had found his sweet ones, and they had found him, and the Holy One of Israel had found them all worthy to be placed at the highest level of the righteous ones of Israel. O, the wondrous working of the divine ways! O, praised be the God of the heavens, hallejuyah!, whose sublime mysteries were beyond comprehension. In the loftiest abode of the spirit eternal, the Hacham repeated joyously the declaration of faith that he had once made on the burning sands of the earth. "Blessed be the Judge of Truth," he declared in the Palace of Love, the mystery of his survival now become clear to him.

*   *   *   *   *

The fall of Naples came soon after the death of King Ferrante in 1494, when Charles VIII of France invaded Italy. As the French armies closed in on the Neapolitan city, Alfonso, Ferrante's son and successor, fled to the island of Sicily. Alfonso pleaded with Don Isaac Abravanel to accompany him, and feeling a strong sense of obligation, Don Isaac agreed to join the King in exile. He remembered the many times that 'Old Ferrante' had come to the aid of the Jews and, at the height of the plague, had refused to allow harm to come to them. As Ferrante aided the Jews in a time of affliction, so too Don Isaac would help Ferrante's son in his time of need.

In Sicily, Don Isaac received many disturbing reports about the French occupation of Naples. French soldiers aided the local populace in a full-scale attack upon the Jewish quarter. Thousands of Jews were murdered or sold into slavery, and others were being forcibly converted. At Don Isaac's urging, the entire Abravanel family fled Naples, as did several thousand of the surviving Neapolitan Jews. Don Isaac's youngest son was studying in a yeshiva in Salonica; his other son Joseph headed for Venice, whereas Judah decided to practice medicine in Genoa. Although their home in Naples had been ransacked and most of his vast personal library had been destroyed, Don Isaac thanked the Lord that his wife Esther was unhurt and that she was planning to leave for Salonica. Nor did he forget his grandchild who had been seized and baptized by the King of Portugal. A secret plan was devised by Abravanel and his aides to discover where the child was and to set him free from his captors, and to return the infant to the proper fold of Israel.

Abravanel stayed with the royal family of Naples when it moved to Messina, remaining there until the death of Alfonso in 1495. From Messina he went to the island of Corfu, where he met many Spanish Jews on their way to Turkey. It was on Corfu that he began to write his commentary on Isaiah, prompted as he was by the events of the day to reexamine Israel's hopes for national redemption and its messianic salvation.

The French surrendered in 1496 to the combined forces of Spain, the Emperor, the Papal States, Venice and Milan. Although Don Isaac was tempted to return to Naples, he decided instead to settle in the small town of Monopoli, deeming the time to be the proper moment in his life to devote himself exclusively to his religious and philosophical writing. He had crossed the elusive border again, disengaged himself utterly from the stifling harness of politics, and rerouted his existence to the pursuit of pious scholarship. It was, in his mind, Segura de la Orden all over again.

Don Isaac wrote much over the next few years: commentaries on Deuteronomy, on the Passover *Haggadah*, on the ethics in the Talmudic tractate of *Avot*, as well as the messianic trilogy, *Ma'ayenei ha-Yeshuah* (Wells of Salvation), *Mashmi'a Yeshua* (Announcer of Salvation), and *Yeshu'ot Meshiho* (Salvations of His Anointed). In the trilogy he described the messianic elements of the coming world order: the fall of Christendom, the resurrection of Israel, the ingathering of the exiles to the Holy Land in Palestine, the judgment at the End of Days under the princely rule of the Jewish Messiah, the restoration of nature to its primeval state, humanity's final attainment of moral and spiritual perfection, and Israel's metamorphosis into the prophesied Holy People of God.

350

REFERENCES
ORIGINAL MEDIEVAL DOCUMENTS

Abravanel, Isaac. *Perush al Nebiim Rishonim* (Commentary on Kings).

Bernaldez, Andrés. *Historia de los Reyes Católicos Don Fernando y Doña Isabel*. Vol. I. Sevilla, 1870.

Capsali, Elijayu. *Seder Eliyahu Zuta*. (Transcribed by A. Shmuelevitz). Ben-Zvi Institute, Jerusalem, 1975.

Colmenares, Diego De. *La Historia de la Insigne Ciudad de Segovia*. 1640.

Ha-Cohen, Yosef. *Emek Ha-Bakha*. (Spanish trans. by Pilar Leon Tello), Instituto Arias Montano (C.S.I.C.), Madrid.

Hayat, Judah. *Ma-arekhet Ha-Elohut* (excerpted in Haim Beinart's *Be-Ikvot Anusim u-Megorashim*, Hebrew University).

Ibn Verga, Solomon. *Shebet Yehudah*, Ed. A. Shochat, Jerusalem, 1947.

Ibn Yahya, Gedaliah. *Shalshelet ha-Kabbalah*. Hadorot Harishonim, Jerusalem, 1962.

Marcus, Jacob R. (Editor). *The Jew in the Medieval World. A Source Book: 315-1791*, (Documents: 'The Expulsion from Spain, 1492', 'The Spanish Inquisition at Work, 1568), Harper Torchbooks, 1965.

Pulgar, Hernando de. *Crónica de los Reyes Católicos*, Madrid, 1953.

Saba, Abraham. *Tseror ha-Mor*, ed. 1586. Jerusalem.

Schwartz, Leo W. (Editor). *Memoirs of My People* (Document: 'Twilight of Spanish Glory', by Don Isaac Abravanel), Schocken Books, 1963.

Seneraga, B. *Commentaria de rebus genuensibus*, in Muratori, Rerum italicarum scriptores, t. xxiv, col. 531. (As quoted by W.H. Prescott.)

Solomon (of Torrutiel), Abraham ben. *Sefer ha-Kabbalah*, (in Adolf Neubauer's *Medieval Jewish Chronicles*, Oxford, 1887).

Suarez Fernández, Luis (Editor). *Documentos Acerca de la Expulsión de los Judíos*. Biblioteca "Reyes Católicos" (C.S.I.C.), Valladolid, 1964.

Usqué, Samuel. *Consolation for the Tribulations of Israel* (translated from Portuguese by Martin A. Cohen), Jewish Publication Society (J.P.S.), 1965.

Zurita, Jerónimo. *Anales de la Corona de Aragón*, Libros IX-XX. Institución "Fernando el Católico" (C.S.I.C.), Zaragoza, 1977.

Cronicón de Valladolid. "Documentos Inéditos para la Historia de España", Vol. 13, Madrid, 1848.

MODERN HISTORICAL WORKS

Abrahams, Israel. *Jewish Life in the Middle Ages*. Atheneum, New York, 1969.

Amicis, Edmondo de. *Morocco: Its People and Places*, Vol. I-II, Philadelphia, 1897. (Trans. Maria Hornor Lansdale.)

Angel, Marc D. *The Jews of Rhodes*. Sepher-Hermon Press, New York, 1978.

Baer, Yitzhak. *A History of the Jews in Christian Spain*, Vol. I & II, Jewish Publication Society, 1961.

Barnett, Richard D. *The Sephardic Heritage*. Ktav Publishing House, New York, 1971.

Benardete, Mair Jose. *Hispanic Culture and Character of the Sephardic Jews*. Sepher-Hermon Press, 1982.

Beinart, Haim. *Trujillo: A Jewish Community in Extremadura on the Eve of the Expulsion from Spain*. Magnes Press, Hebrew University, Jerusalem, 1980.

Bernis, Carmen. *Trajes y Modas en la España de los Reyes Católicos*. I. *Las Mujeres*. II. *Los Hombres*, Instituto Diego Velazquez (C.S.I.C.), Madrid, 1978-79.

Beton, Sol. *Sephardim and a History of Congregation Or VeShalom*, Walton Press. Monroe, Georgia, 1981.

Bokser, Ben Zion. *The Jewish Mystical Tradition*. Pilgrim Press, New York, 1981.

Cantera Burgos, Francisco. *Abraham Zacut*, M. Aguilar, Editor, Madrid.

Cantera Burgos, F. and Carlos Carrete Parrondo, *Las Juderías Medievales en la Provincia de Guadalajara*, SEFARAD, XXXIII-XXXIV (1973-1974), Madrid.

Castro, Américo. *The Spaniards*. Univ. of California Press, Berkeley, 1971. (Trans. W.F. King and S. Margaretten.)

Corcos, David. *Studies in the History of the Jews of Morocco*. Rubin Mass, Jerusalem, 1976.

Croce, Benedetto. *History of the Kingdom of Naples*. (Trans. Frances Frenaye, sixth ed.), Univ. Chicago Press, 1965.

De Los Ríos, Amador. *Historia Social, Política y Religiosa de los Judíos de España y Portugal*, Aguilar, S.A. de Ediciones, Madrid, 1960.

Defourneaux, Marcelin. *Daily Life in Spain in the Golden Age*. Stanford Univ. Press, 1966. (Trans. Newton Branch.)

Erskine, Stewart and Fletcher, Benton. *The Bay of Naples*. A.C. Black, London, 1926.

Fernández-Armesto, Felipe. *Ferdinand and Isabella*. Taplinger Publishing Co., New York, 1975.

Gerber, Jane S. *Jewish Society in Fez: 1450-1700*. Vol. VI, Jewish Studies in Modern Times (Edit. Jacob Neusner), Leiden (E.J. Brill), 1980.

Graetz, Heinrich. *History of the Jews*. Vol. IV, Jewish Publication Society, 1894.

Herculano, Alexandre. *History of the Origin and Establishment of the Inquisition in Portugal*. Ktav Publishing House, New York, 1972. (Trans. John C. Branner, Prolegomenon by Y.H. Yerushalmi.)

Irving, Washington. *The Conquest of Granada*. 2 Vols.

Kamen, Henry. *The Spanish Inquisition*. New American Library, 1975.

Lea, Henry C. *A History of the Inquisition of Spain*. New York, 1906.

Levy, Abraham. *Court Rabbis in 14th and 15th Century Castile*. Doctoral thesis, University of London, unpublished.

Levy, Isaac. *Chants Judeo-Espagnols*. World Sephardi Federation, London, 1959.

Lindo, Haim. *The History of the Jews in Spain and Portugal*. London, 1848.

Lunenfeld, Martin. *The Council of the Santa Hermandad*. Univ. of Miami Press, 1970.

Mariejol, Jean Hippolyte. *The Spain of Ferdinand and Isabella*. (Trans. Benjamin Keen.) Rutgers Univ. Press, New Brunswick, N.J., 1961.

Margolis, Max and Marx, Alexander. *History of the Jewish People*. Jewish Publication Society, New York, 1960.

Marques, A.H. de Oliveira. *Daily Life in Portugal in the Late Middle Ages*. (Trans. S.S. Wyatt), Univ. of Wisconsin Press, 1971.

Martínez Sopena, Pascual. *El Estado Señorial de Medina de Rioseco bajo el Almirante Alfonso Enriquez (1389-1430)*, Universidad de Valladolid, 1977.

Minkin, Jacob S. *Abarbanel and the Expulsion of the Jews from Spain*. Behrman Press, 1938.

Molho, Michael. *Usos y Costumbres de los Sefardíes de Salonica*. Instituto Arias Montano (C.S.I.C.), Madrid, 1950.

Morison, Samuel Eliot. *Christopher Columbus, Mariner*. New American Library.

_____. *Admiral of the Ocean Sea: A History of Christopher Columbus*, 1946.

Nehama, Joseph. *Histoire Des Israelites de Salonique*. Tome II, Libraire Molho, Salonica, 1935.

Netanyahu, Benzion. *Don Isaac Abravanel*. Jewish Publication Society, Third Ed., 1972.

Pearl, Chaim. *The Medieval Jewish Mind: The Religious Philosophy of Isaac Arama*, Hartmore House, Connecticut, 1972.

Pérez Embid, F. *El Almirantazgo de Castilla Hasta las Capitulaciones de Santa Fe*. Universidad de Sevilla, 1944.

Prescott, William H. *History of the Reign of Ferdinand and Isabella the Catholic*. Philadelphia and London, 1837, J.P. Lippincott Co.

Roth, Cecil. *The Spanish Inquisition*. W.W. Norton & Co., New York, 1964.

_____. *A History of the Marranos*. Schocken Books, New York, 1974.

_____. *The History of the Jews of Italy*. Philadelphia, 1946.

_____. *The Jews in the Renaissance*. Philadelphia, 1959.

Rubens, Alfred. *A History of Jewish Costume*. Crown Publishers, New York, 1973.

Scholem, Gershom. *Zohar: The Book of Splendor*. Schocken Books, New York, 1963.

Silver, Abba Hillel. *Where Judaism Differed*. Macmillan Co. New York, 1972.

Smith, Bradley. *Spain: A History in Art*. Doubleday, New York.

Smith, Homer. *Man and His Gods*. Grosset & Dunlap, New York, 1971.

Starkie, Walter. *Grand Inquisitor*. Hodder and Stoughton, London, 1940.

Stewart, Desmond. *The Alhambra: A History of Islamic Spain*, Newsweek Book Division, New York, 1974.

Torroba B. de Quirós, Felipe. *The Spanish Jews*. Meridian Books, New York, 1961. (Trans. John I. Palmer)

Valbuena Prat, Angel. *La Vida Cotidiana en el Siglo de Oro*. Editorial Alberto Martin, Barcelona.

Wiesenthal, Simon. *Sails of Hope*. Macmillan Publishing Co.

Wright, Esmond (Editor). *The Medieval and Renaissance World*. Chartwell Books, 1979.

Other reference works consulted on various topics include the *Encyclopaedia Judaica, Catholic Encyclopedia, Blue Guides* on Spain and Southern Italy, and the *Me'Am Loez (Avot)*.

AUTHOR'S NOTE

To a large degree, this novel is based upon historical fact and historical figures. Many of the accounts provided by the medieval chroniclers of the era, both Jewish and Christian, have been integrated into the body of the work. A few comments follow which illustrate the manner in which original sources and modern-day scholarly works have been utilized.

The partial Jewish origin of Ferdinand is of scholarly interest. As the foremost Spanish scholar Américo Castro writes in *The Spaniards* (pp. 72-73), "We may add that John II of Aragon took Doña Juana Henríquez, the daughter of the admiral mentioned above, as his second wife, so that their son Ferdinand the Catholic turns out to be Jewish on his mother's side."

F. Pérez Embid, in his study of the admiralty of Castile, identifies the illegitimate progenitor in Ferdinand's ancestry as his great-grandfather Don Alonso Enríquez. Certain quoted accounts allude to the involvement of the Master of Santiago, Don Fadrique, Alonso's father, with a certain married Jewish woman who was called 'la Paloma' and who lived in the village of Llerena. With regard to the identity of the mother of Don Alonso, P. Martínez Sopena in translation sums it up thus, ". . . the person of (Alonso's) mother remains relegated to the circuit of hypothesis. It does not cease to be curious that the most ancient testimonies, almost contemporary ones, indicate that she was a Jewess."

It is Elijah Capsali who provides the Hebrew account of Ferdinand's Jewish origin, his nickname, and his secret rendezvous with Isabella in Valladolid. Capsali's source is a certain Rabbi Jacob to whose home Ferdinand first came in search of his Castilian bride-to-be. Capsali writes: "And the King came secretly to the border of Castile, and he did not take with him but seven men. And he estranged himself from his aides and disguised himself in shabby clothes, and he walked slowly. And he came to the house of a certain Rabbi Jacob, a sharp and most clever person, and I have seen this man. He was among the exiles and he sat at our table, and from his mouth he told me all this which I am now writing with ink in the book." Capsali also discusses the specific involvement of Don Abraham Senior in the encounter. Pulgar provides a similar account of the Valladolid meeting, emphasizing the role of Archbishop Carrillo and other courtiers.

Don Abraham Senior was appointed as *juez mayor* or Chief Judge of the Jews by Ferdinand and Isabella. It has traditionally been maintained that Senior was the court rabbi at the time of the expulsion. In his doctoral thesis, Abraham Levy maintains that "In no official Spanish document prior to the Expulsion is Senior either given the title of Rabbi, nor is he described as holding the office of Rab as is the case with every other Court Rabbi in Castile." It has been pointed out by Levy that Senior's two predecessors as *juez mayor*, Shemaya Lubel and Jacob Ibn Nuñez, were not rabbis but rather Jewish communal leaders with juridical and tax collection responsibilities. It is this characterization of Senior as a non-rabbi that has been followed herein. Meir Melamed, his son-in-law, was indeed a rabbi. According to Capsali, the conversion of Senior and Melamed came about because of the threats of Isabella: "And Don Abraham Senior and his son-in-law Meir Melamed, who were among the great ones of Spain, came under the waters of baptism, and they converted either under duress or of their own free will. For I have heard that, behind the curtain, the Queen swore that if Don Abraham Senior did not convert, she (Isabella) would destroy the communities of Spain. In order to save the many, Senior did what he did, but not from his own heart." The linguistic interpretation of their name change is a conjecture originating with myself.

On the life and thought of Don Isaac Abravanel, I have relied upon the excellent work by B. Netanyahu. At the time of the expulsion, Abravanel was regarded as the unofficial spiritual head of Spanish Jewry. He writes, "I was the head of all my people in Spain. They eagerly listed to what I would say and faithfully followed my instructions." (Quoted from the introduction to *Passover Sacrifice* by B. Netanyahu.) Capsali describes him thus: "At that time there came before the King and Queen a scholar comparable to Daniel, Don Isaac Abravanel, who entreated the King and Queen to dispense with the evil deed and to revoke the decree. But they did not listen nor pay heed to him. On that day, permission was given to Don Isaac Abravanel to speak all that was in his heart on behalf of and in defense of his people. There he stood like a lion with wisdom and with strength and with awesome power of speech, for he had a golden tongue whose worth was fifty times fifty shekels. There was no one like him in the land, a man who spoke with clarity in Hebrew and in other languages." As Abravanel and his family were about to set forth for Naples, an attempt was made to abduct Abravanel's grandson, but the plot was somehow foiled. The suckling grandchild, accompanied by his nurse, was taken to Portugal but fell into the clutches of João II.

The martyrdom of Rabbi Simon Maimi, the last chief rabbi of Portugal, at the hands of King Manuel in 1497, is described by Capsali, Saba, and A. Ben Solomon.

The fictional character of Hacham Isaac Alhadeff has no intended relation to the exiled Jewish scholar and mathematician of the same name.

The Marquis of Cádiz, whose marquisate in 1481 was a temporary refuge for thousands of Conversos fleeing the Inquisition, was a known friend of the Jews and he undoubtedly appealed to the Catholic sovereigns on their behalf.

On the Niño de la Guardia trial, the scholarly analysis by Y. Baer has been followed. It is of interest that Antonio de la Peña, the Dominican priest who was reprimanded by Ferdinand and Isabella for making inflammatory speeches against the Jews and urging the ransacking of the Jewish quarter, served on the jury during the Niño de la Guardia trial. He was the author of several anti-Semitic pamphlets.

Although estimates vary, approximately 150,000 Jews were expelled from Spain. The expulsion was justified ostensibly on a religious basis, but there were obvious economic motives as well. In the territories ruled by Ferdinand, widespread governmental confiscation of Jewish homes and other valuables netted the Spanish crown enormous revenues. The total assets of the Jews of Spain were valued at 30,000,000 gold ducats (according to Abravanel, *Wells of Salvation*, 8b, as quoted by Netanyahu). The sale and liquidation of abandoned Jewish properties in the city of Burgos alone brought 7,000,000 maravedis into the royal coffers.

The atrocities and calamities that befell the exiles, as related in Part III, all have ample historical documentation. Ibn Verga records incidents similar to that which occurred to the Alhadeff family in Morocco and to the island-stranded Pardo family. The conflagration in Fez is described by A. Ben Solomon and Bernaldez. Judah Hayat describes the brutal treatment which led to the conversion of his kinsmen in Málaga, the details of which the priest-historian Bernaldez conveniently leaves out. Usqué adds hair-raising accounts of his own, inclusive of King João's shipping of children to the *Islas Perdidas*. Capsali describes vividly the plague in Naples. And the conversion in 1497 in Portugal is attested to by all the medieval chroniclers.

ACKNOWLEDGEMENTS

I would like to express my deepest thanks to Rabbi Solomon Maimon and Reverend Samuel Benaroya, and to their wives Sarah Maimon and Lisa Benaroya, who over the years have offered me their warm friendship and their expertise in matters pertaining to Judeo-Spanish culture. I dearly thank my wife, Esther, for the many instances of encouragement and personal sacrifice which allowed me to bring this project to completion. To our four children, I ask for forgiveness for the many hours which the writing of this book took away from our family life together. Finally, I would like to thank Mrs. Myrtle Solomon for typing my handwritten manuscript from beginning to end.

GLOSSARY

aliyah (Heb., 'a going up'): the ceremonial summons in the synagogue of being called 'up' to the Torah.

aljama (Sp.): an assembly or community of Jews.

Auto de Fé (Sp.): a public event at which heretics were condemned and executed by the Inquisition.

Buenas semanas! (Sp): the traditional Sephardic greeting used at Sabbath's end to welcome the new week.

Gaon (Heb.): an honorific used in reference to a preeminent Jewish scholar, usually the head of a Jewish academy.

Hacham (Heb.), lit. 'a wise man'.

judería (Sp.): the Jewish quarter of the town or city.

Mazal Tov! (Heb., lit. 'a good constellation' or 'good luck'.): a traditional Jewish way of expressing congratulations and well-wishes.

megorash (Heb.): one who is expelled; in Morocco, an exile from Spain

mellah (Arabic): the Jewish quarter in Moslem countries.

Sefarad (Heb.): the Hebrew word used to denote Spain, based upon the Biblical passage in Obadiah 20. A Jew with a historical connection to Spain is called a *Sefaradi* or Sephardi.

Shabbat Shalom! (Heb.): 'Sabbath peace!'. A traditional greeting.

toshav (Heb.): the name used to denote the Jews residing in Morocco prior to the expulsion from Spain.

yeshiva (pl. *yeshivot*) (Heb.): an academy of Jewish learning.

Torah (Heb.): specifically used to refer to the Five Books of Moses (Pentateuch) and, more broadly, to Jewish learning in general.

tzadik (Heb.): a righteous and just man.